A WARRIOR'S DEVOTION
SAGA OF THE KNOWN LANDS
BOOK SEVEN

JACOB PEPPERS

This book is a work of fiction. Names, characters, places and incidents are either the product of the author's imagination or are used fictitiously. Any resemblance to actual persons, living or dead, or to actual events or locales is entirely coincidental.

A Warrior's Devotion: Saga of the Known Lands Book 7

This book is licensed for your personal enjoyment only. This book may not be re-sold or given away to other people. If you would like to share this book with another person, please purchase an additional copy for each person you share it with. If you're reading this book and did not purchase it, or it was not purchased for your use only, then you should return to the retailer and purchase your own copy. Thank you for respecting the hard work of the author.

Copyright © 2025 Jacob Nathaniel Peppers. All rights reserved, including the right to reproduce this book, or portions thereof, in any form. No part of this text may be reproduced, transmitted, downloaded, decompiled, reverse engineered, or stored in or introduced into any information storage and retrieval system, in any form or by any means, whether electronic or mechanical without the express written permission of the author. The scanning, uploading, and distribution of this book via the Internet or via any other means without the permission of the publisher is illegal and punishable by law. Please purchase only authorized electronic editions, and do not participate in or encourage electronic piracy of copyrighted materials.

The publisher does not have any control over and does not assume any responsibility for author or third-party websites or their content.

Visit the author's website: http://www.jacobpeppersauthor.com

This book is for my daughter, Norah.
My little princess who carries the moon with her,
Who sings and dances and loves
That above all else.
I love you, angel.

Sign up for the author's mailing list and for a limited time receive a FREE copy of *The Silent Blade*, prequel to the bestselling fantasy series *The Seven Virtues!*

Go to https://www.JacobPeppersAuthor.com to get your free book now!

CHAPTER ONE

The snow fell heavy around him, a curtain of white that shimmered in the moonlight. Ice crunched beneath his feet as he shifted where he sat. It was a cold night, as it always was this far in the north, but that cold never touched Cutter. It could not. Not with his son sleeping less than a dozen feet away, alive and well.

He had never thought to see him again, yet there he was, breathing softly in his sleep, bundled in Cutter's spare clothes and wrapped inside his bed-roll. A necessity, as whatever magic had transported Matt from the castle in New Daltenia to this wind-blasted landscape had not seen fit to bring any more than the nightclothes he had worn. Thankfully, he'd at least been wearing boots.

Cutter watched him sleep, glancing up at the silhouette of the Black Woods on the horizon. They had all been exhausted when Matt had arrived by a means which they still did not comprehend. Exhausted and hurt, barely able to stand upright, let alone walk. Yet, walk they had, at least for a little while, putting as much distance between them and the home of the Fey as they could.

Cutter hoped that he would never return, for he'd had his fill of the Fey and their strange world, their strange ways. It was a place where no mortal belonged, certainly not a living one, at least. But then, his life had taught him that what a man hoped usually had very little bearing on what would happen. Certainly, as a child, as a young man growing up in Daltenia, he had not hoped for the Skaalden to come, had not hoped for his father to die along with so many others. He would like to think that he had not hoped for a life of bloodshed and war, but he was not so sure that was true. If the Gray Man was to be believed, then war was his purpose. It was who he was, part of him, as inextricably connected to him as his arm or his leg. More so, perhaps, for a man might lose an arm and still remain himself, might lose a leg, too. But that part of him which sought the battle, which craved it...it could not be removed, he thought, unless his life was removed along with it.

Still, while such thoughts might, on a normal day, have caused him grief or shame, today they could not touch him. Not any more than the damp seeping into his boots from trudging through the snow could steal his warmth, or the barren landscape his hope.

He was happy.

Snow and ice and foreboding woods and all...he was happy.

His son was with him, his son who he had never thought to see again. His brother was with him, too. Against all odds, he and Feledias had survived the Black Wood, and Matt had, apparently, survived an assassination attempt. Though it would have seemed impossible to him only hours ago, the three of them were alive and together.

And if something as unlikely as that might occur, then perhaps the impossible task which lay before them was not so impossible after all.

He slowly turned to regard the distant silhouette of the mountains to the north. He thought that, with all that had happened, it was possible that they would succeed in their quest. Possible...but not likely. After all, the Barrier Mountains had not been given their name on a whim. They had earned that title time and time again. When Cutter and his people first arrived on the shores of the Known Lands in their flight from the Skaalden, they had sent excursions north into the mountains, but after dozens had died in the attempt to explore the mountains, they had given up.

But then, when the war with the Fey had broken out, again they had sent expeditions into the mountains hoping that they might expand beyond them, thinking that, should the worst happen, the mountains would serve better than any castle wall at keeping the Fey out. But those desperate expeditions had fared no better than those which had come before them.

Anything might lie beyond the mountain pass—anything or nothing. For no one had gone more than a day in the mountains and returned alive. Even those who had managed that feat—a man and a woman who had been accompanied by a company of fifty soldiers that had gone missing—had not returned unscathed. They had come back with the worst frostbite Cutter had ever seen, before or since. They had lost several toes and fingers to the cold, and those that had remained were as black as night. But even that, as bad as it had been, had been far from the worst they'd suffered. Both had been covered in blood, some their own, some, judging by the amount, not. But even worse than their wounds and the blood which told of some terrible tragedy was that both of them had gone quite mad. Whatever had waited for them in the Barrier Mountains, whatever had killed the rest of their company, it had broken their minds.

Cutter knew that, for he had been in the north at the time, having just finished winning a battle against the Fey forces there, and had spoken with the pair himself. Or, at least, he had tried to. Whatever they had experienced in the mountains had left its mark. The two had barely been able to speak at all and what words they'd said had made no sense. The ice had killed them, they'd said. Winter had taken its revenge.

The claim would have seemed normal enough. After all, anyone looking at the Barrier Mountains, even from afar, could not help but notice the perpetual clouds that covered their peaks, or the eternal ice and snow that covered their surface. The problem, though, had been that in their ranting the pair had spoken about the ice, the winter, as if it had been a living thing, one capable of enmity, of hatred.

Thinking of the mountains, of the cold that waited for them there, cold beyond anything even he had ever experienced, caused Cutter's gaze to return to his son. He leaned forward, grabbing a handful of the scraggly twigs and sticks they'd managed to scrounge up before they'd broke camp, glancing at the fire.

A small, weak blaze, blown about this way and that by wind that cut like a knife. Cutter had thought it would go out a thousand times since he'd lit it and a thousand more since the others had succumbed to their slumber, but so far, at least, the small flame had held on. He carefully laid the small twigs on top of the fire, careful not to smother it and burning his fingertips a little as he did. That was alright. He thought that considering where they were going it was the most warmth he was likely to feel for a long time.

"*Just hold on,*" he told the small fire quietly, a whisper carried away on the whistling wind. Morning, he judged, was only a few hours away. Three. Maybe four. It would be cold then, too, of course. In the north it was always cold, but the sun would at least bring some respite from the worst of it. In the meantime, the small flame didn't seem like much, but in the icy, frozen landscape in which he and the others had made camp, that small fire could be the difference between living and dying, between waking to the morning or never waking again. "*Just hold on,*" he told it again. It was all anything or anyone could do some times. Just hold on.

And if a man held on a long enough, even the worst times of his life would pass. If the flames held on long enough, even the deepest nights would give way to morning.

And the flames *would* hold. He wouldn't have believed that yesterday, but his son was with him, they had made their way free of the Black Wood, and he believed it now.

Night would not last forever, and the cold would not win through.

Morning would come and warmth would come with it.

CHAPTER TWO

He was sweating by the time he reached the dungeon, his entire body trembling with fatigue. A chair had been left in front of the cell, and as he shambled toward it, Chall told himself to remember to buy the guard on duty an ale for that kindness. After all, standing was quickly not becoming an option, and somehow he doubted he'd exude the air of menace he'd like if he were sprawled on the floor outside the would-be assassin's cell like some beached sea lion gasping for breath.

He thought that once he was done here he would need to visit Malden. The ornery old healer would no doubt scold him for not heeding his instructions to rest, but he doubted Robert Palden and his followers would be willing to accept a brief pause while Chall healed of his wounds. That was the thing about assassins and traitors—they didn't tend to be the most thoughtful people. Besides, hurt or not, he needed to find out what had happened to Matt. The others, Vorrun and Ned and a plethora of guardsmen, were out searching the castle now, a task Chall had tried to help with until about his sixth or seventh stumble when Vorrun had ordered him to go back to his rooms and get some rest.

Ridiculous, of course. As if Chall could rest while Matt, his king—

his *friend*—was out there somewhere, perhaps hurt, maybe taken by Robert Palden or one of his accomplices. He frowned, feeling anger awaken in him at the thought, making him forget the pain he was in, at least for the moment. The woman waiting in the cell up ahead was the last person to see the king alive, and she would tell him everything she knew.

One way or the other.

Chall was no expert murderer—an amateur, at best—and knew little of torture, but he thought that given what was at stake, he could learn. After all, he didn't lack in motivation.

He made his way to the chair and sank heavily into it, unable to completely suppress the groan of relief that came from him as he did. Meanwhile, Lady Valencia sat huddled in the corner, her arms wrapped around her knees, her back to him. She could not have helped but to have heard him—Chall had never been known for being quiet and particularly not wounded as he was—but she did not turn from where she studied the corner of her cell.

Chall stared at her. Her dress—once fine—was torn in several places. It seemed that the guards who had brought her here had not been particularly careful when doing so. No great surprise, that. Chall had spent enough time around the castle guards to know that they, like nearly everyone else in the city, loved Matt, their king. At least, that was, those castle guards who weren't traitors bent on assassinating him and anyone close to him.

Anger had brought Chall here. Anger and fear. Anger at the thought that this woman, this woman who they had trusted, had betrayed that trust in the worst possible way. They—*Matt*—had offered her shelter from those who sought her life, had offered her protection, and she had thanked him for it by trying to stick a knife in his back.

Anger had brought him here, but as he sat there, staring at the woman, Chall found it difficult to speak, so great was the weight of his fury, so terrible his fear for his friend. In this moment, in that silence, he could pretend that Matt was okay, that his friend had only stepped out to the privy, perhaps. But should he speak, should he ask her the question he must ask, and should she *answer* it, then he would be able to pretend no longer.

He must have opened his mouth at least half a dozen times, like some fish out of water, gasping for air, but each time the words simply would not come, a situation that, for Chall at least, was rare indeed, a fact to which anyone who knew him might attest.

"Have you come to torture me, then?" she finally asked, breaking the silence.

"No," Chall said. "That comes later, I think. Or...maybe it doesn't have to come at all. If you tell me where Matt is, what you've done with him."

"What I've done with him," she repeated in a low, breathy voice.

"Yes," Chall said, barely managing to contain a scream of impatience, of fear for Matt. "Where is he? Where did your boss take him?"

"My boss?"

"That's right. Your boss, Robert Palden. The man you work for."

She said nothing, and Chall gritted his teeth. Another might have seen the old woman hunkered in the cell and felt pity, but Matt was missing, and Chall had no pity in him. "Well?" he demanded. "It will go easier for you, if you tell me. Believe me, those men who come—and they are coming, do not doubt that—will ask far harder than I. Now, tell me—where did your boss take the king?"

Finally, the woman did turn and madness, or something very near it, danced in her gaze in the dim cell. "*Fool*," she spat. "You speak as if he is some head merchant and I his hireling. You have no idea what is coming...you or the others. You are dead men—all of you. At least, you should hope so, for that is the best outcome you can hope for. He has no compassion within him, no mercy. He is a creature of purpose, that and that only."

"Funny," Chall said, "I feel pretty good for a dead man." Not true, of course. The truth was that he felt like shit, but he'd be damned if he'd give her the satisfaction of saying as much. "Anyway, we aren't exactly a bunch of useless children. If this master of yours wants a war, then he'll find one, but I doubt it'll have the outcome he wants."

She laughed at that. "You poor soul," she said. "You don't get it. You've already lost. You just don't know it yet. He does not go to war. Not any more than the boot goes to war with the roach it crushes underfoot. Your problem is that you still think he is a man, that he feels pain the way you and I might."

"If he's not a man, what is he?" Chall asked.

She opened her mouth to speak—but then something akin to terror flashed across her expression. Only for a moment and then it was gone, but not before Chall noted it. She shook her head. "You will find out, soon enough. You and all your friends. You are in his way, and Robert has very little patience for those things which get in his way."

Staring at her, Chall realized something. She was afraid. No great surprise there, for many who had occupied a similar situation to her own—many, no doubt, who had occupied the same cell as her—had also shown fear. After all, an interminable stay in the castle's dungeons was no one's idea of a good time and that was before one considered the questioners—call them what they were, torturers—who would soon be here to ply their bloody trade.

The problem, though, was that, looking at her, he did not think it was the cell or her predicament, not even the soon-to-arrive torturers, which caused her fear. Instead, it was thoughts of the man, Robert Palden. Not idle claims or bravado then, for whether or not her threats were true regarding him being able to destroy the Known Lands, *she* certainly believed them to be.

And considering that Lady Valencia had spent far more time around Robert Palden than he had—a situation Chall would maintain if at all possible—that was a disquieting realization.

But he realized that she was distracting him from the reason he'd come. "Never mind all of that. Where is the king?"

She said nothing, only studyied him with a small smile on her face. Once, according to Ned, she had been instrumental in the founding of the Wolves, an organization formed to stand against the criminals of New Daltenia. She had also, as it happened, been the carriage driver's friend. But whatever else she might have once been, it was clear now that the woman was evil. He could see that evil in her smile, sharp enough to cut, in her eyes that seemed somehow reptilian, soulless.

Lady Valencia studied him for another moment before turning away to look back at the corner of her cell, making it clear that for the moment, at least, she was done talking. Chall frowned, thinking. She might not want to tell him anything, but now that he'd sat down and the worst of the agony of his legs had abated, he figured he could piece some things together himself.

His first thought was that Robert Palden had found his way into the king's quarters along with her, but now he realized that didn't make sense for a few reasons. For one, if the man had meant to come all along, why bother sending her to do the job? But even more than that, though, was the fact that Vorrun and the other guardsmen had been in their places outside the king's quarters when he and Ned had arrived, and they weren't generally in the habit of allowing homicidal maniacs into the king's bedroom in the middle of the night. So, either the man was invisible, or he was able to scale the near hundred-foot sheer stone wall of the castle to gain access through the king's window, *or*—and Chall thought this by far the most likely—he hadn't come at all.

Which meant that the woman had acted alone, which meant...

"You don't know where he is," he said quietly, remembering the stricken expression that had been on the noblewoman's face when he and the others had arrived in the king's quarters, the way she'd simply stared in apparent shock at the empty space in front of her, her knife thrust forward into air as Vorrun and his men disarmed and manacled her.

The woman said nothing, but he saw her back stiffen and knew that he was right. Whatever had happened to Matt, it had not been part of the woman's—and therefore Robert Palden's—plan. After all, why go through all the trouble of positioning Lady Valencia in the castle only to stymie her in the end when victory had been quite literally within her reach? The man might be insane—certainly everything Chall had seen and heard of him indicated as much—but he was no fool. Which meant that while the woman was ignorant of what had happened with the king, so, too, was Robert Palden. Whatever had happened had not been part of the plan.

"You don't know where he is," he said again, thoughtfully. The woman had been meant to kill Matt, a task at which, judging by the lack of blood—and a corpse—staining the floor of the king's quarters, she had failed. "What's Robert's plan?" he asked. "Sure, he meant for you to kill Matt, but then what? What's he intend to do?"

The woman did not answer, only continued to sit with her back toward him, facing the corner of her cell.

"You say that your master is brutal, that he is barely a man at all, and so, I would assume, largely unburdened by a man's emotions. Emotions like fear and doubt, sure. But there are others too, aren't there? Like compassion. Like mercy."

She slowly turned to regard him over one shoulder, but still said nothing. That was alright—Chall had plenty enough to say on his own.

"A man like that," he went on, "a man who would be willing to risk anything or anyone, to *kill* anything or anyone to achieve his goals...I suppose he doesn't have much time for mercy. Nor much time for failure either, I would think."

A look of what might have been part doubt and was undoubtedly part fear flashed across the woman's face at that. "Why," Chall went on, sensing weakness, "I don't know much about murderers and psychotic criminal masterminds and their plots, but it seems to me that the assassination of a king...well, that's an awful lot of trouble to go through. Makes me think it might be pretty important to whatever he's got going." Chall decided to take a chance, then. To do what he had been doing for nearly all his life and doing well—to lie. After all, he couldn't be *sure* that the woman hadn't succeeded, that Robert Palden or someone working for him wasn't behind the young king's disappearance. But while she was trying to look confident and brave, he could see the frustration and disappointment in her gaze and why not? He'd seen it on the faces of plenty of women over the years, usually when they woke up beside him to find that the knight of their wine-soaked dreams was actually just a wine-soaked cad of very little substance.

And so, the lie. "I can't imagine he'll be happy with the person who failed to do what she was ordered," he offered. "Why, if I were him, I'd be quite upset with the woman who botched the king's assassination, particularly after I'd gone through all the trouble of pretending she was attacked, even taking part of her finger to make it convincing." He shrugged. "It might even be that there would be some punishment in order. Tell me, you know him better than I do: what sort of punishment does this master of yours use? Whippings? Sending you to your room?"

Her lips peeled back from her teeth in an angry sneer. "You don't know what you're talking about. It wasn't my fault that he vanished. Anyway, I'm too valuable t—" She cut off, her eyes narrowing as she realized he'd baited her and that she had fallen for it.

Chall smiled, shifting in his chair and barely even noticing the discomfort in his legs as he did. "So you *did* fail, then. Well, while I appreciate the information, my point stands. Your master isn't going to be too happy when he finds out. Who knows, it might be he knows already." He shrugged. "But then maybe I'm wrong. Maybe he isn't as cold-blooded, as ruthless as I've heard. Might be he'll accept your failure with good grace, maybe pat you on the head, give you a treat for the effort." He leaned forward slowly. "What do you think? You know him better than I do, after all."

She tried to school her features, but like all the most accomplished liars, Chall recognized one when he saw it, so he knew well what hid behind her scowl. Fear. Terror, in fact. "You have no idea what's coming for you and your friends," she hissed, all pretense of calm detachment vanishing in an instant as her face twisted with hatred. Here, then, was the real Lady Valencia. Whatever else she was, whatever else she had been, she was a creature of evil now, that much he could see in her face, her eyes. "You are going to die, all of you. There is nothing you can do about it. Fight or hide, flee or stay, it matters not. There is no hole deep enough for you to crawl into, no mountain high enough to keep you from his reach. You and all those you love will suffer before the end, for you are right in this much, at least—Robert has very little mercy in him." She gave a laugh that sounded forced as she waved a hand at the cell around her. "He will come for me, to save me, and this pitiful cell and your pitiful guards will not even prove an inconvenience to him."

"There's only one thing I don't understand," Chall said as if she hadn't spoken, tapping his finger on his chin. "If his plan was only to kill Matt, then why didn't he do it sooner? After all, it isn't as if he hasn't had an opportunity. There was the serving woman, for instance. Or, I should say, the woman who *pretended* to be a serving girl. Margaret," he went on, speaking more to himself than the woman in the cell. "She wasn't there to kill Matt—I'm sure of that much. She was looking for something. And whatever it was she—and your boss—found it damned important. Important enough to risk revealing your whole operation."

She said nothing, clearly intent on not giving away any of her boss's plans. "That's alright," Chall told her. "You don't have to say anything. I've always been a bit of a talker. This way, there's less competition. Besides, while you might not want to say anything, the poor serving woman, the one you attacked in Mistress Ophasia's quarters, has plenty to say." He made as if to rise.

"*Bullshit,*" the woman hissed. "She's dead. No one could have survived tha—" She froze, her eyes going wide, her face pale as she realized she'd given away far more than she'd meant to.

Chall smiled, settling back down in his chair. "Oh, don't feel too bad," he said. "I've spent nearly my entire life trying to convince women to do things they haven't shown an immediate interest in. I'd even go so far as to say I've gotten pretty good at it over the years."

Lady Valencia's face flushed red with fury, and from the look she shot in his direction, Chall felt lucky that she was on the other end of a cell, the knife she'd carried when they found her taken by Vorrun and his men. Safe from the woman's ire, he considered her words and decided that they told him two things for sure. One, she was the one responsible for the serving woman's death, which meant that although she might have appeared to be an old woman, weak and vulnerable, she was quite clearly insane. Secondly, he was right. Robert Palden was looking for something, and whatever that something was, he was clearly confident it was in the castle. And not just in the castle but in the servants' quarters. After all, what other reason would the noblewoman have had for going to Mistress Ophasia's quarters and risking being discovered?

Chall frowned, his thoughts racing, turning the pieces over and over in his mind. The answer was there, he knew it, but while talking women into making poor decisions might have been one of his talents—if a talent it could be called—thinking or, at least, thinking clearly had never been ranked among them. After all, what could the woman be looking for in such a place? Servants weren't known for their possessions. Certainly not coin, for even the mistress of servants had little enough of that. Besides, while Lady Valencia was undeniably a monster, she was also a rich one, possessed of a fortune that was the envy of almost every man and woman in the Known Lands. No, if it was coin Robert Palden was after, there were far easier ways to get it.

So what, then? he thought.

He sat back, frowning. His right leg began to itch terribly where he'd been wounded and bit back a curse—just what he needed, another distraction. Malden had told him the itching was a good sign, that it meant the wounds were healing well. Chall didn't know about that. All he knew was that it was maddening, an itch somewhere beneath the surface of the skin where he could never reach no matter how much he scratched, and he thought at times—like now—that he would rather have been shot and stabbed again than to suffer it.

He moved to scratch at the itch and, as he did, his arm brushed across something in his trouser pocket. The necklace he had all but forgotten about in his haste.

Later, he would think of that moment, wonder at it, turning it over and over in his mind. He would wonder what might have happened if he had put it in his left pocket instead of his right. He would wonder what would have happened if his leg had not chosen that moment to itch. And he would wonder what might have happened had the trousers he wore not been too loose, a product of Maeve taking responsibility—voluntarily but quite forcefully—of his diet. Loose enough that the necklace slipped out onto the floor, its metal chain tinkling as it hit.

He would wonder, later, if it was luck that made it so, or if perhaps some divine force—Priest's goddess, perhaps—were responsible. And he would consider what might have been different had it *not* fallen to the ground. What might have changed.

Maybe nothing.

Maybe everything.

But in any event, his pocket *was* loose, the necklace *did* slip, and the metallic chime as it struck the floor drew both his gaze and that of the noblewoman hunkered in the dungeon cell.

Chall started to reach down to retrieve it from where it lay but before he could do any more than take a breath the woman let out a hiss and lunged forward with a startling burst of speed Chall wouldn't have credited her with. Enough that he found himself recoiling in his chair and nearly spilling over the back of it as the woman thrust her hand out through the bars in an attempt to reach the necklace.

She strained against the bars, her teeth bared in what appeared to be a mixture of anger and desperation, but the bars, being iron and really having the singular job of keeping people *in,* did not budge. Chall stared at the woman's bestial demeanor in shock, following her gaze back to the necklace where it lay. Likely due to the dimness of the dungeons, the green gem in the necklace seemed to pulse with emerald light.

"I know that women love their jewelry," the flippant part of him—which was very nearly the *only* part—began, "but..."

He paused then as the other, reasonable part of his mind, starved and faded though it was, took the fore. The puzzle pieces suddenly stopped whirling and twirling in his mind. Instead, they finally came together, fitting into place as neatly as some contraption formed by a master smith.

"The necklace," he said, his voice little more than a whisper as those two simple words carried the weight of that answer, the knowledge, now that it was fitted together, of what that puzzle signified.

The necklace. It was the answer. The answer to the questions which had been plaguing him for weeks. He had asked himself, countless times, why Robert Palden would risk exposing his entire operation with the Crimson Wolves to send Margaret into the castle, had wondered, too, why anyone would have killed the servant, Diane, in Mistress Ophasia's quarters. He had wondered what could possibly be worth all that risk, and now he knew. Now, as he bent down and retrieved the necklace, he held that answer in his hands.

As he examined the green gem, he thought that the necklace answered those questions and more besides. He remembered well the way Matt had toyed with it, had seemed to constantly hold it, as if its touch was somehow a comfort. Matt who had been acting so strangely lately, who could not even be bothered to eat or drink most of the time, let alone sleep, had held onto the necklace as if it were some precious keepsake.

Matt who had been in his quarters—Vorrun and the other guardsmen were quite adamant on that—but had suddenly vanished with a burst of magic which Chall had felt even where he'd stood in the hallway while the guardsmen tried to bust in the door.

He stared at the necklace. It did not pulse now, and he wondered if he had imagined that, if he was imagining all of it. After all, when a kingdom was at stake, what possible importance could such a small thing have? Sometimes, a necklace was just a necklace. But other times, he thought, other times it was a key. A key that fit into a box of questions and uncertainties, a key that, frankly, he was afraid to use. After all, there was no knowing what would happen when that box was opened.

His mind was awhirl with thoughts, possibilities, but he still heard the sound of footsteps coming toward him. Chall looked up and saw Ned, the carriage driver, coming down the dungeon hallway.

"The king?" Chall asked.

He had known the carriage driver for weeks, since he and the prince and the others had returned to New Daltenia. The man was almost always of good humor, even, Chall had thought and more than once, to a fault. He did not look in good humor now. As he drew closer, Chall could see that the man's face was a storm of emotion as he gave his head a shake.

"No sign," the carriage driver said. "The others are still looking. Priest is back. Returned to the castle. I told him what happened, and he's helpin' Vorrun and the others search. From the looks of him he's got a story to tell." He frowned over at the cell and the woman inside it. "Not that I've taken the time to hear it, not yet. What did you do with him?" he said, staring at the woman, and Chall imagined that he could almost feel the anger, the *rage* radiating off the man like heat.

Lady Valencia didn't answer. She'd settled back, the shocking desperation, the *need* that she'd shown when the necklace had fallen from Chall's pocket nowhere in evidence. In its place was a small, almost imperceptible smirk. "You have no idea what you carry," she said, ignoring the carriage driver altogether as she stared at Chall. "But you will soon enough. Better for you if it were a poisonous snake, better if it were a thousand, for even so many could not hope to cause you the sort of pain, the sort of suffering that *it* will."

Chall blinked, glancing down at the necklace in his hands. "So you're saying green's not my color, is that it?"

The woman bared her teeth in what might have been considered a grin if a man had never seen one before, but she said nothing.

"Answer me, damn you!" Ned roared, the thunderous sound of his voice echoing in the dungeon hallway. But it was not the volume of his voice that struck Chall, that nearly sent him spilling out of his chair for the second time in as many minutes. Instead, it was the *power*. Power that was not just the product of a man's righteous fury—though it was partly that. Power that was a compulsion, a *demand*, and Chall himself wanted, in that moment, to desperately answer the man, to tell him what he wanted to know, to tell him anything and *everything* he wanted to know.

As Chall stared at him in shock, as he felt that power radiating off the man, he realized that he was staring not just at Ned the carriage driver, a man who had been betrayed by someone he had counted as a dear friend. Instead, he was staring at the power of an Empath laid bare, his strength unveiled. Chall had seen the man use his power before—he and Valden were only alive because of it. But still he was rocked by the strength of the man's gift.

And he was not the only one.

The noblewoman had been at best angry and at worst dismissive when dealing with Chall, and what information he'd managed to get he'd gotten from guile and subtlety. But Ned's demand was not subtle —for the bear, when it chose to attack, had little need of guile. Instead, his power was like a great sledge, busting through whatever defenses the woman might have raised against his questions in the same way that it might have busted through a shield crafted entirely of glass.

Lady Valencia actually rocked backward, her eyes going wide, her body tensing in reaction the way she might have had the carriage driver grabbed her roughly by both shoulders and never mind that he still stood in the hallway. *"Where is he?"* Ned said, and this time, though he did not yell, his voice, the power within it was even stronger than the first.

"I-I don't know," she sputtered, the words seeming to cause her physical pain as if they'd been ripped out of her.

"*Bullshit*," Ned said, and the woman cried out as if he'd struck her. "How could you not know? Where is he?"

"*Truly, I don't know!*" she screeched, all attempts at nonchalance abandoned as she gripped her head in both hands as if might explode at any moment, and with the power radiating off the man Chall would not have been surprised if it had. He was not even the object of Ned's attention, yet it was all he could do to remain in his seat, and each breath was difficult to draw as if some great weight pressed on his chest.

"H-he was there one minute and gone the next," she stammered. "Th-there was a green flash, and...and he was gone."

Ned grunted. "You expect us to believe that he simply up and vanished?" he asked, and this time, at least, his words were simply words as the terrible pressure—pressure which had seemed to build in the air since the man arrived—suddenly vanished.

The woman sucked in a great breath, gasping for air the way a drowning man might when pulled to shore. "B-believe what y-you want," she said between breaths. "I-it m-makes no difference."

"Oh, I wouldn't be so sure about that," Ned said. "Not at all. Whether or not we believe you...well, for you, I think that's going to make quite a big difference, Val. I surely do. See, I passed some fellas on the way here. Fellas carrying a bag of tools, like maybe they got a project to work on. And you, you're the project, see?"

"You can threaten me a-all you want," Lady Valencia said. "I cannot tell you what I don't know."

Ned watched her for several seconds then finally gave a nod. "Alright, Val. Alright. Then why don't we start with what you *do* know? For instance, what's your boss planning?"

She said nothing, only bared her teeth in a humorless smile.

Ned went on, undaunted. "How do we stop it?"

She gave a sharp laugh at that. "You can't *stop* it. Not any more than you could stop a tornado or a hurricane. Only, this tornado, this hurricane is not simply an act of nature doing what it does. This hurricane *wants* to destroy." She gave another laugh. "How do you stop it? You can no more stop it than a roach might stop the boot before it's crushed."

"She's a big fan of boots and roaches," Chall explained.

Ned didn't even so much as glance in his direction. "Suppose we wanted to try anyway," he said. "You know, just for the fun of it. Where would we start?"

He waited, but the woman's mouth remained stubbornly closed.

"Don't like that question?" Ned asked. "Okay, Val. Alright. Here's another one, then—*why?*" His voice was thick with emotion, thick with betrayal and anger and a thousand other emotions too knitted together to separate one from the other. "Why would you do it? When we started the Wolves, you and Robert and I, we did it with a purpose. A *reason*. To help. To make a difference, to be a light in a dark world or, if not, then to slay the shadows and in that way make the world a little less dim. It meant something. The pain, the sacrifices, those we lost…they *meant* something."

"Did they?" she asked softly. "Did they really?" She sighed, shaking her head slowly. "Oh, my poor Neddy. You are a fool. Our work, what we did, it was of no more consequence than a little girl blowing into the air and thinking that by doing so she might hold back an onrushing storm."

The man couldn't have looked more stricken than if she'd *actually* struck him. "You…you can't believe that. I don't believe that. We made a difference. Because of us—"

"Because of us *what,* exactly?" she demanded, her voice sharp and angry once more. "So we rid the world of a killer, a mugger, a rapist—so what? More are born every single day, don't you see that? What difference does it make, what difference *can* it make?"

"It makes a difference to their would-be victims," Ned said. "To those whose lives might have been cut short. Instead, they get to live."

"And what sort of gift is that?" the woman demanded. "Look around you, Ned," she said, waving a hand as if to encompass not just the dungeon but the entire city, the entire world beyond it. "The world is a cruel, evil place full of cruel, evil men. It is nothing more than an unending field of broken glass, and we those poor, doomed travelers forced to traverse it in our bare feet. While you—while *we*—were busy congratulating ourselves for helping those poor, damned souls avoid it on one step, they were already taking another, and another. It is not a question, then, of *if* the pain will come, the agony and regret, only *when* it will come. And I have lived long enough, Neddy, to know the answer to that well enough, to know that it never changes. When will the pain come? The heart-ache? The suffering? The answer, the *only* answer, is *soon*. The world does not stop to ask our opinion on the matter because it does not care. In the end, we are all that little girl blowing into the wind, and whatever difference we make is no more than our own imagination."

"I don't believe that," Ned said. "Who we are, what we do, it matters. Whether we're good—or whether we're evil—it matters."

She snorted. "Are you truly so naive? Don't you see? Imagine that we live in a vast, unending ocean, and that ocean, that *world* is evil. Your efforts, *our* efforts were no more than a single drop of water falling into those murky depths. Even should that water be pure, the cleanest water to ever exist, what difference does it—*can* it—make? For the moment it falls into the rest, it becomes swallowed up by the dark waters of that great sea. It does not make those waters clean—they make it dirty, just as a white cloth against dirt will not leave both clean but will instead leave both filthy. The world is not some sick patient that that wife of yours might cure, and even if it were it does not *want* to be cured. Men are evil, the *world* is evil and just so long as the two exist you can expect nothing else but more pain, more suffering. Given that simple truth, a person who sets out to do good, to make a difference, as I did so long ago, can only choose one of two paths. Either she gives up her quest to destroy the world's evil altogether, or—"

"Or she destroys the world itself," Chall finished, and had he not already known the woman was insane, then the smile that came to her face as he said the words would have decided him.

"And the mage wins a prize," she said. Meanwhile, the carriage driver stood, seemingly at a loss for words, staring at the noblewoman as if he had never seen her before.

"Oh, don't you look at me like that, Neddy," she said. "You think me evil, is that it?" She shrugged. "Perhaps I am, but *if* I am, then I am no more evil than the world itself. I did not make things the way they are. I simply had the courage to see the truth."

Chall wasn't sure what he expected, given the tense manner in which the carriage driver stood. Perhaps another summoning of his empathic powers which had left Chall feeling wrung-out, used-up. He thought that, maybe, the man would shout and rage at this woman whom he had thought a friend. But he did neither of those things. Instead, when Ned spoke, he did so in a quiet, soft voice. "You are wrong, Val," he said, his tone full of regret. "What you do...what Rob does...there is no courage in it. Only fear. Only anger. Maybe the world is as dark as you say, as evil, but if it is, then what courage is there in being evil with it? There is no courage in the man who sees an army approaching and only sits and watches as one of their number moves to cut down a child because he tells himself that the soldier is only one of many and that the child's fate is sealed just the same. That is not bravery, only an excuse for his fear. But the man who puts himself between that dark fate and the child, that man has shown courage. Courage, Val, is in *standing*."

She sighed. "There is the clever fool, the idealist. You can say whatever you want, *do* whatever you want. In the end, it will make no difference. You have no idea the power Robert possesses, the resources. You are clever, Ned, but that cleverness will do nothing to protect you and those you care about against what's coming. There is no point in fighting, can't you see that? No point at all, for you cannot win."

He sighed, shaking his head. "Oh, Val," he said, his voice thick with regret. "You still don't get it, do you? It's not the winning that matters. A man cannot control the winning, not anymore than the little girl blowing in the wind can control the tornado. It's not about winning. It's about standing. Fighting. *That's* what matters. Being a light against the shadows, a torch burning bright in the darkness. That is what matters."

She rolled her eyes. "And if the torch goes out, Neddy? *When* it goes out?"

"Then at least it will have burned as bright as it could for as long as it could. And perhaps in doing so, it will help inspire others to do the same, to hold their own torches high."

She watched him and, for a moment, Chall almost thought that Ned had convinced her. Certainly his words had filled Chall with courage, and that was no easy thing for a lifelong coward. Even without the use of his powers, the man was the most convincing person Chall had ever met. He wondered if that was *because* of his powers or if, instead, who he was, the way he had a mind that seemed built to untangle knots of confusion and morality was somehow behind him having the powers of an Empath to begin with. Or, perhaps, the two were completely unrelated. Whatever the case, there was no denying the impact his words had on Chall and, judging by her stricken expression, Lady Valencia, too.

"Will you help me, Val?" Ned asked quietly. "The darkness is all around us, it's true, but it is not too late. It is not too late to be a light against it. It is not too late to stand."

She opened her mouth to speak then closed it again. A silent tear fell from her eye, winding its way down her cheek, but she roughly brushed it away, giving her head an angry shake. "Stand so that I might be knocked down all the easier?" she said, her voice full of so much hatred and anger and fear that it barely sounded human. "No. No, I don't think so. The world is in flames around us, Neddy. It burns, and there is nothing to do but get as much as you can while you can, to live as long and as well as possible until it all comes crashing down."

The carriage driver sighed, turning to Chall. "I'd say it's time we go, Chall. We won't find anything here, I think."

"I wouldn't be so sure," Chall said, pausing to hiss in pain as he rose, the necklace still in his hand. "I think I've learned quite a bit that might be of some use."

The carriage driver nodded, glancing at the necklace but apparently deciding he could ask Chall about it later. He turned to the woman in the cell. "Goodbye, Val. I do not expect we'll meet again."

They started away then, and had only taken a few steps down the dim, torch-lit hallway when the noblewoman called after them.

"*No, we won't, Ned!*" she screamed. "*Robby will come for me, for I am his friend. Perhaps his only one. And when he has come for me, then he will come for you too. You're going to die, Ned. You and all those you love!*"

The carriage driver paused in the hallway, and in the poor light Chall couldn't make out much of his expression. Finally, the man sighed, seeming to deflate. "Come on," he said. "Let's get out of here."

Chall nodded, following as the man sat off down the hallway once more. "That was...that was something else, back there. Do you believe it? All that you said? About winning not being important, about standing being what matters?"

Ned glanced over at him. "A man has to believe something, Chall. I choose to believe that."

Chall nodded soberly. "And what you did, with the Art...that was... incredible. Honestly...I've never seen an Empath let loose before."

Ned gave him a small, sharp smile. "You still haven't."

CHAPTER THREE

"You can't...you can't be here," Maeve told the woman in front of her.

The woman, though, continued to stubbornly stand as she had, saying nothing, a wide, uncharacteristic smile on her face. Maeve had known Agnes for years before the war with the Fey and had become reacquainted with her recently, yet she thought she could count on one hand the number of times she'd ever seen the woman smile. Shock and confusion roiled through her. Most thought the woman was dead, but of course Maeve knew better, for she and Chall, along with Emille, had staged the woman's death to allow her to escape her role as guild-master and be free of the machinations and conspirings of Bethesa, Piralta, and the recently dead Silrika.

That had been only weeks ago now, and the woman had begged, *begged* Maeve to help her. She meant to get out of the city—no use staying around where she might be spotted, where those like the tribunes who sought her life could so easily claim it. Maeve had not expected to see her again and yet here she was, standing before her with an easy smile on her face, by all appearances as relaxed and un-murdered as anyone could hope to be.

"Hello, Maeve," Agnes said.

"You...you said you were leaving the city."

"Things are bad," the woman said, her smile abruptly vanishing as she glanced behind her at the door through which the tribunes had disappeared. "You have no idea just how bad. I came back—I had to. To help. I'll explain it all, I promise. Only...later. But first, I need your help."

"*My* help?" Maeve asked, confused. "I'm not so sure about that, Agnes. The last time I gave you my help you set me up to become guildmaster without my knowledge and now I'm standing inside of a dungeon cell, my friend in one beside me. It may surprise you to know that I'm not in much of a helping mood."

"I understand, truly," the woman said, shooting another worried glance back at the door, and Maeve thought that was strange, for the woman had already been in the room when the tribunes and their pet guardsmen had brought Maeve here. "But please, this is important. I can fix this, Lady Maeve, *we* can fix it. But I need your help first."

Maeve blinked. *Lady Maeve*. That was unusual, for while she and Agnes had been more cordial than normal the last time they'd spoken— which only meant they hadn't actively been trying to murder each other—the woman had never called her "Lady Maeve" except mockingly.

"What sort of help?" Maeve asked. "But I'll warn you that if it's a piece of furniture needs situating, my back wouldn't thank me for it. Oh, and there's the small matter of me being locked in a cage that might make it more difficult."

"Not furniture," the woman said, "not that. It's...the diary, Maeve. My diary. I need it."

Maeve wasn't sure what she'd been expecting the woman to ask, but it certainly hadn't been that. "Your...diary?" she asked.

"That's right," Agnes said, nodding eagerly. "It's in there, Maeve, all the information we need. Information we can use to bring the tribunes down, information that might save the kingdom. Please, I know that you have it. That you found it."

Maeve frowned. There was something strange going on. Something about the woman's behavior that she didn't quite understand. "If you were so desperate to have the diary, why didn't you take it with you when you left?" she asked.

"I-I couldn't," the woman said, shaking her head. "They, they would have known, and they'd have killed me for it. No, believe me, I had to leave it, just as I had to leave you in charge. You were the only one I could trust."

In a day full of surprises—largely unwelcome ones—those words were some of the biggest yet. It was true that Agnes had asked for Maeve's help, had been desperate to escape the guild, but even then, even when basically begging for her life, the woman had never claimed to trust Maeve, just as Maeve would have never claimed to trust her. Something was going on, something she didn't understand, and she decided that, until she did, she would play it close. "You mean the diary that Tribune Bethesa kept talking about?"

"Yes, yes, that's the one. Please, Lady Maeve, I need it."

There was that "Lady" again. "What's in the diary?" Maeve asked. "*Why* is it so important?" After all, she had looked through it and, at least so far as she could tell, the contents, boring beyond imagination, could not be interesting to anyone except perhaps Agnes herself, if even she could manage reading them without yawning.

The woman hissed, glancing at the door and back at Maeve. "There isn't time for this. I know you have it. And Amber...I know why you had to do what you did. I told her to protect the diary at all costs. It's why she's dead, I know that. Now please—where is it?"

The revelations were coming hard and fast, and Maeve felt unsteady, rocked, like some ship tossed carelessly about in a storm. Still, she focused on bringing some order to her thoughts. "Fine," she said. "It's the same place you left it."

"Right, right, of course. Only...I was in such a hurry when I was leaving, what with trying to escape those damned tribunes before they killed me...I don't remember exactly where I stowed it." The woman suddenly moved forward, grabbing the bars in both hands, her expression desperate. "Please, Maeve. We're running out of time."

Maeve frowned, stepping back from the bars, breathing a heavy, troubled sigh. "What was it Master Silas used to say, Agnes? That an assassin's life is one of blood and fear? I wonder what he would say about all this, if he hadn't left the city."

The woman heaved an impatient sigh. "Perhaps we'll find him and ask one day, but first, Lady Maeve, I really nee—"

"The diary," Maeve said. "Yes, you said that. I've got a question of my own, though," she went on, meeting the woman's eyes. "Who are you?"

Agnes looked shocked at that, confused. "I-I'm sorry?"

"You heard me," Maeve said. "It's a good show, a good act. Almost perfect...almost."

The woman hissed, frustrated, turning her back to Maeve and burying her face in her hands. "Lady Maeve, please. I don't know what you're talking about, but the diary—"

"Is right where you left it," Maeve said. "I wasn't lying about that. Only, you're *not* you, are you? After all, Agnes—the *real* Agnes—would never forget the place she designed specifically to hide her diary. But even if she somehow had, even if she had, for reasons I couldn't imagine, decided to start using my title in any but a sarcastic way, she would never forget Master Silas. Master Silas who was not given to idle chatter or reflection about what an assassin's life was or was not. Master Silas who never left the city and couldn't have even had he wanted to—which, so far as I'm aware he did not. Master Silas who was slain by Agnes herself when it was discovered that he was selling guild secrets. Now, why don't you tell me who you really are."

The woman said nothing, at least at first, but her body began to tremble, as she stood with her back turned to Maeve, her face buried in her hands. Then a soft, almost inaudible sound began to issue from the woman's throat. At first, Maeve thought that the woman was sobbing but a moment later she realized that it was not sobbing that she'd heard.

It was laughter.

Laughter that sounded like Agnes at first, but which quickly changed to something inhuman. A sharp, squeaking sort of sound that reminded Maeve more of the sound a mouse might make than any mortal. The woman—the *thing*—turned to regard her then, and despite the fact that iron cell bars separated the two of them and that she was already well outside of the creature's reach besides, Maeve found herself taking a step back. The figure still looked like Agnes in its face, its body, but where it was different was its eyes. Eyes as black as night. "Oh well," the thing told her in a voice that was not Agnes's but a high-pitched, alien tone, "it was worth the attempt."

"What...what are you?" Maeve asked, a chill running through her.

"I am whatever is required," the thing wearing Agnes's face answered.

"But...but how did you know about us helping Agnes get out of the city?"

"Why, because she told me, of course," the creature said, cocking its head and studying Maeve, a disconcerting fact given its completely black eyes. The creature grinned, and although it still wore Agnes's face, the smile was far too wide, nearly stretching from ear to ear. "Screamed it, in fact, and that more than once."

Maeve stared at the woman, at the *thing* before her. Not Agnes, that much was sure. Not human at all. A feyling, she thought. And unless she very much missed her guess, a doppel. "You killed her," Maeve said.

The creature's eyes went wide in mock surprise, and it brought a hand to its mouth, to *Agnes's* mouth, as if in shock. "*Killed* her? Why, I wouldn't dream of it. At least, not until I am finished with her. No, Guildmaster Agnes is still very much alive and intact. At least...most of her."

Maeve frowned. She and Agnes had never been close—except, that was, when one of them was trying to stick a knife in the other's back—

but the way the creature had said that last bit still sent a shiver of dread through her. "What does that mean?"

The creature bared its teeth in another too-wide grin. "It is no easy thing, the becoming. To put on another's face, to speak as it does, to *feel* as it does...it is difficult work. *Hungry* work."

Maeve suddenly felt sick. "Did you...do you mean you...what, *ate* her?"

"Only parts," the creature said. "Only what is necessary. The secret is in the blood, you see. In the flesh and the bone, the muscle and fat."

"What secret?" Maeve asked.

"Why, who a person is, of course," the creature said as if it was obvious. "It is all part of it, of the becoming. The more of a person one has, the more one consumes, the closer the likeness. Given more time, you would not have known the difference and would have divulged the whereabouts of the diary easily enough and more besides. Still..." The creature shrugged, grinning again. "There is still time. Thanks to you and your companions and your façade regarding Guildmaster Agnes's death, I have all the time in the world for the becoming, to consume. In time, the woman herself will not be able to tell the difference between us. But, of course, by then she will not be around to witness it, for there is a price for the becoming."

"But *why?*" Maeve said. "What do you hope to gain by masquerading as a dead guildmaster?"

The creature smiled. "That which is dead might be brought back to life. And when your attempt on Guildmaster Agnes's life is made known, none will contest her, contest *me* reclaiming her spot as leader of the guild. As for what will happen then...well, I can think of some uses for a guild full of trained killers. Your people will be made to suffer, Lady Maeve, suffer terribly, before their end. And make no mistake, that end approaches. Soon, the plague of your people, the rot which has spread across our home and pushed us back into the heart of the Black Wood, will be wiped from our shores. You and all that you love, all that you have *ever* loved, will be nothing but a distant memory, a miniscule footnote in the great annals of the Fey and then, in time, not even that. In time, you and your people will be naught but dust. So the Green has decreed and so it shall be."

Hearing the creature say it with such confidence sent a shiver of fear up Maeve's spine, but she gave her head a shake. "No. Even if you have me, it makes no difference. There are others, my friends. They won't let—"

"Friends," the creature repeated, "like Prince Bernard? The Green has him in his power, and against one as mighty as he whom I serve, even the Destroyer, the greatest warrior of your people, has no chance, no more than a youngling might against a trained warrior. Less so, in truth, for the Green is powerful beyond your understanding. He is of the Eternal Green. He is part of it, and it is part of him. No, your prince is dead, Lady Maeve. Or else he wishes he was."

"Not just the prince," Maeve said, her mouth suddenly dry in reaction to the creature's words.

"Is it Challadius the Charmer of whom you speak?" the creature asked, its dark eyes glittering with mirth. "Or perhaps it is the priest to whom you refer. One a man of faith with no faith left—he is of little concern. As for your mage, he is skilled, I'll grant, as skilled in the arts of subtlety and deception as your kind are capable of being, yet he is of no consequence. He might craft whatever illusion he wants, whatever world, but here, in the *real* world, he and all those who oppose the will of the Green will be destroyed."

Maeve felt a creeping horror spreading through her as she listened to the creature's words, but she forced it down with a growl. She was no housewife to be frightened by scary stories, nor was she some blushing maid that might be easily cowed. She was Maeve the bloody Marvelous, and she refused to give this creature the satisfaction of seeing her afraid. "You are wrong," she told the thing before her with far more confidence than she felt. "There are other wills at work in the world besides that of your master."

"Such as your king, do you mean?" the creature asked. "Oh, Lady

Maeve, you are almost to be pitied. Do you not yet see? Do you think that I have acted by accident? Do you truly believe that all is not connected? A great play takes place before you and whatever choice you make is of no consequence. The ending is writ and writ already, no matter how you might rage against it. You can do naught but play your part, as we all must. And your part, the part of your people, is to die. A part which your young king is likely playing already."

"Bullshit," Maeve said with feeling. "Anyway, it wasn't the king I was speaking about but the prince. Do you think you're the first creature to think that they have beaten Prince Bernard? The graveyards are full of men—and creatures much like you—who thought the same. Each thing which stood against him believed itself destined to be victorious—as you do. And each was cut down in its time, their threats and promises proved idle, proved false beneath his axe. You think your master possesses a great will? The prince is a creature of will and little else. But that does not even matter, not for you, at least. The Crimson Prince will do what the Crimson Prince has always done. Bring death to his enemies and victory to his allies. But you will not be here to see it, I promise you that." She leaned forward, baring her teeth. "I will make an example of you, an example so that your people might be reminded in the months and years to come what happens to those who stand against us. You will die. If not by my hand, then by Priest's or Chall's or Matt's. It does not matter to me—just know that you will die, one way or the other. Challadius, for one, is far stronger than you give him credit for. But you will learn."

"Strong, is he?" the creature asked. "I see. I do not doubt that should I or another attack the mage or the priest head-on, they would put up a worthy fight. But then...that is not my way. Lady Maeve. When I come for them—and I *will* come for them—I will do so not wearing a face of the enemy..." It grinned that too wide grin again. "But a face of a friend. A face," it said, leaning forward so that she was only inches away from the bars, "of a lover."

The creature moved then, faster than Maeve would have given it credit for. She thought it meant to attack, and so she leaned away, but the creature did not go for her throat. Instead, it snatched at her hair, and Maeve cried out as it ripped a handful free. The creature grinned as it stuffed the hair into its mouth, swallowing it with an expression of what appeared to be ecstasy on its face.

"I will eat you, Lady Maeve," it told her, its dark, alien eyes watching her. "I will feast on you, bit by bit, and when I am finished, when I've had my fill and the becoming is done, then will I come for your friends." The creature let its gaze travel slowly to the cell in which Emille was still unconscious, then shrugged. "Or, at least, the rest of them. But that is for later," it said. "For now, find what rest you may, Lady Maeve. In the days to come, you will need your strength."

With that, the creature turned and Maeve watched as it walked out of the door, taking the light with it and leaving Maeve in the darkness.

CHAPTER FOUR

"You're s-s-sure about th-this?" Feledias chattered.

Cutter glanced over at his brother standing beside him on the snow-blasted hilltop, trembling, ice clinging to his eyebrows, his arms wrapped around himself as if trying to hold on to what little warmth he had. Then he looked to his other side where Matt stood watching him. Matt had grown up out in the frozen north in Brighton, and so he looked in far better shape than Feledias. Finally, Cutter turned to regard the distant village of Windam. A few dozen buildings all covered in snow so that they could barely be made out at all, even from the height of the hill on which he and his companions stood.

"No," he said. "But what I am sure of is that we won't last much longer in this blizzard. Not without supplies, at least."

"I see smoke," Matt said, pointing at the distant village.

Cutter looked back, narrowing his eyes. After a moment, he saw it, a thin trail of smoke drifting into the night air, barely visible in the darkness. "So do I," he said, giving Matt a nod. "Good eye, Son."

Matt smiled. "Thank you...Father." That word struck Cutter powerfully, and for a moment, he forgot that they stood on a snow-blasted, ice-covered hilltop in freezing temperatures, hunted by the gods alone knew how many creatures of the Fey. He had never thought to see Matt again, nor had he ever thought, even a year ago, that he and Feledias might reconcile their differences, yet here the three of them were.

"I'm a-a-all f-f-for a n-nice w-warm, family m-moment," Feledias stammered, "b-but I think m-maybe I w-would appreciate it better if my e-entire body wasn't n-numb."

"Right," Cutter said. "Come on."

The trip down the hillside was not an easy one, particularly for Feledias. The snow was thick and deep, and more than once Cutter's brother, unaccustomed to such conditions, lost his footing. Each time, Cutter and Matt helped him get to his feet, but Feledias—who grew increasingly soaked through and increasingly miserable with each fall—didn't seem in any danger of thanking them for it. He offered no more than sour grunts and muttered curses as they trudged toward the distant village.

They were about halfway there, the ground beginning to level off beneath their feet, when something to the left of the path caught Cutter's eye. He stopped, frowning.

"L-l-let me guess," Feledias stammered, "y-your feet have f-frozen in place."

"Not quite," Cutter said.

"Then wh-what?" Feledias said, shuffling up beside him. "Th-the village is j-just there, B-Bernard."

"What is it, do you think?"

Cutter turned to where Matt had walked up on his other side and was frowning at the field, clearly having noted the same thing Cutter had.

"I don't know," he said. "Stay here."

"You m-must be joking," Feledias said. "The v-village—"

"Will no doubt be there five minutes from now," Cutter said. "Wait here."

There was a fence separating the field from the path, but it had been made to keep livestock *in*, not to keep people *out*, so even half-frozen as he was, Cutter was able to climb over it with little difficulty. That done, he looked across the field at the distant barn and frowned as he noted that its doors were open. A broken latch, perhaps, likely owing to the weather, which meant that inside there would be some unhappy cows, given the frigid winds and snow.

He put it out of his mind as he moved toward the large, snow-covered lump on the ground that he'd first spotted from the road. With the driving wind and snow obscuring his vision, he could see no more than a few feet in front of his face, so that he could not be sure what it was until he was standing over it.

Cutter knelt, wiping some of the snow away to be sure then he frowned, rising again. Here, then, was at least one cow who had far greater problems than a barn door being left open. Or perhaps it was fair to say that this one, at least, was beyond such concerns. The poor creature was dead, frozen. No surprise, as it had clearly been left in the field with no protection from the hazardous weather.

Holding an arm up in a largely vain effort to block the worst of the snow from his eyes, Cutter swept his gaze around the field and saw other, similarly shaped lumps. His frown deepened. In the middle of civilization, such as the fields outside New Daltenia, a loss of a few dozen head of cattle would have been bad, might have quite possibly meant the loss of a family's fortune. But here, in the frozen wastes of the north, such beasts were raised and tended not for profit but for simple survival. After all, in the snow-blasted, ice-covered expanse of the northlands, there was very little game to be found, and what few crops the villagers managed to grow were often poor, pitiful specimens, certainly not enough to survive on.

In such a place, the loss of dozens of head of cattle was not a loss of profit or fortune—it was, likelier than not, a death sentence. A death sentence not just for the owner of the herd but also for their fellow villagers who relied on the purchasing or bartering of the meat to sustain themselves and their families.

He could think of very few reasons the farmer who owned the cows might have for leaving them out in such weather and none of them boded well. He turned to regard the village in the distance again. He might have thought that Windham, like so much of the Known Lands, had suffered from the attentions of the Fey. After all, the Fey had a long reach—one which, he knew from personal experience, had spread not just to the town of Two Rivers but all the way to New Daltenia itself. And to reach the village of Windham they would not have had to reach very far at all. A man would have needed only to travel a few hours west from the village to catch sight of the Black Wood, the homeland of the Fey, in the distance.

Or perhaps it had not been the Fey at all but bandits, for Cutter knew from his time in Brighton that there were bands of outlaws—little more than small, ragtag groups of desperate, escaped fugitives attempting to evade New Daltenia's justice—who roamed the north. Not overly dangerous—more like vultures than wolves, these scavengers—for such bands never grew much in numbers, and far more opportunistic than deadly in the conventional sense. But it could not have been bandits, for unlike the bandits of warmer climes, those to be found in the frozen north valued food far more than gold, and the cow's corpse had been left untouched.

But the biggest problem with either theory, bandit or Fey, was the village itself. It sat in the distance, looking completely undisturbed, the smoke rising from several rooftops making it apparent that someone—*several* someones—still lived there.

"*Stones and Starlight, h-hurry up, will you?*" his brother shouted from where he stood on the path, his voice barely audible over the wind that tore at Cutter's clothes and face. "*Unless you e-enjoy the pr-prospect of carrying a Feledias-shaped ice cube all the way t-to the village!*"

Cutter gave one more look at the cow at his feet, and at those other lumps scattered about the field, then he turned and walked back toward the path.

"What was it?" Matt asked.

"Dead cows," Cutter said.

"Y-you mean t-to tell me you're f-freezing me to d-death over a couple of dead c-cows?" Feledias asked.

Matt, though, was not so flippant. A troubled look had settled over the young king's face, for having grown up in the north as he had, he knew well the value of the livestock such villages as Windham kept, where the unintentional death of even a single heifer could spell a lean winter. "Wolves?" he asked, echoing the first thought Cutter had entertained when he'd come upon the body.

He shook his head slowly. "I don't think so. There wasn't any sign."

"Covered by the snow, maybe?"

Cutter frowned. "Maybe," he said, "but I doubt it...blood stands out on snow."

Matt winced. "What then?"

"Who g-gives a shit is what," Feledias asked. "Fire and salt, if th-the two of you w-want to spend your t-time talking a-about cows o-or sheep or peacocks f-feel free. I-I'll b-be happy to j-join in. O-only, how a-about we have that conversation i-in front of a fire b-before we're h-having it in the l-land of the dead?"

"Something wrong in the village, you think?" Matt asked.

"I don't know," Cutter said, turning to regard the distant village of Windham once more. It looked fine, but then in Cutter's experience most traps did right up until you stepped into them. "And I don't think it matters. Fel's right—we can't stay out here, and the nearest village is several hours away. Too far."

He didn't say too far for *what,* but judging by the worried expression Matt shot at Feledias he didn't think he needed to. Cutter's brother—Matt's uncle—wasn't looking good. But then, none of them were, and while Matt and Cutter himself might have been more accustomed to the cold than Feledias, they would freeze or die just like him if they remained too long in the blizzard.

"Come on," he said. "But be ready."

"I'll fight th-the whole damn village," Feledias said, "i-if, that is, th-they'll let me th-thaw out first."

They started forward again. As they walked, Cutter's gaze roamed the fields to either side of the snow-covered path, searching for anything else out of place or anything that might explain the dead animals.

But despite his concerns, he saw no bands of outlaws or hordes of Fey rushing toward them. Even when they reached the edge of the village of Windham, still he saw no sign of anyone.

"Where is everybody?" Matt asked, echoing Cutter's thoughts.

"P-probably i-inside d-doing their best not to f-freeze," Feledias said. "A-after all," he went on, shooting a meaningful look at Cutter, "only a special kind of f-fool w-would be out in this bl-blizzard. O-or three f-fools."

"There are people here somewhere," Cutter said, glancing around at the abandoned, snow-covered houses, their windows dark. They might have been abandoned for a thousand years, from the look of them. "Someone lit those fires, after all. Let's go find out who."

And so they set out to do just that. It was eerie, walking down what served as the village's main street without so much as a single soul stirring. True, as Feledias had pointed out anyone with any sense or at least any choice would have sought shelter indoors, away from the biting wind and frigid snow, but even still Cutter would have expected to see *some* sign of life. The most obvious of which would have been the orange, flickering glow of fires stoked in the hearths of small homes to keep the worst of the chill at bay.

Fires that, in a blizzard as bad as this one, wouldn't have been just a luxury but a necessity.

And yet there were none, at least not on the outskirts of the village.

No fires, not even so much as a candle flickering in the darkness. It was as if they walked through some ancient, long-forgotten ruin, a place where no one lived or had lived in a very long time. At least, that was, save for the couple of pillars of smoke drifting into the air from the other end of the village. Cutter and his companions had been drawn to those pillars in hopes of safety, and as they moved closer he found himself feeling a lot like a moth fluttering toward the flame. It fluttered toward it, drawn on by some impetus likely beyond even its own understanding, and yet when it reached that which it sought, it would find not safety but its doom.

He did not like that thought, but it was one that would not leave him, however much he might have wished it. Still, while the moth was in no danger of freezing to death, they were, and so they walked on. They walked on past one shell of a house then another, without even so much as a mongrel dog or a bird fluttering past.

The silence, the stillness, was so thick that it felt hard to breathe, and Cutter found himself resisting the urge to reach for his axe as his gaze scanned the street, his eyes roaming over the buildings and the spaces in between, straining to see past the heavy curtain of snow. He had walked into an ambush before, during the war against the Fey, along with a company of soldiers. He had survived it, if only just, but many of those with him had not been so lucky. He did not intend to walk into another such trap if he could help it, particularly when his son walked beside him.

But no ambush came, and as they reached the village square, Cutter was able to make out a building sitting at its center. It was from this building that the smoke they'd seen rose.

"A ch-church," Feledias said, wrapping his arms tighter about himself. "B-been a while s-since I've b-been, but I s-suppose I-I could make an exception. M-might e-even have a few p-prayers to s-say myself."

They started toward the church, and as they did the silence was finally broken by something other than the crunching of their feet in the snow. It was coming from up ahead, somewhere inside the church. At first he couldn't place that sound, so incongruous was it among that silent village far in the northern reaches of the Known Lands, but then he realized what it was. Someone was playing the lute, though while Cutter knew little of such things, he thought that saying they were *playing* it was not doing the music justice. It was beautiful, as beautiful as any music he had ever heard, yet listening to it there, in that ghost of a village, coming from a church where he would have thought to hear prayers or voices raised in benediction, Cutter found a frown coming to his face.

"A f-fine hand at the l-lute, whoever it is," Feledias said. "I h-haven't heard s-such fine playing since leaving New D-Daltenia."

As they drew closer to the church, Cutter was able to make out the sounds of men shouting and laughing, as if they were not in a church at all but the lively common room of a tavern. As they approached the stairs leading into the church something lying half-buried in snow at the church's front caught his eye. At first, Cutter thought it was a body, but as he knelt and brushed the snow covering it away, he realized it was a life-sized carving of an old man in robes. In normal times, the carving would have stood outside the church, an homage to the deity whom it represented, but someone had taken pains to knock it over. And Cutter did not doubt that it *had* been a pain, for he tested the weight and found that, indeed, the carving was one solid piece, not the sort of thing that might easily be moved or knocked over in the wind— even winds like those the blizzard was currently conjuring around them.

"Who treats their god like this?" Matt said quietly, looking at Cutter.

"What g-god?" Feledias asked. "You're sayin' this h-hoary, unforgiving looking bastard is supposed to be a god? I'll a-admit that I never p-paid as much attention to m-my religious t-tutors as I should h-have, but I don't r-recognize him."

Not true, of course, for Cutter knew that his brother had been an avid, eager student in his youth. "It's no surprise you don't recognize him," he said. "Neither do I. The villages of the north might be part of the Known Lands," he said, "but in actuality it is closer to the truth to say that each village is more like its own tiny little kingdom. Different customs and ways of life different challenges...different gods."

"Hoary, unforgiving gods for hoary, unforgiving surroundings," Matt said.

Feledias looked between the two of them, giving what might have been a shrug, though it was not easy to tell for sure with all the trembling. "W-well, you'll have to *forgive* m-me, if just now, I-I don't give a shit. L-let's get inside. I-I'll worship th-the old bastard if they like, j-just so long as we do that worshipping b-by a fire."

Cutter frowned at the church in front of them. "Just...stay close," he said. They walked up to the doors, pushing them open and stepping inside. The first thing Cutter noticed was the heat—perhaps it felt overpowering because of so long spent in the cold, but he thought it was more than that. The inside of the church felt stifling, the air thick and hot. The second thing he noticed as Matt closed the door behind them was that it didn't appear that Feledias—or anyone else inside the church—was in any danger of worshipping anyone anytime soon. At least, not with any form of worship that Cutter had ever seen before.

He hadn't spent much time in church—perhaps, if he had, his life might have taken on a far different cast—but Cutter was quite confident that any priest he'd ever met would have been appalled at the use to which the church was being put.

The church was not particularly large, though large enough, Cutter suspected, to accommodate the few hundred people that called Windham home. All of whom likely attended the services, for having lived in Brighton for as long as he had, Cutter had learned that another way in which the settlements in the frigid north differed from those in the warm climes of the south were that they were, as a rule, far more religious. No doubt owing to their hostile surroundings, for such men and women, facing as harsh a life as they did, looked somewhere for hope, for help.

Indeed, the church was packed with what must have been nearly every man and woman in the village. But they were not seated in the pews, bent in worship as he might have expected. In fact, the pews had been pushed to the sides, creating a large, open area at the room's center in which the men and women of Windham danced.

If what they were doing could be called dancing. Most of the men wore no more than their trousers, the women even less, and they all moved and swayed, gyrated and swung this way and that, in complete disregard to their surroundings or even to their age. Cutter noted several gray-haired, matronly women gyrating perversely along with the rest.

He glanced at his companions and saw that his son's face had turned red, and he did not think it was from the stifling heat. Feledias, meanwhile, was staring hungrily at the room. Or, more specifically, at the large hearth at one side of the room where a giant fire blazed. A fire which, based on the remnants of several shattered pews scattered in front of it, was being fed by the seats which had been carved for the purpose of sitting and listening to the church service.

"Wonder where they think they'll be sitting tomorrow?" Matt asked, his voice sounding as troubled as Cutter felt.

"I don't think they're thinking about tomorrow at all," Cutter said quietly.

"Damn tomorrow," Feledias said. "Today I mean to be warm. You two can stand around gawking if you like. When you're finished, you can find me by the fire...if not rolling in it."

And with that, Feledias moved past them, heading straight toward the large hearth in which the fire burned.

Cutter watched him, making sure no one accosted him, but he needn't have bothered. Feledias moved past several villagers and none so much as glanced in his direction, were instead far too busy with dancing or drinking themselves into a stupor. Though he thought the best way to do that second bit would be to scoop the ale up off the floor the way a man might water from a river. Certainly, Cutter thought there were plenty enough puddles of it lying around that he'd have little trouble doing so.

Barrels of ale were at either side of the church, some tipped over spilling their contents onto the floor even as he watched. Not that anyone seemed to notice, or if they did, then certainly they did not care. They only went on dancing to the lively tune struck up by the lute.

Cutter had never been much of a dancer. Even back in Daltenia, before the Skaalden had come and his father had died, and their people had fled across the great vast oceans to come to the Known Lands. He had never wished to be one of those indolent, spoiled young noblemen who spent their time in one woman's bed or another or dancing at this ball or that engagement. He *had* been indolent. And spoiled. And it had to be said that he had spent more than his fair share of time with one woman or another in his youth, but he had always preferred the training ground—or dueling circle—to a dance. The dueling circle where a man's enemy was clear, his path to victory straight and true, a far cry from the complexities and challenges of social life among nobles.

But while he had never been a dancer, there was something about the lute's rhythm, about the obvious skill of the person playing it, that gave him a wild urge to step forward into the crowd and give it a try anyway. After all, it wasn't as if those at the church's center were likely to judge him for his lack of grace—he thought a bear could have walked in and taken a spot among them and they would not have noticed, so entranced were they by the lute's melody.

Not that he could blame them for it, for the lute *was* entrancing. Cutter was no dancer, yet he found himself stepping forward, *pulled* forward the way a man sometimes was in a dream, moving without ever having *decided* to move. But before he could take a second step, something grabbed him by the arm, and he turned, confused, to see Matt standing there.

He had forgotten about him, for a moment. "Matt?" he asked.

"Is everything okay, Father?" his son asked, a look of concern on his face. "For a minute...you seemed...out of it. Almost like you were dreaming."

"I'm...I'm fine," Cutter said, blinking, but the truth was Matt was right. He felt as if he had just been interrupted from a dream, a particularly pleasant one. He felt the same sort of disappointed hopefulness that a man might feel when waking and finding that he was so comfortable, his dreams so pleasant, that he did not want to wake, even if he knew he should, wanted only to lie there and let that sleep steal over him once more, bringing him back into that dream. Which, of course, rarely happened. In his experience, what usually waited on the other side of that was nightmare.

"I'm fine," he said again, giving his head a shake. "Just...the lute player...they are very skilled."

Matt gave him an odd look at that, as if he'd said something strange. "Father, are you feeling alright?"

"I'm fine," he said again. "Come on—we should go check on Fel."

He turned toward the fireplace where his brother stood facing it, his hands outstretched. Feledias's back was to them, but Cutter couldn't help but notice the man was swaying his hips to the music in a dramatic—and, quite frankly, ridiculous—fashion. Apparently, Cutter wasn't the only one tempted by the music, but if he would have looked half as unskilled as Feledias then he needed to remember to thank Matt for stopping him when the wild urge to join the dancers had overtaken him.

"The sooner the better," Matt agreed.

As they stared across the church toward where Feledias stood by the fire, the lute music gave way to loud clapping until Cutter couldn't hear the lute at all. The sound of all that clapping—and the attending drunken, slurred attempts at singing from those in the church—was deafening. Matt said something at Cutter's side, but he couldn't make it out, so he paused, glancing back.

"*What?*" he said, having to yell to have any chance of being heard over all the sudden noise.

"*I said something feels wrong,*" Matt said back.

Cutter glanced at those nearest them, making sure they hadn't heard, but they didn't seem to be paying any attention at all, too wrapped up in the spectacle of the clapping and raising their voices in what might have passed for a song if a man was drunk enough. He gave Matt a nod to show that he agreed then jerked a thumb toward Feledias. He didn't know what sort of wild madness had overtaken the villagers anymore than he knew the source of the strange compulsion he'd felt to dance, but he decided that, just then, he had no interest in finding out.

He turned back to start toward the large hearth, but had managed no more than a couple of steps when a woman appeared in front of him. She looked young, in her mid-twenties if Cutter had to guess, and in her tight-fitting green dress and with the diamond earrings and necklace she wore, she would have looked far more at home in the capital of the Known Lands attending some lavish ball than she did here, in the church of a village at the end of the world.

"Hello," she said, smiling, and there was something Cutter found very alluring in that smile.

"Hi," Cutter said. Because it was what you did. And because she really was quite beautiful.

Her eyes twinkled, as if they had shared some joke. "You're not from here," she said, her gaze traveling between Cutter and his son.

"Neither are you," Cutter countered.

She shifted in what might have been a faint shrug, her slender shoulders—bared by the green dress—drawing Cutter's eye. "What can I say? I enjoy a bit of travel. And you?"

Cutter grunted. "I travel a lot. I wouldn't say enjoyment has ever had much to do with it."

"And am I to take it that you don't enjoy dancing either? I did not see you among the others," she clarified, gesturing at the villagers still dancing and drinking at the church's center, men and women who, in their rough homespun clothes and hands dirty and calloused from hard labor, looked like crude beasts next to the woman.

"I've never been much for dancing," Cutter said.

"Who are you, anyway?"

This wasn't from Cutter but Matt, and they both turned to regard his son who was looking at the woman suspiciously.

"Who are any of us, really?"

"O...kay," Matt said slowly. "Then where are you from?"

She smiled, turning back to Cutter. "Somewhere...exotic. Tell me, if it is not dancing or drinking that interests you—" she raised a perfectly-shaped eyebrow—"then what sort of diversion sounds more... appealing?"

Cutter felt his face heat, a reaction not strictly caused by the fire, or by his frozen body thawing out. Although it did seem as if there was a part of him, a part that had been frozen over for years, decades, really, that had begun to thaw. Perhaps it had been the music or the heat—a heat that seemed to spread through him as the woman regarded him. Or perhaps it was something else, the woman's face, her smile, her voice. He didn't know. All he knew was that he felt as if that part *had* begun to thaw. He opened his mouth to speak, but Matt beat him to it.

"A bed would be nice," Cutter's son said, then when Cutter and the woman turned to him, the young king's face flushed a bright red. "For sleeping," he stammered.

The woman glanced at Cutter, giving him another demure smile. "Sleeping is all well and good, but I find that it is not the best use to which one might put such accommodations. Wouldn't you agree?"

Cutter found himself smiling, feeling the way he had when he'd been a far younger—far more foolish—man. Nervous and clumsy and excited all at once. "I w—"

"For sleeping," Matt repeated, his voice stern. "Uncle really is quite wearied from his travels, Father."

That made Cutter pull his gaze away from the woman before him—no easy thing, for there was something incredibly powerfully alluring about her—to gaze at the fireplace where Feledias had last stood. Feledias was still there, but now he was raising his own voice in song, adding it to the chorus of drunken shouts filling the room. He hoisted a tankard of ale—the gods alone knew where he'd gotten it—high into the air, doing the already terrible song no favors.

"Tell me, did you like the music?"

Cutter turned back to the woman. "What's that?"

"The lute," she said. "Did you enjoy its notes?"

"The musician was very talented. I have heard very few so skilled, if ever."

Matt made a strange sound at that, and Cutter glanced over to see his son looking at him oddly again.

The woman stared at Matt with a slightly annoyed, perhaps even confused expression on her face before turning back to Cutter. "Well," she said, giving him another dazzling smile, "the musician thanks you for the compliment."

"Wait, that was you playing?"

She gave a small curtsey. "It was."

"Well, it was fi—" he began, then cut off as there was a loud *crash*. Cutter turned to the center of the room and saw that one of the gray-haired, matronly women he'd noted dancing when they'd arrived had tripped. Or, given how still she was as she lay there, he thought that she hadn't tripped at all but fainted. The other dancers paid her no mind, continuing their dancing.

"We should go see if she's okay," Matt said.

"Right," Cutter said, starting forward.

"I can assure you, she's quite fine," the woman said, making Cutter hesitate. "Sometimes, people get so into the music that they dance until they are exhausted...a hazard of my profession, I'm afraid." She gave her fingers a snap, glancing at a couple of nearby men who immediately stopped dancing and moved forward, lifting the woman up between them and bearing her toward a door at the back of the church.

"Where are they taking her?" Matt said, frowning.

"A private room, where she might rest and recover and be seen to, that's all," the woman said. She smiled. "Nothing nefarious, I assure you."

Matt didn't return the smile, only regarded Cutter instead. "We need to get Uncle and go find somewhere to rest, Father, and get supplies."

"Oh, stay a while," the woman said, putting a hand on Cutter's arm, the touch sending a chill up his spine as she looked up into his gaze with eyes that seemed as big as saucers. "We could have some fun together."

Fun. Cutter couldn't remember the last time he'd had it, or the last time he'd *thought* to have it. For days, months, years all he had thought of was his purpose. He had left no time for fun, and he had not missed it. Or, at least, he had thought he hadn't. Now, though, with the woman smiling at him, he thought that maybe he would like to have some fun. What harm, after all, in setting down his purpose, his mission, for a little while? He could always pick it back up again.

"Father," Matt said. "We have to go. We need to get supplies, get some rest, and leave, remember?"

"Leave?" the woman asked. "In this weather?"

"If we have to," Matt said stubbornly.

"And where is it you're going?" she asked, turning to Cutter. "I do so worry about you going out in this horrible weather."

"Our destination is our business and ours alone," Matt said. "Isn't it, Father?" he finished, meeting Cutter's eyes.

Cutter winced, turning back to the woman. "He's right," he said. "Sorry, but we have to go. It...it was nice meeting you. Come on," he told his son. "Let's go get your uncle."

He nodded his head at the woman then he started away toward where Feledias still stood near the large hearth.

"Ah, brother! Nephew!" Feledias exclaimed, grinning and lifting a nearly empty ale glass high in the air in salute with one arm, his other wrapped around the shoulders of a short, buxom woman who had a vacant, dazed look on her reddened, sweat-covered face. "Did you hear that fine music? It was as if one of the gods themselves graced us with a song! I do hope the lute player, whoever he was, might start up again soon."

Cutter frowned at his brother's cavalier attitude, as if he didn't have a care in the world and realized, as he did, that he had been acting much the same only a moment ago when speaking with the woman. Perhaps it had been the music or perhaps it had been the woman's presence or the heat of the church, that felt nearly as if they were standing in a furnace. Perhaps it was a combination of all three. Either way, Matt had been right—they had things to be about. "Come on, brother," Cutter said, thinking it better, as he had since entering the church, if he did not use their actual names. "It's time we left."

"Leave?" Feledias asked as if he were crazy. "Why, it's early yet, Berna—"

"Now," Cutter said, grabbing his brother's arm and interrupting him before he could say his real name. "Sorry," he said to the woman who was bouncing in a sort of distracted dance, meeting his eyes with a look that almost seemed as if she were sleep walking.

"S'alright," she said.

"Hey," Feledias said. "That isn't very civil of you, Ber—"

"We really need to go, Uncle. Supplies, remember?"

Feledias gave a frustrated huff, looking at Matt, then back to Cutter. He heaved a sigh. "Fine, but I want to note my protest."

"Noted," Cutter said. "Now come on."

They started toward the doors of the church, had made it about halfway there when a figure stepped in front of them. "Bernard?"

Cutter froze at that, eyeing the figure. The man was overweight, but he had the broad shoulders and thick arms of a man who had once been a warrior. He had a long red beard streaked through with white and hair to match. A scar ran down one cheek, proof that he had indeed been a warrior and that not all of the fights he'd been in had gone his way. Of course, Cutter had been in enough to know that they never did.

"I-I thought that was you," the man said. "Couldn't believe it."

"Do I know you?" Cutter asked.

The man grunted. "Sure you do. Or, at least, you did. About five stone ago," he finished, patting his ample belly.

Cutter frowned, trying to place the man. There was something familiar about him, but he couldn't think what that was, was still trying to figure it out when the man spoke again.

"If you want to know a man," the red-bearded man said, "watch him—"

"Bleed," Cutter finished with him, staring at the man in shock. "Fabor? The Fierce?"

The man grinned. "And here I thought you weren't goin' to remember me. Anyway, it's more Fabor the Fat nowadays," he said, clapping a hand on his large belly. "I guess the only thing still fierce about me is my appetite. Leastways my wife, Laura, would say so." What might have been a troubled expression flashed across the red-headed man's face, but it was gone in a moment.

"Wait...you know each other?" Matt asked.

Fabor turned to regard Matt, raising an eyebrow at him before glancing at Cutter. "Well? Who's this then?"

"This...this is my son," Cutter said, still shocked to see the man here, on the outskirts of the Known Lands.

Fabor gave a low whistle at that. "Son, is it? Well, seems you've been busy, Bernard. I imagine there's a tale there."

The last thing Cutter wanted to do was relive his past, so he nodded. "We all have our stories."

Fabor grunted, grinning. "Same ol' Bernard—as abrupt as a punch in the nose."

"So...what?" Matt said. "The two of you, you're old friends?"

"Closer'n that, lad," Fabor said, barking a laugh. "Old enemies."

Matt glanced at Cutter, a question in his eyes, but it was Feledias who spoke. "Well, I can't say I'm surprised at that. My brother has a way of making enemies, right enough."

Fabor blinked. "Prince Feledias, is it?"

"Oh, I think, considering that we're on the ass end of the world, we can forego the formalities," Feledias said. "No need of bowin'."

"Just as well," the red-headed man said. "My back wouldn't thank me for it."

"Enemies?" Matt asked.

The red-headed man nodded. "Oh, sure, lad. Why, there were a couple of duels, decades ago, where I reckon I did just about my level best to kill your father, here. Leastways until he left me a gibbering, bloody mess."

"You came awful close a few times," Cutter said.

Fabor barked a laugh. "Well, had a name to live up to, didn't I? Anyway, what brings you all out here? I've seen some things livin' in Windham, but I'll be honest, I never expected I'd run into one prince, let alone two. It's too bad Laura's back at the house, sick. She'll never believe it when I tell her."

"We'd just as soon not advertise that we're here," Cutter said.

The red-headed man glanced between them. "Oh, right. Sorry. Laura's always told me I had a big mouth."

"You don't mind my saying so," Cutter said, "I never expected you of all people to get married."

"Yeah, me neither," Fabor said. "But then life is full of surprises." He nodded his head at Matt. "S'pose you know that well enough, don't you?"

"I do," Feledias said.

Cutter winced at that, confident that he was thinking of the injustice Cutter had done to him in sleeping with his fiancé, Matt's mother.

Fabor glanced between them. "I didn't mean to prod any old scars, if that's what I done. Fumblin' Fabor, my Laura sometimes calls me, and that with good reason. Anyway, the gods know I got enough old scars myself that the last thing I'd do is pick at someone else's."

"It's fine," Feledias said. "As you say, old scars, that's all."

The red-headed man gave a nod. "So then, what's brought you all out here?"

Cutter didn't need to glance to the side to see Matt looking at him, for he could feel his son's gaze on him, hoping he didn't say too much. "We're just passing through, that's all," Cutter said. "Hoping to find some supplies and somewhere to wait out the blizzard."

"Might be you'll be waitin' for a while," Fabor said. "This blow is lookin' particularly ornery. The mountains tryin' to shove us off their land, my Laura says. Still," he went on, "if it's accommodations you're lookin' for, might be you're in luck. We don't have any fancy inns like you'll find in the capital, but Laura and I've got a spare room."

"We wouldn't want to be any trouble," Cutter said.

Feledias snorted. "That'd be a first."

The red-headed man grinned. "What trouble? Why, it ain't every day a fella entertains royalty. Anyway, seems to me you all could use the rest as you look just about done in. You can give me a list of what supplies you're needin' and I'll get it for you while you're sleepin', have it waitin' on you when you're ready. 'Course, I'd know a whole lot better what to get if I knew where it was you were meanin' to go."

"I think we can give a list," Cutter said. He glanced at Feledias and Matt in question.

"I'm...not sure," Matt said.

"Well, I am, Nephew," Feledias said. "This is why we came, isn't it? And while you two might enjoy the prospect of freezing your balls off, I'd just as soon extend this reprieve for as long as possible. Who knows, I might get lucky and die in bed and not have to feel that wind cutting at me like knives."

Cutter turned to regard Matt.

His son shrugged, a concerned expression on his face. "If you think it's a good idea."

Cutter wasn't sure that he could be trusted on what was a good idea, not considering that, five minutes ago, he'd been on the verge of breaking into dance, an affront no one would have thanked him for. Still, Feledias was right—they needed supplies and it wasn't as if Windham had a lot of options when it came to accommodations.

"Alright," Cutter said, turning back to Fabor. "We appreciate the offer, and we'd be happy to take you up on it."

"Good, well that's settled then," Fabor said. "You'll get to meet Laura, if she's feelin' better."

"I hope her illness isn't anything serious," Matt said.

"Oh, nothin' like that," the man said, looking over their shoulder into the room as the lute began to play again. "She's just feelin' a bit under the weather is all. Come on," he went on, flashing another grin which struck Cutter as forced. "Let's head to the house and get you all sorted. It ain't far."

Cutter nodded, and then they were following Fabor toward the church doors. Before he stepped out into the blizzard once more, Cutter glanced back and saw the men and women still dancing as they had been, still clapping, several of them looking as if they would follow the passed-out woman into exhaustion-driven unconsciousness. He saw the woman in the green dress, too, standing atop the dais where, normally, a priest would have preached to his congregation. Only she did not preach but played her lute, and her "congregation," such as it was did not worship—at least not in any sense he had seen before. If their gyrating, lascivious movements *were* to be taken as worship, then he did not know to what or to whom that worship was directed and decided that he would rather not know. The woman in the green dress must have sensed him looking at her, for she met his eyes and gave him a wink before Cutter turned and followed Fabor and the others out into the cold.

CHAPTER FIVE

THERE WERE two guards posted at the end of the hall leading to the king's quarters. He knew that Commander Malex would have no doubt stationed them there to ensure that the king's rooms would be left undisturbed, so that they might try to investigate the scene and piece together what happened. Still, as Chall moved closer, giving them a nod as they stepped to the side to allow him to pass, he couldn't help but feel that their presence seemed a lot like closing the hen house door once the fox was already inside. Or, perhaps, like a drunken husband choosing to stagger home and apologize to his angry wife an hour or two after she decided—in her anger—to find her enjoyment elsewhere. Perhaps she would regret it in the morning, likely they both would, but that didn't mean they could go back and change anything. Chall knew that well enough, for he had been that fox often enough over the years.

But as he stepped past the guards, all too aware of the swords scabbarded at their sides, the feeling that they were largely pointless wasn't the only one that overcame him. There was also fear. He'd spent the last several hours running this way and that—or at least painfully shuffling, at any rate. He'd been distracted; he *was* exhausted, but not so distracted nor exhausted to forget that only a few hours ago several guardsmen much like the ones in the hallway had done their level best to kill him and had quite nearly succeeded.

There was nothing to say that the two guards stationed in the hallway were part of the conspiracy to assassinate Matt as well as Chall and the others. There was no reason to believe that they were conspiring with Catham and Robert Palden and the red-headed woman, Margaret—but neither was there anything to say they weren't. And considering the fact that some of their number had so recently tried to put a few extra holes in Chall, he thought he might be forgiven for the cold itch between his shoulder blades as he walked down the hallway, part of him sure, absolutely *certain* that one of the guards was creeping up behind him and about to drive his sword into Chall's back.

Chall felt great relief, then, when he reached Matt's door unmurdered. A relief that lasted right up until he had the thought that should the guards be in on it, they need not murder him in the hallway and risk being seen or heard. Not when they could just as easily leave someone —or maybe several someones—inside the king's quarters, prepared to ambush him the moment he walked inside.

That didn't make sense—after all, the guards would have had no way of knowing if or when he'd return to Matt's chambers, not unless they had a side job as one of the street prophets, who loved to stand at New Daltenia's street corners. Always preaching that doom was coming and that the end of the world was at hand, a prophecy that seemed depressingly possible just then.

No, it was ridiculous to think that they would lay an ambush inside the king's quarters on the off chance that someone would return.

But Chall thought it anyway.

He eased the door open, his entire body tensed, though his chances of being able to outrun any lurking ambusher were about the same as his chances of doing a cartwheel without falling on his ass. He held his breath as the door swung open and, as he'd feared, there was indeed a figure waiting in the king's quarters. Only, oddly enough this ambusher was not facing toward the door but away from it—one of the first things ambushers would have been taught in ambusher school, he imagined—and, after a heart-stopping, breath-catching moment, Chall had a vague inkling that perhaps the ambusher wasn't an ambusher at all. A moment after that he realized that he recognized the figure standing there even before he turned.

"Hello, Chall," Valden said quietly.

Seeing his friend standing there, Chall's fear vanished in a moment to be replaced by a great flood of relief. But quickly on the heels of that relief came another feeling—anger. A lot of it. "Ned said you were back."

"Yes."

"Well, seems you missed all the fun," Chall said. "While you were out doing...well, whatever it is you were doing, someone tried to kill Matt."

"I know," Valden said quietly. "I just want to say, Chall, that—"

"Maeve's gone, too," he said, and he was surprised to find that his hands were trembling with emotion, and hot tears of anger were gathering in his eyes. It wasn't Valden's fault, he knew, not any of it, but just then it *felt* like it was. "Not that you care."

"That isn't true," Valden said. "Chall—"

"You know, there was a time," Chall went on as if the man hadn't spoken, "that I looked to you for hope. Oh, sure, I never would have said it, maybe, but I did. Sometimes it seemed to me, *most* times, that I was lost in some great ocean, tossed about by waves, and you and your faith were an anchor, something I could hold on to. Now, I realize you are just as lost as the rest of us."

The man winced at that, as if Chall had struck him an actual blow, and while some part of Chall felt bad about that, another part wasn't even close to being finished. "Where *were* you?" he said, *demanded*. "We needed you, Valden. And you weren't here. Shit, even when you're here you're not really here."

"Chall, listen—"

"Bernard's gone," Chall said. "Maeve...Maeve's gone, too. Even

Matt's gone now, and I feel alone, Pri—sorry, *Valden*. Stones and starlight, I *am* alone. And in case you haven't noticed, things are falling apart."

"I'm sorry, Chall," Valden said softly. He stepped forward and put a hand on Chall's shoulder. "I wanted to be here."

Chall looked at the man who had once been one of his closest friends but who had, over the last several weeks, become almost like a stranger. Recently, when he'd looked at him he'd felt as if he looked at a stranger, a man who was so different from the one Chall had once known that he might as well have been a different person altogether. But now...perhaps it was due to his stress—or maybe to the blurred vision caused by the tears in his eyes—but Chall almost thought he could see a bit of his old friend in the man's haggard, ashamed face.

"I'm sorry I wasn't here," he said. "I'm sorry I haven't been here. But I'm here now."

"Are you?" Chall said. "Are you *really*?"

A strange expression passed across Valden's face, one that Chall couldn't have identified. "I'm trying to be," he said.

Chall grunted. "Suppose I'll have to take it as it's the best on offer."

"What were you saying before?" Valden asked. "About Maeve being gone?"

"She's at the Assassins' Guild," Chall said, feeling despair very close, just then, feeling as if any moment he might be overcome with a desire to dash madly through the city, screaming her name. "Emille came by saying there was a problem that needed Maeve's attention, and they left."

"What sort of problem?"

"I don't know," Chall said, "but they're not the Guild of Hugs and Handshakes, are they?"

"No," Valden said quietly, "no they're not. But Maeve can take care of herself, Chall. Better than any of us, I think."

"The prince could take care of himself, too," Chall reminded him, "but he's gone. Dead, maybe."

"We don't know that."

"No," Chall said, "we don't. But how long's he been gone now, Valden? Weeks? Weeks in the Black Wood with thousands, maybe millions of Fey that all want him dead, with no one but his brother to watch his back, his brother who, up until recently, wanted the same. Bernard is the strongest bastard I've ever met, and I'd put him against anyone, but as much as we might not want to believe it, it seems to me that that's the sort of story that writes itself."

"But we don't *know* that," Valden repeated. "He might have succeeded. If anyone can, Bernard can."

"Sure," Chall said. "Maybe the prince who is famous for killing the gods alone know how many Fey during the war, the same prince who is responsible for separating their king's head from his shoulders with an axe *they* gave him, has somehow managed to broker a peace with no leverage that I can see. As you say, if anyone can, Bernard can, but then why haven't we heard from him? After all, it's been weeks, hasn't it? Weeks without so much as a word."

"That doesn't mean anything," Valden said. "The Black Wood is not close, and making peace with the Fey would be no easy task—"

"Likely an impossible one," Chall interrupted.

"Even if things *are* going well," Valden went on, "it would take time to negotiate a peace and more time still to get word back to New Daltenia. Things might yet be alright, Chall."

Chall gave a shaky sigh. "I wish I could believe that," he said. "I really do. But Bernard's gone. *Maeve's* gone."

"We have to have faith in her, Chall," Valden said. "We have to have faith in them both."

Chall tried for a laugh but it came out sounding far closer to a sob than he would have liked. "Careful," he said. "You're sounding a lot more like a Priest than a Valden."

His friend gave him a small smile. "As for Matt, I know that Robert Palden is behind his kidnapping. I don't know why they've taken him, but if they chose to kidnap him instead of...well, instead of something else, then that means they need him for something. And whatever that something is—likely ransom in hopes of making us give in to their demands—at least we know that, until they get what they want, they won't dare harm him. It gives us time, Chall, time to figure out where they've taken him, where they're keeping him."

"It would," Chall said, nodding slowly, raising his gaze to meet that of his friend. "Only, if you ask me, I don't think they've got him at all."

Valden frowned. "What do you mean? What other possibility is there? I know that Commander Malex has been worried about him... where is he, anyway?"

"Commander Malex?" Chall asked. "He's organizing a search party to hunt for the king. Not that it took much organizing. Everyone in the castle with a heartbeat volunteered to help—the people love Matt, there's no doubt of that."

"Well, that's good. That so many are looking, I mean," Valden said.

Chall gave a small shrug. "Yeah, I suppose. But I don't think they'll find anything."

"You don't think Robert Palden and his people have Matt, and you don't think Matt is anywhere in the castle or city that he might be found," Valden said.

"That's right."

"There's a lot I don't know, Chall," Valden said, "but as I understand it, people don't just vanish into thin air."

"Funny," Chall said. "That's almost exactly how she said it."

"How who said it?"

"Lady Valencia," Chall said. "I visited her—Ned came in a little while later. Anyway, we were asking her some questions, and Ned asked her about what had happened to Matt. She said he vanished. Just...disappeared."

"She's lying, then."

"To what end?" Chall asked. "I only ask because it seems to me that Lady Valencia, whatever else she is, is one of those people who does very little without a purpose behind it, a purpose to which she is completely dedicated. I mean, shit, she was willing to chop off one of her fingers just to convince us to trust her enough and make us think it *necessary* enough for her to stay in the castle."

"It is clear they have planned this for some time," Valden said grimly. "That is a lot of effort to go through in order to assassinate Matt."

"It would be, yeah," Chall said. "But I'm not sure that's what it's about at all."

"No?" Valden said, clearly confused by the expression on his face. "Why else go through all the trouble? Not just with Lady Valencia, but the woman, too, the one you and Maeve stumbled on."

"Margaret," Chall said, frowning.

"Right," Valden agreed. "She's the only reason we're aware of the Wolves' return at all. Why send her, why risk it if you were Robert Palden? What possible reason could she have to come to the castle except to kill the king?"

"I have a few theories about that," Chall said. "But now that I think on it, maybe we should find Ned first. He went to the Academy too, after all. It might be that he could have some thoughts on it."

"Thoughts on *what*?" Valden asked, confused. "And what academy are you talking about?"

"Why, *the* Academy, of course, the one to which every snot-nosed little boy who shows either an interest in or an aptitude for magic used to go in Daltenia, back before the Skaalden came."

"I...I don't understand this at all," Valden said. "But what I can tell you is that if it's Ned you're looking for, I'm afraid you're out of luck, at least for a little while. Or else we have a bit of a walk ahead of us."

It was Chall's turn to frown, confused. "What does that mean?"

"He left the castle a little while ago," Valden explained. "He went back home, said he wanted to check on Emille. I guess with everything that's happened, he wanted to make sure she was alright."

"Ah, right," Chall said, thinking of Maeve. With any luck, she and Emille had finished with whatever business had called them back to the

Assassins' Guild and both would be returning to the castle soon. Though not soon enough. He thought he was beginning to have at least a little bit of a handle on things, but then he'd thought that before, been wrong before. He would have liked to have spoken to Maeve about it, though in truth he would have settled for speaking with her about anything.

"Are you going to tell me what this is all about, Chall?" Valden said. "What did you mean by saying that you don't think they have Matt? Or that the red-headed woman wasn't here to assassinate him?"

"In a moment," Chall said. "First, tell me what you've been up to. What happened with Nadia and Catham?"

Valden winced. "I wouldn't worry about Catham anymore. I doubt we'll be seeing him again."

Chall was glad of that, and the gods knew he would shed no tears if the man died, not considering that he'd tried to kill Chall and his companions on multiple occasions. Still, that didn't keep his mouth from going dry at the way Valden said it. "Your friend Nadia?"

"A person like Nadia doesn't have friends, only people she uses," Valden said. "But yes. Catham betrayed her, and Nadia is not the forgive and forget type."

"Right," Chall said, clearing his throat. "And what about the church you went to, the priest you meant to see. How'd that go?" Valden gave him a surprised look, and Chall grunted. "Ned told me. As it turns out some people actually like to share what's going on."

"I was going to tell you, only—"

"Only you thought I would do something stupid like go with you while my legs were wounded."

Valden looked away, a shamed look on his expression, and Chall sighed. "Forget it. Just tell me—how'd it go with the priest?"

"Not a priest. A conman."

"And here I thought those were the same thing."

Valden frowned. "Do you really believe that?"

Chall considered that then sighed, shaking his head. "I guess maybe not. Anyway, how'd the meeting go with your conman?"

"Considering the fact that Willy tried to have me killed, I'd say it didn't go as well as hoped."

Chall blinked. "A conman *and* a murderer. I suppose that times being what they are, a man has to branch out."

"Maybe," Valden said, "but not Willy. Along with being a conman, he also just so happens to be a coward. He prefers to have someone else do his killing for him, assuming he can manage it."

Chall raised an eyebrow, studying his friend's expression. "And did he? Manage it?"

"Very nearly," Valden said, his expression grim.

"Doesn't really seem like the sort of person you'd want to go to for help."

"Wanting had very little to do with it," Valden agreed. "Still, I thought it necessary. I went to him hoping that he could give me a lead on Robert Palden's whereabouts."

"And did he?"

"He did one better, in fact. He brought Robert Palden to me."

"I...don't understand," Chall said. "What do you mean he brought him to you?"

"I was coming back to the castle from visiting Nadia," Valden said, "when Willy and another man who he introduced as Robert Palden were waiting for me."

"Wait a minute," Chall said, "do you mean the *same* Robert Palden who, according to Nadia, killed dozens of people at that brothel?"

"Not according to Nadia—according to me," Valden said. "I saw what was left once Robert Palden paid a visit to Flo's and there wasn't much. Besides the corpses."

"Right," Chall said, a shiver going down his spine. Sure, it wasn't as if *he* was the one standing in a dark alleyway—he just assumed it would be dark—in front of a madman capable of taking on dozens of hardened criminals, apparently without breaking a sweat, but that was little comfort. After all, that madman was out there somewhere, and if Chall was right, he held in his pocket something the man would do just about anything to get his hands on. As for what that might be, who could say? That was the thing about madmen. It was nearly impossible to guess what they were going to do, particularly when they likely had no idea themselves.

"So they were waiting for you in the alley," Chall continued. "Robert Palden and Willy, your conman friend who, unless I miss my guess, was hoping that *someone* was going to die. So—what happened?"

Valden gave him a grim smile. "Someone died," he said. "Willy thought that betraying me to the leader of the Crimson Wolves would earn him some sort of favor—or likely just coin. Either way, I expect that it came as a bit of a surprise when Robert Palden decided to kill him."

Chall grunted, feeling something sour in his stomach. "He killed him?"

"Ripped his head off," Valden said.

Chall winced, clapping a hand to his stomach as his guts seemed to do a flip inside him. "How...you know what? I don't want to know. What I am curious about is how you made it away. I don't suppose we got lucky and you killed him?"

"I'm afraid not," Valden said. "In fact, I got the impression that killing Robert Palden is not going to be a simple task."

"How did you make it away then?"

"I...suppose you would call it divine providence."

"Been a while since I've heard you use words like that," Chall said.

"Been a while since I've felt the urge to," Valden said. "Still, whatever you call it, Brother Elmer—he's one of the priests from Willy's church. A real priest, not a conman. He showed up and ran the leader of the Crimson Wolves over with a carriage."

"Priests," Chall said, shaking his head. "One minute it's, 'be kind to your neighbor,' the next it's 'run them over with a carriage.'"

"Well, in this case I'm glad he did," Valden said. "It didn't kill Robert Palden, but it did give us time to get away."

"And then what?"

"And then I came here. Before I left him with Nadia, Catham, likely thinking it was too late to make any difference, did a little gloating. He told me the truth about Lady Valencia, and so I rushed here as fast as I could. Though…" He turned back, regarding the room, the knocked over table and chair, "I was not fast enough."

"Neither was I," Chall said, "or any of us."

Valden shook his head angrily. "I should have seen it coming."

"Well, sure you should have, we all should have," Chall said. "After all, elderly noblewomen who are old friends are always trying to kill kings. Why, I think there's even a social club."

Valden blinked. "You're being sarcastic."

"Damn right I am," Chall said. "Nobody could have seen what that crazy woman meant to do—and she *is* crazy, Valden. Of that, I am quite sure. Anyway, while we might have been too late to stop her, I think something *else* did."

His friend's eyebrows drew down in a frown. "I don't understand."

"Neither do I," Chall admitted, "at least not fully, not yet. But I think I'm beginning to."

"Anyway, that's my story," Valden said. "I'd say it's time you told me yours."

Chall nodded slowly. "Help me turn the table and chairs over, will you? I think it might be best if we have a seat—this'll take a bit."

"I thought you said Commander Malex wanted us to leave everything the way it was."

"He did," Chall said, "but I've been stabbed in the legs twice, and if I don't sit down soon, I'm going to fall down. I can't imagine a fat mage sprawled in the room would help us figure out what happened. Besides, it isn't as if the table and chairs attacked Matt, is it?"

"Alright," Valden said, "but if Commander Malex goes looking for someone to blame, I'm sending him to you."

"I never would have thought I'd say this," Chall said, "but pissing off the commander of New Daltenia's troops is, at the moment, the least of my concerns. Now come on and help me, damn you."

In truth, Valden did the lion's share of the work—if there was one benefit to being stabbed in the legs, Chall figured it was that people didn't expect much from you. But then, they never had expected all that much from him in the first place, and rightly so.

In another few minutes they were seated at the table, Chall letting out a heavy sigh of relief as he leaned back in his chair, rubbing at his leg where Catham's man had stabbed him. It still hurt, but not as bad as it had, and he thought maybe he should be thankful for that. After all, the only people in the world who didn't hurt were the dead ones. "That's better," he said. "Now then, where were we?"

"You were about to tell me why you're not terrified at the prospect of Robert Palden having Matt," Valden said.

"Ah, that's easy," Chall said, giving his friend a small smile. "Faith."

Valden blinked. "Faith," he repeated.

"What, you think priests have the market cornered, that it?" Chall said.

"Maybe you'd better explain," Valden said.

"'I'm not terrified," Chall said, "because I don't think Robert Palden has Matt at all. As I told you before, when Ned and I spoke with Lady Valencia, she admitted that she had tried to assassinate Matt. She even freely confessed that she was working for Robert Palden. And as I told you, she said that Matt—"

"Disappeared right in front of her, something like that," Valden said. "She might have been lying, Chall. Considering that she had just finished trying to murder a king in cold blood, I don't think she'd have a problem doing so."

"Maybe not," Chall said. "Maybe you're right...but I don't think so. If she was acting, then she missed her calling, and she ought to have been gracing some traveling troupe's stage rather than skulking around castle chambers trying to assassinate kings. Besides, Valden, I know something about liars—I've been one nearly all my life, after all. And I'll let you in on a little secret—lies take effort. Effort that a person wouldn't want to waste if there was no purpose in it. And what purpose would there be for her to tell us Matt vanished when he didn't? Not to help herself, for she was caught already. Pretty hard to claim she wasn't there to hurt Matt when we literally walked in to see her with a knife raised. Not to help Robert Palden because if he *did* have Matt, such as to ransom him like you said, then of course he's going to want us to *know* that. Not much good ransoming someone when you don't have them to ransom."

"She might have just been toying with you," Valden said, frowning thoughtfully. "Hoping to keep you looking for answers in the wrong places."

"The thought crossed my mind," Chall said, "but I don't think so. The real question, anyway, isn't what I'm looking for as much as it is what *she* was looking for."

"What does that mean?"

"She was the one who went to Mistress Ophasia's quarters, who broke in and killed the serving woman."

"Are you sure?" Valden said, clearly as surprised by this revelation as Chall had been when he'd first learned it while interrogating the noblewoman.

"I am."

"But...why?" Valden said. "I understand that she worked for Robert Palden all this time and that his plan was for her to gain access to the castle. But why would she risk giving herself away to break into the room of the mistress of servants, if that would jeopardize her assassination of the king?"

"She wouldn't," Chall said simply, "not if assassinating Matt was her primary goal. See, I don't think she was here to kill Matt at all."

"But you just said you came in on her with a knife raised."

"I'm not saying she *wouldn't* kill Matt, or even that it wasn't one of the reasons why she was here. I'm only saying it wasn't the *main* reason. She was looking for something. The same thing, I think, that the red-headed woman, Margaret, was searching for in the king's quarters."

"But what?" Valden said. "What could possibly be so important? Important enough to risk not only betraying the existence of the Wolves but also risking Lady Valencia's position inside the castle? Not money, surely. Lady Valencia is the richest person in New Daltenia, if not in all the Known Lands."

"You're right," Chall said. "I don't think she came for coin. I think she came for this."

He reached into his tunic and pulled out the necklace, wondering if he only imagined the slight charge he felt in his fingertips when he touched it. He held it out and Valden raised an eyebrow.

"Wait, that is the necklace Matt was always fiddling with, isn't it?"

"It is," Chall said.

Valden took the offered necklace, examining it. "It is special, I assume?"

"If I'm right," Chall said, "this isn't just a necklace. It is the *reason*. The reason why Robert Palden sent Margaret here in the first place, the reason Lady Valencia broke into Mistress Ophasia's quarters and murdered that poor serving girl who just happened in on her at the wrong time. I don't think that necklace is just worth a small fortune, Valden. I think it's worth far more than that."

"More?" Valden asked, glancing away from the green stone fixed in the necklace. "What do you think it's worth?"

"A kingdom," Chall said simply. "I think it's worth the life of every man, woman, and child in the Known Lands. Or, at least, I think *Robert Palden* thinks so."

"How could a simple necklace be worth so much?" Valden asked, his expression skeptical.

"By being far more than a simple necklace," Chall said. "Tell me, do you feel anything when you touch it?"

Valden looked at the necklace he held warily but after a moment shook his head. "No. Nothing."

"Nor should you," Chall said. "After all, while you have many talents—being a pain in the ass comes to mind—the Art is not one of them."

"You're saying you feel something?"

"I do," Chall said. "For you, as for most, such workings are like a language, not one that you don't understand, but one that you can't even *hear*. But *I* hear it. Others would, too. It is one of the reasons I hoped to speak to Ned about it—as an Empath, he would be sensitive to the necklace's true nature, perhaps even more than me."

"I see. And what *is* the nature of it, then?"

"I...I don't know," Chall said. "At least not yet," he added hurriedly. "But I will. There's magic in this necklace, Valden. Powerful magic. I don't know what its purpose is, but clearly it's important enough that Robert Palden is willing to kill over it."

"It doesn't take all that much for him to be willing to kill, I think," Valden said. "But if you say the necklace is important, Chall, then I believe you. What can I do to help?"

"I'll need time," Chall said. "With the necklace. That's all. I have never examined an artifact imbued with the Art—at least not outside of the Academy. But while I might not have paid much attention during my lessons, I paid enough to know that discerning the true use of such an artifact takes effort and dedication. Two things which I historically haven't excelled at."

"If anyone can do it, I'm sure that you can," Valden said.

Chall was surprised by how much those words affected him, how much he felt buoyed up by the faith his friend placed in him. "Thanks," he said.

"Of course," Valden said. "But what does any of this have to do with Matt?"

"Maybe nothing," Chall said, thinking. "Maybe a lot."

"You think...the necklace has something to do with the things that have been going on with him?"

"I'm...not sure," Chall said. "Whatever's going on with Matt, it isn't just from this necklace. Before, when he first told me that he could hear people's thoughts, part of me..." He winced. "Well, I was worried. I thought that maybe there was some sort of...problem."

"You mean that he had gone crazy?"

"Or something like it," Chall said, nodding. "I mean shit, Valden, look at the last year of the boy's life. If anyone's got a right to go a little crazy, it's him."

"That's true," Valden said.

"Anyway, I had hoped that, given time, and given Malden's attention, it—whatever *it* was—would get better. It didn't, though. It got worse. Or at least I thought it did. But then I came to realize that Matt's delusions of being able to read people's minds weren't delusions at all. He could actually do it. In fact, I think he could do more than that."

"More?" Valden asked. "More like, what, vanish into thin air, the way Lady Valencia described?"

"Exactly."

"I'll admit that I am no student of the Art as you, Chall," Valden said, "but I have never heard of such a thing."

Chall winced. There, then, was the one flaw in his reasoning. "Neither have I," he admitted, then held up a hand to silence Valden as he saw the man preparing to speak. "But my tutors, back at the Academy, were always harping about how the possibilities of the Art were endless, and that we had only scratched the surface of what it could do, and that even that surface was always changing. If I can happen to meet an Empath like Ned—extremely rare users of the Art—then it stands to reason that Matt might be able to do such a thing. Might be able to vanish from one place only to appear somewhere else. Perhaps the necklace, the magic in it, even helped him, somehow. Or...or maybe he *used* it, somehow."

"That sounds like a lot of 'ors' and a lot of 'maybe's," Valden observed.

"True," Chall said, "but given how desperate things have been lately, I'll take a 'maybe' any day."

Slowly, a smile came over Valden. A small expression, but one that struck Chall powerfully. He could not remember the last time he'd seen his friend smile, *really* smile. It was as if Valden had been struggling along for weeks, months, toiling beneath some great burden and now, for the first time in a very long time, he had set that burden down. "So...so Matt could still be alive," Valden said.

"I believe that he is," Chall said.

Valden let out a sigh. "I might not have failed, after all. Still...Robert Palden might have him."

"Maybe," Chall said. "But I don't think so. He's out there, Valden. Somewhere. Alive."

"In the city, maybe," Valden said. "Perhaps the men Commander Malex has sent out searching might find him."

"Maybe," Chall said, but the truth was he didn't think so. He felt—without knowing exactly *why* he felt it—that Matt was further away than that. "Either way, he's alive, and that's a miracle in and of itself."

"A miracle," Valden repeated quietly, his eyes taking on a distant look.

"Sure," Chall said, "considering what he was up against, I'd say that qualifies. Just as it seems to me that you making it here without Robert Palden doing to you what he did to all those poor bastards at Flo's seems like a bit of a miracle. It's almost enough to make a man think the gods are out there looking out for us after all."

"Almost..." Valden said.

Chall watched his friend curiously. And the most curious thing of all was that he *felt* like his friend again. In some indefinable way, he had stopped being the stranger he had become and started being the man he had known for years, at least in part. "Can I ask you something?" he said. "Why were you here? In Matt's rooms?"

Valden shrugged. "Partly...I guess...to mourn? To grieve? To..."

"To feel ashamed?"

Valden winced. "Maybe. But not just that. I also hoped—desperate, I know—that I might find something. Some track or trace that might give me a hint to Matt's whereabouts."

Chall gave a soft laugh at that.

"What's so funny?"

"It's just that I came here for a very similar reason," Chall said. "Only…the tracks I'm looking for are a bit…different."

"Magic, you mean?"

"Yes. When we were outside the door—Vorrun and I, the other guards—I felt…something. A powerful release of the Art the equal of which I have rarely, if ever, felt. An explosion of power. A moment later, we broke in to find Lady Valencia standing with the knife, Matt nowhere to be seen. But I thought then—and I think now—that had we broken the door open only seconds before, he would have been there, standing right in front of her. And we would have witnessed whatever it was that happened. Anyway, the greatest of that magic is gone, but some still lingers, the way a man's footprint might linger on wet grass for a short time. Soon, a day, maybe two, and it will be gone. I came hoping to examine the vestiges of what remained, hoping, like you, to find something that might indicate where Matt has gone."

"Then I will not keep you from it any longer." His friend rose from the table, nodding his head. "I will return soon to check on you—if you need anything, Chall, just let me know." He met his eyes. "I *am* here now."

Chall gave the man a smile. "If you don't mind my asking, where are you going?"

"I thought to go speak to Commander Malex to see how the search is going then check on Ned and see how long it will be until Maeve is freed up from her guild duties. As you've mentioned, she would be invaluable in determining the best course of action."

"Sure," Chall said, "she determines mine all the time."

Valden gave a laugh then headed toward the door.

"Valden?" Chall asked, and the man paused with one hand on the door handle, turning to regard him. "Thanks. For...you know. For being here. And for checking on Maeve."

"Always," his friend said, then gave him a wink. "And please—call me Priest."

CHAPTER SIX

Maeve sat in darkness.

The darkness without and the darkness within.

Emille was in the cell adjacent to her own, breathing quietly. She had not yet roused from what Maeve thought must have been a pretty bad beating. Yet even with the healer-assassin lying feet away, Maeve did not think she had ever felt so alone.

She had sat with her back against her cell wall in the hours since the Fey creature had finished its gloating and left. She did not know exactly how much time had passed, but it was enough for even her own frayed, tattered, confused thoughts to come to one inevitable, inarguable conclusion.

She was afraid.

She, Maeve the Marvelous, the most famous assassin in the kingdom, whose very name had once been enough to strike terror into men and women alike, was afraid. And not *just* that. The truth was, she was terrified.

It wasn't just that she was afraid of dying, though that was part of it. She had lived a long life, far longer than many who had deserved it far more, had escaped one struggle after the other, somehow surviving against all odds. She thought that, perhaps, she should be thankful. But she did not *feel* thankful. She felt afraid, and it seemed to her a strange fact that the longer life a person lived, the more desperately afraid they became of losing it.

It wasn't just dying, though, for what she faced was worse than that. If what the doppel had told her was true, then she might not just be killed—a hazard any assassin might face. She might be *eaten*.

Even the thought sent a shiver of fear running through her, making her arms and neck break out in gooseflesh. She found herself thinking of Chall. Chall who had warned her not to come, Chall who she had assured she would be okay, that she could take care of herself. And, mostly, she had even believed that. But then people who could take care of themselves did not generally end up in cells, at the mercy of assassins at best and a monster out of nightmare at worst, a monster who intended to *eat* her.

"You were right, Chall," she said quietly. "I'm...I'm sorry."

"*Careful*," a voice rasped. "*When it comes to men, I find it best to never...admit fault.*"

"Emille?" Maeve asked, shocked for a part of her, a very large part, she realized now, had been terrified that the woman would never wake again.

"*I'm...*" She paused, clearing her throat. "I'm here, Maeve," the woman said.

"Oh, thank the gods you're..." Maeve hesitated.

"Alright?" Emille finished for her, a note of what might have been humor in her obviously strained tone. "No, Maeve," she went on, the humor now nowhere in evidence, "I don't think either of us is alright."

Maeve winced. "How bad off are you?"

"Well, I'm alive," Emille said. "So there's...that. They didn't care for me looking into their affairs, and they—and their men—made that known. At a guess, I'd say I have a broken rib, maybe two. A dislocated elbow on my left, and an eye that I'd wager looks a lot like a swollen plum and *feels* like all the world's misery."

Maeve hissed in a mixture of sympathy and anger. "I'm sorry, Emille. If I hadn't sent you to look into them—"

"Then they would have found some other...reason. Or none at all. It seems to me, Maeve, that they have plans, the Tribunes. I don't know what they are up to but...I doubt they'd want us...around for whatever it is."

"The tribunes are far from the least of our concerns," Maeve said.

Emille gave a soft grunt then hissed in pain. "Speak for...yourself," she said. "Considering how I'm feeling, they're pretty high up on my list of concerns. If I manage to get within arm's reach of either that old hag or that sniveling weasel, I'll make sure to show them *just* how concerned I am." She sighed. "Not that I think we're likely to get the chance. I'm not sure what they have planned for us, but somehow I doubt they mean to have a nice chat then set us free."

"No," Maeve said quietly, "not that." She proceeded to tell Emille of the Fey creature, recounting everything it had said as accurately as she could, leaving nothing out, no matter how seemingly trivial, for she knew well from her time spent as an assassin that it was nearly always the thing a person thought of as inconsequential that ended up hurting them the most. Emille was clever, and if Maeve was lucky, the woman might find some hope, some means of possible escape that Maeve had not.

"Wait," Emille said when she'd finished, "do you mean to say...that thing means to...*eat* us?"

"Me anyway," Maeve said. "You it may just kill."

"You'll have to forgive me if I don't start celebrating. Still, I'd almost prefer it to having to listen to Ned with his inevitable 'I told you so's," Emille said. "I'm not saying that'd be a fate worse than death, but I'm not quite ready to say it wouldn't be, either."

Maeve felt a small, fragile smile come to her face. Not much, maybe, but considering the way she'd felt moments ago, it was a drastic improvement. She wasn't alone, after all. Emille was with her. Emille who was clever enough to somehow be both an assassin and a healer and, on top of that, manage to find a man she loved and who loved her in turn.

"I'm glad you're here," Maeve said.

Emille snorted, then gave a soft, pained laugh. "Wish I could say the same."

Maeve was laughing too, then. Likely it was from the stress and anxiety of their situation—it wasn't every day, after all, that a person was facing the very real possibility of being something's dinner—but whatever the cause, it felt good to laugh. It felt quite a bit, in fact, like medicine.

"So," Emille said as they sobered up, her voice sounding pained and out of breath, "what's...the plan?"

"Don't die," Maeve said.

Emille grunted. "Not bad, as far as it goes but...I was...hoping for a bit more."

"I'm working on it," Maeve said. "I—" She cut off, the two of them going silent as they heard the sound of footsteps from somewhere beyond the door.

"You may want to work a bit faster," Emille said. "Or do you think, perhaps, that is the sound of some gallant knight come to rescue two maidens in distress from the cruel monster?"

Despite their circumstances, that elicited a snort from Maeve. She wasn't sure what the prerequisites for being a damsel in distress were, but she was fairly certain she wouldn't have qualified in her youth and certainly not now. If she were to be cast in a stage play, she would far more likely earn the role of 'evil hag' over 'blushing damsel.'

"In my experience," Maeve said grimly, turning to regard the vague, shadowed outline of the door, all that was visible in the darkness, "the world suffers from a shortage of knights. Monsters, though, well now there's enough of those to go around and then some."

The sound of approaching footsteps grew louder, and Maeve and Emille waited tensely as they listened to the sound of keys jingling outside the door. A moment later, the door swung open revealing several figures, none of which, Maeve noted with very little surprise, were Emille's knight.

It seemed that, for this visit, there were only the monsters.

The guard who'd opened the door stepped inside first, holding a torch aloft as he moved to the side. Next came Tribune Bethesa. The old woman sniffed as she walked into the dungeons, holding a hand up to her eyes. "What is it, then, you tryin' to burn my eyelashes off, that it?" she asked. "Step back, you fool."

The guard did as ordered, stepping further away to the side of the room. Tribune Piralta followed behind Bethesa, his shoulders hunched and head down as if he were in danger of hitting it on the doorway never mind that he had at least two feet to spare. That reminded Maeve of how Agnes—even Emille—had referred to him as a weasel, but then even cowards could be dangerous. Even weasels had teeth, even weasels could bite.

"Ah, hello again, Guildmaster Maeve," Bethesa said as she walked into the room to stand in front of her cell, followed by Tribune Piralta. "I hope you have found your new accommodations to your liking?"

"I'm just not sure about the design scheme is all," Maeve said dryly. "Though I suppose dirt goes with everything. And don't you mean *prisoner* Maeve? I don't know many guildmasters who spend much time in dungeon cells, particularly on this side of the bars."

Bethesa gave her a small, humorless grin. "Yes, well, I s'pose I can see how that might be a bit…confusin'. An unusual situation, to be sure, but one we'll remedy soon enough. You *are* still guildmaster, at least for the time bein', 'til the trial and all. So says guild law and far be it from me to go against guild law."

"So I'm still guildmaster then?"

"That's right."

"In that case, I order you to let me out—and Emille too, while you're at it."

Bethesa gave her a predatory grin, all teeth and no humor. "I'm afraid not."

"So you won't go against the guild's law, but you'll imprison its guildmaster even though she's innocent of any crime?"

The woman actually chuckled at that. "Oh, come now, Guildmaster Maeve. You are many things, but I do not think you can claim innocence as one of them. Do you?"

Maeve did not like the woman, would have happily stuck a knife in her—or a few—if given a chance. But she had to admit that she had a point. Still, just because the woman had a point didn't mean Maeve had to let her poke her with it. "And what of you?" she asked. "You killed Silrika, your colleague."

"Me?" Bethesa said, her eyes going wide in mock surprise. "Oh, Guildmaster Maeve, surely you jest. Tribune Silrika—may the gods watch over her eternal soul—was a dear, dear friend," she went on, her voice sounding emotional, her eyes actually welling with tears. "Why, she and I spent many days together over these last years. We enjoyed a relationship of mutual respect and, dare I say it, love. A love that anyone whose been paying any attention at all over the last years—particularly these last weeks since you took over as guildmaster—couldn't help but notice."

Maeve knew the woman was responsible for Silrika's death, knew that she had gotten out of line one too many times, threatening Bethesa's carefully laid plans, and so had needed to be removed. An added bonus, of course, was that her murder could be pinned on Maeve and Emille, neatly killing two birds with one stone. It would have been impressive to Maeve, had she not been one of the two birds in question. Even more impressive, perhaps, was that while she knew the woman was responsible for Silrika's death—and while Tribune Bethesa *knew* she knew—her facade was so convincing that Maeve almost found herself believing that perhaps she had her wrong after all, that maybe someone else actually *had* done it.

At least, that was, until the old woman smiled. Maeve had faced and fought all manner of creature, all manner of murderer and monster over the course of her life, but she did not think she had ever seen anything as evil as that smile.

"You're...you're a monster," Emille said from the cell beside Maeve's, echoing her thoughts. "You know that, don't you? You're evil."

"Come now, Lady Emille," Bethesa said, glancing in that direction. "Evil and good? Monster? Are we children, then, cowerin' under our coverlets and tellin' each other scary stories?" She shrugged. "To the fly, a spider might seem like a monster, might seem evil. But the spider does what it must to survive. There is no malice in it as it feasts on the fly, only purpose. And more than purpose. It ain't evil that is behind the sinking of its fangs into waiting flesh," she went on, glancing at Maeve. "The spider does only what it was made to do." She grinned. "The fly too, I s'pose."

Hearing the woman speak, hearing the madness in her voice, Maeve felt her mouth go dry. She had faced the truly mad, the truly evil before —far too many times, if she stopped to take count—and it never ceased to terrify her. There was something inhuman about it but, at the same time, something completely human, perhaps *only* human. Or, at least, only brought into the world by a thinking, rational being. "You're crazy," she said.

The old woman gave a small shrug. "And yet I am the one out here and you are the one in there."

"Why are you doing this?" Maeve said. "What did I do to you?"

The woman gave a soft laugh. "Guildmaster, come now. You have done nothing at all to me. In fact, I think that, in another time, another place, perhaps we might have even been friends. It seems that you have been too long away from the guild and so I must remind you of one of the first lessons any fledglin' assassin learns—it is not personal. I harbor no resentment to you." She considered that, then gave a small shrug of one bony shoulder. "Or, at least, not much. I will admit that I have wearied of hearin' your praises over the years. How *marvelous* the lady Maeve, how deadly and beautiful all at once, and all the rest. So perhaps I do take some small bit of satisfaction in this…particularly after how you abandoned the guild that made you what you are."

"The guild isn't responsible for making me what I am," Maeve said. "Only the worst of it."

"An interestin' sentiment comin' from the guildmaster," Bethesa said, glancing at the man standing beside her. "Wouldn't you say, Tribune Piralta?"

"Very interesting, Tribune Bethesa," he agreed. "I wonder if—"

"Anyway," Bethesa went on, turning back to regard Maeve, casually dismissing the other tribune. But while it might have been of no consequence to her, Maeve didn't miss the angry expression that crossed the man's features—only for a moment—before vanishing. "There will be a trial," the old tribune said, either not aware of or, more likely, not caring that she had offended her companion. "A trial in which your guilt will be established."

"Or innocence, right?" Maeve said. "Isn't that the whole point of a trial? To figure out the truth, decide whether someone is innocent or guilty?"

"Many trials, yes," the woman said. "But not this one. You *will* be found guilty, Guildmaster Maeve. And when that happens, Guildmaster Agnes, who you attempted to murder, will return to rule over the guild once more."

"By Guildmaster Agnes you mean that *creature* that has been *eating* her, don't you?" Maeve asked.

"Yes," Bethesa said casually, and if Maeve was expecting some sort of reaction from the woman, she was to be disappointed. "But to the members of the guild it will be nothing short of a miraculous return. Why, I expect that Agnes will be even more loved and revered than she was before."

"Only it won't *be* Agnes," Maeve said. "It'll be that *thing*. I cannot believe that you would do that, Bethesa. That you would betray your people in such a way."

"A good carpenter uses what tools are to hand, Guildmaster," Bethesa said.

"Even if that tool is a creature who, along with the rest of its kind, means to destroy not just you but the entire kingdom, our entire *race?*"

Bethesa gave a small shrug. "What such a creature *means* to do and what I will *allow* it to do may be two very different things."

"You're a fool if you think you can control that monster," Maeve said. "As soon as you turn your back, it will betray you. I know you don't care about me or Agnes, or Emille, but what about the Known Lands? What about your own people? Because that creature and its kind will not stop at you, Bethesa. They will not stop at all until they have destroyed all of the Known Lands and everyone in it."

"Perhaps...perhaps she's right," Piralta said quietly. "I told you before, I did not like working with that creature. Maybe—"

"*Perhaps* you'd be far better off if you learned to keep your inane, foolish notions to yourself, Tribune Piralta," Bethesa snapped. "The wisest thing a fool can do is to remain quiet when his betters speak."

Tribune Piralta's face colored at that, and he shot a quick glance at Maeve and Emille before his gaze turned down to study his feet. "Sorry."

"There's a good boy," Bethesa said, then she turned back to Maeve with a wicked smile. "Even a fool or a feyling might be put to good purpose, Guildmaster Maeve, if one knows the way of it. And while I appreciate your concern for my personal welfare, I think I have matters quite well in hand."

Maeve considered that for a moment, considered the way Piralta still stared at his shoes, the way one of his hands was barely twitching, as if it wanted to clench into a fist. A man might be a weasel, but even a weasel had his limits. With that in mind, she spoke. "You're wrong," she said. "Piralta isn't the fool—you are. Only a fool, after all, would think to treat with the Fey. They are not puppies to be led around by a leash, not a tool that you might put to your use only to discard when it has served its purpose."

"Poor, poor Maeve," Bethesa said sadly. "Of course they are a tool, my dear. Just as you were a tool, one meant to sniff out Agnes's diary for me. You failed on that score, but don't worry—we'll find a use for you yet. As for the Fey, I reckon you're wrong. Seems to me, they *are* little more than dogs that I might lead around by a leash. After all—" she grinned slowly, the first genuine expression of good humor she'd shown—"it ain't the first time."

Maeve frowned. "What do you—" She cut off then as realization dawned. "The regent—the one who had taken over when we got here. Weylan-dreah. You were working with him?"

"*He* was working with *me*," Bethesa corrected, then rolled her eyes. "Come now, Guildmaster. You look like a child who has just learned that the world isn't all gumdrops and sweet treats. Surely, you're not so naive as that, nor as hypocritical. You who are famous across the Known Lands for those who have fallen to your blades."

"You'd better hope I don't get out of here," Maeve said through gritted teeth, "or there will be one more name for the bards to add to their lists. I have done things I'm not proud of, it's true, but I did those things—those done in the light as well as those done in the dark—for the Known Lands. Meanwhile, you have *betrayed* your people and for what? To be the next guildmaster? How pathetic an ambition to turn traitor to all of—"

"You damned *fool*," the old tribune hissed, her wrinkled face twisting with hatred. "You think I have done all this, have sacrificed all that I have sacrificed, have *risked* all that I have risked to be the leader of the guild?" Up until that moment, that was exactly what Maeve had thought but now she was no longer so sure.

Bethesa held her hands up to the side. "Look around you, Maeve. *You* are the guildmaster, I a humble tribune, and yet you stand helpless in a cell to suffer or not at *my* pleasure while I am free to walk around and do whatever I like. I *am* the leader of the guild. Not in name, perhaps, but then that is how I have always wished it. The trick isn't to being on top, Maeve—it's being on top while not *appearing* to be on top. After all, it's the person on top everyone's lookin' at, and if there is a knife slippin' through the darkness, you can lay good odds that it is headin' toward *that* back."

"Then what?" Maeve demanded. "Money? Power? What could possibly be worth betraying your people, what could possibly be worth the lives of untold thousands who will suffer beca—"

"My *life*," the woman snapped, her eyes wide and wild, and if Maeve had ever doubted that she was insane she did not doubt it then. Bethesa took a slow, deep breath, closing her eyes for a moment, and when she spoke on her voice was calm once more, her expression controlled. "Do you not understand, Maeve? I am old. I know that I have little time left to me, now. When we are young, we think that we will never grow old. It is always weeks and months and years away. Even when our first hair turns gray, we tell ourselves that it is nothing, that death is still far, far away. We tell ourselves that though time, that great thief, has come for all others we've met, it will surely stay its hand with us. But it does not. Not for anyone. And so I am left to waste away like some skeleton in its grave, a grave in which I will soon be laid—"

"Sooner, if I have my way," Maeve said.

"I will succumb to my years, while fools like Piralta here, like you, and Emille and Agnes, like *all* the rest live on. No amount of trying can change it. No amount of power or coin, and I should know," she said, then paused to utter a shrieking sort of laugh, "for I have spent fortunes searching. Speaking with healers and alchemists and supposed *learned* men, all to no avail. No fortune in the world could make them rise to the task, nor could any amount of torture."

"Torture?" Emille asked, and Maeve heard in her low, quiet voice what she felt herself—fear. Fear not at the thought of death—though anyone who claimed that they weren't afraid of losing their lives didn't deserve it in the first place, so far as Maeve was concerned—but at what stood before them. An old woman, one who, had her face not been twisted into a rictus of anger and loathing and, yes, fear, could have been mistaken for one of the tens of thousands of grandmothers dotting every town, hamlet, and city of the Known Lands.

Bethesa shrugged as if it didn't matter. "Some of those I went to were more...dismissive than I would have preferred. I felt as though they did not give my inquiries their due attention and so I made sure that they were well...s'pose you'd say properly motivated. Few things'll rouse a man to action like the taste of his own blood or watchin' a little piece of him carved away."

"You're insane," Emille said in a breathy voice, echoing her similar thought from earlier.

"I'm old," Bethesa countered. "When you're old you ain't insane, Emille—just addled. Anyway, those healers and alchemists, those potion-selling conmen couldn't do what I asked of them, and so I went lookin' in other places."

"To the Fey, you mean," Maeve said. "The Fey who, aside from the Skaalden, are the greatest enemy, the greatest threat our people have ever faced."

"A drownin' man holds onto what he can," the tribune said. "Yes, I went to the Fey. Do you expect that I'm to be upset by that? Ashamed, maybe? I am old, Guildmaster. Old and withered, old enough that my knees stopped achin' when a storm was comin' and now just ache. Old enough that I've pissed myself more than once in the night, and the question I go to sleep with ain't if it'll happen again, only when it will. Things I used to do without thought now take a mighty effort, and stairs have become my personal enemy. Yes, I went lookin' to the Fey. And had they not had answers for me then I would have looked further still, would have gone as far into the darkness as I needed. I would have fought however I could fight in the same way that a man, with his life on the line, will cheat or steal or kill, will do whatever he deems necessary to keep breathin'."

Maeve stared at the woman, feeling horrified not just because she seemed insane but because, in many ways, she did not. Maeve was getting older too, after all. Her knees often ached. Stairs weren't a great enemy, not yet, but she could not say that she was overly fond of them. It was not easy to watch what once was fine—or certainly better—give way to the ravages of time, like watching a flower once in full bloom wither and die. Much harder when *you* were the flower.

It was not the strange, the alien in the woman before her that scared her. It was the recognizable. It was not easy, getting older. That Maeve knew well. How not? She'd been doing it for years. Not easy watching what was once tight grow loose and saggy, what was once beautiful and young and vibrant grow old and gray. She wasn't sure if everyone marked the passage of time as she did, if everyone looked with increasingly growing dread at the next celebration of their birth and then the next, until those cheers or shouts—real or, in her case, often imagined—became like the sound of a funeral dirge. A hymn played for a woman on her way to the grave. She didn't know if everyone felt that sort of desperate need to do something about it and never mind that there was nothing to be done. She only knew that *she* did. The truly terrifying thing about the woman before her wasn't that Maeve didn't understand her motivations or her reasoning, it was that she understood them all too well. It was no easy thing to look at a monster and worse still when a person recognized within that monster some bit of humanity. Some bit of herself.

"But," Bethesa went on, "turned out, the Fey did have answers, did have...solutions."

"Somehow," Maeve said, her mouth dry, "I doubt they offered those solutions for free."

"True enough," Bethesa said, giving her a smile. "But then I have been around a long time, and I know that there's no such thing as a free meal. A body has to work for her wage, and that's alright. I don't mind a little bit of hard work. Just so long as my knees don't complain too much. Anyway, it isn't as if those healers or charlatan street-vendors selling magical potions of youth—and yes, I'll admit that I purchased some and admit it freely for as I said I have little shame left in me—don't have their price, too."

"Maybe," Emille said, "but even those cheats and scoundrels will only charge you coin. The cost of what you've done...it is more than that. It is your soul, Bethesa. Surely you can see that."

"*Tribune* Bethesa, you mean," the old woman snapped, turning to peer into Emille's cell. "And what good is a soul, can you tell me that, lady? It ain't as if you can eat it or drink it. A body can't wrap it round herself to keep the chill of night away, and it makes for a flimsy shield, one as can't even stop a harsh word, let alone a sword or arrow. It has done me no good, this soul, and so I will trade it gladly, if it means regaining my youth. I will trade it and consider that I've got the best of that bargain."

Maeve didn't know what to say to that. Mostly because, in some ways, she thought the woman might be right. Was *afraid* she might be right. She was older than Maeve, had experienced far more of that decline, that *loosening*. In ten years, in twenty, would Maeve feel the same sort of bitterness she saw in the woman? Certainly she thought she detected hints of it from time to time now. When she woke and wondered where all her youth had gone, how the years had come and gone, vanishing before she'd known it, and she was left feeling as if she'd been tricked somehow. Duped.

She had no answer to give to the woman, and so she gave no answer at all. Instead, it was Emille who spoke.

"You're wrong, Bethesa," she said, not bothering to use the woman's proper title. Maeve supposed, idly, that the one benefit of being destined for torture and death was that a person might forego some of the formalities of normal society, such as using a person's proper title. *Particularly* when that same person was the one meaning to torture and kill them.

"Oh?" Bethesa asked, giving a small smile before glancing at Maeve with a raised eyebrow. "I can't help but notice it ain't you who speaks,

Guildmaster, but this young slip of a girl. She cannot understand, can she? Some part of her still thinks that aging, *dying* is a thing as happens to other people. Not *her*. But you and I, we know better, don't we? We know what it is to grow old, can *feel* the years in our bones, seeping into us like some sort of sickness," she went on, her face contorting with anger more and more as she spoke, as if aging were a personal affront to her and her alone. "And it *is* a sickness, Maeve. A plague. One that kills us all, in the end. But not me." She shook her head. "Not me. What can she know of it? She with her perky tits who no one has ever told she 'looks good for her age,' in that vaguely pitying, vaguely condescending way. You know it, don't you, Maeve?"

Maeve did. She'd heard that plenty herself—more in the last few years. But not so much that she'd gotten used to the little bit of pain it caused, not that she was sure she ever would. "Wisdom is not reserved for the old and gray like us, Bethesa. Just because Emille is young does not mean she does not know better."

"Is that so?" Bethesa said. "Well then? Tell me, *child*. What is it you think you know?"

"I am in my forties," Emille said. "I am no child. What I *am*, though, is a healer. One who has seen enough of people to know that sometimes they will look fine, look well on the outside, yet their inside is rotten, dying. And it's what's on the inside that kills them, in the end. You are like that, Bethesa. You have sought to save the outside but in doing so have spoiled that within, and it is that within that is who you really are. Even if you somehow got your wish, even if you had your years returned to you, you would only be like an apple that looks fine until one bites into it and finds it rotten. It is not the skin of the apple, the *outside* of it that makes it worthy but the inside. After all, the skin is there to protect what's within, not the other way around, and what good is a rotten apple?"

Maeve found herself blinking, feeling as if the words were for her alone, words that somehow made her feel guilty and, at the same time, better. It felt as if she'd been staring down a dark tunnel of years ahead of her—one that, it had to be said, was shrinking—and that with Emille's words, for the first time, she saw the flicker of light there.

Bethesa, though, apparently took it a different way. "Enough," she growled. "I will not be lectured by a child. Do not think to condescend to me again."

"Or you'll what? Kill me?" Emille said, then gave a pained snort. "You can only do it once, and it seems to me that I'm on that list anyway."

"Oh, you poor young fool," Bethesa said. "You think that killin' you is all I can do, is that it? You think I'll stop with you? What of that husband of yours? Neddard, isn't it? Drives a carriage, as I understand it."

"H-how do you—"

"Know about your husband?" Bethesa sighed, shaking her head as she glanced at Maeve. "Youth is wasted on the young, eh, Maeve?" She turned back to Emille's cell. "'Course I know of your husband. I make it a point to know as much as I can about people I mean to kill. That's one of the first lessons a fledgling assassin learns—why, even you ought to have learned it. I know plenty about you and your past, about your and your husband's sweet love story. One for the ages. But then all stories must end, mustn't they? That is the thing about 'em. No book goes on forever." She shrugged. "Just as well, I s'pose. Puts a real strain on my old, weary eyes."

"Not much of a threat," Emille said, "considering that since you're betraying us to the Fey we're all likely to die, Ned included." She was trying to sound casual, nonchalant, but Maeve could hear the worry in her voice. That was the thing about the greatest love stories, she supposed—they could quite easily turn into the greatest tragedies. After all, it was only a woman who had reached the mountain's peak, the pinnacle, that might fall from that great height and how much more terrible would the fall be from so high. "I mean you're trying to kill everyone anyway," Emille finished.

"Why, of course I don't mean to kill everyone," Bethesa said as if

Emille had just said something insane. "Not much good being queen over a kingdom of corpses, is it? No, killing everyone, that is *his* idea, not mine. I do not do what I do for death at all, but *life*. My life, sure, but life. You as a healer ought to appreciate that, at least."

"The only thing I'd appreciate is a chance to stick a knife in your shriveled, blackened heart," Emille hissed.

"You said 'his,'" Maeve said slowly.

Bethesa turned to her slowly, a reptilian look of cunning on her face. "I told you before, Guildmaster. I would go anywhere, do anything to achieve what I wanted. That is the difference between the average and the extraordinary. Don't you think?"

"Anything including dooming your own people," Emille said before Maeve could respond.

Bethesa shrugged, still watching Maeve. "The bigger the mountain, the more effort, the more sacrifice one must make to climb it."

"Easy to say when you're not the one being sacrificed," Emille said.

"You're working with Robert Palden," Maeve said. "You have been this whole time."

Bethesa sighed. "Not my first choice, I'll admit. Partly on account of we've got a bit of a history—him once leadin' the Wolves and all." She did turn to glance in Emille's direction. "Along with your husband, and just *imagine* how surprised I was when I learned of *that* little secret. That alone would make torturing and killing your husband a pleasure, should you misbehave. As for Robert, though...well, we all have pasts, don't we? And if I'm bein' honest, his past ain't the biggest worry. Fact is, I think he might be a little...well. Insane."

"You'd know," Emille said.

Bethesa smiled. "Many of the world's greatest people were once called insane."

"Many of its insanest, too," Emille countered.

Bethesa sighed. "I tire of you, little one." She turned to regard Piralta. "Go on then. Tell them of the upcoming...festivities."

The man's face was still red in either embarrassment or anger from the old woman's earlier jibes, but he bowed his head in acquiescence. "A trial is to be held in a week's time," he told Maeve. "One in which your and Lady Emille's guilt—or innocence—in the murder of Tribune Silrika and the attempted murder of Guildmaster Agnes is to be determined."

"I'm fairly sure that's been determined already," Maeve said.

"So it has," Bethesa said, "but people do so enjoy a spectacle, and I'd sure hate to be the one to disappoint 'em. Don't know if you're aware or not, but they *murder* people. For a livin'," she finished, smiling and clearly pleased at her own joke. She turned to Piralta. "I have things to do, to prepare—explain to them both what will be expected of them at the trial and then come find me. There is much work to be done." With that, she turned and started away.

"You won't get away with this," Maeve told her. "Chall is—"

"A fat illusionist whose greatest claim to fame is being able to somehow convince women to jump into bed with him," Bethesa said, turning. "Even the Marvelous Maeve, apparently. No, I have little concern for him. The danger he represents is no more real than those images and fantasies his magicks produce."

"He is more than that," Maeve said. "And taking the city will not be so easy as you think, if that is your plan. Matt has Chall and Priest with him, others, too, and they will not allow—" Maeve paused as the woman actually began to laugh.

"Oh, Maeve," Bethesa said. "You still don't see it, do you? You're like a man dyin' of poison stumblin' into a potion shop and just drinkin' anythin' you can get your hands on in the hopes that it'll save you. It won't, though. You're beyond savin' now, though not so much as that child king of yours. He's already dead."

Maeve's breath caught in her throat at that. She opened her mouth to respond but no words came, and she was still standing there in silent shock when Bethesa walked out of the dungeon, the door closing behind her.

Matt is dead? she thought. It couldn't be true. Surely it couldn't. Chall would not have let it happen.

"As I was saying," Tribune Piralta said into the silence, "the trial will take place in a week's time. There, you will be expected to admit the truth of your attempt on Guildmaster Agnes's life, as well as that you had Lady Emille murder Tribune Silrika because the tribune was too close to discovering the truth."

"Am I?" Maeve said, finding her voice. "And I don't suppose it matters that your 'truth' is a complete lie?"

"One week," the tribune said as if she hadn't spoken. "It would be better, when the trial comes, if you told the guild what she wishes for you to tell them. Better for you," he went on then, with an almost apologetic look at Emille's cell, "better for Lady Emille, too."

Maeve didn't have to ask him what he meant by that, for she knew well enough. She had wondered idly during the night—the darkest night of her life—why they had kept Emille alive. If what the creature who had visited her at her cell wearing Agnes's face and Bethesa had said was true, then they needed Maeve. They needed her alive to admit that she was guilty. After all, it was one thing to accuse a guildmaster of a crime and have a fair trial—or at least one that was carefully made to *appear* fair—to determine her guilt or innocence. It was quite another to spirit her away in the night, for her to up and vanish without a trace. The men and women of the guild were assassins, not fools. It would not take much for them to put two and two together.

And so, for the moment, Maeve was relatively safe. At least until she gave them what they wanted. Emile, on the other hand, had no such protection. Or, at least, Maeve had not thought she did. But now she realized that they meant to use the woman to convince her to do what they wanted. Maeve was the puppet and Emille—and the suffering she would undergo should Maeve prove obstinate—was the string.

"Why are you doing this?" she said quietly.

The man blinked, looking surprised as if it was the last question he'd expected her to ask. "Tribune Bethesa—"

"I didn't ask about Bethesa," Maeve said. "I know what she wants—to be young, maybe skip around a field of daisies with little pig tails. But what are *you* getting out of this? This is your city too, Piralta. Your *world* that she means to trade for her youth. And it seems to me that you're just sitting back and letting her do it."

The man opened his mouth as if he might answer, then paused, clearly changing what he'd been about to say. "It would be best for you both to do as Tribune Bethesa requires," he told her. He started to turn to leave but paused as Maeve spoke.

"Why don't you just call her your master and save time," Maeve said. "It's what she is, isn't it?"

He glanced back at her. "Tribune Bethesa and I share the same role and wield the same influence."

Maeve laughed then. A bitter laugh, perhaps, but just then she was feeling pretty bitter. "I don't think even you believe that," she said. "You are not her equal—certainly *she* doesn't view you as such and frankly neither do I. Neither would anyone with eyes to see the way you slink after her and let her order you about like you're some pet. Or do you view yourself more like a tick? A tick who has attached itself to Bethesa and so thinks it is safe."

She shrugged. "Maybe you're right. Maybe Bethesa will win, in the end. I don't think so, but then I am an assassin, not a prophet. But even if she does, even if she carries you to victory—whatever *that* looks like considering that she essentially works for the Fey now—what good will it do you? Do you think she will share the spoils with you, like two equals sitting down at a table to eat?" She snorted. "You're not her equal, Piralta. You will have no place at her table. You are not even the servant who brings her wine. You will be nothing more than the poor, hapless beggar sitting outside pleading for coin as she passes. And knowing Bethesa as I do, Piralta, I doubt very seriously that she will toss any coins into your little tin cup."

She wasn't sure what she expected from the man, then. Anger, perhaps, though she would not have been surprised if he had only nodded meekly, reiterating the need for her to do as Bethesa, her master, commanded. She was surprised, then, when he did neither of those. Instead, he gave a small smile. "You call me a tick, Maeve. You mean it as an insult, but I do not take it as one. You see, in that example you have given, it is I who benefits from the blood of Bethesa. Not the other way around." He nodded his head. "Now, I must leave you. But please—do as Bethesa asks. I will not say what comes will be easy for you, but it might not be so hard as it could be, as long as you are obedient."

"You are a coward," Maeve said, and the man paused again as he'd started to turn away. "A coward who has betrayed his kingdom, his people and for reasons perhaps he does not even understand. Bethesa will fail, *you* will fail. The king, Chall and the others will discover what you're doing. They will stop you, and when they do...well, I don't think I need to remind you of what happens to traitors."

"I believe Bethesa already told you: the young king is not a problem...not anymore. It is a pity, truthfully, for in another time, I think he might have been just what the people of the Known Lands needed. But these are dark times, dark days, and sometimes the only way to make it out of the shadows is for one of their number to lead you out."

"And you think that's you?" Maeve said, caught somewhere between anger and laughter at the ridiculous notion of it. "That you're the one to lead the kingdom out?"

"What I think is that what looks like evil from the outside is, sometimes, no more than necessity," Piralta said.

In his face, his voice, Maeve saw none of the man's usual timidity, and she was reminded of how Agnes had referred to him as a weasel and how Maeve's first impression of him had been that there was more to him than that. Here, then, was the more, and she found that she preferred him as a weasel. "Bullshit," she said, refusing to think about what he'd said about Matt. "You can frame it however you want, obfuscate however you want. Maybe that helps you sleep at night, but it won't change the reality of what you've done, of what you *are*."

Still, he did not grow angry, no screaming or shouting or even protesting. He only smiled wider still. "A tick—I remember. But there is another thing about ticks, Lady Maeve. Any parasite, I suppose. The creature to which it has attached itself might die, it is true, but that means little to the tick. It will live on. Will, perhaps, find another creature upon which to attach itself. Or...perhaps, it won't. Perhaps *this* tick might become a creature of its own. Perhaps *this* tick might even become a king." He winked then.

"Good night, ladies," Piralta said, then turned and started toward the door. He lifted the torch from its bracket on the wall then turned to regard them. "I would recommend rest, if you are able. Unless I very much miss my guess, the two of you are in for a busy week. After all, Bethesa is quite set on you saying what she wants you to say, and I'm afraid she won't just take your word for it. She will send someone to do a bit of...convincing, soon enough. And the men she will send can be *very* persuasive, as I'm sure you both know. Though," he went on, giving a little laugh, "I suppose it is fair to say that you will know it better soon enough."

He reached for the door, and Emille spoke.

"You think you're safe," she said, her voice shaking with anger. "You think that you understand Bethesa, that you have a grasp of what's happening. I wonder...do you think Silrika thought the same?"

"Silrika was a fool," Piralta said, not with any anger or feeling, just as a statement of fact, the way a man might point out that it was raining.

"Maybe," Emille said, "but then often fools don't realize they're fools. Anyone could be one. *You* could be one."

Tribune Piralta smiled, letting his gaze travel between Maeve's cell and Emille's. "I suppose we'll see," he said. "I'm excited to find out." He gave another wink then turned, opening the door. As he did, he changed, somehow. Not the way the doppel might have but instead a change that was more subtle. His back seemed to shrink, his shoulders shrugging down on themselves. He had been a man, speaking with them, but as he stepped out into the hallway he became the weasel once more.

Then the door closed behind Piralta, leaving Maeve feeling stunned and hopeless. The torchlight disappeared, and once more, Maeve was cast into darkness.

The darkness without...

And the darkness within.

CHAPTER SEVEN

Cutter lay awake in his borrowed bed at Fabor's home, staring up at the ceiling. The room was nearly completely black, the only illumination coming in from the window, a sliver of pale moonlight that allowed him to see the vague forms of Matt and Feledias where they lay in the room's other beds.

He was weary, a weariness that felt as though it had seeped into his bones along with the cold, yet he found that, however hard he searched for it, sleep continued to elude him. Maybe it was the strange scene he had witnessed back at the church, men and women dancing as if there were no tomorrow or, if there *were* one, they had no intention of being around for it. Dancing so energetically that some—like the old woman —passed out from the exertion.

Perhaps it was the bed, which after weeks spent sleeping on the hard ground of the Black Wood, felt far too soft, almost like a trap somehow. It might have been just him getting older, his body too busy complaining about this ache or that pain to realize that it ought to be sleeping, or even the bear-like snores issuing from where Feledias lay sleeping as he had since the moment his head had hit the pillow.

Yet he knew that, in truth, it was none of these things which robbed him of his sleep.

It was Matt. His son who lay only a few feet away. Matt who he had thought lost to him, who he had been certain he would never see again. And yet he was here. Against all odds, he was here, and that truth struck Cutter both with a profound, all-encompassing relief but also a terror to match. After all, a man who had much had much to lose.

Dark thoughts for a dark night, and it was these thoughts more than the cold or his brother's snoring or any other of the myriad reasons that kept him awake. That kept him awake so that he could not help but hear the sound of voices as they began speaking from beyond the room's closed door. One, a man's voice that he recognized at once as belonging to Fabor. The second, though, was the voice of a woman, one Cutter believed must be that of the red-headed man's wife, Laura.

He and his companions had not met Fabor's wife when they'd arrived at the house; either still in the grips of whatever illness had befallen her or perhaps simply because she was the only sane person in Windham and owing to nothing more than the late hour, she had been asleep.

Cutter could not make out what they were saying, not with their voices muffled by the door and distance. But what he *could* hear was the manner in which they said it. He detected a note to their voices that he did not like—urgency. And not just that...fear. They were arguing about something, that much was obvious, and whatever it was, it had them both worried.

The husband and wife must have come to some sort of agreement, for in another few minutes the voices cut off to be replaced by another sound—footsteps. Cutter had known Fabor a long time, but it had been years since he'd seen the man. Time enough for Fabor, at least, to find a life, a woman he loved—that much was obvious by the way he spoke of her—and for him to carve out a place in the world as a sheep farmer of all things. That much Cutter knew from his brief talk with the man on their way to his home. Two things that seemed far beyond the Fabor Cutter had known, a man who had been renowned for the wild, aggressive abandon with which he fought. And of course they were. The man in whose house they stayed, whoever he was, whoever he had been, was not Fabor the Fierce. Not anymore.

Which meant that Cutter and his companions were in the house of a stranger.

The footsteps were drawing closer. Cutter rose, reaching down beside the bed where he'd laid his axe, the Fey-gifted weapon they called the Breaker of Pacts. As soon as his fingers closed around the haft of the weapon, he felt better.

By the time the door to their room swung open, Cutter had put on his boots and cloak and stood with his axe in hand, ready for what would come. The shadowy figure standing in the doorway let out a startled cry, taking a step back.

"P-Prince, it's me, Fabor."

"I know," Cutter said.

"What in the shit was that noise?" Feledias grumbled from the other side of the room.

"Father?" Matt said, apparently also having been woken by Fabor's cry. "Is...is everything alright?"

"In my experience, Nephew," Feledias muttered, and Cutter could see him rising from the bed out of the corner of his eye as he spoke, "men rarely show up in other men's bedrooms in the wee hours of the morning if everything is alright. Unless maybe they've had too much to drink, and our Fabor here looks just about like the most sober person I've ever seen."

That, at least, was true. Fabor held a lantern, and even in its orange, fitful glow Cutter could see that the man's face was pale, and there was a wild look in his eyes that Cutter had seen often over the years, usually in the minutes before the dying began.

"Forgive me, Prince," the red-headed man said, "but we have to go. Now. They're coming."

Cutter had been in enough life-or-death situations that he didn't waste time asking who the man was referring to for just then, with Matt now sitting groggily up in bed, rubbing at his eyes, there was only one question that mattered. "How long?"

The red-headed man gave a shake of his head. "I don't know. They're not due for a half hour, maybe a bit more, but I wouldn't put it past her to show up early."

"I...I don't understand," Matt said. "What's happening?"

"What always happens when I hang out with your dad, Nephew," Feledias said, rising. "Someone's trying to kill us. Best put your boots on."

To his credit, Matt didn't ask anymore than that, only set about pulling his boots on as Feledias had suggested. Satisfied that his son would be ready in a moment, Cutter turned back to Fabor. "How many?"

The red-headed man winced, shooting a glance behind him as if expecting someone to materialize and attack. "All of them," he said. "I'm sorry, Prince...I...I didn't have a choice. If we hurry, we might yet make it away before they get here."

"But how do you know?" Matt said, clearly confused as he finished pulling on his second boot and rose. "That they're planning on coming here, I mean."

"Don't you get it, Nephew?" Feledias asked, frowning in the lantern light. "Fabor here knows because he was planning it with them."

"I...I didn't have a choice," Fabor said. "Th-they would have killed us, me and Laura both. Prince," he went on, turning to Cutter, "I'm sorry—"

"Save it," Cutter said. "We need to go. Now."

The man winced but nodded. "Follow me."

"Sure, because it's worked out great for us so far," Feledias muttered, but he moved to stand beside Cutter.

"Ready?" Cutter asked, glancing at Matt as his son pulled his cloak on.

Matt's face was pale, but he gave a nod. Perhaps it was Cutter's failing as a father—one of many—that his son had faced several similar situations in the last months and so had grown, at least to a degree, inured to them. "I'm with you, Father," he said.

"Father?" Fabor asked, his eyes going wide. "Oh, gods be good, Prince, he's your son? I-please forgive me, I didn't realize—"

"Leave it," Cutter said. "Lead on, Fabor."

The red-headed man gave a nod. "O-of course. This way." Fabor turned and led them back through the house. Before, when he'd shown them here, Fabor had been all welcoming smiles and jests, but he did not smile now, and he did not jest. He moved through their small house into the main room where Cutter saw a woman standing by one of the home's windows, peering out it.

"What's it look like, Laura?" the red-headed man asked.

Fabor's wife turned away from the window to look back at them. According to the red-headed man, his wife had not attended the festivities at the church because she had been sick, stricken with an illness that, by the way he'd acted and spoken of it, had nearly proven fatal. But she did not appear sick now. Instead, she only appeared frightened.

"I don't see anything yet," she said, turning back to the window.

"This your wife, Fabor?" Feledias asked.

"Yes, this is Laura."

"Then madam, I suppose I ought to congratulate you on what appears, to me at least, to be a miraculous recovery," Feledias said, frowning at Fabor.

The red-headed man winced. "You saw the way they were, back at the church. I didn't want Laura to be a part of that, so when they... invited us, I said she was sick."

"Why not just tell her you didn't want to come?"

"The woman...Aurora..." Fabor said, sharing a look with his wife, "she isn't the type of person you say no to."

"Another lie," Feledias said. "Keep this up, Fabor, and I might just start to think you aren't trustworthy. Anyway," he went on, turning to Cutter, "what now?"

Cutter opened his mouth to speak but before he could, Fabor's wife, Laura, let out a barely audible gasp from the window.

"What, Laura?" the red-headed man said. "What is it?"

"I think…" she started, then paused for a moment before breathing a sigh of relief. "I thought I saw a flicker of…of something. I must have imagined—oh gods," she said, and when she turned back to them her face was pale, her eyes wide. "They're coming."

Cutter walked up to the window, following the woman's gaze. At first, he didn't see anything, but a moment later a light flickered in the dark night. He was reminded, as he stared at that barely visible light, of a time what felt like eons ago when he'd stood in the middle of the snow on a hill, skinning an elk. He had seen lights then, too, the flicker of torches as Feledias's men came to Brighton to kill him.

And then, like now, he had fled into the night with Matt, hoping only to see morning.

"Time to go," Feledias said.

He started for the door, but Cutter reached out and grabbed him by the arm, stopping him.

"Bernard, there isn't any time," his brother said. He jabbed a finger at the window through which could be seen the flickering of several torches, more and more appearing by the moment. They were still distant, those flickerings, but they were getting closer. "Those bastards will be here in a few minutes," Feledias said, "and I don't know about you, but I don't much relish the idea of being here when they arrive. I'd rather face that damned blizzard than that."

"We're going to leave," Cutter assured him, "but not that way. They'll see our tracks—even the snow won't cover them up, not quickly enough."

"So what then?" Feledias asked, the panic clear in his voice.

"The window," Matt said before Cutter could speak. "Back in our room."

Cutter nodded. "Let's go."

"Go *where?*" Feledias said. "Look, I'm all for climbing out of a bedroom window—the gods know I've done it a time or two. But we stopped in Windham for a reason, and unless I miss my guess that reason hasn't changed. After all, there's still a blizzard out there."

"What choice do we have?" Cutter asked. "If they do come upon us, we'll have a better chance out there than in here, trapped in a small room."

"A better chance to do *what*, exactly?" Feledias asked. "Freeze to death? In case you missed it, it's pitch-black outside, not to mention the snow's coming down out there like someone's paying it. We won't be able to see more than a foot in front of our faces and we'll have no idea where we're going even if we *knew* where we were going. And we don't."

"What do you want to do, Uncle?" Matt asked. "We can't stay here. You heard Fabor—they're coming."

"At least we'd die warm," Feledias said, frowning and hugging his arms about him as if even the thought of stepping out into the blizzard had struck a chill into him.

"It might be that I have a better idea," Fabor said. "There's an old barn out back. Haven't used it in a few years, not since our milk cow died. The roof leaks, and I ain't got around to patchin' it nor cleanin' it out, but if you don't mind a mess, it might do."

"I'll take a mess over death any day," Feledias said.

Cutter gave the red-headed man a nod, and Fabor started toward the bedroom they'd used, only to pause and glance back at his wife. "When she gets here," the red-headed man said, "tell her that they ran, and I went chasin' after 'em. Tell her they were fleein' to the south."

She nodded. "Okay."

Fabor hesitated then, obviously not wanting to leave her, and in that hesitation, in the man's face, Cutter could see the man's love for her.

"Go on," Fabor's wife said, offering her husband a timid smile. "I'll be alright."

Fabor nodded. "Love you, Lor."

The second smile she gave him was far more genuine. "I love you too."

Fabor hesitated for one more moment, the two of them watching each other, then he pulled his gaze away with an obvious effort, starting toward the bedroom.

Cutter and his companions followed him into the room. While the others began to climb out, Cutter turned and watched the closed door, marking the others' progress by his brother's muttered hisses and curses.

When they were all outside, Cutter moved to the window. It was a tight squeeze, and he scratched his arm and shoulder, leaving a bit of himself behind, but he finally managed it. No sooner was he standing outside than the cold hit him with a shock nearly as powerful as if he'd leapt into a winter lake.

"This way," Fabor said, speaking in a normal tone of voice. Not that there was any danger of them being overheard, for with the powerful gusts of wind Cutter could barely make out what the man was saying even though he stood only feet away.

He started away then, Matt and Feledias following. Cutter glanced behind them, peering into the night, and could just make out the flicker of at least two dozen torches, maybe more, as they moved toward Fabor's home. Then he continued after the others.

The barn could have been no more than fifty feet from the house, but in the blizzard it felt as if it was a mile away, as if it took them an eternity of shambling through the heavy snow to reach it. Fabor struggled with the barn door, and Cutter had to help him, the two of them straining against powerful gusts of wind that seemed intent on refusing them the shelter they sought.

They finally managed to open it enough to fit through, and Cutter held the door as the other three stepped through the narrow crack. He followed after, and Feledias let out a yelp of surprise as Cutter released the door and the wind slammed it shut behind them.

"I don't know that our situation's improved much," Feledias said, glancing around with a disapproving frown. "The only change that I can see is that when they come for us, we'll die smelling of cow shit instead of lying in a soft bed."

"Lor will tell 'em you ran to the south, like we discussed," Fabor said. "There's no reason for 'em to think to check here."

"In my experience," Feledias said, "not havin' a reason was never enough to stop a man, much less a mob. Particularly when they've got murder on their minds."

"It's the best plan we have," Cutter said.

"Even if they don't check, though," Matt said, "what then? We can't stay here forever—even if they don't look in the barn at first, they *will* look eventually. It will be daylight in a couple of hours, and even the snow won't be enough to keep them from noticing if we try to sneak away. Once the sun rises, we'll be trapped."

"Which means we have to make sure we're gone before then," Cutter agreed.

"Gone *where?*" Feledias said. "To the Barrier Mountains? In this?" he went on, gesturing out at the blizzard raging beyond the barn doors. "Fire and salt, Bernard, the mountains have killed almost everyone who has ever dared journey into them—there's a reason why they're *called* the Barrier Mountains. And those expeditions waited for the best weather, the clearest days, yet still only a handful of people returned, and those who did were driven mad, lost fingers and toes to frostbite, or do you not remember?"

"I remember," Cutter said, "but—"

"*Father,*" Matt interrupted, his voice a low hiss.

Cutter turned, following Matt's gaze to look out of the barn's small window. He did not have to ask what his son had seen, for it would have been impossible to have missed it in that darkness—light. The orange, flickering flame of a torch...and it was getting closer.

Someone, it seemed, knew about the barn and had decided to give it a look. Cutter studied the two shadowy figures—barely visible in the light of the torch—as they trudged through the snow.

"Hide," he said.

"Are you sure, Father?" Matt asked. "There are only two of them. We could...that is—"

"Maybe," Cutter said, knowing full well what his son did not want to say, "but I'm not worried about whether or not we can handle them. I'm worried about whether or not we can handle them in time. If one of them manages a scream or a yell, they could draw the others, and then we have real problems."

"You expect them to be heard in this blizzard?" Feledias said. "Not much chance of that, you ask me."

"Whatever chance there is," Cutter said, his gaze going to Matt, "it's more than what I'm willing to take. Now hide—there is little time."

They all clearly understood, as well as he, what was at stake. They asked nothing more before moving further into the barn. Cutter watched them, marking where each went. Matt climbed the rickety ladder up into the barn's small loft then disappeared out of sight. Feledias walked to the back of the barn, tucking himself behind a bale of hay, while Fabor did the same beside a second. That left Cutter himself, who glanced through the slats of the barn wall again to see that the men would be here in a minute or less. He moved toward the loft where Matt had gone, but instead of climbing up the rickety ladder—which looked as if it wouldn't have supported his weight in any case—Cutter moved into the empty stall nearest it, hunkering down in the corner.

He had only just knelt when he heard the creak of the barn door opening. The slats of the shadowed stall in which he crouched were separated enough that he was able to see the two men as they entered. Not well, but enough that it was impossible to miss what they held— one, a pitchfork, the other a machete. Not exactly weapons of war, but then the people of Windham were not warriors but farmers. At least in normal times. Something, it was clear, had changed that, and while

Cutter couldn't say for sure what that might be, he thought he had a pretty good idea from the woman he'd met and Fabor's multiple references to a "she."

He did not know exactly what influence the woman had on the villagers of Windham and, at the moment, he did not care. All he cared about was that his brother and his son were in the barn with him, and something as simple as a single shout from one of the two men currently easing their way inside might be enough to spell their doom.

"I told you they ain't here," said one of the two as they paused in the doorway, surveying the barn in the fitful light of the torch. "Shit, Fabor ain't used this barn in damn near a decade, not since that old ratty cow of his died."

"Well, they're somewhere, ain't they, Fred?" the second said. "Anyway, she told us to check, so check we will. I don't mean to get on her bad side. Do you?"

"I'm goin' to have some words with that bastard Fabor when I see 'em," the second grumbled, "I can tell you that much."

"You check the left, I'll check right," the man said, speaking on as they started forward. "Anyway, I ain't all that sure you'll get the chance before *she* has words with him first. She didn't look none too pleased that that big bastard let 'em get away, I can tell you that. You ask me, I'd rather be just about anywhere than in Fabor's shoes right now. Or his wife's, for that matter."

"What do you mean?" the man asked, glancing back from where he'd been peering into one of the stalls.

"What do you think I mean? She don't strike me as the sort that takes well to failure. Nor betrayal, so far as that goes."

"Betrayal?" the man named Fred asked. "You're kiddin', ain't you? Shit, Bill, you know Fabor. We both do. He's a good enough sort. Keeps himself to himself, as my pa used to say, sure, but that's alright. Anyway, Laura said they snuck out, and he went after 'em."

"Yeah, that's what she said," Bill agreed, "but then she would, wouldn't she?"

"What are you sayin'?"

"You know damn well," the other man said, pausing as he pushed aside a horse blanket hung from the wall to make sure no one was hiding behind it. "I'm sayin' that it seems awful convenient, them somehow runnin' just as we were gettin' ready to pay 'em a visit."

"You think Fabor told?"

"I think those three bastards'd have to have a pretty good reason to go out in this blow. Not many folks take strolls at two in the mornin' in the middle of a blizzard. What other reason do you think would drag 'em out of their warm beds into the freezin' cold if not that Fabor did a bit of oversharin'?"

They were getting closer as they spoke, close enough now that Cutter could see the frown on the second man's face as he slowly shook his head. "Bullshit," he said. "Fabor wouldn't do that. Even if he *would*, he damn sure wouldn't leave Lor to take the fall. You know how he dotes on her."

"Sure, who wouldn't, what with those tits."

"You'd best not let Fabor hear you talk about Laura that way," Fred said. "Matter of fact, probably it'd be best if you didn't let me hear it either. Lor and Fabor, they're good people. They deserve better'n that."

The other man, Bill, grunted as he paused just outside the stall where Cutter crouched, peering up the ladder at the loft into which Matt had climbed. "I think Fabor's got plenty enough problems of his own without goin' lookin' for more. Anyway, what's deserve got to do with it?" He frowned back at the ladder. "Damn if I'm goin' up there. Ladder looks like it's about to collapse. If Fabor survives the night, I ought to have a talk with him about keepin' his barn up. He could at least do a bit of dustin'." He shook his head. "They ain't here. Come on —let's go."

The man turned, starting toward the door, but whatever relief Cutter felt was cut short when the other man spoke.

"Hold up, Bill."

"I was just kiddin', Fred, damn," Bill said. "I know you and Fabor are buddies, but a big bastard like that don't need you to mother hen for him."

"I'm not talking about that," Fred said, frowning at the ladder. "You said it was dusty," he went on, jerking his chin at it.

"Sure, but what does that got to do with—" the man began, then cut off as he turned and regarded the ladder. He cocked his head and moved closer, lifting the torch and illuminating what the other man must have taken note of even from where he stood at the opposite side of the barn. Namely that while the ladder was largely covered in dust, there were also several clear marks where the dust had been rubbed away, marks that were undeniably boot prints, left when Matt had ascended the ladder.

The man, Bill, took a step back from the ladder, motioning to his companion then toward the door, clearly meaning to go and get reinforcements. He took another step which brought him close enough to that Cutter could reach out and touch him.

And so he did.

Cutter rose, wrapping an arm around the man's neck who managed only a strangled gasp before Cutter pulled him closer.

The villager dropped his torch on the ground as he brought his hands to his throat but too late. Cutter gave a savage jerk of his arm, and the man's neck snapped. He let him go, and the man dropped to the dirt floor of the barn, dead. Which left Cutter to regard the second villager in the light of the flickering torch, the man staring at him in shock with wide, terrified eyes, his mouth opened wide in surprise.

There was a frozen instant in time, one in which Cutter prepared to rush forward, knowing even as he did that he would not be able to reach the man in time. He would call out, would scream, and that scream would mean the death of Cutter and his companions. His son.

Still, with no options, Cutter started forward anyway. He'd managed no more than a step when the other man clearly overcame the worst of his shock, taking in a breath in preparation to scream. But before he could get the scream out, Fabor appeared from behind him, his expression grim. The big, red-headed man clapped one hand over the other man's mouth from behind then reached around him and drove a knife into the man's chest.

The other man's entire body went rigid, and his scream of agony was muffled by Fabor's hand as the red-headed man ripped the blade free and drove it in again. Fred fought to break free after the second stab, but after the third he had no fight left in him. He fell to the ground, dead, to reveal Fabor standing over him, his hands and arms covered in blood, a look of horror on his face as he stared at the man's body. "Fred..." he said. "He...he was a friend."

"Seems you ought to pick better friends," Feledias said as he stepped into view, brushing errant pieces of hay off his shirt and trousers.

Fabor winced. "Fred's got a wife. A mother and father who live a few hours outside New Daltenia."

"We all have families," Feledias said. "In fact, all of mine is here, in this barn, running from their lives because you and your *friends* decided to kill us, and that for reasons you still haven't explained."

Fabor tensed at that, and for a moment Cutter thought he caught sight of the old Fabor, the man who had often simply been called "the Fierce," and who had earned that name time and again on the field of battle. In another moment, though, Fabor nodded, turning to Cutter. "I'm sorry. About all of it...about Fred, but about the position I've put you and yours in. I can only tell you that I'll do what I can to see you all safe of it, your son most of all."

Feledias snorted. "Though what good that is coming from a man who nearly got us ki—"

"That's as good as it can be," Cutter interrupted.

"But what do we do?" Matt said. "We can't wait here, not anymore, even if we'd meant to." He glanced at the two dead men, at the pools of blood gathering beneath the one Fabor had killed. "They'll come looking for them soon."

"We were going to go to the Barrier Mountains anyway," Cutter said. "I see no reason not to start now."

"Really?" Feledias said. "*Really*, Bernard? No reason? What about the gods-blasted *blizzard* outside? Or the mob of would-be murderers hunting us down? Stones and starlight, even if we somehow *do* manage to evade them, what good would it do? They couldn't help but see our tracks and catch us up. Not that it will make any difference. If they want us dead, all they'll have to do is wait since, you know, we have no *supplies*."

"If you have a better idea, Fel," Cutter said, "I'd love to hear it."

Feledias frowned but said nothing.

"Maybe...maybe we could hide the bodies?" Matt asked, glancing down at the dead man then wincing, turning away.

Cutter considered that, turning to Fabor. "The woman—the one they were talking about. Who is she?"

"I...don't know," the red-headed man said.

"What do you *mean* you don't know?" Feledias demanded. "You were going to what, betray us, kill us in our beds for a woman you don't even—"

"Leave it, Fel," Cutter said. "We can pass around blame later, if we survive." He turned back to Fabor. "What do you mean you don't know her?"

The red-headed man sighed. "She showed up in town a couple days ago. Said her name was Aurora. We don't get a lot of visitors come through this way, as you can imagine. Only a small supply caravan as comes through once a month from some of the other villages. That trade, us to them and them to us is the only reason we all can survive this far out in the wilderness. Anyway, I guess besides that, it's been years since anyone come here."

"So she just shows up and what, exactly?" Feledias said. "Goes into your church and starts playin' music and then you all abandon your reason, that it?"

The red-headed man cleared his throat. "It...somethin' like that. I guess...well, as I said we don't get a lot of visitors here, and those we do get...they don't look nothin' like her. I only got eyes for my Lor, understand, but some of the other fellas in the village, well, they were a bit...taken with her, I guess you'd say."

"Taken with her," Cutter repeated.

"Sure," Fabor said, "and not just the men. The women, too. You'd think maybe they'd be jealous of all the attention she was gettin', but they weren't, leastways not so far as I could see. Anyhow, if they *were* jealous, it was on account of the attention *she* was showin' the men, not the other way around."

"And you all didn't think that was a little strange, a woman showing up out of nowhere and taking over the village?" Feledias demanded. "Playing the lute while you all drank and danced yourselves into a stupor?"

"The way she played..." Fabor said, "I've never heard anythin' like that."

Feledias frowned. "Well. Fair point, but still, it has—"

"You all keep saying that," Matt said. "About her playing being great, but...you're kidding, right?"

They all turned to Matt, and it was Feledias who spoke. "I have been known to kid a time or two, Nephew, but rarely when being hunted by a village full of men eager to see what my insides look like. I don't have any love for the woman as planning my murder and the murder of my brother and nephew has a way of souring me to a person—I'm funny that way—but even I have to admit, she played a magnificent lute."

"That's...not what I heard," Matt said.

"Well, not everyone has an ear for music," Feledias said. "I wouldn't sweat it, lad—I'm sure there is plenty else to recommend you. Your rugged good looks, for example—which you get from me, of course. Now, on to the matter at hand. I think—"

"What *did* you hear?" Cutter asked his son, for there was something about it all that didn't make sense to him. It might have been nothing, but for some reason, the fact that his son didn't agree that the woman was a talented hand at the lute—when even Cutter who knew little of such things had been struck powerfully with her skill—seemed important.

"Honestly?" Matt said. "It was painful. Awful. As bad as if she'd just picked up the lute today and begun trying. Worse, maybe."

Feledias snorted. "Everyone's a critic. Anyway, if we can focus on what's more impo—"

"That is really what you heard?" Cutter asked.

"It is," Matt said. "I would not lie, Father."

"No," Cutter said thoughtfully, "no, I don't think you would."

"What are you thinkin', Prince?" Fabor said.

"I'm thinking there is more to this woman than we first believed," Cutter said. He glanced at Feledias. "You asked earlier, Fel, how Fabor and the rest of the villagers of Windham could allow some stranger, a woman they'd never met, to take over their village and turn them into a mob to kill us. I think, now, that we have our answer. How could a woman do such a thing?"

"When she isn't just a woman at all," Matt finished for him in a breathy, shocked voice.

"I'll admit that it's been a while," Feledias said, "but I'm fairly certain I remember what a woman looks like, and it seems to me she's got all the right parts. Some of them *very* right, from what I sa—"

"You know as well as I that the Fey can sometimes look like us," Cutter said.

His brother blinked, frowning. "That's what you think? That the woman is a feyling and that her lute playing, all of it was some sort of, what, a glamour?"

"That's exactly what I think," Cutter said. He turned to Fabor. "How long ago did you say the woman showed up?"

"Two days, I think?" Fabor said. "Perhaps three? It's all a bit...a bit fuzzy, to be honest."

Cutter turned back to Feledias, raising an eyebrow.

"That'd be about the time we escaped," Feledias said.

"That's right," Cutter said. "I don't think we stumbled into the strange goings-on in Windham by chance. I think it, *she,* was a trap laid for us. Her glamour was used to beguile the villagers, to beguile *us.*"

"Not all of us," Feledias said. "If what you're saying is true, then why didn't it work on Matt here?"

"I don't know," Cutter said honestly, glancing at Matt who shook his head, clearly as confused as they were. "And it doesn't matter, in any case, at least not at the moment. I'm sorry about your friend," he told Fabor. "But he, all of them, have been taken in by the creature, the same as the woman I saw dancing until she fainted back at the church."

"What does that mean for us?"

"It means that they're not going to stop until they find us," Cutter said grimly. "It means that, more than ever, we have to get out of here—now. We cannot stay."

"And how are we going to do that, Bernard?" Feledias asked. "Fey or not, glamour or not, our problems haven't changed. We cannot outrun them, and we do not have supplies even if we could, nor any way to get them."

"It...might be I can help there," Fabor said. They all turned to regard him, and the red-headed man grunted. "I don't know much about Fey and glamours and all the rest," Fabor said. "But what I *do* know about is danger. Death. Seen plenty of both, plenty enough to recognize it when it comes, plenty enough to know that it don't always come with a roar and a battle axe like the one you carry, Prince. Sometimes, it comes with a smile, a wink...a tight-fittin' dress."

"It really was tight," Feledias said. He shrugged as Cutter turned to regard him. "Oh, don't look at me like that, Brother. I'm not blind. I noticed her while I was warming myself by the church's fire. I noticed the woman, sure. Noticed *you* notice her too."

Cutter grunted, turning back to Fabor. "You said you could help. How?"

"Lor and me," Fabor said, "we didn't like it, when this woman showed up. Didn't much care for how she was actin', nor how she was makin' *other* folks act. Folks we've known for years to be good, decent folk hootin' and hollerin' and carryin' on. Shit, some of 'em even ruttin' in the church there like pigs goin' at it." He shook his head. "I didn't know *what* was wrong, not exactly, but I knew somethin' was, and Lor, she knew better'n me. It was her idea."

Feledias opened his mouth to speak but Cutter, aware that every minute they spent here was a minute they would likely regret squandering in the near future, held up a hand to silence him. "What was her idea?"

Fabor hesitated for a moment then shook his head. "I'm sorry, Prince. For what I done...what I was goin' to do to you and yours. It was Lor talked me out of it. Whatever good is in me, I reckon it come from her. Always hated traitors...treason. Seemed to me they were just about the lowest thing goin'. Never knew how easy it'd be...so easy a man could take a single step and before he even rightly knows he's takin' it, it's too late. He's there."

Cutter didn't know what to say to that. He had, for years, decades, felt like a traitor himself. Certainly, he had betrayed his brother. His people, the trust they'd placed in him. He glanced at Feledias, and his brother gave him a look that showed he felt much the same. After all, they had both failed their people, betrayed them. He wanted to help Fabor, but how could you help a drowning man to shore when you were drowning yourself?

When someone finally spoke to offer consolation, it was neither Cutter nor Feledias. It was Matt. "Nothing has been done that cannot be undone," Matt said. "There is still time, Fabor. Time to do the right thing. But not much of it...so what did you mean? How can you help?"

Fabor cleared his throat, nodding. "As I said, Lor and I, we knew somethin' was wrong. I got a cousin who comes by Windham once a month with the supply caravan. He's due back here tomorrow. Anyway, since the woman showed up, Lor and I have been squirrelin' away supplies. Getting ready."

"You meant to go with him," Cutter said.

It wasn't really a question, but the red-headed man nodded. "It was Lor's idea. She's always been the clever one. The good one, too. It was her idea that I warn you of what was comin'. I didn't mean you all no harm, honest," he said. "Only...I was just tryin' to protect her."

"Forgive me if I have a hard time believing that," Feledias said. "After all, I don't know of many people that plan a late-night, uninvited visit with a murderous mob that don't mean harm."

Fabor winced. "Reckon I deserve that. Reckon I deserve a lot worse."

"Thankfully, the gods don't give us what we deserve," Matt said, shooting a frown at Feledias. "Or else we'd all be in trouble."

Fabor grunted. "I heard about you—the young king. Heard that you were a good and proper ruler, the sort the Known Lands have been starvin' for...no offense," he said, glancing at Cutter and Feledias.

"None taken," Cutter said.

"Well...some taken," Feledias muttered.

"Anyway," Fabor said. "It seems the stories were right. What I was getting at before is that I can go and get 'em. The supplies, I mean. Get a wagon while I'm at it. Old Farmer Clem, he's got a couple of horses. Draft beasts. They ain't goin' to win any races, but they're strong, hearty, and if you're planning on goin' north then I reckon strong and hearty is what you're needin'."

"Where would we meet?"

Fabor considered that for a moment, scratching his beard. "There's a big oak tree just beyond the village. Just about the biggest tree you ever saw. Folks call it the Kissin' Tree on account of young folk will—"

"'We get it," Feledias said.

"Right," Fabor said. "Well, anyway, you want to go there and wait for me, I'll meet you with the wagon and the supplies."

"And a mob of homicidal villagers, no doubt," Feledias said.

"Fel—" Cutter began, but his brother wasn't finished.

"Don't *Fel* me, Bernard," Feledias said. "Am I wrong or did your *friend* here not try to betray us and get us all killed? And now we're supposed to trust that he's going to risk himself, risk his wife, to help us? To give us the supplies they meant to use themselves to get out of the village?"

Fabor winced. "I...I'm sorry for what I done...what I was goin' to do. I don't make no excuse for it except to say that it was Lor I was thinkin' on."

"Right," Feledias said. "And what are you thinking on *now?*"

"What choice do we have?" Cutter countered.

"What choice besides trusting a man who has *admitted* to betraying us not to betray us again?" Feledias said. "Oh, I don't know, Bernard, but I'd like to believe I can think of *something* better than that."

Cutter opened his mouth to answer that but before he got a chance, Matt spoke. "He made a mistake," Matt said.

Feledias snorted. "A mistake? Forgive me, Nephew, but a *mistake* is calling someone by the wrong name, maybe congratulating a woman when what you thought was her pregnancy was instead just a few years of good living. Treason, though, that's a *choice.*"

"Maybe you're right, Uncle," Matt said. "Maybe it is a choice. But then we've all made choices, haven't we? And all of us, I think," he went on, meeting Feledias's eyes, "have made a few that we probably aren't proud of. A few that some might even consider treason."

Feledias frowned, glancing at Cutter. "This is what comes of educating our youth, Bernard. They start to know things."

"All I'm saying," Matt said, "is that we can't control what we've done, only what we *do*. And I think Fabor is trying to do—to *be* better. We cannot ask more than that."

"Sure we can," Feledias said. "I've got a few things I'd think to ask for—an army wouldn't go amiss, and..." He paused, his gaze traveling between Matt and Cutter, then finally he let out a sigh. "Fine. I hear you, Nephew. Maybe you're right—maybe you both are. We'll do it your way." He turned to Fabor then, and in his eyes, his face, Cutter was reminded of what they called Feledias—Stormborn. Certainly, a storm raged behind his eyes as he spoke. "I will trust you, Fabor, because *they* trust you. As my nephew has said, we all make mistakes. But do not make another one. Should you do anything to endanger my brother and my nephew, then I swear to you, whatever that woman might do will seem like a gentle reproof in comparison."

Fabor blinked, clearing his throat. "And they call me 'Fierce,'" he said. "You have my word, Prince. I will do anything within my power to keep the king—to keep *all* of you—safe."

"Now that's settled, we'd best not waste anymore time," Cutter said.

Fabor nodded. "I'll leave first, in case anyone's watching. Give me five minutes, then come after." He started toward the door of the barn, pausing as Matt spoke.

"Fabor? Good luck. And...thanks."

The man blinked, clearly surprised by the gratitude, as was Cutter himself. The red-headed man gave a smile, seemingly touched by Matt's words, then he bowed. "As you say, Majesty."

Then he opened the door a crack, glanced outside, and in another moment he was gone into the darkness.

"I still think it's a mistake, trusting him," Feledias said, glancing at Cutter.

"It wouldn't be my first," Cutter said.

Matt moved over to one of the dead men and reached down, retrieving the machete the man had held, pointedly looking away from the corpse as he did. A moment later, he rose, noted the two of them watching him, and winced. "I...I didn't have my sword on me when... when whatever happened...happened."

"You mean when you appeared out of thin air in a burst of green light that nearly blinded me and somehow sent those Unsated monstrosities fleeing back into the woods?" Feledias asked.

"I don't know that I did that or *how* I would have done it," Matt said, "but...yes."

"Well," Feledias said, shrugging, "considering that you saved our lives by appearing like you did, I suppose we can forgive you for forgetting your sword at home. Though I'll admit I am more than a little curious as to *how* you did it."

"You and me both," Matt said, and though he tried for a smile, Cutter could see the grimace beneath it. His son was bothered by what had happened. Cutter was too, though not so bothered that he didn't appreciate the fact that it happening had saved not only his and Feledias's lives but, according to what Matt had told them of Lady Valencia's assassination attempt, his son's as well.

He put a hand on his son's shoulder, waiting until Matt raised his gaze from where he'd been studying his feet. "Whatever it is," Cutter said, "whatever's going on, we'll face it together."

"Careful, brother mine," Feledias said. "I fear that we are dangerously close to a group hug." But despite his words, he clapped Matt on the back. "We'll figure it all out, Nephew. You'll see." He shrugged. "Or else we'll all die horribly in the next few minutes, in which case it won't really matter all that much, will it?"

"Thanks?" Matt said, glancing at between Feledias and Cutter.

Cutter sighed. "Your uncle has a way of looking at the bright side. Now, we'd best get moving." He glanced at the machete in Matt's hand. Not much of a weapon if it came to a fight, but then he supposed it would do better than a harsh word, if the villagers found them.

"I'll go first," he told them. "Stay close. And stay behind me."

When neither voiced any complaint, Cutter moved to the door, peering out. He couldn't see anything but the darkness and the flicker of torches in several different directions where, judging by their shouts, the villagers were hunting for him and his companions. But then, just because he couldn't see anyone waiting, didn't mean they weren't. For all he knew, Fabor had walked out into an ambush and was dead already.

Still, it wasn't as if they had many options, and he'd learned the hard way—and more than once—that often, when facing danger, the worst thing a man could do was nothing.

He stepped out into the darkness.

When no attack came, Cutter turned and peered at the others through the crack in the door. "Come on."

Feledias came out next. "Safe?" he said.

Cutter grunted. "Not sure that's the word I'd use."

Matt came next, glancing around at the light of the torches and lanterns flickering in the darkness of the village. "They're all looking for us alright."

"Or else they decided to organize a last-minute festival," Feledias said dryly. "Want to know what I'd bet on?"

"Do you think he'll make it?" Matt asked, glancing around them though between the darkness and still-driving snow he was unlikely to see anything.

"Fabor?" Cutter asked. He gave his head a shake. "I don't know. But right now we have to worry about us. Stay close."

"Yes, Father."

There it was again. One word, but one that felt like some magical spell, rousing in Cutter a storm of emotions, gratitude and fear chief among them. The sort of gratitude a man might feel if he was scrounging in the dirt and found a diamond worth a fortune, one he knew he did not deserve. Fear because he was aware, even as he lifted the diamond, examined it, how quickly it might be lost.

"Come on," he said grimly, then he turned and started in the direction of the northern gate.

They carried no light, and so they walked blindly, relying on the pale light of the moon and the snatches of silhouettes caught between the wind and snow to make their way. And the torches, of course. Torches not to help show them the way to go, but to show them the way *not* to. Dozens of them, possibly as many as a hundred, and Cutter thought it was safe to say that every able-bodied adult in Windham was out hunting for them under the feyling—for he had grown more and more sure when listening to Fabor that the woman he'd spoken with *was* a creature of the Fey—and never mind the frigid temperatures and piercing wind.

On a normal day, it would have taken no more than a ten-minute walk to reach the church from Fabor's home. Given the conditions, it took them half an hour, and by the time the building loomed up in front of them, Cutter's face and hands were numb from the cold.

"It looks like they gave their partying a rest," Matt observed as they stared at the dark, silent church.

"Better things to do, I guess," Cutter agreed.

"T-too bad," Feledias said. "I guess I m-might even l-let them kill me if i-it meant another cup of a-ale and f-five minutes by that f-fireplace."

"That's a deal they'd likely be only too happy to make," Cutter said. "I'd aim a little higher."

"S-says the m-man who m-might be out for a s-stroll, th-the way he acts. S-stones and starlight, Bernard, a-aren't you cold? You're m-making me f-feel like less of a-a man h-here."

Cutter glanced around at the night, gauging the distance between them and the flickering torches. Most were far away, searching the village proper, but there were two that seemed to be getting closer. He glanced at his brother, giving him a small grin. "Don't worry about it, Fel. Some men are made for summer and others for winter, that's all." With that, he set off, grinning to himself as he heard his brother mutter "bastard" behind him.

They walked along the side of the church, the walls granting them a brief reprieve from the cutting wind, but that didn't keep Feledias from keeping up a steady stream of hushed curses as they struggled through snowdrifts as high as their calves.

Cutter was staring ahead of them, at the wilderness beyond the village edge and at what he thought must have be the tree Fabor had mentioned and so noted nothing amiss—until Matt hissed beside him.

"*Father,*" his son whispered harshly.

Cutter spun immediately, raising his axe as he caught sight of what he first took to be half a dozen figures at the back of the church. But as he peered closer, struggling to see past the snow, he realized that the figures weren't rushing toward them, as he would have expected. Instead, they were sitting with their backs propped against the wall of the church.

"Stay here," he told Matt and Feledias, and when neither of them offered any argument, he stalked forward, his axe raised.

The figures did not move as he approached, and as he drew within no more than a few feet of the closest, he realized that they weren't *just* sitting. They were dead. Men and women of various age with no marks that he could see. Frowning, he walked in front of them, examining them. A gray-haired man, a thin woman who appeared to be in her thirties, then—Cutter paused, stopping in front of the third figure, that of an old woman. One he recognized as the same old woman who he'd seen faint in the church when they'd first arrived. Only now he realized that she hadn't fainted at all. Under the power of the feyling's glamour—no doubting that now—she had danced until she died. And judging by the others sitting to either side of her, not a single mark on them to indicate they'd been in any sort of altercation, he thought she wasn't the only one.

But even that realization was perhaps not the thing which disturbed him most. They had died while dancing, that was clear, and someone had dragged them out here, had propped them up against the back of the church the way a little girl might prop up her dolls for a tea party. And whoever had done so had not stopped there, or else someone else had decided to brave the elements to come out after.

Whatever the case, *someone* had come, and they had brought face paint or dye with them. Likely such a thing was rare in Windham, an expensive luxury most wouldn't have been able to afford and wouldn't likely squander. And yet whoever'd come had used it to paint the faces of the dead men and women in wild, garishly bright colors that would have looked far more at home on the face of some court jester dressed in motley than on the faces of the dead.

Cutter found his grip tightening on the handle of the Breaker of Pacts. If he'd had any doubt as to the nature of what had come over the people of Windham, the sight of those bodies, with their painted smiles and brightly-dyed skin would have dispelled it.

He had been bothered, since discovering what had transpired, at the thought of leaving the village and its people to suffer underneath the feyling's glamour. It had felt—and still felt—to him, like yet another abandonment, yet another failure on his part and that in a long line of failures. Now, though, he wasn't so sure. Even if he had an army, he did not think he could have saved the people of Windham. For those people, he thought as he stared at those decorated corpses, were beyond saving.

The others were waiting where he'd left them.

"What was it?" Matt asked.

Cutter was trying to find the words to say, trying to find how he might be honest with his son while sparing him from the worst of it, when Feledias spoke. "I-if you ask me, N-Nephew," he said, meeting Cutter's eyes, "i-it's an invitation to-to leave. One that I, a-at least, am e-eager to take them up on."

Cutter gave Feledias a nod, trying to communicate his gratitude in his gaze. "This way," he said. "I think that must be the tree Fabor told us about."

They started forward then and had only taken a few steps when Feledias spoke. "D-does anyone e-else feel as th-though we're walking into a trap?"

"We're in a trap already," Cutter said. "Best we try to get our way out of it."

He did not like that walk to the large oak tree. Up to that point they had been able to make use of the buildings and homes they passed as cover to keep them from sight on the off chance that someone might manage to catch a glimpse of them through the blizzard. Unlikely, but then such a glimpse, unlikely or not, would have been enough to spell their deaths, and so Cutter had been grateful for what cover they could find.

Now, though, they walked in an open field, and there was no cover to be had. Anyone looking in their direction, if afforded a moment's respite from the snow, could not help but see them, for the moonlight illuminated their silhouetted figures. Moonlight which seemed far brighter than it had. Ridiculous, maybe, no more than Cutter's nerves that made him think so, yet he *did* think so, just the same.

He walked with his shoulders hunched not just against the wind but against a certainty—one that grew by the moment—that any second they would hear the shout of villagers in the distance and would turn to see all of those torches which had flitted in the night like fireflies converging on them. And should the villagers come upon them here, in the open, Cutter knew that he and his brother, his *son,* would be overwhelmed in minutes.

It felt as if they traveled forever, yet every time Cutter looked up to check their progress the tree seemed as if it had gotten further away instead of closer. It was a thought, a sort of hallucination that persisted until, finally, they had reached the tree. Cutter could not keep himself from reaching out to touch it, half-convinced that it would vanish as his fingers alighted upon it, like the smoky substance of some dream he'd had.

But it did not. The tree remained a tree as Cutter's fingers—too numb to feel anything—ran down its length. He and his companions stepped around to the opposite end of the tree so that it stood between them and the wind and obscured them from anyone who might look their way from the distant village.

"Thank...th-the gods f-for that," Feledias said, wrapping his arms around himself as he shivered from the cold.

Cutter turned to regard the village. It seemed far closer now that they had reached the tree.

"D-do you th-think the b-bastard will make it?" Feledias asked in a voice that trembled with the cold.

"I don't know," Cutter said honestly.

"So wh-what do we do now?" Matt asked, hugging himself and rubbing at his arms with his gloved hands.

"Now we wait," Cutter said, turning to his son. "For Fabor to arrive."

"O-or to f-freeze to death," Feledias said.

Cutter glanced at his brother, then back to his son. Finally, he turned back to the village, huddled against the great expanse of the northern wilderness. Torches flickered here and there, tiny motes of light in the dark and the snow.

"Either way," he said, "we won't have to wait long."

CHAPTER EIGHT

As he drove his carriage through the streets of New Daltenia, toward his home, Ned thought of his wife, of what he might say to her. Things were bad—Emille always accused him of refusing to see anything but the bright side, but damned if he wasn't having a hard time finding one just now. He couldn't imagine what he would say to her, how he would tell her all that had happened.

First, he decided as he made his way around a carriage parked—against all decency, he noted with a frown—in the center of the street, he would apologize. Partly because, in his experience, that was always the best way for a husband to start any conversation with his wife but mostly because in this case, she was owed it. She had tried to warn him about Val. She had told him that her story hadn't added up and yet he had not seen it, had *refused* to see it. And now, because of that, because of *him* the serving woman in the castle was dead, and Matt, the king—the first *real* king the people of the Known Lands had had in a very long time—was gone.

He decided as he rode grimly through the streets—and getting grimmer by the moment—that he didn't just owe Emille an apology. He owed everyone in the Known Lands an apology. In truth, he owed them much more than that.

He owed them a king.

It was a debt that he felt like a weight pressing down on him, a debt that he would settle, even if it killed him. But first, he had to speak to Emille. She would know what to do, what to say—she always did.

He'd set out a long time ago to try to make the world a better place—it was the whole reason he and Robert and Val had formed the Wolves in the first place. But now they were both traitors, and he was a failure.

But just because a man had failed, that did not mean that he must *always* fail. He had done good once—no matter what Val said, he believed that, *had* to believe that. He had not always been a carriage driver. Once, he had been a warrior, one who had stood against the evil in the city. He could be that man again. He was rusty, that was all, but then even a dull blade might be sharpened, even a blade which had long adorned some mantel might be made of use once more.

With the morning sun rising high in the sky, the streets of New Daltenia were bustling with people. Perhaps the world would end in a week, but in the meantime, people still had to eat, still had to *live*. And in truth, most of those men and women Ned passed did not seem worried or disconsolate—they seemed happy. As happy as they had since Matt, the prince's son, had taken over the rule of New Daltenia. And not just happy...hopeful.

He had not ruled for long, but already the young king had a reputation—largely gained from his regular audiences with the people of New Daltenia—for fairness, kindness. It was a reputation which, from what Ned had seen, was well earned. For even in his brief time with the young king, he had seen, as anyone who spent even a few minutes with him could not help but see, the effort he put into being the king his people needed.

As he waited in the street behind another carriage as it was loaded with provisions and its owners climbed inside, Ned wondered what the smiling, laughing people of the city would think if they discovered that their new king was gone. Vanished. He wondered, briefly, what they would do if they discovered that the man who was in a very large part *responsible* for that vanishing was within arm's reach.

One of the men loading the wagon ahead of him spilled a bag, and potatoes and onions spilled out. Ned started to climb out to help but saw that the man's companion had it covered, the two of them beginning to scoop up the errant vegetables. While he waited, Ned studied the people of the city moving back and forth down the street and the sidewalks on either side. *His* city. *His* people.

There was a shout, and Ned—already on edge from all that had happened—spun to look in the direction it had come from. But instead of the deadly assassin or Fey monster he'd half-expected, Ned saw that it was only a group of young kids, none older than ten if he had to guess, who'd been playing with a ball. The ball had gotten away from them and even as Ned noticed it, it rolled underneath his carriage.

One child, the youngest—a boy of no more than seven—was nominated by his companions to retrieve it. There was no vote, at least so far as Ned could see, only the expedient of them pushing him into the street. The youth approached nervously, wringing his hands, and Ned smiled, trying to remember what it had been like to be so young that his greatest worry was losing a ball. Wondering if he had *ever* been that young. He glanced back at the wagon in front of him and saw that the two men still had some gathering left to do, then he climbed out of the carriage.

He knelt, looking beneath it to see that the ball had fetched up against the inside of one of the wheels. He crawled forward to retrieve it and noticed as he did a man looking in his direction from the other side of the street. He wouldn't have thought much of it—people had eyes, after all, and they had to look somewhere—except that, the moment he looked at the man, he turned away.

It might have just been a coincidence, but then Ned had lived long enough, had seen and suffered enough that he thought a man was better off believing in fairy tales than coincidences. Still, he didn't give the man another look, for the thing about predators, he knew, was that sometimes they didn't attack until their prey noticed them.

He inched forward, retrieving the ball, then climbed back out again. The boy was waiting a few feet away when Ned rose. Close enough that he could get the ball but not so close, Ned thought, that he couldn't make a break for it if Ned proved to be angry or dangerous.

Ned smiled as best he could—though considering the direction of his thoughts, it likely wasn't his best effort—then tossed the ball back. The boy took it, nodding his head in what might have been thanks before turning and running back to his friends, grinning at a challenge faced and overcome.

Ned wished that all challenges might be overcome so easily. By the time he climbed back into the carriage, the two men were finishing picking up the last of the spilled vegetables. While he waited, Ned fought the urge to glance back at the man he'd seen looking his way. Instead, he regarded the other side of the street, taking in the stalls where merchants hawked their wares to the people crowding the busy street.

Yet while he might not have looked in the man's direction, he fancied that he could *feel* his gaze upon him. Instead, he glanced over at the side of the street where several merchants had set up stalls and were busily hawking their wares to the passersby. As he did, he caught sight of a woman who appeared to be in her thirties. Normally, he wouldn't have noticed her, but at seeing the man watching him, some part of him, a part of him that had long been asleep, had begun to awaken.

He was like a playgoer who had allowed himself to become fully immersed, fully *fooled* by the pretend world in front of him but, by sheer luck or happenstance, had seen something, a failed costume or prop, a flaw, and now could not help but see others. He would not have noticed the woman before, but he noticed her now.

She stood in front of a merchant's stall while the merchant himself was trying to interest her in a small leather purse and not having much luck attracting her attention. Ned, though, seemed to have done it and that without trying, for the woman was looking directly at him, though she turned away the moment he looked at her, engaging with the merchant.

Old instincts kicked in, and Ned didn't allow his gaze to linger, continuing to glance around the street. He focused on appearing calm, relaxed as if he were doing nothing but waiting on the carriage in front of him to move. Meanwhile, his heart was hammering in his chest and his hands had begun to sweat. One man staring at him in a crowd like he owed him money, well that might have been a coincidence. Or maybe he even owed him money. Driving carriages wasn't known for making many people rich. But *two* people staring at him that way...well now that was a pattern.

He made a show of patting his horse, just relaxing while the men in front of him finished up, but while he focused on keeping cool on his exterior, inside, his thoughts were running a mile a minute. Perhaps he *had* become dull over the years, more sheep than wolf, but nothing sharpened a man like danger, and the wolf was beginning to waken.

It was that part of him, that long dormant part, which told him that these two were not criminals. Or, at least, not the sort of criminals that had marked him out of a crowd and decided to rob him of all that he had. For one, criminals searched for the easiest opportunities, for the best marks, and these two didn't appear to be searching for marks at all but watching him specifically. Secondly, there was something about the woman that bothered him. He couldn't be sure, but he thought that he had seen her before, when he'd left the castle, walking along the street.

He wasn't certain, more instinct than memory, but he'd learned long ago to trust his instincts, had been *taught* to trust them as an Empath back in Daltenia's Academy, and so he trusted them now. Anyway, there was nothing of value in the carriage beyond a silk scarf accidentally left by a noblewoman Ned had given a ride a few days ago. At the time, the noblewoman had been far too concerned with draping herself over a man Chall was confident had *not* been her husband to notice the scarf falling from her shoulders. And if the two had followed him from the castle, as he suspected, then they would have checked, would know that the carriage contained nothing of worth.

Which meant that they had not come for the carriage or its contents—they'd come for him.

Finally, the men in front of him finished loading up their supplies, and the carriage started away. With more than a little relief, Ned clucked at his horses, giving the reins a snap, and started forward, down the street. Here, in the middle of one of the city's markets, it was slow going, constantly having to stop the carriage while men and women and children moved in and out of the street. Ned did his best to keep from looking directly to either side, though he thought he detected the man and the woman on more than one occasion out of the corner of his eye, the two blending in as they kept pace with the slow-moving carriage.

After what felt like an eternity, he reached the edge of the market stalls and the path before him opened up. He urged the horses to pick up their pace. Not fast enough to show any sort of panic, at least he hoped, but fast enough that he would inevitably leave behind his two watchers as he went further down the street.

They would have to move far quicker than a walk if they meant to keep pace with him, and he supposed they thought that breaking into a jog might be just a touch too obvious. Which, he thought, meant that they were still unaware that he had marked their presence. Otherwise, they would have had no reason to continue with the pretense.

Not that the thought offered much comfort. After all, those two were the ones he had seen—there was no telling how many he hadn't. But then, that wasn't *exactly* true. They weren't regular criminals, after all. He had already decided that by their manner. No, they struck him far more like trained professionals, the sort employed by the Assassins' Guild, and the guild, he knew from past experience, tended to send five-person teams on this sort of mission. Plenty enough to ensure that they wouldn't lose their mark. Plenty enough that, when the time came to do more than just watch, they could be confident that the thing would be done with minimal fuss.

Which meant that there were likely three others out there, somewhere, and unless they were the worst-informed assassins in the world, they knew that he drove a carriage, which meant that they would have made plans to track him despite that.

It was an effort to keep from looking up at the rooftops, but Ned managed it, if only just. Still, he was worried. Not for himself—or, at least, not *only* for himself—for any man who wasn't concerned about being hunted by five assassins had some serious issues. Mostly, though, he was worried for Emille. After all, Ned had recently discovered that his wife was part of the Assassins' Guild, and even though he hadn't been the best husband of late, he didn't think Emille would send a kill team of assassins after him—even if he might deserve it.

But as scary as that sounded, the alternative was worse, for that meant that Emille and Lady Maeve hadn't sent them at all, and that didn't bode well for how the two were faring with dealing with the trouble at the guild that Chall had mentioned.

When he'd set out from the castle, Ned had meant to go home, to hopefully find and speak with Emille, for when the world—when his life—got crazy, the greatest comfort he could have was his wife. But when he came to an intersection, the right branch of which would take him in the direction of his home, Ned urged the horses left, instead.

It took him another fifteen minutes to reach the livery stables. Not so long in the normal course of things, but an eternity when he had to fight the constant urge to look all around him to try to spot the person —or people—who he was certain were marking his progress. Once he thought he heard a soft scraping sound from a roof to his left that he thought must have been one of the slate tiles of the home shifting underneath someone's weight, and it was all he could do to keep himself from turning to check.

He managed it, if only just, just as he managed, with no small surprise or relief, to reach the livery stables where he had worked for what felt like a lifetime. As he pulled the carriage forward, he thought of his plan again, turning it over this way and that, looking for any flaw. But then he knew from cold, hard experience that plans were a lot like shields—a man never really knew how well-made they were until someone swung a sword at them.

He pulled the carriage up to the front of the building, bringing the horses to a stop as the waiting groomsman moved forward.

"Good morning, Mister Neddard," the young man—who Ned would have pegged at not a day older than twenty—said as he moved up beside the carriage while Ned climbed out.

"It's morning anyway," Ned said as he stepped off the side of the carriage. "And I must be misrememberin', Dylan, for I could have sworn that the last time I was here we discussed you callin' me Ned."

The young man blushed. "Sorry, Mi—Ned. And the horses?"

"Could use a bit of rest," Ned said. *Couldn't we all?*

"Yes, sir," the groom said, then cleared his throat as Ned raised an eyebrow. "Sorry—Ned. And what of you, sir? Short day?"

Ned sighed. "Long night, I'm afraid, Dylan."

The groom nodded as he began unhitching the horses. "Are you done for the day?"

Ned shook his head. "No, Dylan," he said. "I don't think I am. It seems to me that the day is just getting started."

"Then I wish you luck of it, sir."

"Ned," Ned corrected then gave the young man a smile. "And thanks. I'm thinkin' I'll need it."

He gave the groom a nod then turned and started toward the building. As he did, he let his gaze travel around as much of the city as he could in the instant it took him to turn. He didn't see them, his silent, invisible watchers, but of course that made little difference.

He stepped into the livery stables. Groups of men and women stood around the large room, talking. Some Ned recognized, others he didn't. He nodded to them in greeting either way. The day was likely to end in blood and pain, and so he thought it might as well start in kindness. There were three different women who sometimes worked the desk at the stables. The two that he had hoped to find behind the desk—at least one or the other—and the one currently sitting behind it.

But the plan was the plan already, so Ned continued forward, Delilah frowning at him from her place behind the desk as he drew closer.

"Neddard," Delilah said—grumbled, really—by way of greeting as Ned came to stand in front of the desk.

"Hello, Delilah," Ned said, "and can I just say that your beauty rivals that of the mornin' sun."

"I'm not wearing a dress, Driver Neddard," the woman said, "so there is very little need for you to go blowin' smoke up it. Now, what do you want?"

"Want?" Ned asked, giving her his best smile. "Why, couldn't I just be visiting my favorite secretary?"

She raised a dark black eyebrow, perched on her forehead like all the judgment in the world. "Are you?"

Ned's grin faltered, and he cleared his throat. "Well…no, not exactly. That is, I am, of course, glad to see you," he stumbled, "only, well, you know, I've got a bit of a favor to ask."

"A favor," she repeated as if he'd just asked for one of her kidneys.

"Just a small one," he said.

Her lips pursed into a sour frown that showed Ned exactly what she thought of that. "Small favors lead to big problems, my mother used to say."

"She sounds lovely," Ned said, glancing back at the door. No one moving through it yet, but that didn't mean they wouldn't soon. They would not want to lose sight of him for long, but by stepping into the stables they would be taking a risk, one that might well make them decide that the time for subterfuge was past. They might instead choose to no longer be content with following, and while Ned didn't much care for being stalked, he thought he'd care even less about being stabbed.

"Listen, Lila, I don't mean to be rude, as I enjoy our little...chats. But I'm in a bit of a hurry. So I was going to see if—"

"Delilah."

He blinked. "What's that?"

"I've told you before, Carriageman Neddard, I only let my mother call me Lila, and considering that she's been buried going on fifteen years, I doubt if you're her."

"Sorry for your loss," Ned said. "Anyway," he went on, making an attempt at lightening the mood, "I seem to recall asking you to call me Ned."

She said nothing, only stared at him, but then Delilah had a way of saying plenty without so much as opening her mouth.

"Right," Ned said, clearing his throat. "Anyway, about the favor...I was going to hire a carriage."

She blinked. Whatever she'd expected him to say, it certainly hadn't been that. Not that she looked pleased about the surprise, but then he didn't think Delilah spent a lot of her time looking pleased about anything. "You want to hire a carriage," she repeated.

"That's right."

"And you are aware, of course," she went on, "that you work here."

"Suppose that explains the coin you guys have been giving me the last few years," he said, flashing her a grin.

She did not return it. Instead, she reached for the ledger that sat on the desk in front of her, opening it and withdrawing a pen from the desk drawer. "Destination," she said in what might have loosely been considered a question but was really nothing short of a demand.

"Nice to meet you, Destination, I'm—" He cut off as she raised her eyes, looking at him from underneath her dark brows. He cleared his throat. "Right. Um...destination. Well, I suppose I'm...not really sure. Yet?"

He was, of course, but then considering that assassins were stalking his footsteps, he didn't think it wise to be too free with his whereabouts or his soon-to-be whereabouts.

"You're not sure," she repeated. "And when will you be returning?"

"Not...sure?" he said.

She set the pen down, raising her gaze to look at him. "Are you wasting my time, Carriageman Neddard?"

"I wouldn't dream of it," Ned said.

She sighed, retrieving the pen. "Let me get this straight—you would like to hire a carriage to take you somewhere for some amount of time, neither of which you're sure about."

Ned winced, glancing back at the door. Still empty, at least for the moment, but he doubted it would remain so for much longer.

"Expecting company?"

He turned back Delilah. "I hope not," he said.

She frowned. "Everything alright, Neddard?"

It was the kindest thing he'd ever heard her say to him, and if Ned hadn't known better he would have almost thought he'd heard a note of compassion in her voice. "I...I don't think so. Listen, Delilah, I'm in a bit of a hurry, and—"

"To get to a place you're not sure about yet," she said. "Where you'll be for an amount of time of which you are also unsure," she said.

"That's right."

"Of course," she said dryly. "Let me put on my hurry face. Now, is there anything else?"

"Just one thing," Ned said. "I was wondering if...well, if it wouldn't be too much trouble if I used the back door and if maybe the driver could meet me there instead of out front."

"Around back," she repeated.

"That's right," Ned said, glancing back at the door again. "If it isn't too much trouble."

She was frowning at him when he looked back. "I forgot to ask you, how's your cousin?"

"Cousin?" Ned asked, doing his best to keep from showing his impatience. Delilah struck him as the sort of woman who would dig her heels in the moment she thought someone else was in a hurry. "What cousin?"

"You know," Delilah said, "the one you introduced me to before. Don't you recall?"

Ned blinked. It took a moment but finally he remembered when Prince Bernard had arrived at the stables what felt like a lifetime ago, and Ned had given Delilah a fake name to hide the prince's identity. "Oh, right," he said, smiling to cover his confusion. "No, sure. Cend, you mean. Cend Averteen."

"Aberdeen," she corrected.

"A-are you sure?"

"I can check my notes," she said, reaching for the ledger.

"Oh, no, no that won't be necessary," Ned said hurriedly. "I wouldn't want to put you out."

She sighed, glancing around the stables before leaning forward. "A big man, your cousin. I'd say I've never seen someone so big, but that's not true. I did. Once. When Prince Bernard and his brother, Prince Feledias sat in on an audience in the castle. This was years ago now, when my mother was still alive, and she had been wronged by a nobleman. I won't go into the details. Anyway, I remember they helped her—Prince Bernard didn't say much, but he had a certain...presence. One that commanded my attention, enough that I remember him well, even to this day. Everything about him. Including his size—how he looked."

Ned blinked. "You...you knew. But...but you never said anything."

"Sometimes, I find it best to let men pretend they are cleverer than they are."

"I see."

"It is the easiest way of dealing with fools."

"Men, you mean."

"That's what I said," she said, giving him a small smile, something Ned would have doubted her capable of until that moment. "Anyway, this errand you're on, would it happen to have anything to do with... your cousin?"

"Yes," Ned said, nodding slowly. "And...and my nephew, too."

"I've heard of him," she said. "I've heard he's quite a good...nephew. Is that true?"

"The nephew I, *we* all deserve. Better, really."

She nodded. "Go on then, Ned," she said, the use of his preferred name as much of a surprise as any he'd had that day and that among some stiff competition. "You do what needs doing." She motioned to the door at the back of the stables behind her desk.

Ned was so surprised that for a moment he just stood there.

"Ned?" she said, using his preferred name again. "Not that I don't think you do a fine impersonation of a statue, but I was under the impression you were in a hurry."

"O-of course," he said. "Thanks, Delilah. Really. And listen, if anyone comes asking after me—"

"I'll tell them you've gone to the Salty Sailor," she said. "It's a little pub on dockside. A hole in the wall and just about as far away from... well, anything as any place in the city."

"Thanks, Delilah," he said. "I...thank you."

She waved a dismissive hand. "Go on then. Go help your cousin and nephew—for your sake, for all our sakes, I wish you luck."

He started toward the back door, pausing when she spoke again. "And Ned?"

"Yes, Delilah?"

She frowned her usual frown. "You bring my carriage back in one piece."

"Of course," he said, reaching for the door handle.

"But if not," she said. "You make sure you bring *you* back in one piece."

He paused, glancing back at her. "Yes ma'am."

And then he left.

CHAPTER NINE

None of them spoke as they stood in the shadow of that great tree, each of them nursing their own thoughts, their own worries, as the blizzard raged around them. They had waited there for what felt like a lifetime but there was still no sign of Fabor.

Cutter pulled his gaze away from the distant village and the motes of flickering orange light floating in the darkness—proof that the villagers had not given up their search—to look at his son. He could not see much of Matt in the darkness, with the wind and the snow, but it was enough to know that he was there. He realized in that moment that for some time it had not been his promise to Layna, Matt's mother, which had spurred him into watching the boy. Perhaps it had never been. It had been his own desire. For to protect Matt, to see him safe, he would do anything, would try to be whatever man he needed to be for his son.

Even a good one.

It was something he knew little of, for whatever else others might call his life, what *he* might call it, none, he was confident, would call it *good*. But that was where the hope he had found came in. In truth, though, he had not found it at all but had been gifted it the moment

Matt had first opened his eyes onto the world. He had not known it, then, the gift, had not recognized it for what it was, but that made no difference.

He knew it now.

In truth, he knew little else.

"I...I think I see something," Matt said.

"Yeah, m-me too, Nephew," Feledias said, the worst of his shivering and stammering seeming to have abated with the shelter the giant oak offered. "Snow."

"Not that," Matt said. "Something...I think maybe it's Fabor."

Cutter shielded his eyes with an arm, squinting toward the village, but he could see nothing.

"I think maybe it's your imagination, lad," Feledias said. "Not that anyone could bla—"

"Wait," Cutter said, frowning. "Listen."

At first, there was nothing, only the sound of the snow and the driving wind, and he began to think that he had imagined it. But then it came again. A sound that was barely audible...but one that he had heard enough over the course of his life, on his way toward this battlefield or away from that one that he could not have helped but recognize it. The sounds of horses and wagons on the move.

Or, at least, one.

He was able to see it a moment later, a vague silhouette in the distance, outlined by the pale moonlight. It was a wagon, that was sure, and someone sitting atop it. It might have been Fabor.

It *could* have been anyone.

"What are you thinking, Brother?" Feledias asked.

Cutter frowned at the wagon, shaking his head slowly.

"That's got to be Fabor, right?" Matt asked.

"Maybe," Cutter said uncertainly, still studying the distant figure as it slowly drew closer across the snow-covered field.

"It...it's just one man, though," Matt said. "It looks safe."

"Most traps do, Nephew," Feledias said grimly, "right up until a poor fool steps into them."

"What should we do, then?" Matt asked.

Cutter glanced at him then back at the slowly approaching wagon. "Stay here," he said, then glanced at Feledias. "Fel," he went on, glancing at Matt, "if anything should...that is, if it *is* a trap..."

"You have my word, Brother," Feledias said, not needing him to finish, which was just as well as Cutter wasn't sure, just then, that he could have.

He gave him a nod.

"Father, you shouldn't go alone," Matt said. "If it is a trap, you'll need help, and—"

"If it's a trap, then there's an entire village on their way and the three of us will fare no better than me alone, in such a case. Stay here. And if anything goes wrong...run." He said no more than that, could say no more for in truth there was nowhere to run *to*. If it was a trap, if Fabor had betrayed them—again—then the best they could hope for would be to flee into the Barrier Mountains. And in the unlikely event that they reached them before the villagers rode them down, they stood little chance in the mountains without supplies.

He started through the snow, watching the wagon slowly rolling toward them. He gripped his axe tightly, ready, should it prove a trap, to buy his son and brother what time he could. He glanced back at the village as he walked, half expecting to see the flickering lights of the dozens of torches in the distance suddenly begin to converge toward them.

They didn't, though, so Cutter continued forward. Finally, he met up with the wagon and felt more than a little relief to see that it was indeed Fabor sitting at the front, clutching the reins of the horses in one gloved hand.

"Prince," Fabor said. "You made it."

"We did," Cutter said, glancing past the wagon in the direction of the village.

"Looking to see if I gave you up?" the red-headed man asked.

"The thought had crossed my mind."

The big man's wince was visible even in the moonlight. "Considerin' that I have already, I reckon I don't have a right to act offended. Still, I want you to know that I wouldn't do that. For what it's worth, I made you a promise that I would see you and your boy and brother safe if it was within my power, and I meant it." He climbed down from the wagon then, handing Cutter the reins.

"Listen, Prince," Fabor said, "Are you sure about this? Going to the mountains, I mean. I've lived in Windham a long time now, and in that time I've seen a few folks come and venture into the Barrier Mountains. Small groups, mostly, of four or five, but one large expedition, at least twenty of 'em. I don't know why they come here. Bored, maybe?" He shrugged. "But they weren't clerks or tailors who got a wild hair and decided to become adventurers, that I know. These fellas—and ladies, for there were more'n a few of them—they looked to me like they knew their business. Not that I reckon it made any difference. I don't know what brought 'em here, what they went to the mountains lookin' for, but I got a pretty good idea what they found."

"They didn't return?" Cutter asked, though in truth there was little need, for he was all too aware of the reputation of the Barrier Mountains from his time in Brighton.

"Not a one," Fabor agreed grimly. "I don't know what it is waitin' up in those mountains, but whatever it is, Prince, you can be assured it don't care for us mortals trespassin'." He shook his head. "Maybe it's just hard, sharp rocks, long drops, and the cold. Cold like you ain't ever felt." He shrugged, meeting Cutter's eyes. "Maybe it's somethin' else. I don't know. But you ask me, there's better ways to die. Fact is, I can't think of a single reason good enough to make me walk that path."

"Then you haven't given it enough thought," Cutter said, his eyes drawn to the great oak. He couldn't see Matt, but he knew he was there. Matt who was in danger and would be in far greater danger still if Shadelaresh and those who followed him managed to rekindle the war against the Known Lands, to turn what had, for the last few years, been acts of espionage and a sullen disquiet into widespread bloodshed.

"You're thinkin' of your boy," Fabor said. "It's him as drives you on."

It wasn't really a question, but Cutter answered it anyway, turning back to regard the red-headed man. "Yes. And not just him. Some nights are darker than others, Fabor, but the only way to see morning again is to go through them. And so I mean to."

The man watched him for a moment then grunted, giving his head a nod. "I see there's no talkin' you out of it, and if it's as important as you seem to think, then I don't guess I'd want to. After all, you ain't the only one with people you love, people you want to protect." He clapped a hand on the side of the wagon. "There's plenty of food and drink in there to get you on a piece, enough that if you die, it won't be on account of an empty stomach. There's blankets, too, and some warm clothes. Flint and tinder for startin' a fire. A few other things."

Cutter nodded then after a moment, he held out his hand. The other man took it. "Thank you, Fabor. For your help."

"Considerin' where you're goin, I ain't sure me helpin' you along is doin' you any favors, but you're welcome just the sa—" the red-headed man began then cut off as a shout sounded in the distance.

They both turned at once to the village, peering into the darkness toward those torches. One of which, Cutter noted with grim realization, had stopped on the edge of the village nearest them. For a moment, he hoped he'd been wrong, that he'd imagined it, perhaps, and never mind that Fabor had turned just as quickly as he had. Or else, he hoped that the distant screamer had been startled at something in the night. But whatever hope he had was dashed seconds later when another shout came. The words themselves were inaudible from this distance, but their effect was all too clear.

A chill that had nothing to do with the weather ran up Cutter's back as dozens of flickering orange lights from the torches suddenly began to converge, all moving toward the one nearest him which stood like a waiting beacon.

"Oh, gods be good," Fabor said, "they're comin'."

"How many horses do they have?"

"They'll see me," Fabor said, "and they'll know, they'll know I helped. And Lor—"

"*How many horses?*" Cutter demanded, grabbing the man by the shoulder and turning him to face him.

"I-I let them out of the stables," Fabor said. "It'll take them some time to round 'em up. Listen, Prince, you've got to kill me."

Cutter recoiled, feeling as stunned as if the man had slapped him. "What?"

"It's the only thing for it," Fabor said. "There ain't no way I'm makin' it back to the village without them seein' me, we both know that. And when they see me with you, they'll know I helped you. That woman, she ain't the sort to leave a man's punishment with him."

"Fabor, I don't…"

"Don't you see?" the man said, his voice rising. "They'll kill *Lor*, Prince. They'll kill her because of what I done. Unless—"

"Unless they think you weren't helping after all, that you tried to stop us and we killed you to escape," Cutter finished.

"Right," Fabor said. He took a slow, deep breath, then nodded. "I'm ready."

Cutter looked at the man for several seconds, then at the axe in his hand. Finally, he found his gaze turning back to the tree at which Matt and Feledias stood. He couldn't see them, but he knew they would be watching, wondering what was taking so long. Wondering why Cutter wasn't running, for they could not have helped but to have seen the villagers' torches floating in the darkness as they made their way across the fields toward them.

Cutter thought of none of that for long, though. Instead, what he thought of was what Fabor had asked him and more importantly what *Matt* would think of it. He had never deserved his son. Maybe that could be said of every parent, but he did not think that it was ever truer than in his case. But despite his flaws, Matt had given him a chance, had seen past the sins of a life full of little else, and had seen something good in him. Had seen it even before Cutter had, or perhaps it was closer to the truth to say that it had not been there at all until Matt had seen it, until he'd *decided* to see it, and then, once he had, so too had Cutter.

Matt had forgiven him for a lot, more than he deserved to be forgiven for certainly, but Cutter did not believe he would forgive him for this, for watching him kill a man—a man who had helped them escape certain death—right in front of him.

"*Please,* Prince," Fabor said, his voice desperate, "you have to do this. We're running out of time."

"I...I can't," Cutter said.

"They'll kill Lor!" Fabor screamed, his grief and pain and fear audible even over the driving wind. "Don't you get it, you bastard? They'll kill her, and it will be your fault!" He drew a knife from his belt then, his eyes wild. "If you don't kill me, I'll kill you."

"Fabor," Cutter said. "Don't do this. I won't—"

"I love my wife, Prince," the man said, sounding almost calm now. Then, he raised the knife over his head in a two-handed grip and rushed forward, screaming as he did.

Cutter's instinct was to let his axe flash out as it had so many times before, to cut down the danger, the threat before him. He had done it plenty of times, had done far worse than this. And had told himself, in the doing, that what made a man a man was being able to make the tough choices. It was something his father had taught him, long ago, a lesson that Darius Alder, his father's master-at-arms, had reinforced repeatedly. Where Cutter had erred over the course of his life, however, was in thinking that making the hard choice was the same thing as making the bloody one.

As Fabor rushed toward him, Cutter pivoted, lashing out not with his axe but with his fist, fetching the man a powerful blow in the side of the temple that sent him crashing into the wagon before he slumped to the ground, unconscious. Cutter stared down at the man for a moment, breathing heavily, then back toward the village, noted the torches growing closer now. "Good luck, Fabor," he told the unconscious man. "And thanks."

He climbed into the carriage, gave the reins a snap, guiding the horses toward the tree where his brother and his son waited. The beasts could not move quickly, not with the snow so thick on the ground, but they were still considerably faster than a man on foot, and he reached the tree in a few minutes' time.

"Have a nice chat, did you?" Feledias asked, glancing past Cutter to where Fabor still lay unconscious on the ground.

"Something like that. Climb on—we need to go."

They were well aware of the danger, so neither argued, climbing into the wagon, Matt in the front and Feledias in the back, finding an empty place among the bundles Fabor had placed there.

"You hit him," Matt said, a surprised note in his voice, one that sounded hurt. "Why?"

"It's...complicated," Cutter said, glancing down at his bloody knuckles as he urged the horses forward. "Now, we have to go."

"But...but he's hurt," Matt said, and the look of betrayal he gave Cutter was almost a physical pain.

Cutter glanced back at the torches bobbing in the night, a few stopping at the place where Fabor lay while others struggled after him and his companions. "He'll live," he said.

CHAPTER TEN

Chall hissed in frustration, tossing the necklace onto the desk in front of him.

"Impossible," he muttered.

He sank back into his chair, rubbing at his temple where a headache was beginning to form. He remembered one of his instructors at the Academy—a man with a wart on his nose big enough that Chall had joked that it ought to have a name—always proselytizing on how anything was possible as long as a person believed. Maybe he'd been right. Certainly Chall thought Priest would agree. But then Chall had been near the instructor when the Skaalden came and destroyed the city, had watched the man hold up his hands to shield himself from an attack that split him in half anyway.

Which didn't exactly mean that the professor's theory had been wrong—maybe he hadn't believed enough. It did, however, underline the fact that, sometimes, despite his best efforts, a man failed and that failure often ended in pain.

He scowled at the necklace lying on the desk, the green jewel seeming to shimmer as if in mockery. He considered—not for the first time—taking a hammer to it. The problem, of course, was that while he knew little of artifacts of magic, he *did* know that doing so could be dangerous. Magic was power, after all, and the amount contained inside the jewel, if it was responsible for Robert Palden's supernatural abilities as he thought, was a considerable amount. Destroying the housing that contained that magic could have disastrous effects, particularly for any fool within arm's reach of it.

But while he knew not to take a hammer to it, in truth he knew little else. He'd been at it for hours, examining the amulet with his magic the way a thief might a home he meant to burgle, checking windows and doors, hoping to find some means of ingress. But so far, at least, he had found the home—the amulet—to be locked tight. Or else there *was* a way in but those measures the creator of the amulet—the builder of the home—had put into place to secure it were beyond his talents to supersede.

During his time at the Academy, Chall had been in a few classes and numerous lectures on magical artifacts. Of course, he had been far more concerned at the time—and right up until recently, truth to tell—with the magic to be found underneath a woman's bodice, or in the flash of a dress's hem to reveal a shapely calf or, dream of all dreams, a smooth, toned thigh.

In that moment, as he stared at the necklace, a silent snarl on his face, Chall wished something that he had never wished before in his life—he wished he'd studied more.

"Fire and salt, I'm screwed."

He buried his face in his hands, frustrated. He wanted to give up. To walk out. To let someone else do it. The problem, of course, was that there *was* no one else. In matters concerning the Art, concerning *magic,* he was the best they had. Which was terrifying for a variety of reasons. Who else, after all, could be expected to solve the mystery of the amulet? A mystery that might well be the only possible way to defeat Robert Palden—certainly a brothel full of hardened criminals hadn't been.

He found himself thinking of Ned. The carriage driver had attended the university in Daltenia just as Chall had. Perhaps he might be able to discern something that Chall hadn't or, failing that, between the two of them maybe they'd be able to work it out. Except Ned wasn't there—he had gone to check on his wife to make sure that she was okay and that whatever trouble had occurred at the Assassins' Guild had been resolved. Not that there wouldn't be another trouble, soon enough—the problem with trained killers was that they were always wanting to kill someone.

That brought his thoughts to Maeve. No great wonder, really, for wherever they started, all of his thoughts eventually ended up leading him to her. Maeve who had left so abruptly when Emille had come, Maeve who was trying to maneuver through a guild of killers without becoming a target. It was a task that seemed, to Chall, at least, tantamount to traipsing through a hall choked with deadly, poisonous snakes and hoping not to get bitten. However skilled, however talented—and Maeve had both skill and talent in excess—it would only take one bite to end it all.

"Focus," he growled, slapping himself on the cheek. It didn't help, but it *did* hurt. For at least the dozenth time since he'd sat down to begin his examination of the necklace, he told himself that Maeve could handle herself. Certainly, *he* couldn't help her. Not directly, anyway. The best way for him to help her, to help *everyone,* was to solve the mystery of the necklace.

He was tired and scared and worried about failing, but then that was how Chall had lived most of his life. Whatever charm he'd been famous for had been, in large part, for him at least, no more than camouflage to hide his own fears, his own insecurities. Had been him play-acting, trying to convince everyone, trying to convince *himself* that he was the confident, unworried man he pretended, *wanted* to be.

He sat forward, grabbing the necklace once more. He closed his eyes, letting his fingers run along the gem, letting his magic run along it. He had no sooner begun, though, than there was a knock on the door, and so deep was he in his concentration that he let out a yelp of surprise at the sound.

His heart hammering in his chest, he rose, moving toward the door. By the time he reached it, excitement had mingled with his surprise, his fear, and he opened the door, hoping to see Maeve, fearing to see a monster. In the end, it was neither. Instead, it was Commander Malex, the man bowing low as Chall opened the door.

"Good morning, Sir Challadius."

"Is it?" Chall asked, giving the man a weak smile. "How are you, Commander Malex?"

"I...am as well as might be expected," the commander said.

Chall nodded, and for a moment the two of them only stood there awkwardly, then Chall cleared his throat. "Right, sorry, please, Commander—come in."

He stepped to the side, waving the other man in. The commander gave him a nod of appreciation then stepped inside. It was about the moment when Chall closed the door behind him that he had an uncomfortable thought. Malex could be a traitor.

It sounded silly even to think it. Despite that the man had—at Feledias's order—been searching for Chall, Maeve, Priest, and Prince Bernard for years since they'd all gone into exile, Chall knew Malex to be a good man. A loyal man.

But then, Chall would have considered all the guards in the castle loyal—it seemed to him that loyalty was the primary prerequisite for the posting. He would have considered Guardsman Dalton, whom he had so recently played cards with, loyal right up until the man had murdered one of his fellow guardsmen and proceeded to do his level best to do the same to Chall.

"There's something we need to talk about, Sir Challadius," Malex said grimly, and with Chall's current panicked state of mind the man's deep, gravelly words couldn't have sounded anymore threatening if he'd been shaking a bloody knife while he said them.

At once, he felt silly for the thought and stupid for not having it *before* a closed door stood between him and the castle beyond. Not much, in the normal course of things, one that might be opened in a few seconds, but then murder didn't take all that long either. Chall inwardly cursed himself. He had allowed himself to become distracted by the necklace and his worries, and he had walked long enough in the prince's shadow, in war, to know that few things killed a man as quickly as being distracted—though he thought the sword hanging from Malex's waist could give it a good shot.

"So, Malex," he said, shuffling toward the table where a plate of barely-touched food sat. The knife sitting on it wasn't much of a weapon, but he thought it would do better than begging if the commander turned out to have murder on his mind. "What brings you to my door? In for a game of cards?"

"Not quite," Malex said, his expression still grim—murderous? "I'm afraid that my purpose for coming is nothing so...enjoyable as that."

That sent a chill down Chall's spine, but he did his best to nod as he reached the table. The knife was just there, within reach, but if he did reach for it, Malex would have to be blind not to see it. Instead, he turned back to the commander, then let out a gasp, pointing in the corner.

Malex turned—as Chall had hoped he would—and Chall's hand shot out at the knife. Thankfully, he wore a long-sleeve tunic, one that was terribly uncomfortable but one that presented an opportunity to hide a blade. He'd seen Maeve do it a thousand times, had watched her hide one of her many blades on her person in a flash, as if by magic. And so he reached out smoothly, grabbing the blade and sliding it into the sleeve of his tunic with ease even as he turned back to the commander who found him looking no more suspicious than he had, completely unaware that Chall was now armed.

Or at least that's how he thought it would happen.

As it turned out, secreting pointy objects on one's person in an instant was the sort of thing a fella ought to practice at. The blade was in the process of slipping into his sleeve—and Chall in the process of being smooth as butter on a hot day—when it met an obstacle. His forearm.

Chall cried out in pain, jerking his arm back, and the knife clattered on the floor less than two feet from where Malex spun back to look at him.

"Sir Challadius," the commander said, "are you alright?"

"Perfect," Chall said, glancing down at his arm to see the small scratch the knife had left, barely bleeding at all, and so he was right. He was alright—at least for the moment. He glanced at the knife, a small bit of his blood staining it and thought that as far as not getting murdered went, he was doing a pretty shit job. After all, there was already a blade stained with his blood in the room. If Malex *had* come to murder him, it felt like all he really needed to do was wait a bit, and Chall would take care of it himself.

"Let me take a look—" Malex began, starting forward.

"That's alright," Chall blurted, taking a step back then wincing as he bumped up against the table, his entire body tensing in surprised shock as the glass which had been sitting there fell to the ground and shattered.

The commander paused in the wake of that, his gaze slowly traveling from Chall to the broken pieces of glass scattered on the floor to the bloody knife. "Sir Challadius…" he said slowly, "do you…do you think that I mean you harm?"

Chall gave a nervous laugh, his gaze traveling of its own accord to the door, wondering if he could make it and knowing the answer even as he had the thought. "O-of course not," he stammered, looking back to the commander. "That is…you don't…do you?"

He wasn't sure what he expected of Malex, in that moment. Or, perhaps he was. Either for the man to be offended, angry at the accusation or else for him to decide that, now the pleasantries were out of the way, he might as well get on with the murdering part of the evening.

It was some surprise, then, when Commander Malex did not rush forward to kill him or shout or yell. Instead, the man looked hurt. "Forgive me, Sir Challadius," he said, "if I have somehow given you cause to doubt my loyalty, for I have never meant you or the others harm. I have only ever wanted to help, to serve. But it is my fault, what happened, my fault that you were nearly killed. My fault that the king is..." He paused then, clearing his throat, and if Chall didn't know better he'd think the man very close to tears. "It is my fault," Malex went on, "that the king is gone. Taken from us. You are right to doubt me, for I have failed you, failed the people of the Known Lands. Failed King Matthias most of all."

"Commander Malex," Chall said, suddenly feeling terribly, horribly ashamed, "forgive me—I am a fool. Everyone thinks so, me most of all. You don't deserve to have your loyalty questioned. You've done as much to prove yourself trustworthy as anyone ever could. What happened—it isn't your fault."

"I thank you for your words, Sir Challadius, but I am the commander of the castle guard. It is my duty to ensure that those allowed in the castle mean no harm to the king or the others who call the castle home. And so it is *I* who have failed. After all, King Matthias is missing, you were nearly killed, and there are others of the castle staff who were, all because of my incompetence. In truth, it is no surprise that you question my loyalty, but I assure you that I am not unloyal—only a fool."

"Well, then you're in good company," Chall said with a small smile, trying to lighten the mood. But the commander looked about as grim as a man could. Chall gave a slow sigh. "Listen, Commander Malex, none of us is perfect. You have served your post admirably for years, and I do not think that recent events change that. After all, it isn't as if we are dealing with some lone assassin seeking to topple a kingdom. We are dealing with a conspiracy rooted deep in New Daltenia—just how deep we don't yet know, though I doubt we'll be excited when we discover the truth of it."

"Perhaps," Malex said, "but that changes nothing. If you ask me for my resignation, Sir Challadius, I will give it freely. Should you decide that insufficient and prefer to send me to the dungeons, I will go without complaint, for I deserve that and more for my failures."

"Damn," Chall said, wincing. "I've been told, Commander, that I don't take responsibility for my own actions, but why bother? What with you out there taking the blame for everything, there doesn't seem to be much need."

The commander said nothing, only watched Chall with a slightly perplexed expression on his face, and Chall sighed, shaking his head. "Do you like pie, Commander?"

Malex blinked. "Pie, Sir Challadius?"

"Me," Chall said, "I love pie. Blueberry in particular, though I'll admit that when it comes to pie, I'm not all that choosy. Anyway, I bought a pie, once. From a street vendor. I'd been told about how good the man's blueberry pies were, and you don't get a figure like mine by ignoring that sort of talk. I thought about that damned pie all the way back to my quarters, thought about it more than I've spent thinking about most things in my life, though I guess it's fair to say I've never been accused of thinking things through. Only, when I got home and finally cut into that pie, you know what I found?"

"Blueberries?" Malex asked, clearly still not seeing where he was going.

"Strawberries," Chall said with disgust.

"I..." the commander hesitated. "And...you don't like strawberries?"

"Of course I like strawberries," Chall said. "Who doesn't?"

"Then...forgive me, Sir Challadius, but I don't see—"

"My point, Commander," Chall said, "is that from the outside, that strawberry pie looked just like a blueberry one. Couldn't tell the difference, and I ought to know, for I've seen enough of both in my time. And considering that the man was famous for his blueberry pies, I could be forgiven for thinking that's what I got. I thought so then, and I still think so. Just like you can be forgiven—can forgive *yourself*—for what's happened. It's too much to expect yourself to somehow single-handedly detect and uncover a conspiracy that has eluded everyone in the city, in the kingdom, one that no one was even aware of until people started dying. Lady Valencia, for example—who could have guessed she was in on it? Not me or you—not anyone." He shrugged. "Sometimes, the pie is just strawberry, that's all. When you find out that it is, well, you can give up—walk away ashamed and disappointed, wishing it was something it isn't, wishing things were something they aren't. Or you can deal with them as they are."

Commander Malex slowly nodded, thinking over his words. "Thank you, Sir Challadius. For your kind words...but I admit to some curiosity. What did you end up doing? About the pie, I mean."

"What did I do?" Chall said. "I ate it—every damn bit of it. Sometimes a man has to eat the pie he has."

"As to that..." Commander Malex said, "I suppose I ought to tell you the reason for my coming to your quarters at so early an hour."

"Isn't pie, is it?" Chall asked.

"I'm afraid not," Malex said. "You told me before, Sir Challadius, to not divulge the fact that King Matthias has gone missing, not to the public and to no more of the castle staff than necessary."

"That's right," Chall said. "I don't like lying—it's an old habit, one I mean to be quit of—but the people of New Daltenia, of the Known Lands, have more than enough on their plates right now. They have just, for the first time, begun to experience the king they deserve. They have, for the first time in a very long time, begun to feel hope. I would not steal that from them, not now. I'd like to get to the bottom of this damned conspiracy first. I think it'd be a whole lot easier for the people of New Daltenia to swallow the fact that the king is missing and that there have been killings in the castle if they know that the ones responsible for all of it have been brought to justice. Why, Commander, do you disagree?"

"Not at all, Sir Challadius," Malex said. "However, I fear that what I think on the matter makes little difference. Spring is coming."

It was Chall's turn to blink. "Right," he said slowly. "And after that, as I recall, is summer. Listen, Malex, I'm as excited about the warm weather as anyone. Or, at least, as any overweight man who sweats at the first mention of heat. But I don't see—"

"The Festival of the Sun approaches," Malex said.

Chall paused, grunting. "I suppose it does," he said. "To be honest, with everything that's going on, I haven't given it much thought. But if it's a date you're looking for, Commander, I'm afraid I'm a bit busy. I may have to miss the parades and sweet treats this year, though if they have blueberry pies, think of me, won't you?"

"You have been gone for some time, Sir Challadius," Malex said, "so you may have forgotten, but the Festival of the Sun is an important event for our people. A chance to celebrate surviving the Skaalden invasion, a momentous occasion where commoner and noble alike share in the festivities. Festivities which culminate with—"

"With a speech from the king," Chall finished as realization struck. "Shit."

Commander Malex gave him a small, humorless smile. "My thoughts exactly, Sir Challadius."

"Can we...I don't know, put it off?"

"Put off the first day of spring?"

Chall grunted. "Right. Stupid question. And...this festival. How important would you say it is?"

"The Festival of the Sun celebrates our escape of the Skaalden, Sir Challadius. It celebrates the fact that the people of the Known Lands, *our* people, have endured despite all that has come against us. It stands as proof that no matter how dark the night gets, the sun will come again. That no matter the shadows gathered against it, the light, *we* will endure."

Chall blinked. "So...important, then," he said. "You know, Commander, you would have made for a fine poet." He sighed, glancing at the desk on which the green jewel and necklace sat. Plenty of problems with no solutions in sight. Still, he told himself that if Priest had found his faith again, maybe he could scrape up a little of his own.

He didn't know much about the festival, about the ins and outs of it

—he'd attended several, but he'd nearly always been drunk. Still, he remembered the speeches from Feledias, even remembered Bernard attending. It was, as Malex had claimed, a festival that was very important to the people of the Known Lands, now more than ever.

"What should we do, Sir Challadius?"

I have no damned idea, he thought. They couldn't call it off—that much was clear from Malex's reaction. But neither could they have it. Somehow he doubted they could have someone dress up and give a speech pretending to be Matt—he thought people might notice.

Chall considered the problems before him. The necklace and the festival. He knew little of Fey artifacts and even less about the innerworkings of the Festival of the Sun, at least beyond where the best ale and best women might be found during the celebration. Plenty of questions to go around then, questions to which he had no answer. But then, he realized with a distinct mixture of relief and dread, he knew who did.

Worse still, he knew where to find him.

He took a slow, deep breath, turning to regard the other man. "Do you pray, Commander Malex?"

"I do, Sir Challadius."

"Then pray for me," Chall said, taking a slow, deep breath. "For I go to war."

CHALL GRUNTED in pain and exhaustion as he climbed out of the carriage. Malden had a reputation as being one of the greatest healers to ever live, so he told himself that however much his healing wounds pained him, they could have been far worse. After all, living—even in excruciating pain—was better than being dead. Probably.

"Or maybe not," he mumbled to himself as he stood in the street and regarded the giant stone building before him. "It isn't as if you've tried it, is it?"

"What's that, now?"

Chall turned back to the carriage driver and immediately thought of Ned. Ned who had gone to check on Emille and Maeve, Ned who would have been invaluable to have with him just then, who might well have some answers to the necklace and, for that matter, to the matter of the approaching festival, answers that might have saved him from the grim task before him.

But as much as he might have wished it, the man before him stubbornly continued to not be Ned, and so Chall sighed. "Nothing," he told not-Ned.

"You want I should wait a while? Until you get back?" the man asked, not acting annoyed at Chall's odd behavior. He supposed that to a man who spent most of his time hauling around drunkards and spoiled nobles out for a night on the town, a fat mage wasn't so bad.

He considered not-Ned's words, turning to regard the building in the distance. He sighed regretfully. "I'm afraid not," he said. "There's really no telling for sure when I'll be back." He sighed again then, in a lower voice, "*if* I'll be back."

The man looked past him, down the street and at the building Chall had been staring at. "Bad as all that, is it?"

"Worse, no doubt," Chall said.

The man nodded. "Well. Good luck."

As the carriage driver led the horses away, Chall turned back once more to stare at the library before him. He remembered when he and Maeve had visited the library in search of Petran and she had scolded him for acting ridiculous. He wished that she was there to do the same now. But she wasn't, of course. No one was. Only Chall. He took a slow, steadying breath then started across the street toward the library which sat hunched on the street like some great beast, eager to swallow him up.

Stepping through the grand doorway, Chall saw that the library was largely unchanged from the way it had been when he and Maeve had come. Towering bookshelves stacked with all manner of books and tomes and scrolls stretched as far as the eye could see, seemingly on into infinity. The air still had that old, musty, *papery* smell. Even the librarian's desk was where it had before. The only difference he could see was in the person sitting behind it—not the stern-faced librarian who had practically worshipped Petran that he and Maeve had spoken with the last time they'd come. In her place sat a man who looked like he might have been about as old as the building itself. He had a long white beard, and strands of wild white hair poked out from the cap atop his head as if they were trying to escape.

As Chall approached, the man studied him from beneath two incredibly bushy white eyebrows that looked to Chall like a couple of giant caterpillars—or perhaps just one—squirming around on his face.

"Hello," said Chall, wincing as his voice seemed to echo in the large space.

"What's that?" the man said, his voice somehow reminding Chall of the creak of a door seldom opened.

"I said hello."

"Who's a fellow now?" the man asked, frowning.

Chall realized the man must have been hard of hearing, and he leaned forward. "I said *hello*," he said louder, wincing as his voice echoed in the vastness of the library.

"You don't have to shout, lad," the man said. "This is a library, don't you know?"

Chall opened his mouth to answer, then paused as the old man grinned wide, his white eyebrows waggling on his face.

"Wait a minute," Chall said. "Are...you were messing with me?"

The old man shrugged his bony shoulders. "My knees aren't much for tumbling and children's games, and my creaky bones make a game of hide-and-seek difficult—messing with people is about the most fun a fellow can have at my age."

Chall blinked and despite his own worries, despite the troublesome errand that had brought him to the library in the first place, he found himself grinning in response. The man was a far cry from the pretentious, judgmental woman who he and Maeve had encountered the last time they'd come, that was sure. He considered asking the old man where the woman had gone—to waggle her finger at some children daring to have fun, maybe—but decided against it. Mostly because he held an irrational fear that to ask about her would be to conjure her up the way the fools in the stories conjured up demons by saying their names.

"I suppose a man has to do something to keep himself entertained in this place," Chall said, "so tucked away from the world."

"Which, do you mean?"

"I'm sorry?" Chall asked.

"Which world do you mean, lad?" the old man asked, then he waved his hands at the seemingly unending rows of shelves in the vast space. "We've got thousands here. Tens of thousands. Any of which a man might step into with the simple opening of a book, the unrolling of this scroll or that tome."

"Sorry," Chall said, "I mean the...uh, you know, real world."

"Oh, the *real* world," the man said, grinning. "Who's got time to bother with that? Except maybe some old dusty scholars sitting around drinking and quibbling about this theory or that fact."

"Certainly not dusty old librarians," Chall said.

The man grinned, accepting the jibe with good grace as Chall had thought he might. "Exactly. Now, what can I do for you, lad?"

For the first time, Chall realized that he had just taken it for granted that Petran would be here in the same way that if he'd gone looking for a fish, he would have started at the nearest lake or river, searching for it in its natural habitat. The truth, though, was that for all he knew the historian had left the library days ago, and the entire trip a waste of his time. "There's a man—" he started.

"Quite a few, in fact," the librarian said, smiling again as Chall frowned in confusion. "Men, I mean. I do hope your question is a bit more specific."

Chall winced. "Right. Sorry. No, he's a historian, quite...famous, I think."

"Oh?" the old man said.

"Petran Quinn is his name," Chall said.

"A nice name, I suppose," the old man said. "Though it might surprise you to know that everyone who comes here doesn't always offer theirs. Certainly, you haven't offered yours, at least not as I recall." He grinned. "We dusty old librarians do have a tendency to forget things."

"Right, sorry," Chall said. "My name is Challadius—but people call me Chall."

"I'm sure they do," the old librarian said. Chall wanted to ask him what he meant by that, but he never got a chance before the man spoke on. "Anyway, what was it you said this friend of yours name was? Bertrand Finn?"

Chall wasn't sure that he and the historian would qualify as friends, but he thought it better not to bring that up. He was in a hurry, after all, and the old man seemed all too willing to go off on any tangent that presented itself. "Petran Quinn," he said.

"Ah. Right," the man said, nodding slowly.

Chall waited for him to say more, thinking that he did recognize the name after all. But when he only continued to stare at him, he cleared his throat. "Right...anyway, he's a historian. The historian to the crown, in fact." *Likely to be the last one if things don't improve soon.* "Some...I've heard some call him Truth Teller?"

The old man continued to stare at him and Chall grunted. "Right. Well, he's about my height, brown h—"

"Of course I know Petran Quinn," the old man said, grinning. "I'm not so addled that I don't know the crown historian, lad."

Chall blinked. "Then...why did you..."

"Let you talk on?" the man asked, then shrugged his bony shoulders. "You seemed to be enjoying it."

Chall, who had been accused on more than one occasion—and that by far more than one person—of talking too much, felt his face heat.

"Oh, take it easy, lad," the old man said, grinning again. "It ain't so bad as all that. Now then, the historian is in the third study room from the left—you'll find them near the back there. I can show you if—"

"That won't be necessary," Chall said, partly because he remembered where they were from when he and Maeve had visited the library searching for Petran the last time but mostly because he felt like a fool—an increasingly common occurrence of late, it seemed—and wanted to flee the old man's presence. "Thanks for your help."

Before the man could respond, Chall turned and started deeper into the library. Shelves filled with what must have been millions of books and scrolls loomed over him on all sides. A wilderness of knowledge where one might easily become lost. Which made librarians more guides than anything, guides who spent their lives learning to navigate that vast wilderness, who had maps in their heads that they might follow to show others where they needed to go. They gave them direction and that seemed like a fine thing to Chall, for just then he needed some direction.

He was drawing nearer to the place where he remembered the study rooms being when he became aware of a strange sound. It was a sort of moaning which, while barely audible, sounded no less wild, no less *fierce* for all that.

A chill ran through him, and he hesitated for a moment. It sounded as if someone were being murdered in a life-or-death struggle nearby. It might have sounded silly to think of anyone dying in a library—at least of anything but boredom—but then up until about a week ago it would have seemed silly to think assassins would infiltrate a castle not once but several times. They had done it just the same, killing several serving girls and very nearly killing Matt, too.

He wanted to turn around and leave then. After all, he had more than enough on his plate already without getting murdered. But the problem was that he had come to the library for a reason and that reason had not changed, however much he might have wished that it had. So, he took a slow, deep breath, gathering the frayed ends of his courage, and his gaze roaming left and right along the bookshelves on either side, he continued forward. He followed the path the woman librarian, Elizabeth, had led he and Maeve on the last time they'd come, the moaning growing increasingly louder, increasingly *closer* as he did.

By the time he reached the end of the long aisle, his fear had conjured up a small army of assassins, so that when he finally emerged in front of the study rooms and caught sight of someone standing there, he almost screamed. The two young women though—librarians by their dress—didn't appear threatening. Instead, they were giggling, their hands over their mouths as they stared at the study rooms or, specifically, one room in particular. The room's door was closed but it was apparent that the noises he'd heard were coming from inside.

The two young women noticed Chall, and their faces turned deep red before they turned and scurried away, vanishing down the aisles. A moment later, Chall was left standing in front of the rooms. There were six of them in all. The white-haired librarian had told him that he would find the historian in the third study room. Which, probably unsurprisingly given the course of Chall's life, was the room from which the sounds of struggle were coming.

A terrifying thought struck him then. Perhaps he had been right—perhaps the assassins *had* come to the library after all, only it had not been them they'd come for but Petran. Maybe Robert Palden or those who worked for him had concluded—as Chall himself had—that the only one who could help him was Petran Quinn. Or—and at this thought a cold chill ran through him—maybe he had followed him here. Maybe they had not thought of the historian at all but while he'd been standing outside speaking with the carriage driver, bemoaning his fate, they had sneaked inside the library, ascertaining his motivation for coming and realizing the problem Petran Quinn could pose. And while Chall hadn't met Robert Palden personally, he'd seen enough of his work to know that when it came to problems, he tended to prefer the bloody solution.

Any sane man, thinking assassins lurked in the room ahead, would have turned around and run, but Chall hadn't ended up with two knife wounds and a lifetime of regrets by accident. Besides, he could not bear the thought that he might be responsible for whatever was befalling the historian.

Chall took a deep breath and rushed toward the room in a shuffling run. As he reached the door, the sounds of struggle from inside were louder, and he jumped at the sound of something falling to the floor. A part of him wondered if it was the historian's body, if he was already too late. Petran Quinn might one of the smartest men in the world, but he was no fighter. He would stand little chance against a trained assassin.

Chall tried the door and was unsurprised to find it locked. He suspected that the librarian he'd spoken with would likely have a key to each room—how else to roust teenagers who came to the rooms with no intention of studying beyond a very particular lesson in biology? But it would take too long to go back. By the time Chall returned, the historian's fate would already be sealed. So instead, Chall took a step back, holding the handle of the door, then with a roar, charged into it shoulder first.

He'd seen the prince bust his way through plenty of doors over the years—in fact, he figured it was probably approaching the same number of times he'd seen the man walk through them the way a normal person might. He'd seen the man shatter thick, well-built doors into kindling, a far cry from the thin utilitarian doors the carpenter had built for these study rooms, yet one thing he had never considered was just how much it *hurt.*

Pain shot through Chall's shoulder into his neck, before both promptly went numb. But a moment later as he careened through the doorway, he realized that was far from his only problem. When a man puts all his weight into something, really *all* of it, and then that something—like a door, say—is broken down and suddenly not there, well, that poor bastard's weight doesn't just stop. It keeps going. Carrying him forward and, in Chall's case, over a piece of debris from the door that stole what little balance he had left and sent him staggering—and, a moment later, *falling*—into the room.

He hit the ground hard, rolling to his back with a groan and looking up from what he figured was just about the worst rescue attempt ever made. But as two figures—he'd hit his head when he'd fallen, so they were little more than vague blurs—appeared standing over him, he didn't think he would have to live with the embarrassment for long.

"Chall?" one of the figures asked in surprise. "Is that you?"

Great, they know who I am, Chall thought, but a moment later, he found reason returning. The voice hadn't sounded like that of a hardened assassin. Instead, it sounded like that of a scholar, soft and kind, perhaps even a little timid, if out of breath. What's more, he realized in another second that it was a voice he recognized. "Petran," he groaned. "I'm here to save you."

"Save me?" the historian asked, and as his vision began to clear Chall noted a look of confusion on the man's face to match that which he could hear in his tone.

And that was far from *all* he noticed.

First, there was the state of the historian. He certainly *looked* like he'd been attacked. The man's shirt was ripped and torn, hanging completely off one shoulder, and there were scratch marks on his bare chest. His hair was in disarray, and there were splotches of what must have been blood on his cheeks and neck.

Chall's gaze shot to the second figure who stood beside Petran and the confusion he'd felt doubled. He'd expected an assassin, someone, perhaps, like Balderath the Brutal. Instead, however, he found himself looking into the face of the stern-faced librarian who he'd met the first time he and Maeve had visited the library.

Not that she looked particularly stern just then. Mortified was closer to it.

The woman also looked as though she'd been attacked, her long hair everywhere, her own clothes just as rumpled and torn as the historian's.

Suddenly, the pieces clicked into place, and Chall's eyes went wide. "Well," he said slowly, "I'd say the two of you ought to get a room, but then...I guess you already did. Didn't you?"

"Forgive me," the woman blurted, "but I must be going. I-I have been meaning to check on the pre-Skaalden texts in the preservation room. It is long past due." She scooped up a pile of clothes that Chall hadn't noticed lying on the floor, then before either of them could speak, she was vanishing through the doorway, fleeing as if there really had been an assassin in the room.

Chall turned back to look at Petran, realizing as he did that what he'd taken for spots of blood was actually lipstick, evidence of the woman's attentions. Not that it was easy to notice just then, for the historian's face had gone a bright red that was nearly a match for it. Despite the fact that his body still ached all over, and that he was more than a little embarrassed himself, Chall found himself grinning as he held out a hand. "Well, don't just stand there. Help me up, will you?"

"O-of course," Petran said, moving forward and taking Chall's hand. It wasn't easy, but after a few moments of groaning and hissing and cursing—pretty much exclusively from Chall's end—the two of them managed to get him to his feet.

Chall stood there panting from exertion for a moment as he regarded the historian. "So," he said. "You and the librarian. Every little boy's fantasy."

"Is it?" Petran asked, swallowing and looking around nervously. Just then, Chall thought the man likely would have preferred the assassin.

"Couldn't say," Chall said. "I never spent much time in the library. Still..." He paused, grinning. "If I'd have known the sorts of things you all were getting up to, I might have spent more."

Petran's face flushed an even deeper, angrier shade of crimson at that. "I-it isn't like that," he said. "Beth—that is, Elizabeth—is very knowledgeable. She has proven a great asset in—"

"Sure," Chall said. "I think I might have seen a few of those assets while she was scurrying out the door."

Petran let out a nervous laugh. "I...that is..."

"Relax, Petran," Chall said. "I'm just about the last person you have to worry about judging you. I assure you that going at it like a couple of wild beasts while some younger, librarians in training are outside giggling, while perhaps ill-advised, doesn't even begin to approach some of the foolish things I've gotten up to in my life. Of course," he went on, raising an eyebrow, "I was a bit younger then."

"I did not...that is not why I came," Petran said, wincing. "I am working on a new history of Daltenia, and—"

"A *new* history," Chall repeated.

Petran winced. "I can see how that might sound strange, but I hope that there might be some value in it. Much of our people's recorded history was lost when we fled from the Skaalden and took to the water. What remains is little better than some few tattered scrolls and tomes, no full accounting of the history of our people."

"As it turns out, when fleeing from ice monsters out of nightmare, people tend to worry less about their history and more about their present," Chall said. "Anyway, this full accounting, you mean to be the one to give it?"

"Someone has to," Petran said, a defensive tone in his voice.

"Well, sure," Chall said. "That's important work."

Petran frowned. "You're mocking me."

"Not at all," Chall said honestly. "I might have, once, but I'm older now, and while I'm still a fool, I like to think I'm not quite as much of one as I once was. Not that that takes much doing. I wish you luck with all of it. Still, just now it isn't our history that concerns me but our future."

"Oh?" Petran asked, looking interested now.

"The Festival of the Sun is coming," Chall said.

The historian smiled. "I know. Beth and I—that is, Elizabeth—"

"Oh, just call her Beth, man," Chall said. "As long as you don't call her 'cutesy-poo,' I think we'll be alright."

The other man cleared his throat. "Forgive me, you're right. Anyway, Beth and I are attending together. We are both very excited for the festivities. And, of course, to hear what young King Matthias has to say."

Chall winced. "Right...and do you suppose a lot of people are looking forward to it? To hearing the king speak, I mean?"

"Of course!" Petran said. "Why, Chall, I have never seen the people so excited for the festival as they are now. I mean no disrespect to Prince Bernard or Prince Feledias, but surely you know as well as I that the people of New Daltenia, of the entire *kingdom* have come to love King Matthias. For they see the good in him—as any who pay attention must."

"Right, right," Chall said quickly. "But...tell me, Petran, how bad would it be if the king *didn't* speak at the festival?"

Petran blinked. "Didn't speak?" he asked, as if he was having a difficult time even understanding what Chall meant.

"That's right," Chall said. "Like...maybe if he was too busy to do it, or..."

"Too busy?"

"Well, I mean, what with all that's going on in the city, surely they'd understand, right?" Chall asked. "I mean, with the fey up to no good, and that bastard Robert Palden and his ilk doing the gods know what... well, considering all that, all the uncertainty, the people of New Daltenia would understand if the king wasn't able to attend, wouldn't they?"

"Forgive me, Chall," Petran said. "I do not mean to be contrary, but it seems to me that it is exactly *because* of all that uncertainty that the people *need* to hear King Matthias speak. There is much confusion in the city, just now, and King Matthias, since he has taken over the rule of New Daltenia, has given our people what they have not felt in a very long time—hope. Hope that no matter how bad it gets, there is a king in charge who cares about them, who puts their interests first. Hope that no matter what comes, they are not alone. Hope that—"

"Matt's gone," Chall blurted.

Just then, a young librarian appeared in the doorway, his eyes wide. "Sir Petran, are you alright? I heard a noise, and—"

"I'm fine, Lionel," the historian stammered, his face going a deep, angry red. "Everything is fine. Please—leave us."

"O-of course, sir," the young man said, clearly finding it difficult to suppress what Chall supposed must have been at least a dozen questions. He managed, though, bowing his head. "Just...please let me know, if you need anything, sir."

"Of course, Lionel, thank you," Petran said. The man shot one more suspicious look at Chall before turning and disappearing beyond the doorway. When he was gone, Petran turned back to Chall. "Forgive me, Chall, *who* is gone?"

"Matt," Chall said, wincing. "King Matthias. He's gone."

Petran paled at that. "Oh gods, do you mean—"

"He's not dead," Chall said quickly. "Fire and salt, Petran, it's not bad as all that. Though..." He rubbed at his temples where a headache had begun to form. "In truth, it isn't much better."

"Perhaps...perhaps you'd better explain," the historian said.

Chall sighed, looking toward the doorway where the door itself lay in a heap on the floor and thinking of the two young librarians who'd been snooping. "I'll tell you," he said, "but perhaps we ought to find a different room first. One with a door. Hopefully one built better than that one. And maybe you can find a shirt, while we're at it."

Petran flushed. "Of course. But...I must ask, Challadius, why *did* you break the door in?"

"I thought you were in danger," Chall said, "that an assassin had come."

"And you meant to save me," Petran said.

"Don't be too flattered," Chall grumbled. "I do a lot of stupid things.

Now come on—you're half-naked, in case you've forgotten, and I'd just as soon nobody show up and think I had anything to do with it."

The historian nodded. "Still...I thank you for your concern."

"No problem," Chall said, "but it might be you'll want to save that—once you hear why I've come, I doubt if you'll be feeling particularly thankful."

The historian swallowed hard, glancing behind him then back to Chall. "Is it truly so bad as that?"

"No, Petran," Chall said. "It's worse. Now if it's all the same to you, I'm in a bit of a hurry. You know, fate of the kingdom and all that."

Petran paled once more and nodded. "Of course—please. This way."

CHAPTER ELEVEN

THE CARRIAGE ROLLED to a slow stop, and a moment later the small wooden window separating the driver from the carriage car slid open. "We're here, s—" the driver, a young man who'd only started at the livery stable a few months before, began then paused. "Ned? Is everything alright?"

Ned looked up at the driver from his spot on the floor. "Of course, lad. Why wouldn't it be?"

"Well...it's just...you're on the floor, sir."

"I do my best thinkin' on the floor," Ned said, rising just enough to peer out of one of the side windows of the carriage car. He didn't see anybody, but then he imagined that when a fella showed up to assassin class, not being seen was one of the first lessons.

"Is...are you sure you're okay, Ned?"

Ned peered back at the new driver from where he crouched low in the wagon, peering out the window. "Sure, I'm sure," he said.

He didn't want to get out of the carriage—that felt a lot like walking into the lion's den with no idea whether the lion was home or not. Still, he'd done what he could to lose his unwanted shadows, and it would take more than an assassin or two to keep him from going to his wife, if she needed his help. He climbed out into the street.

He glanced at the dilapidated old buildings flanking either side of the alley in which he stood, searching for anything out of the ordinary—like a man dressed in all black brandishing a bloody knife, say. He did not see any such man, nor, in fact, did he see anyone at all. Once, the two buildings had been competing tailor shops. The two tailors, two older men, had hated each other—hated each other with a passion a man wouldn't have expected from men who sewed clothes all day. Hated each other so much, in fact, that they had competed aggressively with each other, lowering and lowering prices in an effort to undercut the other until, finally, they had both gone out of business.

That had been a few months ago and, since then, the dead-end alleyway in which Ned stood with the carriage—which had once been used primarily for loading and unloading shipments from the respective tailors—had seen very little traffic. It was, after all, the whole reason he'd chosen it in the first place.

"I can drop you closer to your home, if you'd like, Ned."

Ned turned to regard the driver. "That's alright, Levi. I could do with a bit of a walk. Best you get on back to the stables before Delilah throws a fit. She isn't known for her patience."

The young man nodded, swallowing hard, looking nervous at the mention of Delilah's name—which just meant that he wasn't a complete fool. "Very well. Good day, Ned."

"Not so far, but then we can hope, can't we?"

The young man hesitated at that, and Ned waved a hand. "Go on, then, Levi. And thanks for the ride."

He watched as the young man led the horses back down the alley, the carriage trundling along the city cobbles. He waited until it was gone then stepped out of the alley, half-expecting to find an army of assassins waiting to greet him.

They weren't though, and the only people he saw on the street were a couple making their way down the other side. Ned studied the rooftops of the buildings around him, then, seeing nothing out of the ordinary, turned and started down the street.

Fifteen minutes and what must have been a thousand backward glances later, he arrived at his and Emille's home. Or, at least, close to it. Ned stood in a nearby alley—the same alley, in fact, that he thought Val had mentioned fleeing down when she'd been concocting her lies, and he swallowing them like a baby bird at feeding.

That one still hurt, but he told himself to focus as he studied his home, studied it in a way that he hadn't for years, maybe not since first moving in. Looking for any signs of waiting assassins but seeing, instead, how small it was, how unassuming. It wasn't much, really, that house. Four walls, a couple of windows, a roof that mostly didn't leak. Yet he wouldn't have traded it for all the castles in the world. After all, he and Emille had built a life there. Emille who, if he was lucky, waited inside, likely preparing to scold her husband for coming home late. It had been a hard few days with no signs of slowing anytime soon. Ned thought he could do with some scolding just then.

He looked around the street once more, seeing no one, yet still he hesitated. He knew he had to step out into the street, yet doing so felt tantamount to a rabbit hopping innocently—*naively*—up to a cave mouth. No idea if something lurked within the cave, but *if* it did, it would likely be hungry, and everyone liked the taste of rabbit.

But he told himself that he was no rabbit. He was a *Wolf*. Or, at least, he had been, once. And he must be so again. A wolf that was wary and cautious, clever when it needed to be, but who never let its fear or its thoughts paralyze it from action. After all, if a man—or a rabbit—found himself in a jam, he wouldn't find his way out by cowering in the fetal position.

Up to that point, Ned had been reacting, acting like the hare being chased, like prey instead of predator. But he would do so no longer. Maybe someone watched his home, maybe not. It made little difference.

He was going inside—he always had been. His wife might be there, and so he was going. And if Emille *wasn't* home, then at least she might have left some message for him. Hopefully, his invisible watchers—if there *were* any—would continue to be content to watch. But if not, if they accosted him while he searched for his wife, then they would find that he was not a rabbit, not prey, after all, but a wolf, one with teeth of his own.

He stepped into the street. He wasn't sure what he expected—a shout of alarm and a dozen assassins charging at him with blades bared wasn't that far from the truth—but in the end the street remained silent. He scanned the rooftops of the houses flanking his own and, seeing nothing, hurried toward the door to his house. He reached into his pocket, retrieving the key, and in another few seconds he was stepping inside, closing the door behind him.

He didn't bother calling out for his wife, for he knew at once that she was not there. It was his home, after all, *their* home and he knew the feel of it when it was empty.

He fought down the panic that threatened to come then. Emille wasn't here, that was true, but that didn't mean something had happened to her. Ned walked back into their bedroom, moving to his nightstand. As a healer, Emille often kept unusual hours—people had a selfish tendency to get hurt with no regard for a person's schedule. Which meant that, sometimes, he'd wake up to find her gone. In such instances, she would leave a note on his nightstand, telling him when she expected to be back.

But now he discovered with a feeling of despair that no such note awaited him. Wherever Emille was, she had either not seen fit to—or had been *unable* to—leave him a note. He knew his wife, knew that she was a kind, selfless woman who always considered the feelings of others, and so he thought, despite how much he might wish otherwise, that the latter was the far more likely of the two.

He knelt to look beside the nightstand and under the bed with the desperate hope that she had indeed left a note but that it had fallen. He had just bent to gaze underneath the bed at the nothing waiting there

—not even much dust, for Emille was particular about cleaning—when there was a knock at the door.

Another, in his place, might have felt fear at that. In other circumstances, Ned himself might have. But Emille was gone, gone in such a way that she had not been able to leave a note, gone after telling Chall and Maeve that there was trouble at the Assassins' Guild. Meanwhile, people who he believed to also be members of the same guild had waited outside the castle to follow him for reasons he did not know for certain but ones that he might guess at easily enough.

So as he rose to his feet, it was not fear Ned felt but anger. The assassins had been watching his home after all, as he'd thought they might, and apparently they had decided they were no longer content to watch. That was just fine. They must know something of his wife's whereabouts and if they did, they would tell him.

One way or the other.

He stepped out of the bedroom, staring at the door to their house as a second knock came. Ned had owned a sword once—several, in fact. Ones he'd kept sharp, for a wolf with dull teeth was barely a wolf at all, or so he'd told himself when tempted to complain at the onerous task of sharpening them. But that was years ago. He had no such blades now.

Another knock came, but instead of going to the door, Ned moved to the room Emille used for her trade. Or, at least, the trade of healing, not the secret trade of killing that Ned had recently discovered she took part in.

Inside, he stared at the various tools and implements Emille always kept laid on a small table, cleaned and ready for use, should the need arise. They were a healer's tools, but as he looked at them, settling on a large needle nearly as thick as his finger, Ned wondered if there was much distinction between the tools of a healer and those an assassin used in her trade.

Largest needle in the world in hand, Ned took a breath, then moved toward the door.

PRIEST WAS JUST ABOUT to turn and leave, to look for Ned and his wife elsewhere in the city—though where that might be, he had no idea—when the door opened to reveal the carriage driver with a look of fury on his face.

"*Where is she, you ba*—" the man began in a furious growl then paused, frowning. "Valden? That you?"

"Please," Priest said. "Call me Priest."

The man raised an eyebrow at that. "Seems I've missed some things."

"I could say the same," Priest said, glancing at the man's raised hand and realizing that what at first he'd taken as a knife was, in fact, a very large and, by all appearances, very *sharp* needle. "Have you taken up sewing?"

The carriage driver grunted. "Something like that." He let his hand—which had been half-raised as if to strike—fall to his waist, shaking his head. "You shouldn't be here."

"Sorry," Priest said, surprised. "I didn't mean to intrude, I only—"

"What? No," Ned said. "It isn't...damnit. It's too late now. Best you come inside." He stepped to the side, motioning Priest in.

Priest didn't much care for the sound of that, but he trusted Ned—the man had saved his and his companions' lives far too much to do anything else—so he nodded, moving into the house.

He turned as he did, noting Ned frowning out at the street, looking first one way then the other before closing the door.

"Has something happened, Ned?" Priest asked.

The other man grunted. "Yeah, yeah I s'pose you could say that."

"It isn't Emille, is it?" Priest asked. "Chall told me that she came to the castle to get Maeve, that something was wrong at the guild. Is it something we can help her with?"

"I'll be sure to ask her when I see her," Ned said.

Priest blinked. "The two of you haven't spoken?"

The carriage driver gave his head a slow shake, an expression on his face that seemed to vacillate between fear and anger. "I came here lookin' for her. When I saw she wasn't here, I'd hoped maybe she'd left a note. She does that sometimes, when she's going to be gone."

"Did she?"

Ned shook his head. "Nothin'."

"I'm...I'm sure she's alright, Ned," Priest offered. "Emille, she struck me as a capable woman, one that is fully able to take care of herself."

Ned grunted. "Better than I can, and that's a fact." He gave a slow, shuddering breath. "Anyway, it's worse than that."

"Worse?" Priest asked.

"That's right," Ned said. "The problems with the guild, I'm thinkin' they're pretty bad."

"You know what they are?"

"No," the carriage driver said, "but I'm betting one of the assassins that was following me when I left the castle does."

"You were being followed by assassins?" Priest asked. "Are you sure?"

"Sure as I can be without getting into stabbing distance and asking for myself."

Priest nodded grimly. "So, what will you do now?"

"I mean to find my wife," Ned said. "But first, we ought to get out of here before those assassins come callin'. I don't know what's goin' on with Emmy and Maeve, but what I do know is we ain't goin' to be much help to either of 'em as corpses. Who knows, maybe if we find 'em, they'll know somethin' about where the king is. Might be it's the guild that has him."

"I...don't think the guild took Matt."

"No?" Ned said, shrugging. "Well. S'pose it could have been Robert, sure. Makes sense, what with Val workin' with him and all."

"Sorry, I don't think it was them either," Priest said. "Chall...Chall has a theory that *no one* took Matt."

Ned frowned. "So he what, exactly? Disappeared into thin air?"

"Something very much like that," Priest said. "I'll tell you all about it once we get moving."

"Storytime," Ned said. "I can't wait. Maybe you can also tell me the story about your sudden name change." And with that he turned and moved to the door, swinging it open.

He didn't step out into the street though. Instead, he only stood. "Hey Priest?"

"Yeah, Ned?"

"Remember those misplaced assassins of ours?"

Priest frowned, not much caring for the sound of that. "I remember."

"Well. Seems I might have found 'em."

Priest drew one of the knives from his waist and walked up to stand behind the carriage driver, peering over his shoulder at the figures standing twenty-five feet or so away, in the middle of the street.

There were seven of them in all, four of which held loaded crossbows pointed in their direction. Two others held swords down and at their sides. The last stood in front of the others, his weaponless hands clasped behind his back, a pleasant smile on his face. He didn't look much like an assassin. In fact, he looked far more like a man who belonged behind a desk scribbling in some ledger than the apparent leader of a group of trained killers.

"Ah, Neddard, isn't it?" the man called from the street. "I apologize for the abruptness of our visit, but there is something I would like to discuss with you."

"That so?" Ned called back. "It got anything to do with you screwin' off?"

The man smiled pleasantly. "I'm afraid not."

"Well, get on with it," Ned said. "Somethin' about lookin' at you makes me want to yawn, maybe take a nap. If you came here for a reason, best share it. The suspense is killing me."

"Ah, you must forgive me," the man called. "I misspoke before. It is not *I* who would like to speak with you, but the one who sent me."

"Yeah?" Ned answered. "And who might that be?"

The man only smiled, saying nothing.

The carriage driver grunted. "You know what? Today's not good for me. I'm afraid I'm going to have to pass. Besides, I'm not in the habit of accompanying strangers to unknown places to meet with unknown people, particularly when those strangers are holding crossbows and swords like they're just lookin' for a reason to use 'em."

"My name is Balderath," the other man answered. "There—now we are no longer strangers. As for the rest, I am afraid that my...employer, was really quite insistent. I do not believe they will accept 'no' for an answer."

Ned glanced back at Priest. "Too many to fight," the carriage driver said under his breath. "Look to your left there. See the alley?"

"I see it," Priest said quietly.

"We'll make a break for it," Ned muttered, turning to regard Priest. "In case you reach it before me, about halfway down there's a door, leads to a small stable. It ain't much. A far cry from the facilities at the castle, but Alber normally has a horse or two. Enough to put some distance between us and these bastards, anyway"

"Okay," Priest said, preparing himself to run.

"May I ask, Neddard," the man called from the street, "after the identity of your friend?"

"Don't s'pose there's any law against you askin'," Ned called.

The man frowned, not angrily but thoughtfully as he studied Priest. "It's strange, it's almost as if I recogni—" He cut off then, his eyes going wide. "Wait a minute. Are you Valden? The one known as Vicious?"

"When I need to be," Priest called back.

The man gave an amazed laugh, shaking his head. "Why, what an unexpected pleasure. What's more, I am quite sure that my employer will wish to speak with you as well and so I extend the same invitation to you as I have your friend."

"Not sure I'll be able to make it, I'm afraid," Priest called back. "Busy day and all that."

"Ah yes, I understand," the man said. "But I can be quite…persuasive, when I have a need, and I do not doubt that my employer would very much like to…talk with you both."

"On three, we make a break for it," Ned muttered under his breath. *"One…"* he began, then they both turned to the alley. *"Two,"* Ned said, and Priest waited tensely for the man to call three.

But before the carriage driver was able to say "three," a man stepped out of the alleyway Ned had indicated, a loaded crossbow in his hands.

"Ah!" Balderath called. "I see you have spotted my friend, Silus. Not much for talking, I'm afraid, but he does enjoy his sport, and he is a fine shot with that crossbow he carries. You would not believe just how fine. Now then," he went on, "shall we go?"

Priest frowned at the man, Silus. Only one man. He was confident that he and Ned could take him, if it came to it, and make their way past. He was far less confident, however, that they could do so before Balderath and the other assassins caught up to them or decided to put a couple of crossbow bolts in them instead. "Any other ideas?" he asked quietly.

"Just the one," Ned said grimly. "Tell me somethin', Priest, you got somethin' that steadies you?"

"Steadies me?" Priest asked, confused.

"Sure," Ned said, his eyes on the assassins standing in the street. "Somethin' that keeps you *you*. Somethin' that matters to you, that acts as an anchor for you. Somethin' that holds you together."

Priest found his mind going back to Brother Elmer, the way the man had appeared—miraculously—and saved his life when Robert Palden and Willy had been waiting for him in an alleyway. He would have died, then—*should* have died—had the man not appeared when he did, and that was far from the first time in his life. He had been a fool for the last weeks, a man floating in the sea and refusing to believe in the flotsam he held on to when it was the very thing, the *only* thing keeping his head above water.

But he believed now.

"My faith," he answered.

Ned gave a small nod. "Well, that faith is about to be tested. You hold on to it, understand? Hold onto it as hard as you can for as long as you can. Hopefully, it'll be enough."

"Enough to wha—" Priest began, but he never got a chance to finish.

Ned held up his hands the way a man might if he meant to show that he meant no harm, and then suddenly a wave of invisible force crashed over Priest. He staggered, gasping for breath as if he'd just been dunked into an icy lake, but before he could manage one, a second wave of force, eclipsing the first in power and ferocity, charged into him, *through* him, knocking Priest from his feet.

He lay on his back, gritting his teeth as a silent storm raged around him, *inside* him. He heard a shout and turned from where he lay on the ground to see that the assassins were no longer studying him and Ned the way they had a moment before. Instead, they were looking at each other. In fact, they were doing far more than that. The scream he'd heard had been from a man with a crossbow bolt sticking out of his stomach where one of his companions had decided to shoot him. The man barely seemed to notice it though. Instead, he charged into another of his companions—not even the same one who'd shot him—growling and hissing and spitting as he leapt at the man. Then they were all fighting, not like men at all but beasts, discarding the crossbow bolts and swords they held in their rage and choosing, instead, to attack each other bare-handed, ripping and tearing at each other with their nails and teeth.

It was insane, a wild bloodthirsty melee of bestial hate, animalistic fury.

And Priest wanted to be a part of it.

He growled in anticipation as he rose to his feet, starting forward, only to be stopped by a hand on his arm. He looked down at the offending hand then up at the man to whom it belonged.

"*Easy, Priest,*" the man said, his voice seeming to come from a long way off. "*Your faith. Remember your faith. And follow me.*"

He did not want to follow. He wanted to attack, to *kill*. But something about the man's words gripped him, *tethered* him, and he found himself staggering along as the man pulled him forward, his hand on his arm like an anchor in that storm of fury raging all around him.

So he remembered his faith...

And he followed.

CHAPTER TWELVE

THE BARRIER MOUNTAINS, they were called, and that with good reason, for they served far better in that role than any castle wall that had ever been built.

A barrier not just of height—though the mountains were taller than any others Cutter had ever seen. But a barrier of *cold,* a cold that made even the harsh temperatures Cutter had experienced in Brighton or, more recently, in Windham seem like nothing more than the brisk chill of autumn. A cold that seeped into a man's bones, that cut through their clothes—even the thick furs that Fabor had provided—as if they weren't there at all. The horses pulling the borrowed wagon had thick coats and thick bodies that helped them to survive in the harsh colds of the northern Known Lands. Yet even they were not immune to the freezing temperatures, for as Cutter guided them up the mountain pass, he caught glimpses of them shivering.

It was a cold like nothing Cutter had ever felt before, not like a simple temperature at all but like some living creature of ice digging into him, *burrowing* beneath his flesh. After half an hour of traveling the mountain pass, he thought a man couldn't get any colder than he was at that moment. Half an hour after *that,* he realized just how much of a fool he was.

Matt sat beside him at the front of the wagon, and even though the youth had lived his entire life in the cold and so was as acclimated to such temperatures as anyone *could* be, perhaps even more than Cutter himself, he was clearly struggling. He was bent forward, his hood pulled over his face, his arms wrapped tightly around him to conserve what little body heat the frigid temperatures and cutting wind had left him.

As for Feledias, once they had begun scaling the mountain pass and the temperatures had grown worse, Cutter's brother had crawled into the back of the wagon where he now lay huddled among the supplies Fabor had packed.

Cutter turned enough to look at Matt, and as cold as he was, even that small movement seemed to take a monumental effort. His son did not look back. It might have been that he had not noticed, but Cutter did not think it was that. After all, with the blizzard raging around them, the snow and wind that blocked out anything beyond reach from sight, the world seemed very small, and in such a small world even the tiniest of changes, such as a shifting of weight, could not help but be noticed. Anything, after all, to distract oneself from the cold.

Cutter turned back to the path. Not that it did much good. He couldn't even make out the ground in front of the horses, hadn't been able to since they'd started up the mountains and had been left to trust that the beasts knew better than he. So far, at least, it seemed to have worked, for they hadn't plummeted to their deaths over the cliff's edge yet.

Cutter turned further, wincing as the movement brought life into some of his numbing extremities, and gazed behind them. He didn't see anything, but then that meant little. If the villagers *had* followed them, then he wouldn't have been able to see them until they were close enough to stab him. Still, he doubted if they had. If it was their deaths the strange Fey woman was after, then she might well get her wish without having to so much as lift a finger or cast another glamour. After all, when it came to killing anyone foolish enough to venture into them, the Barrier Mountains held a nearly perfect success rate, one that might *be* perfect if one considered that the only two who had ever ventured into them and made it back had been mad and died shortly after.

The Barrier Mountains, they were called, but they had other names, too. Death Mountains, for one. Cutter had even once heard a scholar, waxing poetic, refer to them as the Doom of the North. And, of course, for those poor souls who had died trying to brave the terrible conditions they presented, "graveyard" would suffice.

And it was to this place of frozen death, that Cutter had brought his brother and his son, some of the most important people in the world to him. He was only grateful that Chall and Priest and Maeve were safe in New Daltenia instead of risking their lives on the frozen trail with him and the others.

He found himself looking at Matt again. He thought he knew what was bothering him, thought it surely must have something to do with the fact that Cutter had struck Fabor. He'd considered defending himself, trying to explain a dozen times in the last hour but now, like those other times, he gave it up. Partly because it would have been near impossible to communicate anything beyond a shivering nod given the howling wind and partly because he thought that anything he said would come out sounding like an excuse. Sure, striking Fabor had seemed like the best solution to him, but then to a violent man violence was, more often than not, the answer. That didn't mean there wasn't another, a better one. It meant only that he could not see it.

But he told himself now, like those other times, that now was not the time to try to speak to Matt about it. He would explain it to his son later.

If there *was* a later.

For now, he had more than enough to concern him. Enough like the feyling somewhere behind them, one that had been willing to use a glamour on an entire village just to set a trap for them. Enough like the journey ahead. The Gray Man had told them that the secret to defeating Shadelaresh lay in the Barrier Mountains, but he had not told them much more than that, and stumbling through such a dangerous place blindly sounded like a good recipe for dying if ever there was one.

And then there was the cold, of course.

All the furs and blankets in the world wouldn't save them if they remained in the elements much longer. The snow and sleet covered all of them, the horses and wagon too, and despite the fact that Cutter's gloves and boots had, like all those made in the north, been fat-tanned to be water resistant, the melted snow had found its way in anyway. His feet and hands had stopped aching from the cold some time ago—now they only felt numb. And while a person might be relieved at the absence of pain, it was not a good sign.

Pain, after all, was life.

He knew that they wouldn't last much longer, not as they were. It was unlikely that the feyling, Aurora, had followed them, not without preparing first as Fabor and his wife had, but even if she and a village of would-be murderers were right behind them, it would make little difference.

They had to stop. To go much further would mean death, death not just for Cutter but for his brother, for his son. If the villagers appeared to kill them at the creature's behest, well, at least villagers could be fought. A man could not fight the cold. Not and win, anyway.

So, Cutter set aside, for the moment, his concern for Matt's regard, and instead, peered into the flurry of snow, searching for anything they might use as shelter.

Twice over the next hour, he felt a surge of hope as he just made out what might have been the vague outline of a cave entrance covered in snow. And twice his hopes were dashed as the wagon drew closer and he saw that what he'd taken as a cave entrance was actually only a slight indent in the side of the mountain.

They traveled on. Cutter was beginning to think about how they might all shelter in the wagon—though doing so would mean no fire and the cracks between the wooden slats would do nothing to block the cutting wind—when he caught sight of another vague outline.

He might have dismissed it as no more a cave than the first two he'd spotted, but if the last days had taught him anything it was to hope. And so he did.

And as he pulled the wagon up alongside the vague outline he'd seen, he felt a powerful wash of relief that he had not hoped in vain.

He urged the horses to stop then glanced inside what was unmistakably a cave. He could not see much, for the inside lay cloaked in shadow.

"What is it, Cutter? Why have you stopped?"

He turned to regard Matt who was watching him from beneath his hood.

"Cutter," he'd said. Not "Father." That hurt. Hurt more, in its way, than the sharp pains of the freezing cold lancing into him.

"Is it shelter?" Matt asked.

"Maybe," he said. "I'm going to check it out. Wait here and watch over your uncle. If anything happens give a shout."

"H-h-happily, Brother," Feledias said. "I've been wanting to scream for some time now."

Cutter nodded, climbing down from the wagon. His fingers were numb, his toes, too, making what normally would have been a simple enough task difficult and, as he worked feeling back into his frozen extremities, painful as well.

Still, he finally managed it, stepping onto the ice-covered trail carefully. "I'll be back in a minute," he told them. "I won't be long."

"We should come with you," Matt said.

"Better if you don't. As you said, the cave means shelter, and it may be too much to hope that those others who call this mountain home have not taken advantage of it. Best I go and see, make sure it's safe."

"And if it isn't?" Feledias asked.

Cutter gave him a grin, his face, dry and chapped from the wind, feeling as if it cracked as he did. "Then I suppose I'll be the one doing the screaming. Back in a minute."

"*You'd better be,*" Feledias called after him as he started away, his brother's voice barely audible over the wind. "*Otherwise, you won't come back to find your brother and son but a couple of macabre ice sculptures, one of which, I can attest, will be extremely pissed off.*"

Cutter didn't bother turning to respond—likely his brother wouldn't have heard it even if he had. Besides, Feledias had always been the clever one, the funny one. The kind one, too, come to it. A man of many gifts, many talents. Cutter, meanwhile, only had the one.

He stepped into the cave.

Immediately, once out of the worst of the winds, he felt a hundred times better. At least for a moment. A moment after *that,* he felt like shit. Muscles which had been practically frozen stiff began to unthaw and, as they did, pain lanced through them, and they trembled the way a man might when coming awake from some terrible nightmare.

Cutter did his best to ignore this as he retrieved his axe from its sling and hefted it in front of him, his eyes scanning the cave interior. Much of it lay cloaked in shadow, but what he could make out showed a cave that was larger than he might have hoped.

For a moment, he only stood there. He could see little in the near-darkness of the cave, so he relied on his other senses. At first, there was nothing, but after nearly a minute of standing silent, still, he heard it. The slight, almost imperceptible movement of air. It might have been the wind from outside or perhaps the wind working its way through small cracks in the mountainside. It might have been a thousand different things, might have *meant* a thousand different things, but as he stood there Cutter knew that, in truth, it meant only one.

He was not alone.

And it wasn't just the sound that told him so. It was the smell, too. The smell of unwashed fur, of old blood and raw meat. And then there were the low growling sounds, of course, barely audible over the wind beyond the cave mouth.

Cutter wished in that moment that he had brought a torch, could only blame his own exhaustion and distraction with the cold for the lapse. Not that it would matter, if this went sideways. All dead men, if given a chance, would likely be able to find the cause, the decision which had led to their demise. Some of those decisions might even be forgiven, under certain circumstances—such as stepping into a cave and, in your eagerness to see your brother and son, your*self* safe, forgetting to grab a torch. Such a lapse might be forgiven—but the dead men would be no less dead for all that.

As his eyes slowly acclimated to the gloom, Cutter was able to make out vague forms at the other end of the cave. At first he couldn't see much, just shadowy silhouettes, but as they began to move, rising from where they'd lain, he was able to discern more. Enough to know that they were wolves. Wolves which, from what he could see, were very lean, their ribs visible beneath their fur. Starving, then, or near enough as to make no difference. Their teeth, though, would have lost none of their edge.

Their growls grew louder as they spread out in a semi-circle in front of him. Cutter glanced back at the cave mouth. It lay no more than half a dozen feet behind him, yet it might as well have been miles away. He had some experience with wolves from his time in Brighton—enough to know that they could move incredibly quickly. If he tried to run, they'd be on him long before he reached the cave mouth. Yelling for the others for help was also out of the question. They wouldn't have heard him, not with the blizzard raging as it was.

That only left one option, then, the only option his life had ever seemed to present him with.

Violence. Death. His or that of the foe he faced.

As the wolves continued to spread out, Cutter noted grimly that there were not just one or two as he might have hoped but half a dozen at least. Half a dozen slouching figures, their teeth bared, their eyes glowing golden in the darkness. Cutter hefted his axe, showing them his teeth as they were showing him theirs, but they did not back down. Another sign, then, that they were hungry.

Wolves were not, by choice at least, predators who took on other predators. Instead, their survival was predicated on them taking on things which were weaker than they. The easier the prey the better, for wolves, unlike men, cared nothing for the sense of pride they might feel at defeating a powerful foe. They only wanted to eat.

And these wolves, it was obvious, had not eaten well in some time. They were desperate, and desperate wolves, like desperate men, would take on risks that they otherwise would not. Like, for example, attacking a man wielding a large axe. They would do so accepting the fact that Cutter would likely take down one or two of their number, perhaps even three. But not all of them. And those who were left would eat well, would experience the feeling of their bellies being full for what would likely be the first time in a very long time.

"Come on then," he told them, resigning himself to the fact that now, like most of his life, the only way forward was through blood and death. "Let's get it done."

They seemed to be ready to do just that. The figures—nine, he counted, not six as he'd first thought—stalked forward in a ragged semi-circle, their backs arched, their teeth bared. They were starving, but none were eager to be the first to brave his axe, and so they waited for one of the other of their number to make the first move.

But they would not hesitate for long, he knew. Sooner or later, one would decide that their hunger, their desperate *need* for sustenance outweighed their fear, and they would come at him.

They seemed preparing to do just that, their bodies tensing, lowering as they got ready to launch themselves forward, when the worst thing that Cutter might have imagined happening happened.

He heard steps and turned slightly to see Matt walking up to stand beside him.

"Cutter? Feledias wants to know what's ta—" He cut off, freezing where he stood beside Cutter, as he noticed the shadowy forms spread out before them, their lambent eyes glowing with deadly promise in the darkness. "What are they?" he asked, his voice a low whisper.

Hungry. "Wolves," Cutter said. "They must have sought shelter from the storm, same as us."

"What do we do? Fight them?"

"Nine of them?" Cutter asked, shaking his head. "It's too many. Listen, Matt, I need you to go. I'll buy you as much time I can. Get on the carriage and keep goi—"

"Not nine," Matt said, his voice sounding strange, as if he was reading a difficult passage in an old scroll and trying to understand it or as if someone had posed a particularly difficult hypothetical question he was mulling over. "I can feel more than that...eleven, I think, and—" He cut off as a growl came from behind them, and he and Cutter glanced back to see that two more wolves now stood in the cave entrance.

They were larger than the others, likely the parents. Perhaps they had gone out in search of food, or maybe their keen senses had picked up on Cutter and the others' approach and so they had lain in wait, letting their food come to them. In the end, it made little difference which was true. What mattered was that their teeth looked just as sharp as those of their companions, and they looked all too ready to use them.

"I'll try to make a hole," Cutter said, "when I do, you charge through it, understand? Don't look back. Get to the wagon and get out of here."

"No," Matt said, "no, even you can't fight so many. It's suicide. I won't let you do it."

"You don't have a choice, Son," he said. Then, before Matt could argue any further, Cutter roared and charged at the two wolves standing in the cave mouth.

The two beasts tensed as he came on, preparing to leap, but before he reached them, a voice split the air like thunder.

"*Father, no!*"

The words, the voice hit him like a physical force. His head suddenly ached as if it might explode, and Cutter's charge faltered as he staggered, one hand leaving the haft of his axe and going to his head. Matt's voice, he knew that, but there had been something different about it, a *power* to it that he didn't understand. It was as if it hadn't come from Matt at all but from inside his own head. A head that, just then, ached terribly.

And he wasn't the only one affected by the shout. The wolves yelped as if in pain or fear, their anticipatory growls changing in a moment to desperate, mewling whining. They began to move then, and Cutter raised his axe in preparation, but the wolves did not attack as he expected. Instead, those deeper in the cave moved to its edge, slinking past Cutter and Matt, their backs arched as if terrified, their eyes studying them.

Only, as Cutter watched this strange procession with disbelief, he realized that the wolves were not looking at *him* and Matt, but Matt only. They crawled past him, nearly on their bellies, a respectful, almost worshipful appearance to their postures. They acted the way, Cutter thought, a lowly farmer might act when brought before his king or, perhaps, a priest his god.

They continued to where the other two wolves waited, not looking so intimidating now but simply frightened, their tails tucked between their legs, their heads lowered so much that they touched the cave floor. In another minute, maybe two, all the wolves had reached the cave mouth, and to Cutter's astonishment they began to flee out into the blizzard. The largest of the two who had waited at the entrance was the last to go. It cast one backward glance at Matt, and its lambent, glowing eyes, as it studied him, seemed to Cutter not to be the eyes of some wild beast, but eyes that felt, that *reasoned* as a man might. The beast's head lowered in what looked shockingly close to a bow, then it turned and followed the others, disappearing into the snowstorm.

Slowly, Cutter turned to his son. Perhaps it was some trick of the light or his own confused thoughts, but for a moment Matt's eyes seemed to glow as the wolves' had—only his did not glow gold or yellow but a deep, abiding green.

A moment later, though, it was gone, and Cutter was left trying to decide if he had only imagined it. "What...what just happened?" he said.

"I...I don't know," Matt answered, sounding afraid but not just that. Sounding angry. "I think..." He paused, glancing at Cutter, and even in the shadowed interior of the cave Cutter could see his son's anguish writ plain on his features. "I think something's wrong with me."

"There's nothing wrong with you, Son."

Matt gave a ragged laugh without humor. "Isn't there? I just...I saw you moving toward the wolves, and I thought...I thought I was going to lose you. I was angry...scared, and...and it just happened."

Cutter didn't bother asking *what* had happened, for it was clear from his frustration that Matt didn't have the answer to that anymore than Cutter himself. "It's what you said before, isn't it?" he said. "Something to do with how you appeared beside us, how you saved us from the Unsated?"

"I...I think so," Matt said, and in that moment he looked very young. Not a king, not even a young man, but a child. A child who had seen, had felt something he did not understand and was afraid.

Cutter sheathed his axe and stepped forward, putting his hand on his son's shoulder. He waited until Matt slowly raised his gaze from the ground to meet his eyes, then he spoke.

"I don't know what's happening, Matt. I don't know what these... powers you have are. If they *are* powers. I know it must be confusing. Frightening. But what I *do* know is that because of them—because of *you*—Fel and I did not die back there when the Unsated attacked us outside the Black Wood. Because of *you* we're not spending the afternoon as lunch for a pack of hungry wolves. It might even be these powers, whatever they are, that made you be able to see past the feyling's magic, back at Windham. So while they might be confusing, whatever else these powers are, they aren't all bad."

Matt nodded slowly, looking a little relieved, at least. "Do you think..." he began, then cleared his throat. "That is...they're getting worse."

"Worse?"

Again, Matt raised his gaze from the floor where it had drifted, meeting Cutter's stare. "Stronger," he said. "Whatever it is...it's growing. I felt it back in New Daltenia but not like this. I'm afraid...I'm afraid I'm going to lose control of it...honestly, I'm not sure I have control of it now. Whatever *it* is. I feel...I feel like it's taking over me. Like...like maybe soon there won't *be* a me."

"Is it like when that feyling, Emma, was in your mind?"

Matt gave a frustrated shrug. "Sort of, but...but it's different, somehow. It isn't as if someone is taking over my mind, taking control of it. The way it was with Emma. It's...it's like my mind *itself* is taking over." He gave another one of those ragged, desperate laughs. "I guess I'm not making any sense."

"Listen, Matt," Cutter said. "I won't pretend that I know what you're going through or that I know how to fix it. Perhaps Chall would, if he were here. Maybe Priest would have some idea. But what I can tell you is this—whatever comes, whatever you have to face, you will not face it alone. I will be with you. Whatever it is, we will face it together."

Matt gave a slow sigh, then a small smile. "Thanks...Cutter."

Cutter blinked. He had been sure that Matt was preparing to call him father, and the expression on his son's face—a mixture of apologetic and defiant at the same time—assured him it was true.

"Listen, Matt," Cutter said. "About before, with Fabor. I want you to kn—"

"Wh-what in the name of all the g-gods i-is going on in here?"

Matt turned, clearly eager to have an excuse to avoid the conversation. "Uncle," he said, moving quickly away toward where Feledias stood in the cave mouth, "are you alright?"

Cutter turned to regard his brother fully and decided that "alright" was not how he would have described him. Feledias stood with what must have been all the furs and blankets Fabor had packed in the wagon wrapped around him, one hand holding them together at his front, the other clutching a sword. Not that he looked in any danger of stabbing anyone just then except maybe himself, considering the way the blade trembled in his hand.

"S-so I'm o-out there f-freezing my ass off," Feledias stammered, "and th-the two of you are just standing h-here having a n-nice chat?"

Despite his attempt at humor, his brother's appearance worried Cutter. He looked done-in—no surprise, given that he'd spent the last weeks in the Black Wood, being hunted, wounded, and nearly dying to a fever. The last place he needed to be was in the Barrier Mountains, the most inhospitable place in the Known Lands, perhaps in the world.

"Something like that," Cutter said, moving toward his brother. "Come on, Fel. Let's get you inside. I'll retrieve the supplies and start a fire, how would that be?"

"F-fire," Feledias said, and it was proof of his condition that he allowed Matt and Cutter to guide him toward the back of the cave without complaint. "I s-seem to r-remember hearing s-something about that before."

They reached the back of the cave where the wolves had lain, and Cutter and Matt eased Feledias down so that his back was against the cave wall.

Feledias sniffed, picking up, Cutter suspected, on the smell of wet fur and meat that had first alerted Cutter to the wolves' presence. "Don't take this the w-wrong way, B-Bernard," his brother said, "b-but it might be time you t-took a bath."

"Just rest, Fel," Cutter said. "I'll be back in a minute, and we'll get that fire going."

"P-probably a good i-idea," Feledias said. "I-I'm not doing so h-hot." He gave a soft laugh at that. "H-hot, get it? A-anyway, I m-must have been ha-hallucinating. I thought I s-saw some wolves w-walk out of the cave."

Cutter and Matt shared a worried glance at that. Of course his brother *had* seen the wolves, but it wasn't a good sign that he trusted his own thoughts and vision so badly that he just assumed it was a figment of his imagination. "Watch him," Cutter told his son. "I'll be back in a moment."

"You said that last time," Matt observed.

Cutter raised his hands to his side. "And here I am. Anyway, don't worry. I'm pretty confident that any wolves—" he paused, glancing at his brother—"real *or* imagined, are gone. Besides, I need to get the horses inside. They're bred for the cold, but this will be too much, even for them. Keep him warm, if you can."

Matt frowned at that and Feledias gave a soft, weak laugh. "A-at least give the b-boy a task he has a ch-chance of completing, B-Bernard." He snorted. "K-keep him warm," he repeated, shaking his head. "M-might as well t-take a s-swim in the ocean and t-try to stay d-d—" Feledias cut off as he was overcome with a bout of shivering, and he wrapped his arms around himself.

Cutter didn't say anything more, only met Matt's eyes. His son gave a small nod, and then Cutter moved outside. He stepped out into the blizzard once more, and as he did the cold hit him like a runaway carriage, nearly stealing his breath. Axe in hand, he let his gaze travel around his surroundings. He'd been telling the truth when he told Matt he didn't think the wolves had stuck around, but then he'd been wrong before and had paid for it in pain and blood.

If the wolves were lurking somewhere, however, then he did not see them. Not that there were all that many places to lurk. Besides the wagon and the horses harnessed at its front, the snowstorm had made of the world nothing but a great white expanse. A white path leading up a white mountain into white clouds and, beyond the pass itself, over the cliff's edge, unbroken fields of white that appeared as if they stretched on into eternity.

Cutter felt badly for the horses, forced to endure the elements as they were, but he decided to focus on getting Feledias warm first. The horses would survive being left on their own for a while longer—he was not sure he could say the same of his brother. He moved to the back of the wagon and retrieved the small leather pack which held the flint, steel, and some tinder, tucking it against his chest. The leather had been oiled to help waterproof it, but the last thing he wanted to do was try to start a fire with tinder and flint that had been soaked through. It could be done, but the doing of it would take time and considering the state that Feledias was in, he wasn't sure they had any time to spare.

He hurried into the cave, moving to the back where Feledias and Matt were. As soon as he drew close he felt his breath catch in his throat. His brother was not sitting as he had been. Instead, he was lying on the ground, his eyes closed.

"Is...what..." Cutter began.

"He's sleeping," Matt said.

Cutter looked back at his brother. At first, he couldn't make out the rise and fall of his breath, not with all the thick furs and blankets wrapped around him, but after a moment he saw that Matt was right and let the breath he'd been holding go. He nodded. "Good. That's good."

He knelt, quickly rifling through the pack and retrieving the flint and steel before reaching into the bag of tinder and pulling out some of the mixture of crushed bark and dried grass. He arranged it into a pile carefully, using his broad back to block what wind came in through the cave opening, then he grabbed the flint and steel and set about striking it. It did not take long for a spark to catch and with that done, Cutter coaxed the fire into life, smoke filling the cave as it did.

Feledias coughed once, but he did not wake, fully given in to his exhaustion. "I'll be back," Cutter said. Matt nodded, taking his place at tending to the small blaze as Cutter went back out to the wagon, retrieving one of the small bundles of dried sticks that Fabor had thankfully seen fit to pack. A wise choice, for in the north there was never any telling when a person might come upon dry fuel for a fire. He came back, and after a short time tending the small flame they had a steady blaze that did much to banish the worst of the chill from the cave.

Cutter held his hands out to the flame, as did Matt, and for a time they did not speak, only enjoying the heat. He was not warm—far from it. But he was the warmest he had been in what felt like a very long time, and so he was grateful.

He did not allow himself long, though. Only a minute or two, enough to work some small bit of feeling, of warmth back into his hands, then he rose.

"Where are you going?" Matt asked.

"The horses won't last long in this—I need to bring them inside."

"I'll help you," Matt said, rising.

"No," Cutter said, holding out a hand to forestall him. "Stay and watch over Feledias. Please. Keep the fire going."

Matt frowned but gave a slow nod. "Okay."

Cutter hesitated for a moment, considering broaching Fabor and the rest of it...but in another moment he decided against it and turned and headed for the cave entrance.

He spent the next half hour unloading the wagon. He unharnessed the horses, moving them into the cave and tying them, giving them food and melted snow for water. Satisfied that they were as comfortable as they could be made to be, he set about retrieving the packs Fabor had placed inside the wagon and bringing them into the cave, intending to see what resources they had available to them. When Fabor had brought the wagon, Cutter had been far too concerned with getting him, his brother, and his son away from a village full of people wanting to see them dead to ask. But now that they had a moment's respite, he thought it important to check through the packs' contents. After all, he had a sinking feeling that everything those packs contained —down to the last crumble of hardtack—would likely mean the difference between life and death.

A weak anchor, perhaps, to tie his life and the lives of his brother and son to, but then it was also the only one available. Carrying the last of the packs, he stepped into the cave and set them down near the others. He glanced at Feledias and saw that he was still fast asleep, though Cutter was relieved to see that the worst of his brother's shaking had subsided.

As Cutter sat down among the packs, Matt looked up from where he'd been tending the fire, having worked it into a good-sized blaze. Matt, like anyone who had lived or grown up in the frozen north, knew well the importance of fire. Starting a fire and tending it might have been a novel skill to those accustomed to the far warmer climes of New Daltenia, but in the north, it was a necessity, one that could quite easily mean the difference between life or death.

"Is that everything?" Matt asked quietly, clearly hoping not to wake Feledias.

Cutter didn't think that that, at least, was a worry they needed to concern themselves with, not based on the way his brother was snoring. He glanced at the packs. They had seemed like a lot when he'd first looked in the back of the wagon, packing it pretty much completely full, but now, spread out as they were, they seemed woefully inadequate. "That's everything," he said.

"What is it exactly that we're looking for out here?"

Cutter shook his head slowly. "I don't know."

"I see. And...how far do we have to go?"

"I don't know."

"So...why are we here again?"

"Because the Gray Man told us that the only way to beat Shadelaresh, to bring peace between our people and his own lay in the Barrier Mountains."

"Shadelaresh...that is the Green Man? The one who came to us before?"

"Yes."

Matt nodded slowly, giving a heavy breath. "And this Gray Man... who is he?"

"A feyling, an ancient one of great power. The father of King Yeladrian."

Matt blinked. "King Yeladrian as in the one who you killed, the reason why the war started?"

Cutter scratched his chin. "That's right."

Matt nodded, a clearly troubled expression on his face.

"You're wondering why we're here, why we trusted the Gray Man," Cutter said.

"The thought had crossed my mind," Matt admitted.

Cutter nodded, his gaze going to Feledias where he still slept, then back to Matt. "Our journey through the Black Wood was...difficult. We faced creatures, some of which even I have not seen before. We nearly died, *would* have died if not for the Gray Man interceding on our behalf and that more than once. He healed Feledias of a fever that would have killed him. He even went so far as to send someone to help us, to keep us out of the reach of the Unsated—the creatures that were attacking us when you appeared."

"Where is he, then? This helper?"

Cutter winced. "He died. He gave his life so that we could escape. Had he not sacrificed himself, had the Gray Man not sent him, we would have never escaped the Black Woods, and I never would have seen you again. And for that—for that *gift*—I would trust him with far more. If the Gray Man says that the key to defeating Shadelaresh lies in these mountains, then I believe him."

"And if we do find it, if we somehow manage to survive the cold and the dangers of the mountains—dangers any kid growing up in the north has heard about a thousand times and more—and to not *just* survive but to find this, this *thing,* whatever it is, what then?"

"Then we use it to defeat Shadelaresh," Cutter said.

"Kill him, you mean."

Cutter raised his gaze from where he'd been checking on Feledias to meet his son's gaze. "Yes."

Matt gave his head a shake, a troubled, even hurt expression on his face as he turned to stare out at the cave mouth. "That's your answer for everything. Killing. Hurting."

Cutter opened his mouth to argue that, but after a moment's hesitation he closed it again. After all, he'd been entertaining very similar thoughts recently himself, thinking that the only solution he ever saw to problems was the bloody kind. Not because those were the only answers available, he'd thought, but because those were the only answers he ever saw.

So they only set in silence until, after a minute or two, Matt spoke again. "Back at Windham...you didn't have to do that to Fabor."

"Matt, I didn't w—"

"I know, I know," Matt interrupted. "He meant to betray us to the feyling, whoever she was. But can you blame him? He was just trying to protect his wife, himself. And you hurt him—badly, I think. It seems that hurting people is all you like to do."

"No, Son, it isn't—"

"As if you would have done anything different," Matt said, his voice growing louder with his anger, his indignation. "Anyway, he risked everything to save us, to get us out of there, and you thank him by beating him half to death. I would think *you* of all people, *Father*, ought to appreciate that sometimes men do things that they aren't proud o—" He cut off as the sound of a wolf's howl came from somewhere beyond the cave mouth. The horses whinnied at the sound, shifting restlessly as instincts bred into them from thousands of years urged them to flee.

Cutter frowned. "Stay here. Watch him." He rose, grabbing his axe from where it lay on the ground then started toward the entrance of the cave.

"Maybe I should go too," Matt said. "There might be too many."

"No," Cutter said quickly. "Stay. It might have nothing to do with us."

Matt wanted to argue—he could see that in his son's face—but thankfully Feledias chose that moment to let out a troubled sound in his sleep, drawing Matt's attention who moved toward him to make sure he was okay.

Cutter left him to it, walking toward the entrance of the cave. The blizzard had abated somewhat—likely the only reason they'd been able to hear the wolf's howl in the first place—and so Cutter was able to see beyond the cave without the nearly impenetrable curtain of white snow that had blocked his view earlier.

Not that there was much *to* see. The wagon sat where he had left it, the wood barely visible beneath the snow piled atop it. He hefted his axe and stepped out onto the snow-covered path, tensing as he prepared for one of the wolves which had so recently vacated the cave to pounce at him.

No such attack came, however, and he let his gaze slowly travel around. Nothing stirred, not a wolf, not even so much as an errant piece of grass. The world was so still that he might have been standing inside of a lifeless painting.

He studied the mountain pass on either side, noted that the ground showed no signs of footprints or passage of any creature or man. Not that that said much, for the snow, even falling lighter now than it had before, would have covered such marks in a quarter hour or less.

He'd only stood there for a minute, perhaps two, when there came another wolf's howl, this one, he was sure, further away than the first had been. Satisfied that an attack was not imminent, he moved back into the cave.

"Anything?" Matt asked, looking up from where he'd been watching the fire. "A horde of wolves rushing toward us, maybe?"

Cutter shook his head. "They are leaving, I think."

"It doesn't mean they won't be back."

"No, it doesn't."

Matt frowned thoughtfully. "Maybe I was out of line before, but I meant what I said."

"I know."

"I just...when you were gone to the Black Wood, I missed you. Every day I thought about you, about how I hoped you were okay. And now—" Matt paused as a heavy yawn overcame him.

Save for the Skaalden invasion, Cutter had never fled from a fight. He had stood against man and monster and had, somehow, come out alive, though not without the scars to prove it. But he found himself eager to flee then, and so he took the opportunity of his son's yawn to speak. "You're tired," he said. "You need rest—it has been a long day. Go ahead—lie down, get what sleep you may. I'll take watch."

"I've been tired before," Matt said. "Anyway—"

"No doubt you have," Cutter said, "but as you mentioned, we don't know how long we'll be in these mountains or what we'll face trying to find the key the Gray Man told me and Fel about. There's no way of knowing. But what I *do* know is that whatever we face, you'll need your strength."

Matt sighed. "Okay. But wake me, and I'll take second watch."

"Of course."

Matt started to turn away then hesitated. "How do you live like this? Where everyone's an enemy, where every problem has only the one solution?"

Cutter considered that. He might have lied. He *wanted* to lie, but even his cruelty, it seemed, had bounds. "I know no other way."

Matt watched him for a moment, then he gave a soft sigh. "Goodnight."

"Goodnight, Son."

As Matt retrieved blankets from one of the packs Fabor had stowed and began to settle in near the fire, Cutter turned to face the cavern entrance. The wolves had gone, and he did not think they would be back; but then, there were many other, many *worse* dangers to concern them than a hungry pack of wolves.

He turned his back on the flames, on Matt and Feledias too as he moved closer to the entrance, until he was only a few feet from it. Then he sat, placing his axe, the Breaker of Pacts, on the stone floor of the cave beside him within easy reach.

He sat in the cold. He did not look back at the fire. Nor did he glance back at his brother or son. His gaze only remained on the cavern entrance, waiting for what might come, prepared, when and if it did, to meet it with blood and steel.

He knew no other way.

CHAPTER THIRTEEN

Maeve slept a troubled sleep.

She did not dream as such. Instead, her thoughts, however she tried to calm them, to still them, were cast frantically about from one half-formed fear to the next, each looming larger than the last. Great, shadowy behemoths, any one of which might crush her and anyone and everyone she cared about, should it fall.

And they were *all* falling. Teetering and threatening to topple over, and Maeve was able to do nothing but watch and wait for that great fall.

She came awake slowly, aware of a strange feeling against her hand, her fingers. A wet roughness.

A dog? a confused, still half-sleeping part of her mind thought. Her eyelids felt as if someone had tacked them down with glue, and it was an effort to open them.

And the moment she had, she wished she had kept them closed.

Somehow, in her slumber, she had turned in such a way that one arm and hand lay between two of the bars, as if even in her sleep she had been searching for escape from her cell. She felt that wet roughness sliding against her hand again and as her eyes adjusted to the darkness, she followed the length of her arm then gasped, jerking her hand, along with the rest of her, back and away from the bars.

She staggered to her feet, staring first at her hand, and then in disgust at the figure beyond the bars. She had imagined, in her half-sleeping state, that she had felt a dog licking her, but the figure outside the cell was no dog and never mind that it knelt on all fours the way a dog might. It was a person—an old man with frazzled gray hair and a patchy gray beard who had an unkempt, unwashed look. He looked to Maeve like a beggar who had lived the last long while on the streets. But unlike all such beggars Maeve had seen, the man did not look somber or depressed or as if he were simply waiting to die.

Instead, as she regarded him, he raised his head and grinned, a too-wide grin that displayed a mouth largely devoid of teeth, those few rotten ones that remained appearing to hang on by a thread. The man studied her with that grin seemingly frozen on his face, his eyes wide and wild and strange. Hungry, alien eyes.

Maeve looked down at her hand then wiped the wetness off her shirt in disgust. "Who are you?" she demanded.

The old man cocked his head in a very unusual way then leapt to his feet the way a child might, the sight incongruous and more than a little troubling from a man in threadbare clothes that appeared to at least be in his seventies. "Today?" the man asked, only his voice was not that of an old man or a man at all. Instead, it was the voice of a child, a strange, sing-song quality to it. "I don't know…I'm afraid I never got this one's name."

"This one?" Maeve asked, horror slowly dawning as she realized to whom she must be speaking.

"This flesh. This suit," the doppel told her. "I am quite certain he *had* a name, but he did not offer it and I did not ask. We were both… occupied, I'm afraid. I suppose I might have given him a name, but me and my kind do not name our food anymore than you and yours do." The feyling tittered a laugh. "It would be awfully strange, wouldn't it?"

it asked, its old man's face studying her with a childlike glee as it spoke calmly about eating someone.

"You...monster," Maeve said. "This man—whoever he was. He was a *person*. He had a family. He had hopes and dreams, and—"

"Oh, I am well aware that he had his hopes and dreams," the doppel said, grinning widely once more. "For I have tasted them. Sour, by and large, brittle and old, forgotten and abandoned, but there is still a sweetness to them just the same. Perhaps it is because however neglected, they are still living dreams, when I find them. When I am finished, though..." It shrugged, even the gesture seeming wrong, its shoulders and arms all sharp, wooden angles, more like a puppet than a person. "Still," it went on, Maeve herself unable to speak for her own horror, "he was not the best meal I have had. Half dead already. I prefer them live and struggling. Like you will be, when it is my time to feast on you. I have tasted you already, tough and sweet at the same time. Your reputation among your kind is, it seems, not without reason. I am eager to taste more."

Maeve looked with disgust at her hand, rubbing against her shirt again and never mind that it was already dry. "That's not going to happen. Touch me again and I'll kill you."

The creature did not look intimidated—but then Maeve figured she didn't look very intimidating just then, not locked behind a cell as she was, her clothes filthy from sleeping on the floor.

"You are a fighter, and that is good," the feyling said. "Some of my kind like easy meat, but I have always enjoyed a struggle. It makes the victory, makes the *meat* taste so much sweeter. The other. Agnes. She is a fighter, too. Or, at least, she was." The doppel shook its head, an exaggerated expression of regret on its face. "I am sad to say that she has lost some of her...*hunger* for the fight in recent days, since I have started the becoming."

Maeve felt a chill run up her spine at that. The becoming. The creature had mentioned it before, and she knew that what it alluded to was no less than the fact that it was *eating* Agnes. Eating her so that, in time, it might *become* her. Maeve and Agnes had been far from the best of friends, but thinking of what the creature before her had been doing to the woman, Maeve felt anger rising in her, banishing, for the moment, her fear.

"You may think yourself safe now," Maeve said, her voice a furious rasp, "but know this, creature. I will make you pay for what you have done. You mentioned my reputation before, and you were right. I did not get it without reason. Assassins get famous for one reason and one reason only: because they're good at their job. And I, creature, I am very, *very* good at my job. You think yourself safe, and that's fine. There were others that thought themselves safe, too. But *when* I came for them, no amount of locked doors or bodyguards, no amount of prayers or planning could keep me away, and neither will these cell bars."

The creature grinned that too-wide grin, but its dark, alien eyes watched her, and in them she saw no humor. "I do not fear you, fleshling."

"And yet," Maeve said, "my blades will cut just as easily. Courage is a flimsy shield, feyling, when the dying begins."

"Do you think to frighten me, meat?" the feyling asked, and its smile was nowhere in evidence now, its black eyes shining with anger, its voice a hiss. "I have feasted on dozens of your kind, since you and yours came to our shores, to our place. And *you* think to frighten *me*? You are nothing to me but food. I have killed dozens like you, *eaten* dozens like you."

"Not like me," Maeve said. "I am no old, toothless beggar, feyling. And it makes no difference to me whether you are afraid or not. What will happen will happen just the same. In my trade, creature, we kill for coin and contract, rarely for pleasure. But for you, I'll make an exception."

The creature bared its rotten teeth in response, the way a furious dog might. "No Fey would ever fear your kind, fleshling. You are no more than bugs to us, scuttling here and there, living your short, pitiable lives. You, your king, even the Destroyer, who you followed so blindly for so long are, at best livestock to be feasted on whenever we wish."

It was angry. Maeve rarely ever felt as if she understood her own people, and she understood the Fey far less, but this much she knew. She knew she probably should have left it there, but here was the thing—she was angry too. Angry because this creature meant to kill not just her and Emille but all her people. Angry because Bethesa and Piralta, the fools, were helping it to do it. Angry, most of all, because Chall was out there somewhere, him and Priest, and Matt. If, that was, the creature hadn't been telling the truth when it had said Matt was dead, and that was something Maeve could not, *would not* believe. Then there was the prince, if he were still alive. Her friends, her family. And this thing meant to kill them all.

The rational part of Maeve knew she should remain silent, knew that there was no purpose in antagonizing the creature. But, just then, the rational part of her held very little sway. "Livestock, are we?" she said. "I wonder if your king thought as much. You know, before *my* Destroyer chopped his head off."

The creature let out a roar of anger at that. "You *dare* to make mockery of the great Yeladrian, the Voice of Twilight, who—"

"Not too great anymore," Maeve interrupted. "And not much of a voice either. You know, with his head missing and all."

The creature screamed then. "*Enough!*" it screeched. "*I will crush your bones and feast on your flesh, meatling. I will devour your essence, drink your blood and glut myself on your soul, and I will not wait another moment!*"

In its anger, the creature seemed to have discarded any and all of its plans. It dropped to all fours, its arms and legs splayed out to the side at an impossible angle and Maeve watched one of the most horrifying things she'd ever seen—and that with no small competition—as the creature scrambled toward the wall like some great spider.

It reached the wall and rose, snatching the key from where it hung on the hook then scurried back to the front of Maeve's cell. Maeve felt hope mixed with fear as she watched the creature fumble the keys in its anger, trying to fit them into the lock.

"*Leave her alone, you monster!*" Emille screamed, but the creature, fully given to its fury, paid her no mind.

Maeve was tired and hungry—they had not bothered feeding her yet. She was frightened, as anyone with any sense would be, given the situation she found herself in, but she did her best to gather her courage and her strength. If she could manage to overcome the feyling and get the key, she had a chance of saving not just herself and Emille, but the entire kingdom. She had to survive, not just for herself, but to warn the others that the Assassins' Guild was working with the Fey.

So, she tensed as she listened to the sound of the door creak as it opened, preparing to launch herself at the creature and make use of whatever strength she had left. But even as she started forward, she realized with a shock that it was not *her* door that had opened but the door that led out of the dungeon.

The creature, too, was surprised by this, spinning and glaring at the door, and so it watched, along with Maeve, as the door swung wide and four guards filed into the room. One of which, Maeve was stunned to see, was none other than Phillip, one of the men that had been her bodyguard when she became guildmaster. The man noted her gaze and looked away quickly, studying his boots as he and the others stepped to either side of the door.

Maeve shouldn't have been surprised by the man's betrayal—the virtuous rarely found themselves joining a guild of contract killers. Nor should she have been hurt—she had only known him a few weeks, and while he'd seemed kind, likable enough, many of the world's best predators did—right up until they sank their teeth or their blades into you. But the fact was, Maeve *was* surprised, *was* hurt, for some part of her had thought that the two of them had shared a rapport.

"Guess that'll teach me to give second chances, won't it, Phillip?" she asked, referring to the fact that she had kept him and his companion—who Maeve also saw among the four guards—in their positions despite the fact that they had allowed the tribunes into her quarters without her consent. He had told her, at the time, that he had not realized she had not wanted them there, claimed that they had said she'd given them orders to wait, and she, fool that she was, had actually believed him.

The guard turned a bright shade of red visible even in the flickering light of the torch another of his number held. He opened his mouth, perhaps to answer or give another excuse—though likelier to gloat—but never got the chance for either.

"I thought I heard shouting," Bethesa said as she stepped into the dungeon, Piralta following behind her like a dutiful pet. "And I just had a feeling that someone—or some*thing*—was getting ready to do something particularly foolish." She turned her head to regard the creature before Maeve's cell whose stolen face was still twisted with hate, its hand, which still clutched the cell key, frozen halfway raised. "Seems I was right."

"*This does not concern you, withered one,*" the creature hissed.

"No?" Bethesa said. "Sure seems as it does to me. See, from where I'm standin', it's lookin' as if you meant to let Maeve out, maybe have a nice chat. That about the size of it?"

"*She has mocked the Voice of Twilight and so must suffer the consequences.*"

"You mean to kill her."

The creature gave a slow, sly smile. "*Not at first,*" it said. "*In time she might be made to die.*"

"Then it seems that your kind are just as capable of being fools as my own," Bethesa said.

The creature's body twisted and writhed in a strange way, almost, Maeve thought, like a snake preparing to strike. "*Do not think to hinder me, withered one. She has offended the name of the king and so must be made to suffer.*"

"And she will," Bethesa said, her gaze traveling to Maeve for a moment. "But not like this."

"*You think to dictate to me how it will be, is that it, fleshling?*"

"Never been much at dictatin'," Bethesa said. "And as you pointed out, I'm old—too old to be tryin' new things. No, I reckon instead I'll do some remindin'. I'll remind you, for example, of why it is you're here, of why it is you were sent among all us fleshlings. Not by me, understand, but by that boss of yours."

The creature's hands were clenching and unclenching into fists at its side as it clearly struggled with its anger. "*Boss, you call him. You are an old fool. He is the Will of the Green, its strength embodied, its wildness tamed. He is the Speaker for the Wood.*"

"Lot of fancy titles," Bethesa said, nodding. "Seems to me that he ain't the sort I'd care to disappoint. But you tell me, feyling—reckon he'll be happy he finds out you jeopardized his whole plan—*our* whole plan—in a fit of offended pique?"

The feyling actually growled then, not the growl of a man but of a beast. "*Am I to be lectured on loyalty by one who betrays her own people?*"

"Not much more at lecturin' than dictatin' I'm afraid," Bethesa said. "Now stop actin' a fool and step away from that cell."

The feyling hissed. "*Perhaps, when I am done with this one, I will feast on your withered flesh. I will suck the marrow from your bones.*"

"Careful, creature," Bethesa said, frowning. "In case you've forgotten, you ain't standin' in the Black Wood. You're here, in the Assassin's Guild, and here, *I* am lord. Not your Green Man and certainly not you."

"*You think to threaten me?*" the creature asked, sounding shocked, some powerful emotion audible in its voice, though what that emotion might be, fear or anger, Maeve could not tell for sure.

"I'll do a sight more'n that, you don't stop this foolishness," Bethesa said. "Can you really be so stupid? Why do you think she was antagonizing you in the first place? You think you were in control, but you weren't. See, Maeve here is clever. She knows that inside that cell, she is helpless, *hopeless*. Unless, that is, some angry fool comes along and opens it for her. Do you see? She *wanted* you to open that door. And if you had, I imagine she'd have done a lot more than offend you."

The creature sneered again. "*I am to be frightened of this frayed sack of rattling bones?*" it said, turning to regard Maeve with its dark, alien eyes. "*She is nothing to me.*"

"Let me remind you, creature, that you stand in a guild of *assassins*. You're offended? Well, then count yourself lucky. You can be a lot worse than that, here. This place ain't for trainin' folks to give offense—it's for trainin' 'em how to kill. And that 'sack of rattling bones,' as you call her, is largely regarded as the best ever to come out of it."

"*Once, perhaps,*" the creature said, regarding Maeve, and even though the creature was a being Maeve knew little of, she could hear the doubt in its voice, "*but even if such is true, it matters not. No blade is sharp enough, no wit quick enough to defeat time.*"

"True," Bethesa said, "but then even old lions have sharp teeth. That's a truth quite a few folks have found out the hard way. Fey too, I imagine. Now, leave—go back to Agnes, if you'd like. Chew the fat." She grinned at her own joke then, and in that joke Maeve saw a cruelty, an *evil* that might well have surpassed even that alien evil of the doppel. "Do whatever it is you do. If things don't go to plan, well, it'd make things a lot easier if Agnes herself—or someone that everyone *thought* was Agnes—was around to sell it. Now go on—get."

The feyling's body tensed at that, and Maeve thought it was considering launching itself at Bethesa. She hoped that it would—however it went, she figured she and Emille could only come out winners. But the feyling did not rush forward, though when it spoke its voice shook with anger.

"*What reason of sky and moon makes you think that you might speak to me in such a manner?*"

"The same reason that knows why you're here," Bethesa said, and if she was afraid, she did a fine job of hiding it. "The same reason that knows these four guardsmen here will happily cut you down, if you make one step out of line, and that even if they somehow fail—and they won't, they're quite good at cutting things—then I doubt you'll have long to celebrate. After all, this isn't just my plan, but that Green Man of yours too. I expect he'd be a bit upset with the creature that made it all go sideways, particularly when it's so close to succeedin'."

For several tense seconds, the creature only stood, no doubt weighing its desire to attack and its wounded pride against its own survival. In the end, the creature only turned back to regard her. *"We will speak again,"* it promised.

"Can't wait," Maeve said.

The creature bared its few rotten teeth then turned and started for the door.

"And feyling?"

It turned back to stare at Bethesa.

"Do not come here again," the tribune told her, "without asking my permission first."

The creature gave that revolting grin again, its dark, alien eyes flashing with fury, then it turned and left.

Bethesa sighed, turning back to regard Maeve. "Good help's hard to find."

"Given your winning personality," Emille said, "I figured you'd be beating them off with a stick."

The tribune flashed a smile at the woman's cell. "Lady Emille. I do so enjoy your wit. It is a shame that you chose to place your loyalties with Maeve, here. Better if you hadn't, for I might have made good use of you." She shrugged. "But, I suppose, there ain't much use cryin' over spilt milk, is there?" She turned to Maeve. "Clever. Trying to make the creature angry. I did not think their kind so easily offended."

"I've always had a knack for it," Maeve said dryly.

Bethesa smiled. "Yes, well, I reckon we've all got our gifts, don't we? Still, you might come to regret antagonizin' it in the days to come. A person in your position hardly needs more enemies."

"Guess I'll have to get rid of some, then. Who knows? Maybe I'll start with you. Anyway, the feyling isn't exactly your biggest fan, either."

"I couldn't care less what it thinks of me," the tribune said. "Not any more than the carpenter cares for the thoughts of the hammer. All I care about is that it does its job. When it's finished..." She shrugged. "Well. It's a big world out there. Easy to disappear in, whether a body wants to or not."

"You really are an evil bitch," Emille said.

"That's *Tribune* Evil Bitch to you, lass," Bethesa corrected. "Now, if we're done with the pleasantries, I'm afraid this isn't a social call."

"And here I was preparing to bring out my finest plates and glasses," Maeve said.

"Another time, perhaps," Bethesa said. "For now, we have business to be about."

"Well, get on with it then," Maeve said. "Can't you see I'm a busy lady? What do you want?"

"From you?" Bethesa said, raising an eyebrow. "Nothing. Or, at least, nothing that cannot wait. Unless, of course, you'd like to tell me where the diary is. I promise that, if you do, I will make what is coming as painless as I can for you. I do not say pain *free,* as that would make me a liar. Still, I reckon there's pain and then there's *pain,* isn't there?"

"Diary?" Maeve asked, watching the woman. "First I've heard of it."

Bethesa nodded. "That'd be about what I expected. Which is why I am here for another purpose." She turned to stare at Emille's cell. "The trial has been moved up to three days' time. Recent events have, understandably, caused some members of the guild to find themselves beginning to distrust guild leadership, and so circumstances are such that we have been forced to speed it along."

"The guild that has been coopted by one of the tribunes and weaponized against their kingdom?" Maeve said. "One cannot imagine why."

"Piralta, do one of those guardsmen have a crossbow?"

"Yes, Tribune Bethesa."

"Good. Instruct them that if Lady Maeve decides to speak again, to put a crossbow bolt in Lady Emille's leg, if you please."

"What do you want?" Emille asked.

"Oh, don't look so grim, Lady Emille," Bethesa said. "I do not want anything so terrible. Nothing that will cause you to break a sweat, anyway. I simply need you to explain to the guild that Lady Maeve, here, is a traitor, one who is responsible for the murder of Guildmaster Agnes's personal servant and who, when Tribune Silrika discovered her treachery, killed her."

"You want me to lie," Emille said.

"Ain't as if you haven't done it before, is it?" Bethesa asked, smiling. "After all, it is my understanding that for the vast majority of your marriage your husband was unaware of your membership in the guild, was he not?" She made a *tsking* sound. "I have never been married myself—some folks just ain't made for it, I guess. Never really had the desire. Oh, men have their place, but I was always of the opinion—when I thought of them at all—that they were useless anywhere except in the bedroom, and often there as well, more's the pity. Still, it was my understandin' that it is frowned upon to lie about something so monumental to your husband. Or am I wrong?"

"Leave Ned out of it," Emille said. "He doesn't have anything to do with any of this."

"Come now, Lady Emille," Bethesa said, giving the woman a smile that looked almost pitying. "Surely you don't really believe that. You already said you reckoned me a monster, ain't that right? So is it that you've changed your mind, or are you under the impression that even a monster would not make your husband pay for your crimes? Either way, I can attest that you're wrong."

"What does that mean?" Emille asked, and Maeve could hear the fear in her voice as she spoke.

Bethesa smiled by way of answer, a smile that was, in its way, even worse than that inhuman, alien smile the creature had favored them with. "It means that an unfortunate truth of war, Lady Emille, is that there are always casualties. In war, even the innocent suffer, and let us be honest—your husband is far from innocent. After all, a saint would not have done what he and Robert did. But enough of that for now," she went on, waving her hand dismissively. "Understand, I do not judge your husband harshly for his decisions—he did what he believed he needed to do to achieve his goals. And so, Lady Emille, will I."

Emille said nothing in response, but Maeve fancied that she could feel the woman's despair from where she stood. Bethesa, it seemed, felt it too, for she smiled. "You think me evil, Emille...perhaps you are right to think so. But as long as you do not cross me, your dear, beloved husband, need not find out just how evil I can be." She turned to regard Piralta. "Prepare them for what we expect—there is no time to waste. After all, the Festival of the Sun approaches. It would be best if this were all settled by then."

Maeve didn't like the sound of that. "Why?" she asked. "What happens at the festival?"

Bethesa gave her a cunning smile. "Why, festivities, of course. Have you never been to one, Maeve? You really ought to—they are quite enjoyable. Oh, but then I s'pose you won't be makin' this one either. A shame, but then life's like that, sometimes, ain't it? It's a shame you'll miss the show, but I s'pose there's no help for it."

"What does that mean?" Maeve said. "What show?"

"Don't you never mind about that," Bethesa said. "You got plenty enough to concern you already, don't you think? After all, once the guild learns what you done, well, these ain't the sort of folk that are known for forgiveness. Or maybe I'll let that creature have you—didn't seem to care for you much, that one. Did seem hungry, though, didn't he? Or she? I ain't real sure which myself. Hungry though, that I'm sure of. But then, I reckon their kind always are."

"The festival," Maeve said, doing her best to ignore the rest. "You're doing something there, aren't you?"

The tribune frowned. Either annoyed that her threat didn't have the desired effect, or else—and Maeve thought this more likely—annoyed that she had given away more than she'd intended. "Were I you, Maeve, I'd focus on the troubles before me instead of goin' lookin' for more. I ain't ever been ate before, but it seems to me that it'd be the sort of thing that'd demand one's attention." She glanced at Piralta, motioning. "Go on then, Piralta. Continue."

The man bowed his head. "Of course, Tribune. As I mentioned," he went on, turning to regard Emille, "the trial to determine the guilty party regarding these crimes—"

"A determination you've already made," Emille said.

"What can I say?" Bethesa said, giving her a smile. "I do hate surprises. Leastways, unless I'm the one doin' the surprisin'. Now, keep quiet and let Piralta speak—trust me, you'll want to hear this. It concerns you. But then, not *just* you."

"The trial takes place in three days' time," Piralta said. "You will be called to testify to your time spent in Lady Maeve's company while she served as guildmaster, to make a determination on her guilt or innocence. It is expected that you will be sure to include specific instances in which you became increasingly sure that she had betrayed the guild and, more, the people of the Known Lands. Starting with the fact that she tried to kill Guildmaster Agnes so that she might take over her position within the guild."

"See, we don't just need you to tell 'em," Bethesa said, "we need you to convince 'em. And don't worry—you ain't the only one'll be testifyin' to Maeve's evil. Why Joseph and Phillip here will as well, just to name a few."

Maeve glanced at the two men who had once served as her bodyguards. Joseph gave her a small, cruel smile while Phillip refused to meet her gaze.

"Even with them lying, even with me lying, it'll make no difference," Emille said. "No one in the guild is going to believe Maeve is a traitor, and you're a fool if you think so."

"Now, I'm not so sure about that, Lady Emille," Bethesa said. "I believe in you. Oh, I don't think it'll be easy, mind. Plenty of the folks in the guild grew up on stories of just how marvelous our Marvelous Maeve here is, how brave and deadly and beautiful and all the rest. But I still believe in you. See, it's amazing what folks can do with the proper motivation."

"You're a fool," Emille said. "Even if I were the best liar in the world, they wouldn't believe it."

Bethesa sighed. "Well, I hope you're wrong, Lady Emille. For your husband's sake. Tell me, what's our Neddard been up to lately anyway? Gettin' up to some foolishness or another, I expect—it's what men are best at. And your Ned, well, from what I've heard he shows a real knack for it. If nothin' else, he did marry an assassin, didn't he?" she finished, smiling as if she'd just told a particularly funny joke.

"You wouldn't...you couldn't..."

"Oh, come now, Lady Emille," Bethesa said in a voice that was almost soothing. "Of course I would, honey. If it meant gettin' what I wanted," she went on in that soft voice, "I'd tear your husband's entrails out with my bare hands while he still lived. I don't reckon it'd even bother me all that much, save havin' to clean up afterward. And—"

"You're a monster," Emille said, sounding horrified.

"You said that already," Bethesa said. "I won't waste time quibblin', will only say that I'm a woman who will do what needs to be done to get what she wants. And in case you haven't noticed by my wrinkled face and spotted hands, I ain't got all that much time to waste. Would I kill your husband, destroy everyone and everything you have ever cared about to get you to do what I want? Sure. Of course I would. And as for *could*. Well, that's already in the works."

"What do you mean? What are you saying?"

"What I'm sayin', Lady Emille," Bethesa said as if it was the most obvious thing in the world, "is that I've bet everythin', my reputation, my position, my *life* on this. I wouldn't make such a bet lightly, wouldn't make it 'less I already knew what the cards were goin' to show before they were turned. You'll do what's required of you, of that I'm certain."

"You don't have him," Emille said. "Ned, he's strong. Stronger than you think—he won't—"

"You're right," Bethesa said. "I don't have him. Not yet. But its bein' seen to. Your Neddard, he's been spendin' an awful lot of time at the castle lately, hasn't he, Lady Emille?" She waggled her eyebrows. "Hope he ain't got no secret lover. That'd be a damn shame, wouldn't it? A hard way for your love story to end. But then…not the hardest way. We'll have dear Neddard as a guest in the next few hours, I expect—by mornin' at the latest. I ain't concerned about that in the least. My only concern is that Balderath leaves enough of him intact to threaten you with. Not much good pokin' holes in a corpse, is it?"

"You sent the Brutal?" Emille said, her voice barely more than a whisper, like that of a terrified child.

"For such an important guest as your Neddard? Why, only the best, of course. Balderath, he's a fine one for deliverin' an invitation, and he can be quite persuasive. But then, you already know that, don't you?"

Emille didn't speak then, and Maeve understood. There were a lot of bad people in the Assassins' Guild. Those who killed simply for coin and, worse, for the pleasure of it, the coin no more than an added bonus. Balderath was one of the latter. But not just *one* of them—he was the epitome of the latter. A man who enjoyed killing simply for killing's sake. He had made a name for himself by not just enjoying taking life but by enjoying taking it in the most terrible, horrific, most *brutal* way possible. Balderath the Brutal they called him, and he had not come by the name on accident.

Maeve found herself scared and furious for Emille's sake. "You might think you are winning, Bethesa," she said, "and you can smile as smugly as you please now. But know this—I am going to kill you. Maybe not today and maybe not tomorrow. But I *will* kill you. You said that I enjoy a reputation in the guild for being the best that came out of it? Know then, that you have made an enemy of me, and come what may, I will stare down at your corpse, before the end."

The old tribune's eyes widened as Maeve spoke, then she gave an exaggerated shiver. "My but that's quite a speech, Maeve. Enough to keep a woman up at night, sure enough. But then, at my age, I don't get much sleep anyway, so that's no great loss. Now, while I've enjoyed our little chat, I'm afraid I really must be goin'. As it turns out, orchestratin' a trial to find someone guilty of betrayin' the guild and of high treason is a lot more work than you'd expect. Almost enough to make me regret doin' it in the first place." She grinned, giving a wink. "Almost. You all sit tight now—don't go anywhere." She cackled at that then turned and motioned at Piralta and they headed toward the door.

The two tribunes filed out, and the guards began to walk out behind them. Phillip shot what might have been an ashamed glance at Maeve as they were leaving.

"Some bodyguard you turned out to be," Maeve called after him.

The man flushed and looked as if he might say something, but another of his fellows, the one named Joseph, gave his shoulder a slap. "Don't worry about that, bitch," he said. "She's just barkin' on account of that's all she can do. Come on—let's go."

Phillip looked at Maeve for another minute, as if he wanted to say something. He even went so far as to open his mouth to speak but, in the end, he only closed it again. He gave his fellow a nod and then they were disappearing through the doorway along with the others, leaving Emille and Maeve alone. But not *quite* alone. Another had come among them. One who, perhaps, ought to have been there before, but had not. Or, at least, had only been there in part.

Fear. Maeve could feel its presence in the room, in *her*. Fear not just for herself, not even for what the feyling planned to do to her, if given its way. Fear, mostly, for Chall and for Ned.

"What do we do, Maeve?" This from Emille, and although there was a wall separating them, Maeve didn't need to see the woman to know that she was terrified.

"Ned will be okay, Emille," she told the woman, told herself. "They all will. *We* will be okay. We'll find a way out of here, out of this, and when we do…the promise I made to Bethesa was not an idle one. We will put an end to her, an end to everything that she and Robert Palden and Lady Valencia and whoever else are responsible for."

"But how, Maeve?" Emille asked.

"I'm working on it," Maeve said.

"She sent Balderath, Maeve. You know...*everyone* knows..." She trailed off then, apparently unable to finish.

"You're right," Maeve said. "Everyone does know. But I have met your husband, have spoken with him on several occasions, so while everyone might not know, *I* know that he is a formidable man, and I would bet on him against half a dozen Balderaths any day of the week."

"Yes...but Balderath won't have gone alone," Emille said quietly. "It's important to Bethesa. She would have sent others. To...to make sure."

"No," Maeve said. "No, he wouldn't have gone alone. But Ned is not alone either, Emille. He has friends. Chall and Valden, Malex at the castle. Vorrun. They're all good men, all men who wouldn't stand by and let something happen to Ned."

"If they saw it coming," Emille said. "Balderath and the others... they're assassins, Maeve. Not soldiers."

Maeve winced. That was true enough. She was trying to convince Emille that Ned was going to be alright, that *they* would be alright, but she felt that the woman was convincing her otherwise instead. "Ned is a clever man, Emille," she said. "So are Priest and Chall. I'm sure that Ned and the others are absolutely fine. Probably they've already figured out what's going on with Lady Valencia's betrayal and Robert Palden, got all of it solved, and are sitting around with their feet propped up, having a drink."

"I hope you're right, Maeve," Emille said. "I really do."

So do I, Maeve thought. *So do I.*

CHAPTER FOURTEEN

"Come on, Priest," a voice said, coming from a very long way off. "*Just hang on. One foot in front of the other. You've done it a thousand times—there's nothin' to it.*"

It was a man's voice, one he thought he recognized, but he could not be sure. He felt lost, unmoored. Like a boat long anchored finally cast free and left to the fickle will of the ocean's wild currents in storm. He felt as if, his entire life, he had been anchored, but that now that thing to which he'd been moored, that *self* to which he'd been moored was gone, and he was left to be tossed this way and that, not in a literal storm but instead in a storm of emotion brought on by Ned's use of the Art.

Anger, mostly, anger greater than any he had ever felt in his life, anger that made him want to lash out at everyone and everything, including himself. But as the storm seemed to grow in strength instead of subsiding, there was another emotion. Fear. Fear that, by the time the storm settled, he would no longer be himself. Fear that it would never settle at all.

"Come on, Priest," the voice urged, and the small part of his mind that wasn't consumed by the storm was aware of someone pulling at his arm. *"It ain't much further now."*

"I...I can't..." he told the voice or thought he did. "It's too...the storm..."

"*Yeah, I know,*" the voice said. "*It'll get worse before it gets better, I'm afraid. But it* will *get better, Priest. You just have to hold on. Just hold on.*"

And he tried. He really did. As his blurred, confused vision got snatches of buildings, as some part of him was vaguely aware of the fact that he was being led down one alleyway and another, aware, too, of a sharp pain in his side, he tried to hold on. The problem, though, was that there didn't seem to be anything to hold on *to*. He was like a man falling, plummeting off a cliff face—*pushed* off it, perhaps—his hands now grasping desperately for a handhold and finding nothing.

At least, that was, until a voice echoed in his mind.

You have something that keeps you you. You hold on to it, understand? Hold onto it as hard as you can for as long as you can.

And Priest *did* have that anchor. He had lost it, for a time, but he'd found it again. Or, rather, had been *shown* to it. By Brother Elmer, by Chall, and Matt, by Maeve, and by the man guiding him forward, through the storm.

Faith.

Faith that things would work out, that as dark as the night got, the morning would come again. Faith that for all the cruelties of the world, all its many evils, there were just as many kindnesses, just as much good. Faith that Raveza, the Goddess of Temperance, had not forgotten him.

It was that faith that kept him going, that kept the battered, wave-tossed vessel that was *him* from being swallowed up by that dark, churning water. And he did what the voice had told him.

He grabbed hold of his faith, wrapped his arms around it...and he held on. It was not easy—no more than a man, finding purchase on an up-jutting bit of rock in the middle of a great, tempestuous ocean might find it easy to hold on to its algae-slick surface. But he held on anyway. As hard as he could. For as long as he could.

"*Just...a little further,*" the voice told him, but Priest barely heard it, was barely aware of anything at all save the effort.

Some time passed. How much or how little, he had no idea. All he knew was that the part of him that existed in the physical world was finding it increasingly difficult to walk, each step harder than the last, just as the part of his mind caught in that terrible storm was finding it harder and harder to hold on. Harder and harder to remember *why* he was holding on in the first place.

Eventually, his guide led him off the street and to the front door of a dark building. His vision was still blurred, but he got the impression that it was a shop of some sort, though he couldn't make out the words written on the sign, and so the purpose of the shop itself remained a mystery. No light shone from within the building, at least not that Priest could see, and he heard his guide mutter a curse.

"Just hope Bert hasn't chosen tonight of all nights to stay home," the voice muttered, then a moment later he knocked on the door. He knocked normally, Priest was sure of it, yet the sound felt too loud, too *sharp,* and he found himself wincing.

"Right, sorry about that," his companion said, glancing at him. "That sort of working can be a bit...harsh. But don't worry over much—it'll wear off."

Priest nodded numbly—at least he thought he did, though he could just as easily have been wrong, for that algae-slick rock that kept him steadied in the storm seemed to be growing slicker and slicker by the moment, and it took all his attention to keep hold of it.

They waited for a moment, and his guide grunted. "Damnit." He knocked again, louder this time, and Priest seemed to feel each knock as if it was coming from inside himself.

They waited, and Priest staggered, would have fallen had his companion not caught him, draping his arm over his own. "Come on," he said. "This ain't workin' and we gotta find some place, see to your wound quick. I ain't a healer like Em, but even I know we can't go on much longer like this."

Wound? Priest thought. He meant to ask the question aloud but, just then, he barely had the strength to stand, to *think* let alone speak.

His guide was just beginning to lead them away from the shop when the front door opened a crack and a craggy face with a gray beard and short gray hair scowled out at the night. "We're closed," the man said. "Find your way back tomorrow, and—" The old man cut off, raising a bushy eyebrow. "Wait a minute. That you, Ned?"

Ned, Priest thought. *Of course, his name's Ned.* How had he forgotten that?

"It's me, Bert. Find your way back—that a cartographer joke?"

"If it is, it ain't a good one," the man said. "Anyway, sorry about answerin' the way I done—I thought you were a customer."

There was a snort from somewhere inside, out of sight. *"Don't let him lie to you,"* another man's voice called. *"Been so long since Bert seen a customer, I doubt he'd remember what one looked like."*

The man, Bert, scowled, shooting a glance behind him. "Well, you'd know, wouldn't you, you dirty old bastard? Considerin' you're here as much as I am." He glanced back at them. "Good to see you anyway, Neddy. Where's our girl?"

"Em's...gone, Bert."

The old man frowned, squinting out at the night. "What's wrong with your friend, there? Everythin' alright, Ned?"

"Not really, Bert, no," Ned said, glancing behind them at the street "Can we come in?"

It wasn't easy to tell for sure with his blurred vision, but it seemed to Priest that the man looked at Ned as if he were a fool. "You know you're always welcome here, lad. Come on in."

He swung the door wide and then they were moving through it. Priest was feeling weaker by the moment, and he knew that had Ned not been holding his arm, he would have fallen.

They stepped into a large room, and Priest noted shelves lining the wall, all with rolled parchments of various sizes decorating them. The few parts of the wall that weren't taken up by shelves were plastered with various maps, some depicting the borders of the Known Lands, some of New Daltenia and its outlying areas, and others, he saw, that appeared to depict Daltenia the way it had been before the Skaalden had come.

"You're a mapmaker," Priest said, his voice sounding weak and thready even to himself.

"And you're bleedin'," the man observed, glancing at the floor. Priest followed his gaze and was surprised to see that he was right; there were several drops of blood staining it. The man raised his gaze then let out a grunted curse. "Shit, fella. Is that a damned crossbow bolt stickin' out of you?"

"What?" Priest asked. "No, it—" He looked down and even through his numb, confused mind, he felt a shock as he saw that, indeed, there was a crossbow bolt sticking out of him. "I...it's a crossbow bolt. It...we were in a bit of...well—"

"You can tell me the why of it later, how'd that be? For now, let's get you patched up before you bleed out all over my floor. I ain't much on cleanin'."

Another snort. "You can say that again—why Bert here's started namin' his dust bunnies."

Bert scowled at the back of the room where an old man stood, holding what appeared to Priest to be a crossbow. "Keep it up, wise-ass. And put that damned crossbow down before you kill somebody."

"Can't be too careful these days," the man said. "I been tellin' you, you ought to get a better lock for that door. Wouldn't take no more than a cool breeze to push the thing open and what with you sleepin' here... well. I'd sure hate to show up and see someone had stolen what little virtue you got left."

"To show up you'd have to leave first," Bert grumbled. "Now, if you're done wavin' that thing around and puttin' all our lives at jeopardy, why don't you go and heat some water. Best get my bandages and tools while you're at it."

"Been a while since you used 'em."

"Not long enough," Bert said grimly. He turned back to Priest and Ned, grabbing Priest's free arm and draping it over his shoulders. "Come on then—there's a cot in the back. Nothin' fancy, but it'll serve."

With one arm draped over Ned's shoulder and the other over the older man, Priest allowed himself to be led toward the back door by which the crossbowman had first emerged. Not that he could have done much to argue. Between whatever Ned had done and his wound, he felt drained, hollowed out. He didn't walk so much as he was carried between the two men, for he had no strength left. Even speaking seemed too much of an effort.

They walked past row after row of maps covering seemingly every landscape, grandiose or minute, that a person might imagine until they reached the door. The room they stepped into appeared to have once been an office, but Bert had, it seemed, eschewed the typical desk and chosen instead to go with a table. A circular table at which three other people currently sat, all of them appearing to be near an age with Bert himself, what Priest would have expected to be around their mid-sixties. There were two men and a woman. Despite their age, the two men looked muscular, broad-shouldered, and there was something in their faces, in the way they sat, that made Priest believe they were capable of violence if violence was called for.

Like two hammers waiting for something to hit, maybe. The woman was smaller, but what she lacked in size compared to the men she made up in some indefinable quality, one Priest couldn't quite put his finger on except to think that she seemed...dangerous. A dagger to the men's hammer. A dagger might not smash the way a hammer would, but then, if it was sharp enough, the dagger didn't need to, and something about the woman, about the way she watched him and the others as they made their way across the room, told him that she was plenty sharp.

"Need some help, Cap?" she asked, looking at Bert, and there was something about her tone, about the way she said it that made Priest think she meant more than just to ask if he needed a hand. A dagger, it seemed to his half-delirious mind, wondering if it needed to leave its sheath. "Boots and blades, is it?"

At first, Priest thought he must have heard the woman wrong, her seemingly nonsensical words no more than the product of his delirious mind. But a moment later, Bert answered, and he realized that he was not the only one who had heard them after all.

"Not yet anyway," Bert answered the woman, and if he thought anything strange about her words, he didn't show it. "This way," Bert went on, turning back to Priest and Ned. "Not much further."

Priest wanted to tell him that was good as he didn't think he had much further in him, but the truth was he didn't even have it in him to tell the man as much, so he remained silent as they led him to another door at the back of the office. This led into a small storeroom. Dusty shelves littered with more scrolls and maps lined the walls, and in between them, at the opposite end of the room, sat a small cot. A fold-out table of the kind Priest had seen on campaign during the Fey War sat beside the cot and upon it he saw a small, framed painting of a woman. Beside this sat a bottle of wine, one that appeared to be nearly empty.

This he saw as the two men led him to the cot and Bert let loose of Priest to move forward, sweeping an arm out to knock the several books that had been scattered on the cot onto the floor. "Sorry 'bout that," he said, glancing back at Priest and Ned. "Like I said before and as Neddy here'll tell you, I ain't much on cleanin'."

They laid Priest down, and though he knew they did their best to be gentle, he hissed in pain as the movement tugged at the wound where the crossbow bolt still rested.

He was sweating by the time he was settled on the cot, his side burning like fire, his vision blurry from exhaustion and pain.

"That's alright now," a voice said, and Priest was so given to the pain and weariness, so consumed by it, *transported* by it, that he was not sure even which of the two blurred figures above him had spoken.

"How bad is it?" a voice asked.

"Well, bein' as you ain't a healer, you might not know this, but most men's sides come without a crossbow bolt stickin' out of 'em. So, considerin' that, I'd say it ain't ideal."

"He'll be okay, though?" the voice, *Ned*, Priest thought, asked.

Priest was pretty eager to hear the answer to that one, but when the voice he thought to be Bert spoke, it gave him no comfort. "That bottle there, on the shelf. Hand it to me, will ya? Helps ease the pain."

The next thing Priest knew, his head was being lifted up, and a foul, thick liquid was poured down his throat. He gagged but managed to keep it down, and in another moment he was lying down again.

"Tastes like death, I know," a voice said, "but it'll dull the sharpest edges of the pain."

And almost instantly Priest realized, even as the viscous, oily liquid worked its way down his throat and into his stomach, seeming to leave a trail of coolness he could feel, that the man was right. The worst of the pain did, indeed, abate. Nearly all of it, in fact, and in seconds he had settled into a thick numbness, as if he'd just sank into a snowbank of soft, new snow.

The last thought he had before sleep took him was that the small, military-style cot with its threadbare sheets was far more comfortable than it had any right to be.

He awoke some time later.

At least, mostly. Priest's eyes felt heavy, as if someone had tied weights to his eyelids while he slept, and his brain felt fuzzy, as if it had been stuffed with wool. Still, with an effort, he managed to open his eyes and saw Bert's face peering down at him from a couple of feet above him.

"Ah, you're alive," the old man said. "Guess Gene owes me some coin."

Priest opened his mouth to answer but was overcome with a sudden yawn. "Sorry," he said, feeling very disoriented. "And...good afternoon?"

"Night, I'm afraid," Bert said, "and don't worry about it. The stuff I gave you, it steals more than a little of a man's wits along with the pain. Probably why it works in the first place as, it seems to me, it's our wits that cause us the most damage, in the end. Anyway, the effects ought to wear off soon."

Priest nodded numbly, then glanced down at his stomach. It was thickly wrapped with bandages that were tied around his waist. "Am I...?"

"Going to die?" Bert asked, raising a gray eyebrow. "'Fraid so. It's the only way out of this shit-show we call life. Still, it won't be today, so that's somethin'. And if it's your little accessory you're lookin' for, it's just there," he went on, jerking his thumb at the small table Priest had seen when they'd entered the room. The portrait and the bottle of wine were gone, replaced by several instruments, most stained with what he could only imagine was his blood, as well as a crossbow bolt, also so stained. "I can bag it, if you'd like. A bit of a souvenir."

"No...no thanks," Priest said.

Bert grunted. "Can't say I blame you. Anyway, why bother luggin' that thing around—the scar'll do nice enough to remind you, if you're ever wantin' remindin'. And even if you don't. That's what scars do, after all."

"Spoken like a man who has some scars of his own," Priest observed.

The old man grunted. "Might be that's true. But then I reckon that's true of everyone. A man lives long enough—and in my experience that ain't long at all—life's bound to knock him around some."

Priest had plenty of his own scars, those visible and those not, so he had no intention of disagreeing. Anyway, scars weren't on his mind.

Instead, he found himself curious about the man before him, about the others, too, those he had seen seated at the table.

"The woman—she called you 'Cap' before."

"She did," the older man said, watching him.

"Short for 'Captain'?"

"Reckon so," Bert said. "Anyway, I try not to hold it against her. After all, I've called her worse than that—never to her face, mind. Joan ain't the sort of woman a man offends, not if he can help it and certainly not more than once."

Priest had only seen the woman for a few brief moments, but there had been something in her posture, in her face—and in all those that had been gathered at the table—that had given him that impression.

"So…"

The other man gave a small smile, shaking his head. "Me and Joan—the others, too. We've known each other for a long time. A man gets to my age, his past becomes like a weight, like some great chain stretched out behind him. Might be he wants to leave pieces of it, *forget* pieces of it, but he can't. Not anymore'n he can leave or forget pieces of himself. After all, that's what a fella's past is, it seems to me. Himself. All the best and worst bits followin' him wherever he goes. Now, I ain't in charge of nothin' but this here shop, and that's the way I like it. The only leadin' I do is myself to the privy or maybe when I help that silly bastard Eugene home on nights when he's had too much to drink. Which is just about every night."

"Eugene," Priest repeated. "The one with the crossbow?"

"That's right."

"He looked comfortable with it," Priest said. "Like he'd held one before."

Bert gave him a small smile. "You're the sort of fella likes to ask a question without askin' it, ain't you?"

"I didn't mean to cause offense," Priest said.

"That's good, as I didn't take any," the other man said. "And to answer the question you didn't ask, yes, Eugene has held a crossbow once upon a time. A bow too. And while I would never tell him so, he's the finest shot I've ever seen. Or at least was before his vision started to go."

"He's got something wrong with his eyes?"

"Yeah," Bert said, nodding. "They're old. Like the rest of him. Like the rest of us. You'll learn one day that a fella gets old, his body starts to go on him a little at a time. I ain't complainin', understand—there's plenty of folks that don't make it this far. Besides, it has occurred to me that maybe all the knee aches, all the back pains and blurred vision ain't nothin' but the gods' way of tellin' us to slow down. *Makin'* us slow down and relax a little. After all, runnin' around, chasin' this thing or that woman, well, that's a young man's game. Old men—old women, too—we ain't much for runnin'. Make some damn fine sitters, though."

"Well if it weren't for you and your help, I don't think I would have had a chance at making it to old age, so thank you," Priest said.

Bert waved a dismissive hand, clearly uncomfortable with gratitude. "It ain't nothin'. You weren't so bad as all that. Barely more'n a scratch. Nothin' a little needle and thread couldn't put to rights."

Priest was no healer himself, but he had been around enough of them to be pretty confident that the man was making light of it. Certainly, it felt like more than a scratch. "You seemed to know what you were doing," he said.

"There you go again," the old man said, barking a laugh. "Yeah, there was a time when I used to be considered a healer, I s'pose. A long time ago, part of that past I was tellin' you about."

"So, if you don't mind my asking," Priest said, giving the man a smile, "what made you become a mapmaker instead?"

The other man's smile faded at that, and his eyes took on a distant cast, as if he were looking into the past at some painful memory, perhaps quite a few of them. "Ain't easy, gettin' older. It's a trip a fella starts on with a bunch of others. Ones he meets along the way. But as he keeps walkin', a lot of 'em, they fall by the way-side, 'til he's traveled long enough, he takes a moment to look around and sees there ain't all that many left. Not many at all." He shrugged. "Guess I'd seen enough of blood. Maps, they don't die. They don't scream their wife or their mother's name while they breathe their last, lookin' for you to help and you with no help to give." He shook his head, seeming to banish those memories with a visible effort. "Any rate, I had to do somethin' and jugglin' was out of the question." He held up his hands as he spoke. Only Priest realized as he stared at them that the man only had one. His other arm ended at the wrist, a nub over which was strapped a leather cap.

"You lost your hand."

"Wouldn't say lost," Bert said. "I know exactly where I left it. Remember that all too well, in fact. You know—sorry, I just realized I never got your name."

"Valden," Priest said. "But everyone calls me Priest."

"Better'n some of the names I've been called," Bert said. "Anyway, it seems to me, Priest, that folks always talk about a fella leavin' his past behind him. What they rarely mention is that, sometimes, he leaves pieces of himself along with it. Certainly, I did. But that's alright. Losin' my hand, in some ways, was the greatest thing that ever happened to me."

"You don't often hear that."

"Maybe not," Bert said, "but it's true. Anyway, a lot of folks lost a lot more'n their hand that day, so I can't complain. Not when there's so many corpses that'd have plenty more to complain about than me, if only they could."

"Did you lose it during the Fey War?"

Bert shook his head. "Before that. My hand, see, is back in Daltenia. Leastways, whatever's left of it." He reached his other hand to the leather cap covering his wrist. It was secured with a buckle and leather strap around his forearm which he unbuckled before pulling it away. A moment later he removed the cap. Then he began to unwind the bandages wrapped around the nub of his wrist.

Priest had been in too many battles to count, had fought men—and creatures—to the death, had been *surrounded* by death more times than he cared to think about. He had seen men killed and wounded by nearly every means imaginable, had seen wounds of all shapes and sizes, those that killed a man and those that only left him wishing he were dead. He would have said, if asked, that he had seen just about every type of wound one could think of, certainly more than he would *want* to think of...

But he had never seen anything like this.

In other instances in which he'd seen that someone had lost a limb in battle, it was often an uneven cut—battlefield warfare often lacked the accuracy and precision of a capable barber surgeon. This, Bert's wrist shared in common with the others. But that was about all. As Bert finished pulling the last of the bandages away, Priest saw that the end of the wound—seemingly everywhere that might have been struck by whatever weapon or beast had taken off the man's his hand—was a whitish blue. Almost like..."Is that..." he began.

"Ice," Bert confirmed. "It's frozen. Been like that since the day I received it. S'pose I ought to be grateful—the barber surgeon on the ship I was on when we fled Daltenia didn't have to cauterize the wound. Or rather, he couldn't. Couldn't get the ice to melt."

"So what did he do?" Priest asked.

Bert shrugged. "There were other folks to see to, so he saw to 'em. Wished me luck before he left—to be honest, I don't think the bastard expected me to live through the night. But then I always have been stubborn—least, Eugene's always tellin' me as much, and while I do like to make it a point of disagreein' with him, I don't s'pose I can here."

"It's...frozen?" Priest asked. "But shouldn't it have...that is..."

"Thawed?" Bert asked. "Yeah, you'd think so. But it hasn't."

Priest stared at the wound in disbelief, finding it difficult to look away. A barber surgeon, when operating on such a wound, was always forced to cauterize it lest the unfortunate soul who'd received it die from blood loss. Because of this, the wounds were always covered in scar tissue, making it difficult to see much. This, though...this was different. He could see it all clearly, the man's bones and the rest of it—could see far more than he wished to, in truth. According to what he'd said, he'd had the wound for years, but it appeared to Priest as if he had only just received it. "You said that this, this is the best thing that ever happened to you?"

Bert grinned. "Yeah. Life can be funny like that. A man might stub his toe and stop to comfort his aching foot only to avoid bein' run over by a wagon. Or he might trip and fall into a hole in the forest only to discover that there's treasure hidden there, treasure he never would have found if he hadn't fallen in the first place. And me, I found my treasure."

"Oh?" Priest asked, his eyes moving around the humble shop of their own accord.

The older man grunted. "There's treasure, lad—gold and riches, diamonds and all the rest—and then there's *treasure*."

"What sort of treasure did you find when you...tripped, then?"

"The best kind," Bert said. "Anyway, let's leave it at that for now. It's a long story and we got more pressin' matters to attend to."

"Your wrist, if it's frozen, then...isn't it..."

"Cold?" Bert asked. "Yeah. Always."

"I...I can't imagine what that's like."

"Sure, you can," the old man said, grinning. "Just stick your hand in a frozen lake and leave it there for decades. You'll get a pretty good idea."

"That must be unbearable."

"Nah, it ain't so bad as that. Losin' to Eugene at cards, now that's unbearable. Or watchin' Blunder—that's one of the two brothers you saw seated at the table when we led you in—try to figure one of the puzzle boxes he always carries around, that's unbearable. Enough to make a man want to track down the bastard that made it and give him a piece of his mind. Or blade. This..." he went on, looking at his wrist. "Well. S'pose I never have to worry about my drinks gettin' hot, do I?"

"One of the Skaalden did it?"

"Great big bastard," Bert confirmed, nodding, his face taking on a faraway cast as he looked back over the years. "He wasn't there one minute and the next he was. And not just him—a great big axe, too. One that I swear to this day seemed made of ice. Felt like it, too."

"The axe. It's what took your hand."

"That's right," Bert said. "Like winter itself took a bite out of me, it was. Ain't never felt pain like that, not before and not since. Thought for sure I was goin' to die just from the shocked pain of it—like jumpin' into a frozen lake, only a thousand times worse."

"But you didn't," Priest said.

Bert barked a laugh. "Not on account of anythin' I did, I can tell you that. Eugene and Joan, Blunder and Thunder, they're the only reason I made it onto the ship. Them and a few others," he went on grimly. "Others that weren't so lucky." He sighed. "Lost a lot of friends that day."

"I'm sorry."

Bert waved a dismissive hand. "I ain't the only one and that's a fact. It was a tough day, is all. Tough day all 'round. But enough of the past. A man can get lost there, and that's a dangerous thing, particularly when he's got trouble in the present. Trouble like what you and Neddy are into."

Priest started to respond then hesitated. The man had saved his life, and it was clear from what he'd seen of their brief interaction when he and the carriage driver had arrived that Ned trusted him, but he didn't know the *extent* of that trust. It was one thing, after all, to trust a man to let you in, to patch up a friend of yours. It was quite another to trust him with the knowledge that the two of you were being hunted by assassins, assassins who would possibly reward anyone who decided to assist them in their endeavor and who would *certainly* punish anyone who made it more difficult.

Bert barked a laugh. "You're a careful one, aren't you?"

"In my experience," Priest said, giving the man an apologetic smile, "the careful ones live longer."

"Fair enough," the old man said. "A fella spends the night hunted by assassins, it's only natural he's a little foggy on who he can trust."

Priest raised his eyebrows at that.

"Oh sure," Bert said. "Neddy told me about your meet up with the Brutal and a few other assassins." He grunted, grinning. "Best relax those eyebrows, fella, else you'll end up misplacin' 'em in your hairline."

"Sorry," Priest said, "I'm just…that is—"

"Just surprised that an old codger like me would know about Balderath the Brutal?"

Priest winced. "Something like that."

Bert gave him a grin. "A fair point. Probably most mapmakers don't stay too apprised of assassins and criminal organizations and all the rest, so I get the confusion." He shrugged. "Call it a hobby, if you like. But in my experience, a man's ignorance makes a poor shield. And while the careful ones live longer, so, too, do the ones who keep themselves informed. It's a sort of maxim Ned'd likely tell you that I live by."

"Speaking of Ned, I was wondering—"

"Where he was?" Bert asked. "Well, I can tell you that I ain't got him locked up in a closet somewhere, if that's what you're thinkin'. He's restin'. He likely didn't say so—and wouldn't. Whatever else he is, Ned ain't much on complainin'. But when he uses the Art, his power…it has a way of takin' it out of him."

Priest couldn't help being surprised again. "He told you? About what happened?"

"Back at his house?" Bert asked. "Yeah, he told me. In between bouts of frettin' over whether or not you were goin' to be alright." He shook his head, rolling his eyes, but Priest could see that there was a fondness there, one the old man felt for the carriage driver. And maybe not just fondness but love, love of the kind a father might feel for a favored son. "But then he didn't need to. I could see it in him the moment I opened the door and saw you two standin' there. Well. He was standin'. You were mostly just leanin'. He doesn't like it—the power. Most men, they had a power like that, I reckon they'd spend their time practicin' it on talkin' this woman or that one into their bed, but not Neddy. Doesn't use it at all, not if he can help it. It's as if he's ashamed of it, though the gods alone know why that'd be. If there's a reason, it's one he ain't never shared, and I ain't asked. A man's business is his to share as he pleases. Anyway, if he used the Art to save the two of you then it means he thought there weren't any other choice, which means that it was pretty bad. After all, Ned might not act like it, but he's a damned fine fighter. One of the best I've ever seen. I'd put him up against one, even two Balderath the Brutals any day and be confident of the way the thing would end."

"There were nearly a dozen of them," Priest said. "They got the drop on us."

Bert grunted. "Never known Ned to let anyone get the drop on him." He grinned. "'Cept maybe Emmy, but then no matter how clever a man is there's always a woman somewhere ready to make him look a fool."

Priest winced again, feeling his face heat. "It was actually my fault. I didn't know he was being followed, and I showed up at his house. It...it was a mistake."

"Oh, don't worry yourself over it, lad," Bert said. "The only man doesn't make mistakes is one that ain't breathin.' The gods know I've made more'n my share. Anyway, I expect that ain't the only mistake you've made, is it?"

It sounded like an innocent enough question but there was something in the way the man watched him that made Priest think there was more to it.

But before he could speak and ask the man about it, Bert went on. "You said your name was Valden before. Ain't exactly a common name —not like Bert. In fact, I only ever heard of one Valden in my life. The one they used to call the Vicious. Can't say as I know the exact origin of the moniker, but I don't reckon its on account of he liked to pick flowers and pet puppy dogs. Fair to say?"

Priest winced. "Fair to say," he agreed. "I'll go," he went on, starting to rise.

The old man put a hand on his shoulder, easing him back down. "You ain't goin' any damn where," he said.

Priest tensed at that, considering what he should do, whether he should run, whether, given the wound he'd just taken, he even *could* run.

"I don't mean you no harm, fella," Bert said. "It's just that, a person gets shot with a crossbow bolt, the last thing he needs to do is try walkin' it off. So you got a past—who don't? And I can tell you, mine ain't all sunshine and rainbows. Anybody who tells you their past ain't got nothin' they're ashamed of is the world's damnedest liar. Now, just take it easy—you're safe here. Leastways, you're as safe as any livin' man can be."

Priest nodded slowly, allowing himself to ease back down onto the cot. "Thank you, Bert. For...well. For all your help."

Bert shrugged. "It ain't nothin'."

"It is, though," Priest said. "Most people, they wouldn't do all that you've done for a stranger. Let alone one with my...history."

"If Neddy knows you, then you ain't no stranger to me," the old man said. "Anyway, a man's past is his past for a reason. Don't mean it has to have anythin' to do with who he is. Besides, If Ned trusts you, then I trust you. He's always been a fine judge of character—except in Eugene's case. Why he likes that old bastard I'll never understand."

"Ned means a lot to you, doesn't he?"

"Naw, not that much," the old man said, rising and giving him a wink. "Just everythin'. Me and..." He paused, shaking his head, seeming to banish some sad memory. "I never had a child. Just wasn't in the cards for me, as Eugene'd say. The gods, they saw fit to make it so that my wife and I weren't able. Was a bit of a sore point for us, over the years, a wound that was left to fester. Then we met Neddy and Emille. They were old by then—grown into their bad habits, as my own father used to say, long ago. But turns out they didn't have all that many. We ended up gettin' pretty close, the four of us. See, Ned and Em, well they don't have parents—not ones still livin' anyway. And we didn't have kids." He shrugged. "Guess maybe it was fate, if you believe in that sort of thing. Ned ain't mine by blood—Em neither. But I'll tell you, Valden who goes by Priest," he went on, his expression growing serious, even grim, as he met Priest's gaze, "I love them as much as any one soul could love another. If anyone or anything means to do them harm, then *I* mean to make sure they got to come through me first."

"You're saying you'd give your life for them," Priest said.

"I'm sayin' I'd do a damn sight more'n that," Bert said. "Not that Ned would ever let me know enough to help him—he plays it close to the chest, that one. Does plenty of talkin'—if you've spent any time with him, you know how much he likes to run that mouth of his around, give it some exercise. But for all that it's damned near impossible gettin' the man to talk about—even *think* about—himself. And I guess he'd rather bleed out from a wound than complain about it and make himself an inconvenience."

Priest nodded. "That has been my impression of him. Since I returned to the city with Prince Bernard and the others, Ned has been extremely helpful. In fact, it is only because of him that I—and my friends—survived our first day and night in New Daltenia."

"By your friends, you mean Maeve the Marvelous, Challadius the Charmer, and of course the Crimson Prince, that right?"

"Yes. And Matt—the king."

Bert grunted. "High company, indeed. Anyhow, I guess I'd stand here and jaw for hours—I can be as bad as Gene or Neddy when the mood's on me. But since you're not in danger of bleedin' out—at least unless you get a couple of new holes poked in you—I reckon I ought to go give Neddy a look. As I said, usin' his Art takes a lot out of him. I've seen it. But I still ain't never seen him so exhausted as he looked when I found the two of you on my doorstep."

"Of course," Priest said.

The man moved to the door then paused, his hand on the door

handle as he glanced back. "Look, I know we're little better'n strangers to each other, but Neddy and Emmy…well, I guess they're about the only things in my life I've given a shit about in some time. If…that is…"

"If there is anything, by living or dying, that I can do to keep them safe, I will do it," Priest told the man. "You have my word."

The man let out a heavy sigh, nodding. "I appreciate that. Anyway, I'd suggest you get some rest—you've had a long day, and there ain't a thing in the world that can put a fella to rights as well as a good long nap. That said, if you feel the urge later on, you're welcome to come out into the room, play a hand of cards with Eugene and the others. Just so long as you don't mind the bastards cheatin' anytime they get an opportunity."

Priest grinned. "That…sounds great. And thanks again…for everything."

Bert winced, no more comfortable with gratitude now than he had been before. "Anyhow, you have to listen to them run their mouths a bit, you might not be feelin' so thankful. Now, I'll leave you to it." He turned, opening the door and stepping out.

Before the door closed behind the older man, Priest could make out the voices of several of the others that had been seated at the table when they'd arrived yelling friendly jibes and taunts, inviting him to play.

He found himself smiling at that as the door closed, muffling the sounds of their voices so that their words were indistinguishable. The man, however he might act, clearly cared for his friends, Eugene and all the rest, and they, no matter how *they* might act, clearly cared for him.

That made Priest think of his own friends, and slowly the smile faded. He missed them. As he lay there, he said a prayer to Raveza that, wherever they were, they were faring better than he. He wanted nothing more in that moment than to climb out of the cot, jump onto the nearest horse—stolen or bought—and ride to the castle so that he might speak with Chall, at least, might hopefully discover that Maeve had returned.

But of course that would be tantamount to suicide. Ned had made it clear that the Art he had used on the assassins was temporary. They would have come out of the grips of it by now and would no doubt be scouring the city in search of them.

No, he could not leave. Not yet, at least. He wanted to help his friends, wanted their help in turn, but he could not go to them, not yet. For the moment, they were on their own…and so was he.

As he lay there, the muffled sounds of voices coming from the other room, Priest wondered when he would see his friends again.

He wondered if he ever would.

Just then, he found Ned's words echoing in his mind. *Do you have something that anchors you, that makes you you?*

My faith, Priest had thought.

Then hold on to it, the man had told him, the memory told him again, in that moment.

And so Priest lay there, his side aching, the future uncertain, and he grasped his faith…

And he held on.

CHAPTER FIFTEEN

"...*are* many traditional activities that have begun to be included in the Festival as it has evolved over the years," Petran read, "*but none so traditional or well-received as the king's speech. And, just as important, perhaps even more so, is what follows, where the common people of the city are given a chance, by lottery, to speak to the king himself without having to wait the weeks, sometimes months required to attend such an audience at the castle. It is a chance for them to air their grievances, should they have any, or simply to speak with their sovereign ruler in person.*"

Petran glanced up at Chall apologetically, setting the book down, and Chall sank heavily back in his chair. "It goes on," the crown historian said. "Would you like me to..."

"Unless it ends with, 'and all of this was just a joke and not true in the slightest,' I really don't see the point."

Petran glanced back at the book. "I...I do not believe so."

"Well, I suppose it was too much to hope," Chall said, heaving a sigh.

"What now?"

"What now?" Chall echoed. "Well, now, Petran, I'd say we're pretty screwed. Unless you happen to have a spare king lying around, that is."

"The festival is still a week away," Petran offered. "Perhaps...perhaps Matt will return by then."

"Sure," Chall agreed. "Or maybe we can just, I don't know, convince everyone that it isn't the first day of spring after all, that they've got their dates wrong."

Petran winced at that, blushing, and Chall sighed.

"I'm sorry, Petran," he said. "I know you're just trying to help—I just act like a bit of an asshole when I'm stressed. Or sad. Or angry...well. Most times, really. Don't pay me any mind."

Petran inclined his head. "So then...what are we going to do?"

"I have no idea," Chall said honestly. "I'd like to ask Priest what he thought of it, but the bastard is out for a lark somewhere or another, probably resting with his feet up while I do all the work."

"Forgive my saying so, Challadius," Petran said, "but Valden—Priest—has never seemed, to me at least, to be the sort that would sit back and let others do work that needs doing."

Chall frowned. "Yeah, me neither. The bastard."

"I am sure that if Priest could be here, he would," Petran offered.

Chall scowled at the man. "Is that supposed to make me feel better? That if he could be here, he would, which means that he must be in trouble?" He shook his head. "Gods be good, Petran, for Beth's sake I hope your pillow talk is better than your pep talks."

The historian colored a deep shade of crimson at that. "I only meant that—"

"Relax, Petran," Chall said, waving his hand dismissively. "I know what you meant. And I appreciate it. I'm just worried, that's all. For Maeve and Priest...and Matt...and Prince Bernard...and me too, come to it."

Petran nodded slowly. "I understand. And for what it's worth, I'm sorry."

"Thank you, but you've nothing to apologize for. You've been nothing but a help to us, a help to the kingdom." He heaved a breath. "Well. The others will have to look after themselves as best they can. As must we. We won't help anybody by sitting around weeping." *And never mind that that's exactly what I wanted to do.* "We'll figure out the Festival later. We've got a week, anyway. Who knows? Maybe Matt *will* show up by then. So...I hate to even ask, given the way the day has been going. But...about the necklace. You don't happen to know anyone that's a Fey expert, do ya? Specifically one who knows anything at all about magical artifacts, at least anything more than that they glow pretty."

"Did you not learn about such things back in Daltenia, at the Academy? It was my understanding that they had classes on them."

Chall scowled. "They had lots of classes on lots of things. Seemed to me that anything a person could think of they had a class for it, and each and every one as dull as dishwater. For a young boy as I was, it was nothing short of torture and, by the way, that's coming from someone who has actually *been* tortured. Anyway, I was too distracted by girls."

"Girls?" Petran asked. "I was under the impression that boys and girls had separate classes at the Academy."

"What possible difference does that make?" Chall asked. "Petran, there is no one in all the world with an imagination as vivid as a young boy's when he begins to take notice of girls. No great bard or famed scribe, at his best, can hope to approach that. They almost felt like different creatures. *Better* creatures, come from a world better than our own. Don't you remember what it's like?"

Petran gave him a small smile, and there was something in the man's expression that made Chall certain he was thinking of the librarian, Elizabeth. "I am a historian, Challadius," the man said, meeting his gaze. "It is, quite literally, my *job* to remember. And as for the rest—that is, expertise on magical artifacts—I will admit that it is a bit of a niche field. There were not as many studies done on such things as there might have been back in Daltenia, and much of what we *did* know was lost. Or, at least, the knowledge that was written down in books and scrolls was abandoned when we fled the Skaalden invasion. I remember the library well. In those days, I served as page to the Crown Historian of the time—Leven Alquis. A fine man, if a bit...bookish."

Chall blinked. "Petran, I'm afraid to wonder at what it might take for you to call another man 'bookish'."

Petran smiled. "Yes, well. I and some of the other pages used to make some small jokes at Historian Alquis's expense, as young boys will, but in truth I admired the man. It is he who first taught me the worthiness of the pursuit of truth, no matter who or what it may offend, even if that offense is given to oneself. Perhaps *particularly* if it is given to oneself. He might have been distant, but he was kind, in his way, and everything that I am, everything that I have become, the luck that has befallen me, I owe all to Historian Alquis."

"That luck include being thrown into the dungeon and left to rot?" Chall asked.

Petran gave him another smile. "There is no cost too great, no price too high, when it comes to truth. Anyway, the reason I brought it up was because in those days my duties required much of my attention, but I still had some little free time available to myself. And much of that free time I spent at the Academy library."

Chall grunted. "You're saying that you spent the little bit of free time you had in a *library?*"

"Yes," Petran said, nodding, the poor fool seeming to have no idea why that might be considered strange.

"You know, Petran," Chall said, "I'm not sure whether you make me feel worse for myself or for you. I mean I went to the Academy for years as anyone who showed any aptitude for the Art did, and I counted it then—and now—as a point of pride that I can count on one hand the number of times I set foot in that library."

"Yes, well...I suppose we all enjoy different things."

Chall said. "And all of us enjoy some of the same things too," he grinned. "Seemed like you and that librarian were enjoying each other plenty when I showed up. Anyway, I know that you're a historian and all, but I'm afraid I don't have time for a history lesson just now. What I need is an expert in magical artifacts, particularly ones crafted by the Fey."

"And the necklace, you think it is such an artifact?"

Chall nodded. "I do."

"May I see it?"

"Have at it," Chall said, retrieving it from his pocket and handing it to the historian.

Petran took the necklace carefully, cradling it in two hands as he moved to the table and gingerly set it down before taking a seat. "It certainly seems to have the tell-tale color of Fey magic," Petran said thoughtfully, his voice barely loud enough for Chall to make out his words. The historian turned it this way and that, frowning, then after a moment he looked up at Chall. "What can you tell me about it?"

Chall winced. "Listen, Petran, I'd love to tell you all about it—shit, once I get this sorted, if you want, you and I can have a sit-down—though preferably somewhere, *anywhere* but here. For now, though, I'm in a hurry and quite frankly I've already wasted more time than I can afford. If you know anyone that is an expert on such matters as the necklace, I'd really love it if—"

"Three," the historian said.

"Three?" Chall asked.

"You asked me, before," Petran said, "if there were any experts on Fey artifacts in New Daltenia. Bearing in mind that it is my belief that no man or woman can ever truly be an expert on anything, not even themselves—perhaps *least* of all themselves—I believe that there are three people that might serve for your purposes."

"Well thank the gods for that," Chall said. "Finally, some good news. So where are these experts?"

The historian winced. "Yes, well, I am afraid it isn't *all* good news. You see, the first is Falidar—Falidar the Unnecessarily Verbose, he is called...if only by me."

"Falidar," Chall said, frowning thoughtfully. "Wait, that's the one who wrote that book that you read Maeve and I before, isn't it? The one about the Wolves? The bastard that loved the sound of his own voice so much?"

"I'm afraid so," Petran said. "Falidar has made a study of Fey artifacts over the years since our people arrived in the Known Lands. At least in part, I suspect, so that he might have an excuse to lay his hands on as many as possible in the hopes of making his fortune from them. After all, there are those who might seek to use the magic of the Fey for their own gains."

"Then they're fools," Chall said. "I might not have paid much attention at the Academy, but I listened enough to know that the last thing a man wants to do—assuming he intends to keep on breathing—is to toy about with magical artifacts he doesn't understand."

"I would be tempted to agree," the historian said, "but then, if there is one thing the world is in no danger of running out of, I'm afraid it is fools."

"And this Falidar," Chall said reluctantly, mostly because if the man was half as annoying and self-absorbed in person as he was in his writing, then Chall was in for a *very* long day, "where would I find him?"

Petran gave him a sympathetic wince. "When he isn't attending some ball or gala, Scholar Anquist—that is Falidar's surname—can be found, I'm told, taking his ease at his manor house not far from the castle on King's Street."

"An expensive part of the city," Chall observed.

"Yes, well, as I believe I mentioned previously, Falidar does have a certain penchant for the finer things."

"I see..." Chall said. "And I'm guessing by the way you speak of him, the two of you aren't exactly fast friends. As in, probably you wouldn't have a standing invitation to visit him out of the blue."

"No, I would not call us friends," Petran said. "I suppose he would view me as a competitor of his, if he considered me at all."

"And you? What do you view him as?"

Petran winced. "Perhaps it would be better not to say. I will say this, however—I serve the truth. My life is built around doing just that. And so I have very little respect for anyone who obfuscates that truth or chooses to embellish or change it to suit their own purposes. To me, there are few things less forgivable than that. As for the rest of your question, I am confident that Falidar would be all too pleased to host an audience and answer any questions we may have, if only to gloat over possessing knowledge that I do not."

"You would do that to help me?" Chall asked. "Subject yourself to that?"

Petran gave him a small smile. "I would do—have done—more than that in search of the truth, Sir Challadius. Still, I am more than a little relieved to say that I do not believe it will come to that. As I said before, while Falidar might be an expert in Fey artifacts—certainly he would claim so—he is, at least, not the only one who has made a study of them."

"And the others?"

"The second is a woman I know of only from Beth—that is, Librarian Elizabeth mentioning her in passing."

"See, I knew there was a reason I didn't like libraries," Chall said. "A man or woman can't come and research whatever they want to, can't have an honest study session on bust lines throughout the centuries, without the librarians using that information as pillow talk later."

The historian flushed a deep crimson at that. "It isn't, I don't…" He paused, clearing his throat and making a visible effort to regain control of himself. "Librarian Elizabeth would never, I assure you, do anything improper regarding her role in the library, Sir Challadius. Certainly, we do not spend our idle time speaking of something so banal as who does and does not enter the library, nor what they research."

"And yet…" Chall said, raising an eyebrow.

Petran cleared his throat. "That was…different. Elizabeth only mentioned the woman because she acted…oddly. Desperate, even. As if her life depended on learning as much as she could about the Fey and their magic in as short a time as possible."

Chall frowned. "Motivated, then?"

"I'd say so," Petran said, nodding. "With a temper, at least according to Elizabeth, as fiery as her hair."

"Wait," Chall said, a sinking feeling coming to his stomach. "You didn't say she was red-headed."

"I...didn't think I needed to," Petran said, clearly confused.

Chall took a slow, deep breath. A coincidence. It had to be. The problem, of course, was that he didn't much believe in coincidences. While he might not have paid much attention at the Academy, he distinctly remembered one of his tutors stressing the fact that coincidence was no more than the name the uninformed gave to those things they did not understand. "This woman," he said quietly. "Did Beth tell you what her name was?"

"I...believe she did," Petran said. "But...is it important?"

"Well, now, that'd depend on the name," Chall said.

"Right..." Petran considered, scratching his chin. "Oh, what was it... it started with an 'M', if I'm not mistaken. Maureen...no, no, that isn't it. Mary..." He shook his head, frustrated. "Perhaps it was Madeline...that isn't quite right either. I think—"

"Was it Margaret?"

The historian grinned widely. "Ah, that's it! Margaret." His smile slowly faded as he took in the grim expression on Chall's face. "By the look of you, I would say that this is unwelcome news."

"Just about the unwelcomest," Chall agreed. Petran opened his mouth to speak, and Chall held up a hand. "Leave it, Petran. We have far more important things to worry about, I think, than my struggles with grammar. You see, the woman you've just described sounds an awful lot like someone I've met before."

"Oh?" Petran said. "And I take it you didn't enjoy this meeting?"

"I wouldn't say it was so bad, as far as if it went," Chall said. "What I enjoyed considerably less, however, was the dead body we found after. One who, as it turned out, the red-headed woman named Margaret was responsible for."

The historian's eyes went as wide as saucers at that. "Wait, are you saying that this woman—the one with whom Beth has spoken briefly on multiple occasions—is a murderer?"

"I'm saying," Chall said, "that if she's who I think she is, the murder of a serving woman in the castle is probably the smallest fraction of her crimes. You see, Robert Palden—that's the homicidal, psychotic and seemingly unkillable leader of the newly-formed Wolves—had, as I understand it, two right hands. One of which was Catham the Cautious—a criminal of no small renown. And the second," he went on, meeting Petran's gaze, "was a red-headed woman named Margaret who might count murdering innocent serving girls among her favorites pastimes."

"Oh, gods be good," Petran breathed.

"We can hope," Chall said. "Catham, at least, isn't a problem anymore—that's a long, bloody story and frankly one I've got little interest in reliving just now. But this woman…if what you're saying is true, then I'd say she presents quite a large one. See, I have some inkling that this necklace is the source of Robert Palden's power—power that includes being able to butcher an entire brothel full of hardened criminals without taking a single scratch. A necklace imbued with power by the Fey, the source of his strength, but one that, it appears, was kept in the castle by the Regent Weylan-dreah, a man who turned out not to be a man at all but a feyling in disguise."

"If…if what you're saying is true," the historian said, seeming to grow paler by the moment, "then why would he keep the necklace? It would risk giving his true nature away, at least to those who know to recognize such things as Fey magic."

"Not if he entrusted it to an unknowing person to hold for him," Chall said. "Say, perhaps, the mistress of servants. As for the why, that seems obvious enough. It is all well and good imbuing someone with power and strength to turn them into an unkillable murder machine, but what assurances does the creator have that their creation will not turn on them, in time, using the very powers they gave it to destroy them?"

"The necklace," Petran said. "You believe that the feyling kept it as leverage to convince this Robert Palden to do what they wanted."

"Or to destroy him if he chose not to," Chall agreed. "And from what

I've heard of him, this Robert Palden isn't the sort that would enjoy having that sort of thing hanging over his head. It makes sense, then. Why the woman was in the castle, why they would risk alerting us to the presence of the Wolves. All of it—Lady Val, the murder of the serving woman, it was all in an attempt to locate that," he said, jabbing a finger at the necklace, "to remove the leverage the Fey have on him so he can be free to do what he wants to whom he wants."

"A puppet chafing at the pull of its master's strings," the historian said quietly.

"Sure," Chall said, "except this puppet is damned near unkillable, unstoppable, and wants nothing more than the complete and utter destruction of the world and everything—and every*one*—in it."

"So...what do we do?" Petran asked, sounding afraid.

"Right now? Right now, we hope that either Falidar will see us or that this third expert is close. I need to figure out this necklace and how to destroy it before Robert Palden or that damned red-headed woman tracks it down."

"The third expert is indeed close," Petran said, giving Chall a sickly smile.

"Good. Great. Do you know him or her? Can you get us a meeting?"

"I can," Petran said. "Though as I said, I do not now that I can truly claim to know him."

Chall stared at the man. "Petran, if I haven't made it clear, I'm in a bit of a hurry. We can speak riddles to each other later, if you like. But for now—"

"It's me," the historian interrupted.

"What?"

"The third expert," the other man said, wincing at the use of the term, "it's me."

"You."

"As I mentioned, I began studying magical artifacts in general long ago, when I was a mere page. Even though I am not gifted in the Art myself, I enjoyed learning of it, enjoyed the...complex simplicity of it."

"Complex simplicity," Chall repeated. "Careful, Petran. You're starting to sound more like a bard or a poet than a historian."

"Anyway," the historian went on, "my interest in the workings of such artifacts grew and, once we were forced to flee our homeland and come here, to the Known Lands, and the Fey War began, such artifacts began to surface...well, it seemed only natural to direct my studies toward them. In the hopes that, perhaps, such knowledge might prove useful in the war against the Fey. Though, I'm afraid, it never did."

"I wouldn't be so sure about that, Petran," Chall said. "The war's still going, after all, and I've got quite a bit of use for that knowledge. Now, the necklace, what can you tell me about it?"

"Off-hand?" Petran asked. "Not much, I'm afraid, only that, while I can't be certain, I do believe that you are correct in your assumption that it is magical in nature and that the origin of that magic is the Fey."

"Good, as far as it goes," Chall said, "but I was hoping for a little bit more."

Petran nodded. "It will take time—and your help."

"My help?" Chall asked.

"Of course," Petran said. "While I might discover, given time—and a thorough examination of the object in question, as well as my notes—the key to unlocking the magic and, as you say, destroying it, it will require a practitioner of the Art to actually *use* such a key."

"Right, fine," Chall said. "I'm ready."

The historian winced. "I'm afraid it is not so simple as that, Sir Challadius. The creation of such an artifact as this would have taken time and energy—attention and focus—and the unraveling of it will take no less."

"But *can* you? *Can* you do it?"

"I...believe so," Petran said. "But I will need my notes."

"Fine," Chall said. "Then let's go get them. Where are they? Let me guess, they're on the other side of the city."

Petran gave him a small smile. "Not so far away as that, I'm happy to say. In fact, if you will but come with me, it will be the work of no more than minutes to retrieve them, for they are here, in the library. Elizabeth has been kind enough to store them in a part of the library normally reserved for those works deemed too precious or too rare to risk being open to the public, ones which can only be seen upon special request, once the requestor has been vetted by the library staff."

Chall grunted. "I guess it pays to be sleeping with the head librarian, eh? Anyway, this locked door, I'm guessing only Elizabeth has a key?"

Petran blinked. "How would you know that?"

"In my experience, Petran, if you take a guess at the most inconvenient thing possible, you'll almost always be right."

"Well..." Petran said slowly, almost sheepishly, "in normal circumstances, you *would* be right. But, you see...that is, Beth...Elizabeth, she knows how much I adore studying the ancient texts, as well as how often my work means that I must confer with my notes, and so she did me the great kindness of having a key made." As he finished speaking, the crown historian reached underneath the collar of his tunic and produced a bronze key that dangled from a silver chain about his neck.

Chall gave the man a small grin. "As I said, it pays to be bedding the head librarian. Lead on, Petran. Let's get this done."

The historian nodded. "Come," he said. "It's this way."

He turned and opened the study room door, leading them out into the library proper. Chall followed and as he stepped out of the door he bumped into Petran who had stopped just outside the room, nearly sending them both sprawling.

"Gods be good, man," Chall hissed as the sudden movement he'd made to keep from falling made his wounded legs pulse with a sickening, dull throb. "I always said going to the library'd kill me but I didn't mean by breaking my neck."

The historian, though, didn't seem to hear a word Chall said. Instead, he was looking down one of the many aisles formed by the massive bookshelves that crowded the library. Frowning as if in thought.

"What, man, what is it?" Chall asked. "Look, if you're thinking about your librarian, save it for later. There'll be plenty of time for all the...*research* the two of you can stand soon enough. For now, we're in a hurry, in case you've forgotten."

"Do...do you smell smoke?" Petran asked in a distracted way, still staring in front of them.

"What are you talking about?" Chall asked. "I don't smell anything. Now can we—" But he cut off a moment later, for then his nose caught the scent, and he realized that Petran was right. He frowned but finally shook his head. "It's nothing, Petran. Probably someone's burning some trash. Or one of the baker's on the street had a kitchen fire."

"There are no bakers nearby," Petran said, his gaze unwavering.

"Carried by the wind, then," Chall said. "Or maybe one of the young librarians is snatching a few puffs of a pipe. What di—"

"They would not do that," Petran said, turning to regard him. "Loose flames, in a library, are strictly forbidden. After all, it would only take one errant spark, one flame to burn down decades, *centuries* of knowledge. Such a thing, to light a flame in a place like this...it is unimaginable."

Chall grunted. "Might be you need to work on that imagination of yours a touch, Petran," he said. "Now, the—"

Before he could speak any further, though, there came a scream from somewhere at the other end of the library. At first, the sound was so incongruous to their surroundings, so out of place that Chall thought he must have imagined it. Then he only *hoped* he had. But as Petran turned to him, his eyes wide, his face paling, Chall realized that he had not imagined it, after all.

"Did you..." Petran began, but before he could finish, there was another scream. Hearing it, the pain and fear in it, any hope that it might have been a few kids or teenagers fooling around vanished from Chall's mind in an instant. That was not the sound of someone messing around or joking. That was the sound of someone dying—he ought to know, for he had heard it often enough.

"Yes," Chall said, his mouth suddenly, terribly dry. "I heard it."

A moment later, the sounds of distant shouting seemed to come from all around them, the noise echoing off the grand bookcases, bouncing off the walls and the high, vaulted ceiling overhead and coming back at them. The shouts of fear, the screams of pain and terror, seemed to come from everywhere all at once, and Chall found himself looking around for the source of it, even glancing back at the room they'd just exited, so confusing were those echoes.

"What...what is it?" Petran asked. "What's happening?"

Before Chall could answer—though truth to tell he had no answer to give—a woman suddenly appeared running around the corner at the other end of the long aisle ahead of them. She sprinted at them, screaming even as she did, a look of wide-eyed terror on her face.

As she approached the end of the aisle in front of Chall and the historian, she finally seemed to notice them through her fright, but she did not slow as her gaze fell on them. "*Please,*" she screamed, "*hel—*"

But she abruptly cut off, staggering in shock and stumbling hard into one of the massive shelves, knocking several books and scrolls to the floor as she did. She blinked, staring at Chall with a confused expression on her face as if he'd just asked her a particularly difficult question. As she did, Chall recognized her as one of the two young women librarians he'd seen giggling outside the study room. Worse, though, as he stared at her Chall recognized the object protruding from her stomach as the blood-slicked bolt of a crossbow.

"*Help,*" the young woman groaned weakly. "*They're...they're killing them.*"

Chall moved forward then, fully intent on helping her, but he had managed no more than two steps before a figure he hadn't noticed with his attention fully on the woman stepped up behind her. The man grabbed a fistful of her blonde hair, jerking her head back, and Chall managed no more than a half-formed shout of shock and realization at what the man intended before the stranger dragged his blade across the young woman's neck, opening a crimson furrow from which blood gushed out.

The newcomer gave the dying woman a rough shove, and she collapsed to the ground in a bloody heap. The man stared at Chall and the historian over the dying woman as her struggles ceased, flashing them a grin. "Well, hello," he said.

"What...what do we do?" Petran asked from beside him. The man sounded afraid, and as well he might. Certainly Chall was.

But he had been afraid before—he pretty much lived his life that way. He had seen men and women killed for all sorts of reasons or for no reason at all, and as the man approached, fear was not the only thing he felt. "What you always do when confronted with evil, Petran," Chall said in a whisper.

The man came on, grinning, at least, that was, until there was the sound of troops roaring from behind him, and he spun to regard the dozen city guardsmen rushing toward him, their blades drawn, seemingly having appeared out of nowhere.

Which, of course, they had, summoned by Chall's magic.

The man's gloating grin fell away then—apparently murder wasn't quite as much fun when he was the one it was getting ready to happen to. He turned away from the city guardsmen, back to Chall and Petran. "*Out of my way!*" he roared, rushing toward them in his fear, which brought him charging directly onto the blade Chall held out in front of him. He usually didn't carry a weapon, but recent events combined with Maeve's admonishments had changed that and, as usual, he found that in the end, she had been right.

The man's bloody blade—which he had so recently used to murder an innocent young woman—fell from his fingers, clattering to the ground as he stared at Chall, then down at the knife stuck hilt-deep into his chest.

Chall figured he'd hit the heart or near enough, but then when it came to life or death, only a fool left things to chance, and while he *was* a fool more often than not, he had just witnessed a woman murdered right before his eyes and had been unable to do anything to help. So then, he was of a mind to make sure. Even as the stranger stood in shocked pain, Chall ripped the blade free with two hands and struck at the man's neck. The wounded man moved at the last minute, so it was a sloppy blow—Chall was confident he'd struck a bit of chin, maybe a bit of collar bone too, before he was through. But a sharp blade stuck anywhere would inevitably have an impact, and enough of it hit the man's throat that blood began to sluice out of the wound.

The man stared at Chall for a second, then reached a weak hand at him, a silent snarl on his face. Chall pushed the hand away in disgust and, a moment later, the man fell at his feet. "What do you do, Petran," Chall said, "when you're confronted with evil? You destroy it."

"The guardsmen..." Petran said, his voice shocked, confused. "Where did they..."

"An illusion, Petran," Chall said.

"But...gods, they seemed so real."

"I guess," Chall said. "Never can get the damned noses right."

"She...she was a new addition to the library," the historian said, his voice little more than a whisper as he gazed at the dead woman. "She... she has only been here a few months. But Elizabeth said she shows... *showed* great promise. Her name was Shannon."

Chall nodded grimly, feeling very close to tears, then. Feeling very close to screaming. "I will remember it," he said quietly.

"But...why?" Petran said. "Why would he do that?"

Chall shook his head slowly. "I can only think of one reason men would show up at a library of all places with murder on their minds," he said quietly. He found himself reaching into his pocket, retrieving the necklace and its glowing emerald gem.

"Wait," Petran said, "do...are you saying you think..."

He trailed off then, and Chall crouched, wincing at the pain in his leg as he did. The dead man had fallen on his face, and his hands were covered in blood, but not so much that Chall could not see the ring bedecking one of his fingers, a stylized wolf's head on its face. Blood stained the ring, and Chall found himself gritting his teeth. *Crimson Wolves indeed,* he thought grimly as he rose. He wondered what Ned would think, wondered what Ned would *do* if he found someone bearing the sigil of the Wolves killing innocent librarians, but he didn't have to wonder long. He knew enough of the carriage driver to know that the man would have come up with much the same solution as Chall himself had.

"Come on," he told the historian as he rose. "We have to get out of here. Now."

"What? You want to leave?" Petran said. "W-we have to, to do s-something," he went on, even as the screams continued seemingly from all around them.

"Like what?" Chall asked. "We won't help them by dying with them, Petran, and if there's anything I know about this Robert Palden, the man doesn't care for half measures. He would have sent enough to make sure the job got done and then sent some more, just to be extra sure. We have to get out of here, to get *this*—" he brandished the necklace and the glowing green gem—"out of here. I don't know how he knows I'm here, how he knows *it's* here, but it's clear that he does. And if he gets his hands on this, there will be no way to stop him. You're not just talking about a dozen librarians dying then, Petran. You're talking about the city." He met the man's gaze. "You're talking about the kingdom."

Petran watched him for a moment, then, finally, he took a slow, deep breath and nodded, at which Chall felt a great sense of relief. Given what was happening, he didn't have time to spend convincing the historian of the need to flee—in truth, they had already wasted too much. But whatever relief he felt only lasted until Petran spoke again.

"I won't leave without Beth."

Chall had been afraid the man might say something similar. "Listen, Petran...really *listen* to what's going on. She's probably already... that is..." He cleared his throat. "And even if she isn't, what can you do? I like Beth, I do, but would you risk the world to save her?"

"She is the world to me," the historian said simply.

Chall sighed. "I'm not going to be able to talk you out of it?"

"Would I be able to if it were Maeve?"

Chall hissed at that. "Come on—let's go find your librarian. Grab his blade," he said, motioning to the dead man.

The historian hesitated but, to his credit, only for an instant. He bent, retrieving the blood-stained knife, and by the way he held it, Chall thought that should they be forced to count on Petran's skill with the blade to save them, they were well and truly screwed.

"The pre-Skaalden texts," Chall said, remembering what the woman had said when darting out of the study room. "Where are they?"

Petran looked confused by the question for a moment, then realization worked its way past his frantic thoughts. "Oh. Right. This way."

As they made their way through the library, the smell of smoke grew stronger, and Chall found himself fighting the urge to cough. It was unlikely that he would be heard—what with the sounds of screams and shouts and hoots of cruel laughter filling the air—but he thought it better not to chance it.

Twice they were forced to stop, hiding in the aisle of books as the sound of footsteps made their way past them, the intruders who had come to the library hunting for something or, more likely, some*one*. Bookshelves crammed with all manner of scroll and tome made for poor hiding places, however, and it was luck more than anything that kept them from being found.

They continued on, and after about ten minutes, Petran was leading them down yet another aisle of books, this one distinct from the others by the dead man lying in the middle of it.

"How much further?" Chall asked.

"The preservation room is just up ahead, on our right," the historian answered in a low whisper.

Chall nodded. "Good. Then I'll lead for a bit, if it's all the same to you." Petran didn't voice any complaint or argument at that—and seemed pretty damned far from being ready to from what Chall could see—only moving to stand behind him.

A woman shouted from somewhere up ahead and Chall thought he recognized it as the head librarian's, though he couldn't tell for sure. The historian, on the other hand, seemed certain enough for both of them.

"*Beth!*" he yelled. "*I'm coming!*"

"Petran, wait—" Chall began, but he may as well have been talking to himself for all the attention the historian gave him. The man burst into a run, starting forward. Chall hissed, following after him and thinking it even odds that the historian would trip and impale himself on the stolen blade he carried rather than reaching the head librarian and whatever had caused her to shout.

The historian beat him around the corner—a fact Chall would have liked to blame on his not-completely healed leg wounds, but which more than likely was owed to a lifetime of over-indulging in food and drink. Chall reached the corner seconds later, rounding it to find the historian standing a short distance ahead, the stolen blade clutched in front of himself in a two-handed grip.

Beyond him, Chall saw two men, both wielding swords which, judging by their blood-slicked blades, had been put to recent use. On the other side of the two men, Elizabeth stood with her back against a door. When he'd first met her, Chall had thought of the head librarian as almost painfully prim and proper. The sort of person who did a lot of lifting their nose, a lot of judgmental sniffing, who spent their life living—such as it was—in terror of the great evil of *impropriety*.

She did not look so now.

She had clearly made an attempt, after leaving Chall and Petran in the study room, to put her long hair up, but what had no doubt started as a tight, no-nonsense bun had become frazzled and tousled, and her hair now hung in disarray. One of the sleeves of her blue dress was torn, and there was blood on her arm and face, though from what wound Chall couldn't tell. She held what appeared to be a letter opener of all things in both hands in front of her, but it was the expression on her face—one of wild ferocity—that most clashed with the image Chall had of the woman.

"*Leave her alone!*" Petran shouted, and the two men who had, up to that point, been easing toward the librarian, spun to regard them.

They looked concerned at first, but as they took in the two men standing before them—one a historian, who with his dusty robe, ink-stained fingers, and thin frame looked the part, the other a fat, out-of-breath man who was clearly struggling to stand—that concern slowly turned to amusement.

"You wait your turn, fellas," one said. "We'll get to you soon enough. Just as soon as we're done with this feisty one here."

"You will not touch her," Petran said, and though Chall knew—just as anyone who saw the way he held the borrowed blade knew—that the man had no training in fighting, he was still impressed with the iron in the man's voice.

The two men grunted, sharing mock-impressed looks. "Just like a knight out of one of them storybooks," the speaker of the two said. "Though…" He hesitated, his gaze moving up and down first Petran, then Chall. You two don't look much like knights to me."

"Sure," the second said, grinning, "I mean, where's your armor?"

"Not that this'n here'd fit," the first said, grinning at Chall.

"Look," Chall said, "there's no need for this to get bloody. How about you just let the woman go, okay? Plenty of other people to kill, after all."

The speaker of the two laughed. "I like you. You're a funny bastard. But then, my experience, fella, funny bastards, they die just like all the rest." He nodded to his companion. "Go on—finish them. Half an hour, she said, remember?"

"I remember," the other man said grimly. "Don't worry—this won't take but a minute." Then he started forward, raising his blade.

"Stay behind me, Petran," Chall said, stepping forward. "If he gets past me, then—"

But the historian didn't seem prepared to listen. Instead, he gave a roar, and Chall watched in shock, much the same way he might have watched a rabbit pounce a lion, as the thin historian rushed toward the other man. And Chall was not the only one shocked by the historian's unexpected charge. So, too, was the man who'd been approaching them. The man's eyes went wide, clearly not having thought there was any chance Petran would act as he had. But the man's shock didn't last. He grinned as the historian came on, swinging his sword in a blow that would have split the historian in half, had he been there to receive it. But, to the man's surprise, to *Chall's* surprise, and, no doubt, to Petran's as well, the historian wasn't.

Right as the man had begun to swing, Petran's foot had caught on the hem of his robe—they might be fine for sitting around looking scholarly, but robes made for poor battle garb—and his battle roar turned to a panicked cry as his feet slipped out from underneath him.

Which left Petran lying at the other man's feet, the borrowed knife, by some miracle, still in his hands. The man looked down at the historian, and Petran looked up at him. The man raised his sword for a second strike, but Petran's unexpected tumble had made him sprawl only inches away from the man, within easy reach, and so Petran reached. He lifted his knife and stabbed it into the man's inner thigh.

The historian's attacker roared in surprise and pain, staggering back. But Petran must have struck an artery, for blood sluiced out at an alarming rate, and the man did not stagger nor roar for long, managing only two steps before falling to the floor, dead or well on his way.

That left the second man who stood where he had, Elizabeth all but forgotten behind him, his eyes wide. "*Son of a bitch*," he said. "You'll die for that." The man started forward, raising his blade. Petran, meanwhile, had no weapon to defend himself with, even had he the skill to do it, for the man he'd stabbed had taken the blade with him as he'd fallen. Which left the historian to stare up at the man, left the man to kill him, and left Chall to do something particularly foolish.

He hoped his battle cry was more convincing than the historian's had been, but he doubted it. He gave it a go anyway, charging forward —as much as a man with two recently-stabbed legs *could* charge—and brandishing the small blade he held.

The man looked at Chall with something like amusement on his face, clearly not thinking much of this latest threat. That was fine—as a general rule, Chall didn't think much of himself. Still, he'd been in enough scraps over the years that he managed, to keep his feet as he rushed toward the man. The man decided to forget about Petran, at least for the moment, and Chall had a feeling of dubious relief as he raised his blade, stepping over the historian to meet Chall's charge.

He reached him a moment later. The man swung his blade in a two-handed, overhead strike, but Chall managed to stagger out of line. The sword passed harmlessly by, though Chall fancied that it took a piece of his hair along with it. He countered, slashing out with his knife, and the man shouted in pain and surprise as the blade cut down his arm. His sword fell from his hands, which was good. Less so was the fact that he growled in anger and backhanded Chall with a blow that sent him stumbling, nearly costing him his balance. *"Son of a bitch,"* the man growled as he grabbed Chall's shoulder with one hand and buried the other, balled into a fist, in Chall's stomach.

The breath exploded from Chall's lungs, and he gagged and choked as he fell to his knees. He'd dropped the knife, and he reached for it. The man brought his boot down on Chall's fingers in a stomp that made him scream, then knelt down, retrieving the knife. Chall struggled to get his hand out from beneath the man's foot as his attacker studied the knife. "Barely more'n a butter knife," the man told him. He shrugged. "Still. I reckon it'll do the job."

He raised the blade, and Chall was still struggling to free his hand, knowing he would be too late even as he did, when suddenly a figure appeared behind the man. The historian's eyes were wild, his face and robe stained with the blood of the man he'd killed. He held, of all things, a book in his hands, though it was one of the biggest Chall had ever seen. Heavy, too, he figured, a theory that was proved a moment later as the historian let out a roar, bringing the book down on the man's head.

Chall's attacker only managed to turn about halfway before he was struck, and his legs crumpled beneath him as if they were made of paper. He fell beside Chall, groaning. There was a little space between them, and in that space Chall spotted his knife. The other man spotted it too, though, and they both moved for it.

In normal circumstances, the man would have no doubt beaten him there—Chall had spent his entire life crafting his body, with good food and good ale, and knew well that it was not built for speed. In fact, the man *did* beat him to it, but the blow must have disoriented him, for he groped awkwardly at the blade, missing its handle twice. He didn't get a chance at a third before Chall caught up. He grabbed the knife and plunged it into the closest part of the man to him which, as it turned out, was his outstretched hand. The man screamed, but Chall wasn't finished. These men had come to kill, *had* killed already if the blood on their blades was anything to go by. And he knew that, should he give the man a moment to recover his wits, there were good odds he'd kill the three of them.

So Chall didn't give him that chance.

As the man rolled away, clutching his bloody hand to his chest, Chall followed, scrabbling across the floor. The man started to try to rise, but Chall lunged forward, raising the blade in both hands and plunging it downward in a lunging fall. The blade drove deep into the man's chest. More by luck than design, the blow had taken the man in the heart, and he let out a sharp gasp as blood leaked from the wound, and he died.

Chall, exhausted and feeling just about as tired as he could remember ever feeling, rolled off the man onto his back on the floor. For several seconds, he just lay there gasping, shocked to still be alive.

"What in the name of the gods?" a strange voice said.

Chall craned his neck from where he lay on the floor, looking behind him to see another man—this one, judging by his own sword and dress, a companion to the two dead men, standing a short distance away.

The man started forward but managed no more than a step before a figure appeared behind him. Such was the look on the head librarian's face, the wild bestial appearance of her, that at first Chall didn't recognize her.

The man must have noted his confused gaze as Chall looked past him, for he frowned, beginning to turn. Before he could, though, the head librarian raised her arm, revealing her hand—which to that point had been hidden by the man's form—as well as the knife she clutched.

Before the man could do anything, likely before he was even *aware* of the danger, the blade flashed downward, and he screamed as it stabbed into his back. He staggered forward from the blow, but Elizabeth wasn't finished. She followed behind him, the blade pulling back and flashing forward again and again. "This is a *library!*" she hissed.

The man finally fell face-first onto the ground, and the librarian followed him down, plunging the blade in over and over until his struggles slowed then ceased altogether, and she was left sitting atop him, gasping for breath, her...well. *Everything* covered in blood.

"If you...ever break up with her, Petran..." Chall wheezed, "best...do it with a note."

The historian, though, didn't seem to be listening. He rushed toward the woman. "Beth?" he said. "Are you alright?"

The woman looked up and saw Petran approaching. At once, the look of wild ferocity that had been on her face vanished, replaced by a look of panicked relief as she rose. "Oh, Pet," she said, staggering to her feet, and Chall watched from his spot sprawled on the floor as the two embraced.

Pet. Chall made a mental note to give the man a hard time about that later. But first, he had more important things on his mind—namely, *surviving* until later. It was no easy task, getting to his feet. His legs ached from being overly used, and his body ached from being poorly used. Still, he managed it. Wheezing for breath, rubbing at his elbow where he'd hit it when falling to the ground, he staggered forward.

"Listen, I'm all for cuddling, but how about the two of you do it later? We need to get out of here."

The two pulled apart with obvious reluctance, glancing back at him. "You're right," Petran said. "I'm just..." He turned back to the librarian. "I'm glad you're okay."

"And I you, Pet," she said, giving him an innocent smile as if she hadn't just stabbed a man to death.

"I'm fine too, in case anyone was wondering," Chall said dryly. "Now come on—let's go get those notes of yours and get out of here. It looks like everybody in this library is coming down with a case of the dead, and I'd just as soon get out before we did too."

"Right, of course," Petran said. "This way—"

"No."

They both turned to regard the head librarian who had spoken. "No?" Chall asked.

"It's okay, Beth," Petran said. "We can't stay here. We'll get out—Chall and I, we'll protect you. Isn't that right, Chall?"

He glanced back to Chall for help. "No...yeah, sure. I mean, that is, of course we will," Chall managed.

The woman looked at Chall with a dubious expression one that, while it hurt, he could not fault her for. After all, the dead man had been right about this much at least—Chall shared little in common in appearance and stature as the knights that rode their valiant steeds across the pages of storybooks. He was shorter, for one, had no steed, and was considerably rounder than any of those blond-haired, blue-eyed heroes.

But if the head librarian had such thoughts, she kept them to herself. In fact, she didn't respond to Petran or Chall at all, at least not with words. Instead, she turned and moved back toward the door she'd stood in front of when he and the historian had first arrived, then grabbing the handle, swung it open.

Chall grunted in surprise as he stared at what appeared to be at least a dozen faces staring back at them from where they had huddled against the door. They didn't all fall out onto the floor the way they might have had it been some street troupe performance, but Chall thought it was a near thing.

"What..." he began.

"When I saw what was happening, I gathered those I could," Elizabeth explained. "Come on," she told them, motioning them out of the room, "we must leave. Quickly."

Chall watched in stunned silence as what turned out to be thirteen people stepped out of the doorway. Most, based on their dress, were assistants and librarians; a few were men and women who had clearly had the unfortunate luck of deciding to visit the library today of all days.

Chall had always known libraries could be the death of a man, but he decided to keep that observation to himself, at least for the moment, though it was one he would share with Maeve as soon as possible. Assuming, of course, that they weren't killed or burned alive in the next few minutes, for while he didn't see anymore would-be murderers, at least not for the moment, what he *did* notice was that the smell of smoke was growing stronger.

And he wasn't the only one that noticed, for several of those terrified figures were coughing and clearing their throats as it grew increasingly difficult to draw a clean breath.

"What do we do?" Petran asked, glancing at him, and all of those eyes followed the man's gaze, looking to Chall to save them.

He hesitated then. He knew that he should get the people to safety, but he knew also that if he wanted any chance of finding out the secret of the necklace and defeating Robert Palden, they needed the historian's notes.

"We'll split up," he said finally. "Beth and the others will head for the exit; Petran, you and I will go for your no—"

"Chall, we don't have to—"

"We do, Petran," he said. "You know the importance of this."

"No, but—"

"Fine," he said. "You're right. I'll help make sure everyone makes it out. Then you can tell me where they are, and I will retrieve them."

"No, Chall," the historian said, "I only meant that the storage, where my notes are—it's on the way to the exit."

Chall blinked, deciding that just as soon as he was able, he was going to leave this whole leader thing to someone—*anyone*—else. "Right," he said, feeling his face heat. Stupid, maybe, that a man facing a very good likelihood of dying by fire or sword in the next few minutes could still feel embarrassed, but there it was. "Fine," he said, rallying. "Let me know when we get close. Now, follow me—this way."

"Chall," Petran said quietly as he started away.

Chall turned to glance back at the historian. "Yes?"

Petran winced. "It...that is...it's actually this way," he said, motioning almost sheepishly in a direction that was quite nearly opposite the one Chall had been going.

Chall wanted to ask the man if he was sure, for he had really thought it was the other way, but then over the course of the Fey War, he and some others had become lost in strange woods and that more than once. Enough that he knew that when a man was lost in the woods, what he thought about where he was didn't matter all that much—north just kept on being north, whatever his opinion on it.

"Chall—but, but you're Sir Challadius the Charmer," a young woman said, her voice thick with unshed tears. "I have read of you. You are a great mage, y-you can save us."

"No one c-can save us," a young man said. "W-we're going to die. Th-they killed Finn. C-cut his h-head off. I s-saw them do it."

Chall glanced over and saw the dozen or so people who Elizabeth had been protecting were all watching him, many with tears in their eyes. Some of them were little more than kids, barely out of their teens if he had to guess. No doubt their parents had sent them to the library to work, thinking them safe. After all, what could be safer than a library full of dusty old men and dusty old books?

Chall looked at them, noting the way they huddled against each other, their fear stripping the years from them so that they all looked like children. Terrified children looking for comfort. Terrified children who might, as terrified people do, make a bad decision—to cry out or run when they should remain quiet and hide, for example—and give them all away. After all, none of them, he was confident, had ever been in a life-or-death situation such as the one they now found themselves in.

He wished, in that moment, that the prince was there—the prince who had always been able to help people, Chall included, find their courage even when, like Chall's, it was a pitiful, mewling little thing. And if not the prince, then Priest whose faith—recently renewed—would have served to give them strength. Or Maeve who would have known just what to say, just what to do. But they were not here. These people needed help, and no one was there to give it. No one, at least, except Chall.

The poor bastards.

"Listen to me," he told them, letting his gaze sweep over them. "I am not a brave man—never have been. Always been more of a cowerer than a fighter. But I've *known* brave men. Some of the bravest men that have ever walked this world," he continued, glancing at Petran, noting the way the historian's eyes went wide before turning back to the small group. "And what I know is, when a man—or a woman—has something scary before them, the best thing to do is to get it done as quickly as they can. After all, things are rarely so bad as we imagine them to be—the monster in our closet, is, more often than not, nothing more than a winter coat hung askew or the shadows sitting just so."

"And the other times?" the young man who'd so recently pronounced their doom asked. "The times when the monster *is* a monster?"

Chall could have punched the boy then, for despite the fact that he was probably in his early twenties, he *seemed* like a boy to him. He'd had some of them, he thought, but at the boy's words, he noted the way their faces fell; the brief hope, the small hint of iron he'd caught sight of in them vanished, replaced by wide-eyed terror again.

"I can promise you this," he said to the youth, said to all of them, "if those men want to hurt you, they'll have to come through me first." It was a line he'd heard the prince use, on occasion, and one that he thought was far more effective coming from a giant of a man standing six feet, three inches with shoulders damn near broad enough to lie down on than a man who'd only ever been six feet tall in his dreams and who was far better at wielding a glass of ale than a battleaxe.

Still, they seemed to respond to it, giving him slow nods.

"Y-you're a mage, aren't you?" the young man asked. "C-can't you just, I don't know, kill them all with fireballs?"

"Sure," Chall said, "and when I get done, maybe I'll fly us out of here like eagles, how'd that be?" He winced, deciding as he looked at those terrified faces that flippancy might not be the best policy in this situation, and that was too bad as he had a lifetime of experience at it. "That isn't how the Art works," he explained, then found himself thinking of Matt, of the way he'd seemingly vanished out of a locked room with an assassin's blade only inches away from him. "At least..." he amended, "it isn't how *I* work."

"A mage that can't use magic," the young man said. "Thank the gods that you're here."

Another might have been mad at that sarcasm, but Chall had spent his entire life being sarcastic, and so like a wine connoisseur presented with a particularly fine vintage, he could not help but appreciate it. He was tempted to answer with some of his own—it was the way he would deal with...well, pretty much anything in normal circumstances.

The problem, though, was that these were not normal circumstances. He stood in a library—a place he'd avoided all his life—one full not just of books but of murderers and, somewhere, fire. And he was not alone—more than a dozen people stood with him, and by some cruel twist of fate, they were all looking to him to keep them safe.

"Follow me," he told them, told the young man, "and stay quiet. I may not be much for fireballs, but I have my uses."

"What choice do we have?" the young man asked.

"Sorry, what's your name?"

"Clay," the young man answered sullenly.

Chall nodded. "Well, to answer your question, Clay, you have no choice at all." He gave the young man a small smile. "Now, let's go." He nodded at Petran and then they were off, Chall walking slightly behind and to the side of the historian as he led them through the aisles of books. They moved quietly, not speaking, only focusing on putting one foot in front of the other while they listened to the sounds of others—those who had not been so lucky as to be shown to relative safety by the head librarian—fleeing and screaming and dying around them.

The sounds echoed and bounced off the great, high shelves, the tall, vaulted ceiling, and so it seemed to Chall as if they were surrounded by an army of killers. He looked behind him so many times that he was confident his neck would be sore the next day—assuming he *saw* the next day, that was, which, given the screams all around him, seemed pretty optimistic.

The smell of smoke grew thicker the further they walked, the air hotter, until, by the time Petran signaled for them to stop near the end of an aisle, Chall had an acrid taste in the back of his throat and had begun to sweat.

"The preservation room is just up here, on the right," the historian whispered, for while they had been accompanied by shouting and screaming the entire length of their short journey, now there was another sound, one that was coming from somewhere ahead of them. Laughter. Out of habit, Chall waited to be told what to do—there had always been someone to do that. The prince or Priest or Maeve.

A moment later, however, he realized that the historian was staring at him, waiting for what he would do, waiting for him to lead, and a quick glance at the others showed that they were doing the same. Chall winced. "Right—wait here. I'll check it out."

Even as he walked the remaining length of the aisle, the flames grew hotter, the smoke thicker, until Chall had a pretty good idea of what he'd find even before he peered around the corner. The preservation room sat where the historian had said. At least, what was left of it.

Perhaps those who had come had known it for what it was and so had decided, in their cruelty, to destroy it. Perhaps it was no more than random chance or that the gods hated Chall particularly and enjoyed nothing more than confounding him at every turn. In the end, the reason did not matter. What did was that the preservation room was burning. Burnt already, in truth, the flames licking here and there, nothing of what had been in the room visible beyond the fire and the smoke.

Three men stood a short distance in front of the room, their backs to Chall. They were laughing and joking as they grabbed books out of a pile they'd made on the floor. They took turns tossing them in, making a game of it, who could throw the farthest, who could hit this pile of ash or that burnt, irreplaceable bit of knowledge.

Chall had never been much for books or libraries, yet as he watched the three men pass a bottle of some spirits between them, laughing and capering like demons as they tossed one book after another into the flames, he found himself growing angry.

"*Gods be good*," a voice said, and Chall turned to see Petran standing there, completely in the open, his eyes and face frozen in shock as he stared at the blazing inferno that accounted for some of that knowledge and history the librarians had deemed most important to protect.

"*Petran!*" Chall hissed. "*Get back here, damn you.*" He moved into the aisle, grabbing hold of the historian by the arm and pulling him back behind the cover of the aisle. The man allowed himself to be pulled, his eyes never leaving the grim scene.

"What is it, Petran?" Elizabeth asked, clearly having picked up on the historian's dismay. "What's happened?"

"It's...it's gone," Petran said, seeming to be in a state of shock similar to the kind that sometimes overcame men in war or after some grievous loss. The historian slowly turned to regard the head librarian. "They've burned it, Beth," he said, his voice sounding hollowed out. "The preservation room...it's in flames."

"It can't be," she said, and Chall saw that actual tears had begun to form in her eyes.

"I'm sorry, Beth," Petran said, putting a hand on her shoulder. "It is."

"B-but th-the works...they were invaluable." Her eyes went wide. "Your notes...I promised you they would be safe, that—"

"It is not your fault, Beth," Petran said, grabbing each of the woman's hands in his own. "You couldn't have known this would happen."

"I'm sorry about the books and your notes," Chall said, surprised to find that he meant it. "But if we don't get out of here, they won't be the only thing that gets destroyed. We need to go—now."

The two continued to stare at each other, sharing in their grief, and Chall hissed, "*Petran.*"

The historian winced, glancing at him, then followed Chall's gaze to the others with them before looking back at him. "Right...of course. It... that is, the library exit is that way," he said, motioning in the opposite direction of the three men and the burning, priceless treasures.

Chall nodded, and they began moving again, making their way through the aisles until they reached the last one. They followed it to its end and as they continued down it, Chall could make out the front desk at which the kind old man had been sitting when he'd first arrived. The man did not sit there now, however. Instead, as Chall drew close, he saw that the man lay unmoving on the ground, a pool of blood spreading out beneath him. Dead—killed, no doubt, when the men first came into the library, and he was not alone. Three more, two men and one woman lay dead, sprawled near the desk. Either they had been taken unawares when the Wolves had arrived, or else they had sought to flee and been cut down. Either way, the result was the same.

"Who…who would do such a thing?"

Chall turned to stare at Petran. There was an ache in his hands, and he glanced down to see that he had squeezed them into fists so hard that his nails had bitten into his flesh and they had begun to bleed. He only shook his head, unable, in that moment to do anything more than that. He was still trying to answer when a voice spoke. Only it was not his, nor was it any of those with them. Instead, the voice came from beyond their sight, past the desk and near where, he knew, the massive double doors of the library stood.

"Stay here," Chall told the others. He made his way to the end of the aisle, removing a book so that he could peek through toward the library entrance.

What he saw—or more specifically *who* he saw—made his breath catch in his throat. Four men stood spread out around the doors, clearly there to keep anyone from escaping, their blood-slicked blades and the other two corpses Chall saw lying nearby evidence that they had already done that job and more than once.

But it was not the four men that caught Chall's attention and held it. Instead, it was the one standing at their front. A woman with long red hair, and a small, amused smile on her face as if she were attending some comedic play instead of a massacre. She was dressed in leather trousers and shirt, a far cry from the linen servant's dress she'd worn the last time Chall had seen her, but he recognized her just the same. The woman who had broken into the castle what felt like a lifetime ago, leaving a dead serving girl and a lot of questions. Margaret, she had told him her name was. And according to the information he'd gleaned from Catham the Cautious while the man tortured him, she, along with Catham, served as Robert Palden's second-in-command. Though, considering what Priest had told him about Nadia and what she meant to do with Catham, he thought it safe to assume that it was a position the red-headed woman had all to herself now.

Even as Chall watched, another figure appeared, stepping out of the aisle. The man hurried toward the woman, bowing as he stepped in front of her. "Forgive me, mistress, but we haven't been able to find him."

She frowned, staring at the man. "It is not my forgiveness you will ask for, if we fail, but the master's. And he is not a man known for his forgiveness. You have your task—find him. And find him quickly. We cannot tarry. The city guard will be here soon enough, and we must be gone before they arrive. A quarter hour, and we are leaving. No more than that."

"I understand," he said, "but it's a big library. With plenty of places he could hide, and with so little time to look..."

He didn't finish, but then it didn't seem that he needed to. The woman nodded slowly, thinking it over. Finally, she gave a shrug. "Then we'll burn it."

"Burn what, mistress?"

"All of it," she said, her gaze traveling over the corpses and the aisles of books and scrolls. Lifetimes, centuries of knowledge, and deciding to burn it all down did not seem to bother her in the slightest. "Already the boys have gotten a good start at it. Go. Tell them they've got a quarter hour, no more. Should they linger, should *you* linger, then you will burn with all the rest."

"As you s-say, Mistress," he said, bobbing his head.

"I would hurry, were I you," she said. "There is little time."

The man needed no more urging than that. He turned and hurried back the way he'd come, breaking into a run.

Chall leaned back to look at the others.

"Th-the library," Elizabeth said numbly. "She's going to burn it to the ground."

"What...what do we do?" one of the young librarians, a woman who appeared to be barely out of her teens, asked.

"Isn't it obvious?" the young man, Clay, asked. "We're going to burn with the rest of it."

They all looked terrified at that—as well they might—glancing at each other, whispering quietly, shedding tears. Chall took a slow, deep breath. "No," he said. "We're not."

"And what do you think you're going to do?" the young man asked. "They're guarding the entrance and killing anyone that tries to leave. Or is your plan to just walk right by them?"

"That's my plan exactly," Chall said.

The young man sneered, opening his mouth to speak again, but Chall beat him to it. "You asked me before what sort of mage I was. I am an illusionist, a man whose ability with the Art allows him to make people see things that aren't there or—in this case—not see things that are. That is the type of mage I am."

"And you think you can get all of us past them without them noticing? They'd have to be blind and deaf."

"I don't know if I can or not," Chall said. "What I do know is, we can either cower here and burn, or we can grip our courage tight and try. I've told you what sort of mage I am," he said to the young man, meeting his gaze. "The question Clay, is what sort of man are you? The kind who will hide in fear even as his doom comes upon him? Or the kind who will fight?"

The young man opened his mouth as if he might say something, the sour expression on his face making Chall think that he knew the nature of the man's response, if not the exact words. But a moment later, that sourness faded, disappearing, and revealing what had hidden beneath it all along, what nearly always hid beneath sarcasm, and no one knew that better than Chall—fear.

But there was not just fear there, Chall thought. There was something else too—courage. The young man gave him a nod. "Let's fight."

Chall gave the youth a small smile, then nodded, thinking that the young man, in many ways, reminded him of himself at a younger age, even if Chall had been far more likely to be found in a tavern than a library in his youth. *Time rolls on,* he thought, *and all stories have been told already and told again.*

"It won't be easy," he said, speaking to the group. "But I believe that we can do this. I will cast a working that will hide us from their view."

"Y-you can do that?" Elizabeth asked.

"I can," Chall said, not bothering to tell them that he had never attempted such a thing with so many. "You must all remain as quiet as you can," Chall said to them. "Do not make a sound and proceed in a line. We'll move to the exit."

"You...you mean to walk past them?" This from one of the young women.

"I do," Chall said.

"Th-they'll see us," the girl said. "Th-they'll kill us, like they did the oth—"

"It's okay," the young man who'd been arguing with Chall said, putting a hand on her shoulder in comfort, and Chall decided maybe they weren't so similar after all. The young man he had once been had not given a care in the world for anyone but himself. "We're going to be okay, Kyra."

"Y-you don't know that," she said quietly.

"No," he said, glancing back at Chall. "But I believe it."

That makes for one of us, at least, Chall thought. "Be as still as you can," he told them. "No noises." He closed his eyes then. He had never cloaked so many at once, at least not for long. It was no easy task, one that required concentration and focus, both of which were hard to come by when a man stood in a burning library full of murderers.

In the darkness of his mind, he reached out for the Art, grasping the power. He managed it, but now, like always, he felt it wriggling in his hands, threatening to break free of his grip like some slippery eel pulled from the water. He held on grimly, the red-headed woman's words echoing in his mind. *A quarter hour.*

Using the Art took many different shapes—illusionists like Chall, Empaths like Ned, and plenty of others. And just as what those men and women gifted with its use were able to do with it differed, so, too, did the method by which they did it. An Empath, like Ned, learned to read people, for the closer he got into contact with the natural empathy of understanding others, the more powerful his use of the Art would be.

Illusionists, like Chall, had a different path—they lied. That was, after all, what illusions were. Convincing someone something was true when it wasn't. That was perhaps why Chall was often considered one of the world's most powerful illusionists. He was also one of its best liars. In some ways, he had been built to be an illusionist, he who had lied and tricked his way into the beds of too many women to count, then tricked himself back out again.

But it wasn't enough for an illusionist to convince someone else that something was real, for to do that, first they had to convince themselves. Thankfully, that was another talent he had, one he'd seemingly been born with that had been sharpened over the years by moral justifications made to assuage his guilt after his regular nightly conquests. Sharpened more each time he looked in the mirror and convinced himself that it was just the lighting that made him look fat, not decades of a lot of drink, more food, and as little exercise as he could manage.

It made for a protruding gut and an inflated sense of self, but it *also* made for a pretty damned fine liar. And so, as they stood there, the others waiting expectantly, no doubt impatiently for what would come, Chall did what he was best at...

He lied.

That lie strengthened by the moment, as he convinced himself more and more of the truth of it. Convinced himself that they were not there, could not be there, not in this burning library. Finally, when the lie had solidified into reality—at least as much as they ever did, like a house built of straw, waiting to be knocked over—he opened his eyes.

The others shared looks, and Petran frowned. "What happened?" he asked quietly. "Did the spell fail?"

"No," Chall said. "It's working."

The historian glanced at Elizabeth beside him, and Chall noted the look of skepticism on her face. "Are you sure?" she asked. "I didn't feel anything."

"And why would you?" Chall asked. "The lie isn't for you."

"The lie?"

"You're sure then?" Petran asked. "That it's working?"

"Remember," he told them all, "stay as quiet as you can, move in a line, and move no more than you have to."

"Why?" Elizabeth asked.

"Because you're not there," Chall said. "Now, you want to know if it's working—let's go find out together."

He didn't want to step out of that aisle, but neither did he cherish the idea of remaining in the library and seeing whether the flames or the murderers found them first. And one of the hard truths about existence, at least so far as he had seen, was that what was best for a man was rarely what he *wanted* to do.

So he took a deep breath, whispered a low curse, and he stepped out into the open, nothing to protect him except his own competence—and few thoughts were more terrifying than that. The men still stood at the door, along with the red-headed woman, their swords in hand, glistening with the blood of those they'd already slain, and the only shield Chall and the others had to protect them was the lie.

He wanted to break into a run, to sprint for the door with all the speed two recently-stabbed legs and a hefty gut could muster, but he resisted the urge, knowing that to do so would risk breaking the spell. So he started forward slowly, taking his own advice and moving as little as possible, knowing that each unnecessary movement against the lie would press against it, *strain* against it like a hand squeezing a balloon. And should it take too much strain, then that balloon would pop...and blood would follow.

He glanced behind him as they walked, and saw a line of pale, frightened faces staring back at him. Scared, as they should be, but all of them, he thought, looked resolute too, determined. All, that was, save for one old woman who looked even more terrified than the rest, fully in the grips of her fear, her eyes darting in their sockets like fish in a bowl, looking for a way out. She was trembling, Chall saw, her chest heaving with rapid, panicked breaths. Chall met Petran's gaze, focusing on keeping the spell steady, like a man holding a tarp over some treasured object—in this case himself and those with him—while the driving rain came down and the wind kept threatening to rip the protective cover off.

The historian glanced at him, then followed Chall's gaze to the woman. He gave Chall a small, single nod then slowly started back to her. With each second that the man took moving further back, the woman's trembling became more erratic, her entire body shaking with her terror. Petran had only made it about halfway down the line when, suddenly, the woman let out a wail of fear and charged for the doors.

She wouldn't make it—*couldn't* make it. Had she been in her right mind, she would have known that, but she had fully given in to her panic and so, in trying to save herself, she doomed herself instead.

Wailing in fear, the old woman charged directly at the door—which meant that she charged at those men and the woman standing there. The red-headed woman still stood at the front, as she had before, and as the old woman approached, she stepped forward, grinning. If there was any comfort to be found, it was that the old woman, fully given to her fear, likely was not even aware of the woman being there, and so did not see her death coming.

Chall saw it, though, was forced to watch as the red-headed woman raised her blade and pivoted. Sharpened metal sliced through the air, then through the neck of the old woman. Her head flew into the air, and her body continued for another few steps before collapsing, still a dozen feet from the doors that had been her destination. Her head, meanwhile, tumbled across the floor, and by chance or some cruel taunt of the gods, rolled to a stop only a few feet away from Chall and the others, her dead eyes seeming to study him in silent accusation.

"Where in the name of the gods did she come from?" one of the Wolves asked.

"Don't know," another said, grinning, "but I reckon I know where she's gone."

Chall heard the sharp intake of breath behind him, and he glanced back, seeing as he did that the young librarian who'd spoken earlier was staring at the old woman's head, her eyes seeming to take up her whole face. Her mouth was open in preparation for a scream, one that would doom them all. Already, the spell was weakened by the old woman's outburst—a hole torn in it which Chall was working desperately to knit back together before the flaw made the whole thing collapse on itself. Should the young woman voice the scream which was building in her, he knew that he would not be able to hold it together, not any more than a house of straw might stand against the mighty blow of a blacksmith's hammer.

He gritted his teeth, seeing the scream coming and knowing there wasn't a thing he could do about it, but just as the slightest sound escaped the woman's throat, a hand clamped over her mouth, silencing her. Chall looked over the woman's shoulder to see that it was the young man who held his hand clamped over her mouth. He saw Chall's look and gave him a single nod as the woman began to calm down.

"You know, she fell sort of funny," one of the men said.

"Sure," the first who'd spoken said. "And she'd lose her head if it wasn't atta—"

"*Quiet, fools,*" the red-headed woman snapped, frowning and turning to stare directly at where Chall and the others stood. "I thought I heard something."

"You mean when she screamed, boss?" the man asked.

"Was loud, sure enough," the second man said, grinning again. "Awful inconsiderate of her."

The woman growled. "Not that, idiots," she said. "Perhaps it would be best if the two of you kept an eye on the outside for a time." They hesitated.

"Boss?"

"*Now,*" she hissed without turning from where she looked in Chall and the others' direction, seeming to be looking directly at him.

The two men gave each other a look then walked out of the library like sullen children angry at being reprimanded. Chall only noted them in a distracted way, for what little of his attention wasn't taken up by the act of putting the illusion, the lie back together was on the red-headed woman. She continued to stare at the space where they stood, her eyes narrowed as if trying to see something at night or through driving rain.

She was still looking when one of the other men spoke. "Boss? Everything alright?"

The woman watched for another few seconds then finally grunted and turned away. "Fine," she said. She frowned, glancing at him. "Go and start the burning. This time tomorrow, I want this library to be nothing but a pile of ash. If he's hiding somewhere in here," she went on, her gaze sweeping over Chall and the others as she looked around, "then I want him to cook."

"B-but boss," the man said, "you told Erik fifteen minutes, and it's only been—"

"I know what I said," she said. "Then and now."

"O-of course, boss," the man said, "but I only meant, that is, that the boys are still lookin' for the one we come to find."

"Well then they'd better hurry, hadn't they?" she asked dryly.

The man swallowed, nodding. "Of course boss," he said before hurrying away.

With the man gone, only two of the Wolves remained, the woman and one other. A small enough number that Chall thought there was a chance he and the others, using the element of surprise, could have overtaken them. But that would be a fool's choice as a single scream from the woman or one of the others would be all it would take for them to alert the gods alone knew how many others they had in the library, not to mention the two she'd banished to the street.

Which left only one option: continuing the lie and walking straight past the woman and her sword—still wet with the blood of the old woman—and the others, and out of the door.

A short distance, no more than a few dozen feet, but to Chall it seemed to stretch on for miles. He looked back at the others, gave a slow, steady nod. They returned it with several nervous, wide-eyed nods of their own, and Chall turned back once more, starting toward the doors. Because of the way the two men and woman stood near the door, Chall and his companions would, by necessity, have to walk between them, or else risk going around and wasting more time—time they simply did not have. He'd done what he could to patch the hole the old woman had left in the spell, but he could feel that area of it weakened, like a patch on a favorite shirt. It would hold for a little while longer, but if they tarried it would rip, and when it did the whole thing would collapse.

So he moved forward, walking in between the woman and one of the men, forced to move so close that either might have reached out and touched them—or stabbed them—with little effort. As he walked past, Chall did not dare turn to look at the red-headed woman, did not dare to even so much as breathe.

Yet he was sure that at any moment, she would turn to look at him, flashing him a smile that would say, in that single expression, that she had known they were there all along, had only been a cat toying with her food before finally devouring it.

But despite his fears, he made it past the woman unstabbed—or, at least, no more stabbed than how he'd started the day off. To his amazement, he even made it halfway to the doors themselves before he turned to check on the others' progress.

It all moved along smoothly, going easily enough...until it didn't. A middle-aged man—a clerk by his dress—third from the last in line was just stepping past the red-headed woman, when one of Chall's worst fears came to pass. Perhaps the clerk, if clerk he was, was too focused on his own fear, on his would-be murderers, to watch where he was going. Or perhaps it was an honest stumble. Whatever it was, whatever *caused* it, the man *did* stumble. Nothing terrible, nothing that caused him to fall, but enough that he let out a hiss as he caught his balance.

A hiss that, in that silence, sounded to Chall like the roar of nearby thunder. Or someone running around screaming "Please murder me!"

The woman spun immediately, looking directly at where the man stood only a few feet away. For his part, the man froze, as did everyone else. Except Chall. Whatever else the woman was, she was no fool, and it was too much to hope that she would pass off the sound as a figment of her imagination.

So Chall could not sit back and do nothing and hope that the woman let it pass. Instead, he concentrated for a moment on the sound, the *lie* of footsteps across the grand space of the library's entrance and, to go with those footsteps, a figure, a woman in a green dress—he had always loved green—running past.

"*Hey!*" one of the two remaining Wolves shouted, and the red-headed woman who, up until then, had been looking directly at the space where the man who had tripped stood frozen, spun, looking at the illusion Chall had created as the fake woman disappeared into an aisle of books.

"Go and get her," the woman said, frowning. "See if she knows where *he* is. Then you know what to do."

The man in question nodded, grinning in anticipation—Chall had, it had to be said, made the woman's bustline a little larger than it had strictly needed to be, the dress a little shorter than was necessary, a fact that the man had obviously picked up on as he went after her at a run.

The red-headed woman continued to stare down the aisle where the illusion had fled, which was good. Less good, though, was the fact that to create the illusion, Chall had had to draw some of his attention, his concentration away from the spell he was using to conceal them. Only for a moment, but it was enough. The house of toothpicks had begun to fall. The wind had found its way underneath the tarp, was forcing it up, and soon, *very* soon, it would be blown away to reveal what was underneath.

Chall gritted his teeth, motioning to the others, to hurry, and they began forward again. He was sweating by the time he reached the door, feeling the mental and physical strain of trying to hold the spell together, like a seamstress frantically sewing a piece of cloth together even as it came apart at a greater rate than she could hope to sew no matter her effort or skill.

He focused on the door for a moment, doing his best to include it in the working—after all, he thought that should one of the Wolves see the door open of its own accord they could not help but have questions. It would have normally been a trivial task to conceal such a thing, but given that he was already weary, straining at holding onto the spell as it leaked through his fingers like water, it was far more difficult than it ought to have been.

Still, he managed it. Judging that they had seconds, not minutes, he gave Petran a shaky nod, motioning him forward. The historian stepped to the door, easing it open, and Chall motioned frantically at the others who began filing through the door, staggering into the street like prisoners stumbling out of their cell after decades imprisoned.

Chall staggered after them, barely aware that he was moving at all, so much of his attention was focused on holding the failing spell together. Outside, the two guards Margaret had sent out had taken up position at the base of the stairs leading up to the library, standing on either side of them. Petran, Beth, and the others were huddled in front of the library, all staring back at him with terrified wide eyes, clearly scared to move. At least *nearly* all of them.

One of the group, Chall saw, had separated himself from the others and was, in fact, moving down the stairs, *stalking* down them towards one of the two men. Chall realized after a moment that it was the young man, the skeptic who had been so full of questions. Well, he was not asking questions now, but better if he were, Chall thought. Instead, he held a small knife—the gods alone knew where he'd gotten it—and from the look of fury twisting his face as he moved behind one of the two guards, Chall figured he had a pretty idea what he planned to do with it.

The young woman, Kyra, the same whom Clay had comforted

earlier, had separated herself from the group and was trying to call him back without alerting the guards, an effort which involved a lot of gesturing and horrified expressions, neither of which he paid any attention to. He continued down the steps toward the guard, his upper lip peeled back from his teeth in a silent snarl, clutching the small knife in a white-knuckled grip. Chall glanced at Petran, motioning at him, then at the other Wolf, the one standing opposite the one the young man was moving toward.

The historian looked down at the thick tome he still held somehow—the same that had saved Chall's life minutes ago—then back to Chall and gave a grim nod.

Chall, meanwhile, hurried down the steps as quietly as he could toward where Clay was moving toward the guard. He was only halfway there, though, when the young man stepped up behind the other man. Perhaps the Wolf heard something, the sound of the young man's shallow, anticipatory breaths, or the near-but-not-quite-silent sound of his boots scuffing on the stone of the stairs. Maybe there was no reason at all, just poor luck. Whatever the case, the Wolf chose that moment to turn and look behind him.

That regard, landing directly on the frayed, ragged spell, was all it took. It was as if the spell were some great weight Chall had been carrying, and while he couldn't have said for sure how much weight the man's regard added, he knew this—it was enough. The spell was no longer unravelling but unraveled in truth. He felt it as it did, felt the Art, the working slipping away, an eel wriggling free of his grasp at last.

Which left the Wolf staring directly at the young man and the knife he held in a shaky hand. The young librarian had likely never raised a blade, and the worst hurt he'd probably ever given another person was wounded feelings. In a contest of who was the more educated man, he would have no doubt come out the victor, but just then, in that moment, it was not education that mattered.

It was experience.

The Wolf saw the blade raised above the young man's head, and while the young man hesitated, the Wolf did not. He didn't reach for his own sword sheathed at his side—likely realizing that he would be dead before he ever retrieved it. Instead, he took the single step separating him from Clay, who let out a grunt of surprise as the Wolf tackled him around the waist, sending him crashing backward into the stone steps. The unexpected blow made the librarian lose his grip on the blade, and it clattered to the stairs beside him.

Before the librarian could recover, the Wolf fetched him a hard punch in the face, then another. Blood flew as the young man's lip busted underneath the blows. His fingers scrabbled desperately on the stone stairs, trying to reach the knife that lay nearby. The man atop him grinned as he noted the librarian's intent, then he reached down and grabbed the knife himself.

"Should have stayed with your books, lad," the Wolf said, grinning cruelly. "Better to burn than bleed, I think. But why don't you tell me?" He raised the knife, grinning, his entire attention focused on the young man, this latest victim. He didn't notice anything else. Not the shouts of his companion, not the group of huddled, terrified people standing up the stairs, and not Chall as he approached.

The knife, though—that he noticed.

Chall staggered forward, plunging the blade into the Wolf's back. The man's breath exploded in a grunt, his body arching in shock.

The Wolf reached behind him, trying to get his hands on the knife, but Chall didn't have a mind to let him. Instead, he ripped the knife free and reached around the man, burying the blade in his heart. Or, at least, trying to. He must have missed, for the man didn't have the good grace to die. He did, however, fall forward atop the librarian, then rolled off him, hacking out blood. The man wasn't quite dead—though well on his way, if Chall had to guess—but the fight had clearly gone out of him.

Suddenly there was a noise behind Chall, and he spun, sure that Petran had failed to take care of the second man and that, in another moment, he would be lying beside the dying man, participating unwillingly in a race to death, one he had very little interest in winning.

But it wasn't the other Wolf. Instead, it was Petran himself, as well as the librarian, Beth. Petran gave Chall a grim nod, and Chall turned back to the dying man. "Why did you come here? What do you want?" he asked, though he thought he knew it well enough from hearing Margaret speak. "How did you know I was here?"

But the man didn't answer him. In truth, he didn't even look at him. Instead, his semi-delirious gaze seemed to be gazing at Petran. "*It's...you,*" he gasped in a breath barely more than a whisper.

"Yeah, it's me," Chall said. "Now tell me why you came h—"

"*The...historian,*" the man wheezed.

"What?" Chall asked, feeling dumbstruck. "What do you—" But he didn't bother finishing, as he doubted the man would have an answer. What with being dead and all.

Instead, he filed that bit of confusion away for the moment, turning back to check on Clay. He still lay where he had, his face a stark, pale white, his robe and cheeks and...well very nearly all of him stained with the dead man's blood and some little of his own from where he'd been struck.

"Come on, lad," Chall said, offering him his hand. "Up you get."

The librarian hesitated for a moment, clearly struggling to regain his wits, but finally he took the offered hand and Chall pulled him to his feet.

"Y-you killed him," Clay said, not sounding like a man at all then but like a child as he stared at the corpse.

"Sure hope so," Chall said. "I'd hate to have put in all that effort for nothing."

The librarian might as well not have heard, though, for all the reaction he gave. He only continued to stare at the dead man as if he had never seen anything like it. Which, of course, he probably hadn't. Not a lot of corpses in libraries, Chall figured. At least, that was, until today.

"I wouldn't lose any sleep over that one, lad," Chall said. "Bastard like that, I reckon he probably deserves what he got and more."

Before the young man could answer—not that he seemed in any danger of doing so, considering how he was staring wide-eyed at the corpse—the young woman librarian who he had comforted earlier rushed forward, wrapping her arms around him.

"Oh, Clay," she said, "thank the gods. I thought...I thought that you..."

"I'm...I'm okay, Kyra," the man said.

Not yet, Chall thought, *but you will be. Given time enough.* "Listen," Chall said, "look at me, lad."

The young man did, finally, and again Chall was struck by how he didn't seem like a man at all but a child and how, sometimes, time was not the only thing that made a person one or the other.

"He was right, you know," Chall said. "He said that you should stay with your books, and that's true. There's better ways to die than at the hands of some bastard like that," he went on, jerking his thumb. Then he let his gaze go meaningfully to the young woman who still embraced the man. "Better ways to live, too. Think on it, alright?"

The young man hesitated only for a moment before giving a nod. "Th...thank you. I will."

Chall nodded back then turned to Petran and Elizabeth. "We need to get them out of here—now."

"My house is nearby," Elizabeth said. "We can go there."

Chall was surprised that the woman would have a home nearby considering that the library was in one of the richer parts of the city.

"My grandmother left it to me," she said by way of explanation. "It's big—plenty big enough to hold everyone and then some." She turned to Petran. "We'll be safe there."

"You will," Chall said, nodding, then glanced at Petran. "But not if Petran goes with you."

"What are you talking about?" Elizabeth said before the historian could speak. "Of course he's going to go with us. Those men—"

"Those *men*," Chall interrupted, glancing at Petran, "were looking for you. I know a little something about the man who sent them, enough to know that he isn't the sort that will accept failure with good grace. If he wants you, he won't stop looking until he finds you. If you go with them—"

"Then they'll be in danger," Petran finished. "But...but I thought you said they were looking for *you*."

"I was wrong," Chall said simply. "And we don't have time to argue about it here." He jerked a thumb at the library. "That lot'll be leavin' soon, and I think it'd be better if we weren't standing around here when they did, don't you? Let them go. We've got business to be about."

"Petran, you can't—"

"I have to, Beth," the historian said, taking her hands. "I'll be okay. I promise. Now go. Get them to safety, get *you* to safety."

Tears fell from the woman's eyes at that, and she pulled him into a tight embrace. "Be careful."

"Of course," Petran said, hugging her back. "I'll see you soon."

Beth nodded, stepping back and wiping at her tears. She gave the man a quick kiss then turned and hurried back to the others. "Come," she said. "This way."

They were off and moving then, hurrying down the street.

"Come on," Chall told the historian. "We've got work to do."

"What sort of work?" Petran said as they started off down the street in the opposite direction of where the woman and the others had gone.

"I've got some questions," Chall said, "ones that need answering."

"About the necklace, you mean?" Petran said. "Because, listen, Chall, without my notes—"

"Questions," Chall interrupted, "like why Robert Palden wants you dead. Wants it so bad, apparently, that he's willing to send his second-in-command, his *last* second-in-command, to see that it happens."

"But...why?" Petran said. "It doesn't make sense. I mean, I haven't done anything. I don't—"

"I don't think it's because of anything you did, Petran," Chall said, taking the necklace from his pocket as they turned a corner into an alley. "I think it's because of something you know."

The historian stared at the necklace in Chall's hand as they walked, then his gaze moved to Chall's face. "Wait, you think, those men, all of that, the killing, the burning of the library, was because of what I know about Fey artifacts?"

"Can you think of another reason why a small army of assassins would be so eager to see you dead?" Chall countered.

The historian came to a stumbling halt then, his face paling. "But that...that means that those who were killed, the burning...it's all m-my fault."

"No," Chall said, then he clapped a hand on the man's shoulder, waiting for Petran to meet his gaze. "Don't do that to yourself, Petran. Grief, it's heavy enough. No need to add shame to it, not when that shame's unwarranted. Those men, that woman, they're the ones responsible for that. Not you. And I mean to make them pay."

"But...but how?" the historian said. "If what you're saying is true, if they really intended to kill me in order to keep me from helping you discover anything about the necklace, then while they might have failed in the first, they have succeeded in the last."

"You're telling me you don't remember?" Chall said.

Petran colored. "There is far too much knowledge in the world for any mind, however keen or desiring, to contain it all. It is why I make notes in the first place."

Chall nodded. "That's alright, Petran," he said. "I wouldn't worry about it overly much. These bastards are going to get what's coming to them just the same."

"But how?" the historian asked. "I will do what I can, of course, to help you with what I remember, but Chall—"

"Three," Chall interrupted.

Petran frowned, coming up short. "I'm sorry?"

"You said there were three experts in the city."

"I'm not sure what you mean."

"Aren't you?" Chall asked, meeting the historian's gaze. "I mean, Petran, that I think it's time we paid your friend on King's Street a visit."

The historian frowned then, slowly, Chall watched the realization come into his eyes. "You mean to visit Falidar?"

"I do," Chall said.

The historian sighed, nodding. "Very well, if you think it's best."

"I do," Chall said, "and I think it's best we do it quickly. Unless I miss my guess, your friend Falidar is likely to receive a visit similar to the one we just had at the library before long. We can only hope that he hasn't received it already."

And with that grim thought, they started into the city as fast as a wounded fat man and a historian could which, Chall knew, was not fast at all.

He could only hope it would be fast enough.

CHAPTER SIXTEEN

Matt dreamt of summer.

He dreamt of long days and warm nights, of plants and growing things in profusion, and the feel of the sun on his skin.

Matt dreamt of summer.

But he woke to winter.

He was shivering even before his eyes opened, shifting as he tried to burrow deeper into the thick blankets that Fabor had provided—not that they felt thick then. They might as well have been woven of gossamer and starlight for as little protection as they seemed to provide against the intruding cold.

He wanted to step back into the dream, to pull it about himself like a cloak. But try as he might, he could not, so finally he gave it up, opening his eyes and rising to a seated position.

"You let the fire go out," he grumbled at his father, blinking his eyes blearily.

His father did not answer.

Matt rubbed the sleep out of his eyes and glanced at the cave entrance where the man had sat like some carved statue that might have been there for eternity. Only...he was not there now.

Matt frowned, looking around the cave, and didn't take him long to realize that his father was nowhere in sight. He grunted sourly. "Typical," he muttered. "Probably off hurting someone or something."

"You are not so far wrong, I think, Nephew."

So unexpected was the voice that Matt nearly screamed, *would* have screamed had he been able. Instead, his surprise was so strong that he managed no more than a choked, strangled grunt. "U-Uncle," he said, glancing back to where Feledias was slowly sitting up. "You're awake."

"I am, more's the pity," his uncle said, sighing whimsically. "I was having a most pleasant dream. As for your father, you are not wrong in saying that he is off hurting something."

Matt winced. "You heard that?"

"And more besides," Feledias said, meeting his gaze. "In fact, I would wager that I heard more than you meant to say." Matt didn't know what to say to that and so he said nothing. Feledias gave a small, knowing smile. "King indeed," he said. "Anyway, your father is out searching for food on which we might break our fast."

"I thought you said he was hurting something."

Feledias smiled. "Only a suspicion. I am not a native of this frozen wasteland of the north like you, Nephew—thank the gods for that, at least—but even my limited knowledge is such that I am fairly certain Bernard is unlikely to run across a baker's or a butcher's. That'll mean he will have to do the butchering himself, unless the creatures of the north will kill and skin and gut themselves, and from what I've seen of it, things here are far from so obliging. So, as I said, your father will be out hurting something—at least, we must hope so, for I find that all that shivering has left me with quite an appetite. So then, as is often required, to eat, a man must hurt. Living too, often requires it, I think, particularly in such times, in such places as this."

Matt frowned. "We're not talking about breakfast anymore, are we?"

"Aren't we?" Feledias asked, his eyes wide with mock innocence.

Once more, Matt did not know what to say and so, once more, he said nothing.

Feledias sighed. "Sometimes, Nephew," he began as he rose and shuffled forward, hugging his blankets tightly around him as he crouched and began to get to work starting a fire once more, "the world is hard." He glanced up. "Cold too, in case you hadn't noticed. It can be a cruel place, full of pain and little else. In such a place, it can sometimes help a man to have someone to blame. His anger makes him a little warmer—or, at least, he fancies that it does. Your father, he will be that for you, if you need him to be. He would be a lot more than that."

Matt shook his head. "It isn't—that's not what this is about."

"It isn't?"

"No," Matt said. "Look, I know that Cutter—that my *father*—loves me. Or...or at least he thinks he does. But—"

"Don't do that."

There was something scolding, even angry in Feledias's tone, and Matt found himself looking away from the cave entrance where he'd glanced to look at his uncle. Indeed, the man had an angry, what might have even been *furious* expression on his face. "Be angry with him, if you wish," Feledias said. "Question his choices, if you must—though I find that it is always far easier to judge another's choices after the fact than to be the one making them in the moment. But whatever else you may do, do not ever question my brother's love for you. He deserves better than that. For that love, Bernard went to the Black Wood. For that love, he came back out again."

Matt felt his face heat, feeling somehow embarrassed and angry at the same time, like some child who has been scolded but is still convinced that he is in the right. He did not like the feeling, but neither was he ready to let it go. "I am not so sure he is even capable of love."

"Then you are a fool after all, and the Known lands poorer for it," Feledias said sadly. "Bernard loves like few men do, Nephew. I have seen him risk his life time and time again to save others. I will admit that, in the past, Bernard was a violent man, but—"

Matt snorted. He couldn't help it. "The past?" he said. "If you ask me, Uncle, not so much has changed."

"A fool indeed," Feledias said. "For Bernard, Nephew, *everything* has changed. You think that it is anger or hate or some lust for blood that drives him, but you are wrong. It is love. Love and that only. It is his love—his love for *you*—that guides him. A love for which he would happily lay down his life, should it be required."

"But not his axe," Matt said, surprised by the bitterness in his own voice.

"Rare are the foes that are conquered by a word," Feledias said. "In my experience, if a man means to take on monsters, it helps if he's holding something sharp."

Matt saw that he was getting nowhere, that he *would* get nowhere. He turned to regard the cave entrance again. He could see the snow beyond it, not a blizzard as it had been but coming down softly enough. "Fabor was no monster," he said quietly.

"And so we come to it at last," Feledias said, sounding bored. "Is that what this is about? You took exception to our treatment of Fabor?"

"*His* treatment, you mean. He hurt him. All because he felt betrayed, all because he wanted to punish him."

Feledias sighed, rubbing at his temples. "Do you really believe that? Gods, but perhaps the people of the Known Lands would have been better off had I stayed their king. Yes, lad, your father hurt Fabor, but he didn't do it to punish him. Or to satisfy some sense of being betrayed. He hurt him and, in doing so, he saved him."

Matt frowned. "Didn't look much like saving from where I was standing."

"What things *appear* to be does not matter in the slightest. All that matters is what they *are*. Did you not ever stop to think, lad, what those insane villagers, what that feyling *creature* would have done, had they decided that Fabor had betrayed them?"

"What do you mean?"

"It's obvious, isn't it? They saw him, with your father, with the wagon. It would have been easy enough to put it together that Fabor helped us. And tell me, Nephew, had they done that, do you think the feyling would have been merciful? What of those villagers who had been all too ready to murder us in our beds? Do you think they might be forgiving of such a betrayal? Because I can tell you from hard-won experience that the Fey are not known for their mercy and neither are men known for their willingness to forgive slights."

Matt felt his face heat with embarrassment. "You're saying...that he hit Fabor to save him?"

"I'm saying that he hit Fabor not just to save *him* but to save his *wife,* too. After all, those mad villagers, they didn't strike me as the sort to let a man's wife go out of pity. Did they you?"

Matt shook his head. "No...they didn't." He sighed heavily. "I've been a fool."

Feledias made what might have been an approving sound. "And there is the king I have heard about," he said. "All men are fools, lad. The wisest of us know it."

Matt nodded. "I owe him an apology, I think."

"I wouldn't worry over much, Nephew," Feledias said. "I owe him far more than that. Not that I'd relish the idea of telling him as much, understand. It'd go to his head, and Bernard is nothing if not vain."

"I've never known him to be vain."

Feledias sighed. "No, neither have I." He held up his hands to the small blaze he'd managed, frowning. "Doesn't do much for the chill, does it? Though I suppose we ought to be glad those wolves or any other critter haven't come inside looking for something to eat."

Before Matt could answer he heard a shuffling sound and turned to the cave mouth. As he did, he saw a broad-shouldered figure in furs stepping inside.

"It seems I spoke too soon, Nephew," Feledias said. "Here's one of those critters now. How are you, Bernard? Have a pleasant early morning stroll, did you?"

Normally, Matt's father humored Feledias and his jokes, often even seeming amused by them. Now, though, his expression was grim. That was the first thing Matt noticed. The second was the blood. It was splashed on the furs on his chest and arms. He held his axe in one hand and what appeared to be two dead rabbits in the other.

"F-father?" Matt asked. "Is everything okay?"

"An awful lot of mess for a couple of scrawny conies, Bernard," Feledias said. "What did you roll around on their bodies?"

"The blood isn't theirs," Cutter said.

"Then—"

"Nor is it mine. We need to go. Now."

"What is it?" Matt asked. "What's happened? Did the villagers catch up with us?" he finished, finding his gaze going to his father's axe, to the blood staining the blade. Blood that, he was confident, did not belong to the dead rabbits.

"Why the rush?" Feledias asked, rising. "Whatever it is, whatever it *was* it seems to me by the look of that axe of yours that you killed it."

Cutter frowned. "I think it was dead before I got to it," he said.

There was something about the way his father spoke the words that made the hairs on the back of Matt's neck stand up. "What does that mean?"

"That, Nephew," Feledias said as he hurriedly began shoving the blankets they'd used into the pack Fabor had stowed them in, "means that we need to go."

"Is it the woman, the one from Windham?" Matt said. "Or the villagers? Did they find us?"

"No," Cutter said, glancing back at the opening as if he expected someone or some*thing* to appear there. "I think this is something else. I'll be outside."

"We'll have to get the wagon ready," Feledias said as he continued packing.

"That won't be a problem," Cutter said, and there was something about the way he said it that Matt didn't like.

Before he could ask his father anything more, though, Cutter tossed the dead rabbits to Feledias. "Stow them," he said. "We'll need to eat. Keep our strength up." Then, he abruptly turned, hefting his axe in two hands, and stepped out of the cave.

"What is going on, do you think?" Matt said.

"I don't know, Nephew," Feledias said, "but what I *do* know is that your father is not given to flights of panic. He does not scare easily. So if he's saying we need to go, I think it best we believe him." Feledias glanced up at Matt from where he'd been packing. "Don't you?"

Matt swallowed hard. "I'll help," he said, moving forward.

———

CUTTER STOOD outside the cave mouth, the snow falling quietly around him, as he studied the mountain trail. He could not see anything, nor could he hear it, but that gave him little comfort. He had not heard the creature, either, when it had come upon him. A wolf, he thought, or at least it had been, once. It had been dead—that much was obvious by the state of decay of its body, the bones showing in several places, what little, desiccated flesh had remained clinging to its skeletal frame like moss to a tree stump.

Dead, yet that had not stopped it from trying to kill him. That had been a strange fight. He had been alone, checking the snare he'd made the night before for the two rabbits and then, suddenly, the creature had been on him. No shout or roar, no battle cry, not any noise at all. A silent battle that had not ended until Cutter had used the Breaker of Pacts to separate the creature's head from its shoulders. Whatever call had pulled it back from death to do its bidding had been strong—but it had not been strong enough to ignore that.

There was a sound behind him, and he turned to see his brother and son emerging from the cave, wincing at the brightness of the early morning sun.

"I'll just put this in the—" Feledias began then cut off, frowning at the space where the wagon had been. "Where's the wagon?"

"Gone," Cutter said.

"You know, we really have to work on these one-word answers of yours, Brother. I can *see* that it's gone, but a little more detail might be useful. For example, where did it get gone *to?*"

"I don't know."

"And this is why you said it wouldn't be a problem getting the wagon ready," Feledias said, sighing.

"The horses?" Matt asked. "When they weren't in the cave, I thought you had already harnessed them."

"Gone as well," Cutter said.

"Yes, but *how?*" Feledias demanded. "Did someone take them? Or are they just cleverer than we are and decided to flee this blasted, snow-crusted mountain?"

"I'm not sure," Cutter said. Feledias gave a sour face, opening his mouth to speak. Before he could, Cutter beat him to it. "I was out searching for some food when I was attacked by a mostly skeletal wolf. I killed it...again. No sooner had I done so then I heard the horses," he said. "I came running back to check on them, to check on the two of you, but when I arrived, whatever had caused them to kick up such a stir was gone. As were the wagon and the horses themselves."

"So...perhaps they simply came loose of their tethers and wandered off," Matt said, sounding hopeful and doubtful at the same time.

"I do not think so," Cutter said. "We will have to walk."

"You don't know that," Feledias said. "We should search for them. It might well be that the beasts are just around the corner there," he went on, jerking a thumb down the mountain pass where it disappeared around a bend in the trail.

"Unlikely," Cutter said.

"Is it, Brother?" Feledias said. "I only ask because, I don't know about the two of you, but I don't relish traveling this mountain in a wagon, much *less* walking it. Surely we can spare a few minutes looking for the horses."

"You are assuming that we have a few minutes to spare," Cutter said. "And as for the horses, I don't think we'll find them. Not alive, anyway."

"You can't know that," Feledias said.

"No," Cutter agreed. "I can't. But you did not hear them—I did."

Feledias frowned, sighing. "Very well, Brother. If you say that there is no point, then I will believe you. Okay with you if I still do some bitching along the way?"

"I'd be worried if you didn't," Cutter said, his eyes scanning the path once more, taking in the mountainside rising up beside them.

"You think more are coming," Matt said.

It wasn't really a question, but Cutter was preparing to answer it anyway. Before he could, though, Feledias spoke. "That's the thing about a man's death, Nephew," he said grimly. "It never stops coming."

"Come on," Cutter said. "Time to move."

They started up the mountain pass, Cutter at the front. He might have sheathed his axe and saved his strength, but he did not. He did not see anyone or anything, but that meant little. He felt *hunted*. Pursued. And so his axe remained where it was.

Matt came next, holding the machete he'd taken from Fabor's barn in front of him as he scanned the trail ahead, often shooting glances behind them. Last was Feledias, trudging forward with a grim expression on his face like a man marching to his death. His swords remained in their sheaths, and his hands were tucked underneath his arms, his shoulders hunched in an effort to stay warm.

They walked for over an hour, the mountain path becoming steeper and steeper the further they went. Occasionally, Cutter called for them to halt so that they might listen for any sounds of pursuit. But if they *were* pursued, then those hunting them remained silent, hidden. Not that Cutter would have likely seen them even if they had been only a few dozen feet further down or further up the trail, for a thick fog had risen around them as they walked, obscuring their vision and making an already arduous climb far more difficult, far more dangerous than it might have been.

"Damned fog," Feledias wheezed from behind him as if on cue. "Damned mountain."

It was at least the dozenth time he'd said it, perhaps more, but Cutter found himself agreeing completely.

"There's...something wrong," Matt said.

Cutter turned to regard his son, barely able to see his face even from only feet away for the thick curtain of gray that hung in the air. "What is it?"

"The fog," Matt said slowly, barely loud enough for Cutter to hear. "There's something...wrong with it. It is not...normal, I think."

"Who's to say what's normal in a cursed place like this, Nephew?" Feledias asked. "The entire mountain seems like a trap set to catch any fool stupid or desperate enough to come here."

"I'll be desperate," Cutter told his brother, "you can be stupid."

Feledias grunted. "Just get moving, will you? Perhaps once we reach the top of this damned trail we'll be out of the fog. If something is going to eat me, I'd just as soon see it coming."

Cutter glanced at Matt, raising his eyebrow in question, and his son nodded. "I'm...I'm alright," he said.

"Okay then." They started climbing again.

The steep path was littered with small and not-so-small stones, some of which threatened to trip them and, at least once, very nearly sent Feledias spilling over the edge of the mountain, likely *would* have, had Matt not reached out and caught his shoulder. In several places, large boulders blocked the pass completely, forcing Cutter and the others to climb over them before continuing onward.

They were nearing the top of the steep climb, where the path seemed to level off before disappearing beyond sight of their vantage point further down the trail, when Matt paused. A fact Cutter was only aware of because of a curse from Feledias.

"Gods, lad," his brother said, "you can't just stop like that. Or is it that you want me to go tumbling down this mountainside?"

Cutter turned back. The fog had grown so thick as they walked that at first, he couldn't see anything, and he had the terrified feeling that his brother and his *son* were gone, no more than disembodied voices haunting the mountainside.

It was a feeling, a *certainty* that grew in strength with each moment, and he hurried forward into the fog, brushing it away with his hands the way a man might move a curtain out of his way. By the time he finally caught sight of Matt and his brother standing on the mountain pass, his heart was hammering in his chest.

"Everything alright?" he asked.

If his brother or son noticed the quiet panic in his voice they likely thought it only from exhaustion at the exertion of climbing the steep trail. But in truth, as Cutter stepped forward, taking in Matt's faraway expression, the way his son's head was cocked as if listening to something, he doubted if the young king noticed him speak at all.

"Matt?" he asked.

"Do you hear it?" his son asked, sounding more as if he spoke to himself than to either of them. "Music."

Cutter glanced at Feledias and saw his brother giving him a troubled look. "What music, Matt? I don't hear anything."

"How can you not?" his son asked. "It...wait. It's gone." Slowly, his face lost the distant expression it'd had, and Matt looked at Cutter. "It sounded like her—the woman. The music she was playing in Windham."

Cutter blinked, surprised at that. Just then, on the mountain pass, the village of Windham felt a lifetime away, part of another world, one where the creeping fog and creeping cold did not try, by degrees, to swallow a man as they did here, on the mountain.

"You imagined it, lad," Feledias said, and there was something about the way he studied Matt that Cutter did not like. It was the same sort of look someone might give to a person if they were mad...or else, dying. "That's all. Place like this, with the fog and all, well, it'll play tricks on anyone."

"It was...calling," Matt said. "Not us...I don't think."

Feledias gave Cutter another troubled look at that, and Cutter could almost read his brother's thoughts. He was thinking, no doubt, about before, about the way Matt had appeared out of nowhere and somehow saved them from the Unsated, about, perhaps, the way Matt had thought her music terrible while, to Cutter and Feledias, it had seemed like the most beautiful thing in the world.

"Are you sure?" Cutter asked.

Matt glanced at him, a worried expression on his son's face. "You didn't hear it?" he asked.

Cutter winced, giving his head a slow shake.

"It...it's getting worse, then," his son said quietly. "What I told you about before...the...spells. The sound...the music...it sounded...it sounded green. Gods help me, what's happening to me?"

That scared Cutter. He had faced down all manner of creature and monster over the course of his life, but here, now, there was nothing to face, nothing to fight. Something was going on with his son, that much was sure, and whatever that something was, Matt was afraid. It was as if there was a battle raging inside his son, one Cutter did not fully understand, and he could not fight it for him, however much he might wish to. So, instead, he could only hope to help his son find the strength he needed to fight it himself.

He stepped forward, putting a hand on his son's shoulder. "It's okay," he said. "Whatever it is, Matt, it's okay. And who knows? Perhaps Fel was right—perhaps it is just your imagination. If there is any place that might inspire someone's imagination, I'd say it's this."

His son nodded slowly at that, but he did not look convinced.

"Do you need to rest for a bit?" Cutter asked. "We could all use it."

Matt shook his head slowly. "No...no, thank you. But I think...it's better, if I'm moving. It's better to...be distracted."

Cutter nodded. "Okay."

Then they were moving again.

With the thick fog obscuring their vision so much that they could not even see their feet coupled with the stones littering the mountain path, it took them another half hour to reach the top of the path. Cutter stepped forward into what was a large clearing, an open space in the mountain. Rock walls rose all around them in a rough circle, one with two exits, the one they had just stepped in through and one further ahead, at the opposite end of the clearing that appeared to lead to a long, narrow path flanked on either side by the sheer walls of the mountain.

Cutter frowned at the path, then at the clearing. There was something strange about it.

"The air..." Matt said quietly, "it tastes...strange. Warm."

Cutter glanced at Feledias who shrugged. "Don't look at me," his brother said. "I can't remember the last time I would have described anything as warm."

Cutter looked back at the clearing. It was covered in snow. There was no vegetation—no real surprise there, for they had passed little enough on their trip through the mountain, the conditions of the frigid landscape too much for any except the heartiest of bushes and grasses which might sometime be found clinging on in hostile environments.

But that was not what struck him the most. Instead, it was the fact that the clearing didn't *look* like a clearing at all. Or, at least, not a natural one. The mountain walls which rose up all around it made it into the shape of a bowl, and the rock outlining that bowl appeared to be leaning outward, away from the clearing, as if some giant explosion had blown the rock outward.

"Something happened here," he said.

"Yes," Feledias answered, moving to stand beside him. "But what?"

Cutter shook his head slowly. The truth was, he wasn't sure he wanted to know. Whatever it was, it had clearly been a long time ago, yet even now the air had a strange feeling to it. He would not have described it as warm the way Matt had, but it certainly felt...strange. Almost *charged*, the way the air might sometimes feel before a storm. The hairs on his arms and the back of his neck stood up even as he looked around the strangely-shaped clearing. He found himself studying the rocks on the outer edges, those that looked as if they had been blown outward.

He decided that he did not like that place. It felt, somehow, as if he did not belong. As if, perhaps, *no one* belonged there. At least no one living. He felt the way a man might feel walking through a graveyard alone at night, with the fog rising up thick and cloying around him. Or perhaps the way a man might feel stepping into a church, a place of worship that had been turned to one of debauchery and violence and then left for decades to stew in the memories of those crimes, that betrayal.

He felt, in short, like a trespasser, an intruder upon that place, like an ant crawling on the dinner table and in imminent danger of being smashed. "Come on," he told his companions, surprised by how dry his throat was, surprised too by how he found himself speaking in a whisper, for to speak any louder felt almost like a crime. "Let's get out of here."

"Happily," Feledias answered in an equally quiet voice.

Then they were moving again.

The feeling, whatever it was, grew worse with each step they took into the clearing, but Cutter forced himself onward, feeling as if he were dragging some increasingly heavy weight behind him. Or, perhaps, it was more accurate to say that he felt as though invisible hands pushed at him, trying to hold him back, to tell him that he was not welcome. He did his best to ignore it. After all, what choice did they have? The Barrier Mountains held the key to defeating Shadelaresh, or so the Gray Man had told him, and Cutter believed him.

They continued into the clearing.

They were about halfway to the other side, when Matt let out a quiet hiss behind him.

"*Father,*" he said in a low whisper.

Cutter heard the fear in his son's voice, and he spun at once, his axe —still in his hand—rising in preparation. "What? What is it?"

"Our friends, Brother," Feledias said, his gaze slowly moving around the outer edges of the clearing. "It seems they have returned."

There was a sort of dark resignation in his tone that Cutter did not care for but one that, as he followed the gazes of his brother and son, he understood.

The Unsated were back. They stalked along the outer edges of the clearing, climbing along the rocks, surrounding Cutter and his two companions. Dozens—hundreds—of them and as terrible, as menacing as they had appeared in the perpetual twilight of the Black Wood, here, in the bright light of day, they looked far worse.

Their dark, almost black hides stood out starkly against the snow-covered backdrop of the clearing, their lithe forms moving with a grace that was somehow captivating and revolting at the same time, reminding Cutter not of dogs but cats. Skulking with a cat's grace along the rock outcroppings, their eyes, amber and crimson, shining the way a cat's might in the darkness and never mind that it was early in the day.

"What do you...what do you think they want?" Matt asked.

"I have a few ideas, Nephew," Feledias said grimly. "Unless I miss my guess, you're going to be putting that borrowed blade of yours to use soon enough." He glanced at Cutter's son. "Unless, of course, you want to transport us somewhere else, the way you appeared out of nowhere before. I can think of a few recommendations of places to go, if needed. There's a fine tavern in New Daltenia—I say fine largely on account of it doesn't have any giant monster dog creatures wanting to eat us. The ale tastes like piss, but then after a mug or two—"

"Fel."

His brother sighed.

They both turned to glance at Matt, and Cutter's son gave an apologetic shake of his head. "I...I don't know how to...to do it."

"Ah well," Feledias said, shrugging. "Don't worry on it, Nephew. There are worse ways to die. Probably. Not that I can think of any."

Cutter was barely listening, though. Instead, he was studying the

Unsated, the nearest of which was fifty feet away. A goodly distance but a distance, he knew from hard experience, that the creatures could cover in moments. Yet, none did. Instead, they continued to stalk around Cutter and the others, forming a sort of large circle around the clearing, not touching the ground of the clearing itself but instead moving along its outer edges, keeping to the rocks.

"What are they doing?" Matt said quietly. "Why aren't they attacking?"

"I don't know," Cutter said quietly.

"That thing that you said attacked you near the cave, the dead wolf," Feledias said, "any chance it was one of these bastards?"

"No," Cutter said, giving his head a small shake. "It was different."

"Good to know," his brother said, sighing. "How do you want to play it, Bernard?" he asked, studying the creatures with a look of undisguised disgust on his face.

Cutter considered them, then finally gave his head a small shake. "We keep going."

"What if it...what if that makes them violent?" Matt asked.

"We have a little bit of experience with these bastards, Nephew," Feledias said. "And I'm fairly certain that violent is the only way they come."

Cutter nodded. That was true enough. They had very nearly died to the creatures not once but twice, the first to be saved by Door, the Gray Man's agent, and the second to be saved by Matt. "We keep going," he repeated. "If we can reach the other side we can put the walls of the mountain at our backs. We'll be able to hold out that way for a little while."

"And then?" Matt asked quietly.

Cutter shared a look with his brother. "And then we'll see."

They started forward again. Cutter expected the movement to serve as a signal to the creatures, the way Matt had suggested it might. He expected for them to charge forward, dozens, hundreds of them from all directions the way they had back in the Black Wood.

But the creatures remained where they were, skulking along the rocks, and so Cutter and his companions did the only thing they could do—they continued on.

They were two thirds of the way across the clearing when suddenly, Matt snatched Cutter's arm in a death grip.

"What?" Cutter said, looking around at the Unsated surrounding the clearing. "What is it?"

"Something's coming," Matt whispered, his eyes looking ahead of them. Cutter followed his gaze but saw nothing, only the empty clearing ahead and, beyond that, the mountain trail.

He was still looking, trying to figure out what had bothered his son, when his brother spoke. "Why did they stop?" Feledias asked quietly.

Cutter saw that his brother was right. The creatures, as one, had stopped moving around the edges of the clearing and were instead staring either ahead of Cutter and the others or behind them.

A moment later, as if responding to some silent signal, they suddenly burst into action, and Cutter tensed, raising his axe, sure that the creatures had finally decided that they were tired of waiting and meant to see him and his brother and son dead. But the Unsated didn't move toward him and his companions. Instead, they sprinted toward the direction Cutter and his companions had come from.

In moments, they had all vanished from sight, and Feledias looked at Cutter, a troubled expression on his face. "If something *is* coming, I'm not sure I want to meet it, not if it can send those evil bastards scurrying like frightened mice. Maybe we should hide, or—"

"Hide where?" Cutter countered.

"Tell me you hear that," Matt said, his voice a quiet whisper.

Cutter was opening his mouth to tell his son that he still didn't hear anything when, suddenly, he did.

It was faint at first. So faint that he might have imagined it. Music, what did, indeed, sound like the strumming of a lute. It was so quiet as to be nearly imperceptible, but he did perceive it, and from the frown growing on his brother's face so, too, did Feledias. As they stood there, the music grew louder and louder still. When Cutter had first heard it, it had seemed to come from everywhere and nowhere, with no definable source at all. But now, it was definitely coming from right ahead of them, and even as Cutter looked, the source of that melody stepped into view at the opposite end of the clearing.

The woman, the *feyling* that the people of Windham had known as Aurora was dressed the same as she had been when Cutter had first seen her. Yet even the strange Fey magics she possessed had, apparently, not been enough to allow her passage through the Barrier Mountains unscathed. Her dress was stained and torn in several places, its hem wet with damp. She held a lute in her hands, strumming it softly, but as she stepped forward, out of the mountain pass and into the clearing, she stopped. "Why, if it isn't Prince Bernard and Prince Feledias," the feyling called, smiling. "And the young King too. What an unexpected pleasure, meeting you here."

"Somehow I doubt that," Cutter called back.

"Very well," she said, heaving a theatrical sigh as she stepped further into the clearing, "I must admit that I contrived to meet you once more. But can you truly blame me? After all, our first meeting was cut so short, and we have unfinished business."

"The business of killing us, do you mean?" Feledias called.

"Yes, Prince Feledias," she called. "That is exactly what I mean. Still, it is no matter. You will die here, in these mountains, as all who dare to venture here have."

"It's three against one," Feledias called back, "us with swords and an axe, and you with a lute. I don't think it's us that's going to be doing the dying."

"Father," Matt said quietly, "something's wrong."

If the woman was concerned at all by Feledias's threat, she did not show it. She only smiled. "Yes, three against one," she called. "Three strong men and I just an unarmed woman. Tell me, Feledias Stormborn, do you feel safe?"

Cutter glanced at his brother and saw that for one of the first times in his life, Feledias seemed to have no words, and he understood that, for Cutter, without knowing exactly why, *felt* that Matt was right. Something was wrong. "You are no woman, *creature*," he called.

She cocked her head then, a mock frown on her face. "Ah, you wound me, Prince Bernard. *Destroyer*. And here I thought we got along so well, last we met."

"That was before you tried to kill me and my companions," Cutter called.

"Aw, you're going to let a thing like that come between us?"

"I'm funny that way," Cutter answered.

The feyling sighed again. "Very well. Then I suppose we might as well get on with things. After all, I do not like it here. It is cold, and I so detest the cold. Tell me, Destroyer, do you even know where you stand? Are you aware that you and your companions tread on sacred ground? No, I can see by your expression that you do not. But it makes no matter. You stand on sacred ground, it is true, and soon, you will be buried in it. Buried in it as so many others were before you."

Then she began to play.

The music was faint, a wisp of sound so quiet that Cutter might have imagined it. "Do you know what my people call these mountains, Destroyer?" the feyling asked, her fingers strumming gently on the lute, and though those strummings were almost silent, there was something about the sound that Cutter did not like. Something ominous, reminiscent of the sound of approaching thunder.

She did not wait for him to answer before speaking on and as she spoke, she played, the music growing slowly louder. "*Vertai Hjarta.* Winter's Heart. These mountains have been here long before your people washed up on our shores like the misshapen rodents you are, and they will be here long after you are gone. For winter does not die, Destroyer, and it cannot be killed. I do not know what ill-conceived errand brought you and yours here, to this place of ice and death, but not even your great, cursed strength will be enough to see you leave them again. You will die in these mountains as so many before you have." She smiled then. "Were I to tell you just how many, you would not believe it...not yet, at least."

There was something about the way she said the last which Cutter did not like.

"You shouldn't have come alone, feyling," Feledias called back. "These mountains might be killers, but then so, too, is pride. It's been killing people since there were people to kill."

The feyling gave a slow smile. "And here I was led to believe that you were the clever one. But look at you, how *brave* you are, three armed men facing one lone woman wielding a lute."

"I told you before," Cutter called, "you are no woman."

"No," she said, her gaze moving toward him, seeming to dance with dark amusement. "And nor am I alone."

She began to play in earnest then, and as she played, she spoke, *chanted,* really, in a loud, clear voice one might use when addressing an auditorium. Or, Cutter thought grimly, when casting a spell.

"*Since dawn of time the ice held sway, o'er mortal kin and even Fey,*" she sang. "*Countless sleepers here then lay, frozen in Winter's Heart, lest they stray. Lulled to sleep these dreamers dream, and though contented they might seem, they'd give anything to part, with the icy touch of Winter's Heart.*"

The music grew louder then, so loud that it seemed to Cutter there was no other sound in all the world.

"Something...something's happening," Matt said. "Father, something's wrong."

But this time, Cutter did not need his son to tell him that something was wrong, for he could feel it. Feel it in some primordial part of himself, a vestige, perhaps, left from when the first men walked the world. The hairs on the back of his neck stood up, and a cold chill ran through him as the feyling continued to sing, not in the common tongue now but in the language of the Fey.

"What do we do?" Feledias asked beside him, and Cutter could hear the strain in his brother's voice. "Gods be good, that music, Brother...it feels like a curse. The worst thing I've ever heard, I think."

Cutter nodded in agreement, for he felt it too. Every note of the melody the woman played felt wrong, and not just wrong but perverse, a twisting, somehow, of what ought to be straight. A defilement, though what exactly was being defiled he did not know, only that it was. "You're right," he said grimly. "Suppose we ought to go ask her to stop...and quickly."

He started forward then, his brother and son following. He could see no reason to hurry, at least nothing tangible, but he hurried anyway, every word the woman spoke sounding more perverse and unbearable than the last, like fingernails on slate.

But the thick mountain snow and the tumbled scree and rocks it hid made for poor ground to run on. Cutter and his companions had only made it about halfway to the woman—and Cutter nearly fallen twice when his foot struck some unseen obstacle buried in the snow—when something began to happen.

The ground beneath Cutter's feet seemed to abruptly shift, heaving. He staggered but managed to keep his balance, if only just. There was a shout from behind him and Cutter turned to see that his brother had fallen. He reached down, offering him a hand and pulling him to his feet.

"What in the name of the gods was that?" Feledias breathed, touching his fingers to his bloody lip from where he'd fallen.

"I don't know," Cutter said, turning back to the feyling.

"So many," she called, smiling. *"So many to hear my song, Destroyer."*

Before Cutter had a chance to ask her what *that* meant, he noticed something unsettling. The ground around them had begun to *move*. The snow shifting and seeming to ripple the way the water of a still lake might if someone tossed a stone into it.

Then, mounds began to rise in the snow.

"A great battle was fought here, Destroyer," the feyling said as Cutter and his brother and son gazed around at all the moving lumps of snow. "Not won, you see, for no matter how they strive, Winter and Summer are locked in an eternal battle, one in which neither can prevail. A battle that has raged since the beginning of time and will continue until its end. And like all battles, this eternal war has its cost. The dead know it, for it is they who have paid it. Do you think, Destroyer, that the dead have forgotten the world of the living? That they lie peacefully, perhaps, thinking nothing at all? If so, then you are wrong. The dead remember. They remember what it was to live, to breathe, to feel the touch of the sun. They remember...and they strive, they yearn to feel it again."

"*Bernard*," Feledias hissed from behind him, and Cutter could hear the fear in his brother's voice. He turned and saw that Feledias's face had gone a pale nearly to match the snow covering the ground. Cutter followed his brother's gaze and saw immediately what had caught his attention. Something was rising from the ground, snow and ice sloughing away as it emerged. And when enough of the ice and snow had fallen away, it revealed a wolf. Or at least what had *been* a wolf once. Now, it was mostly exposed bone with strips of ragged flesh clinging to it here and there. One eye was gone, nothing but a cavernous socket where it had been, and the one that remained studied Cutter and his companions with a dead, intent stare.

But the feyling's spell was far from finished. The ground continued to heave, snow shifting, ice cracking as it broke apart, as form after form emerged from the thick blanket of white. There were more wolves—or, at least, what once had been wolves—but that wasn't all. There were others that appeared to have once been feylings, though it was not easy to tell due to their various states of decay. And others, Cutter saw with a mixture of horror and revulsion, had once been mortal men and women, likely members of those failed expeditions which had ventured into the Barrier Mountains.

But while those creatures and men that rose from the ground varied in their form, this they shared in common—they all, once broken free of the ice's clutches, stood unmoving, regarding Cutter and his companions with emotionless expressions.

"Gods...what...what is it?" Feledias asked.

Cutter didn't answer, for he knew that the question arose not from a lack of knowledge but from revulsion and shock, a revulsion, a shock that he shared.

It was not just that such a thing was terrifying. It was that it was *wrong*. The living lived and the dead stayed dead. Or, at least, they were supposed to. The natural order of things had been twisted, perverted, and he thought that any man or woman, having witnessed it, could not help but be affected by it. It was as if a field of beautiful flowers had certainly all turned to thousands, millions of writhing, squirming maggots. Or else, as if the sun itself had gone dark in the sky.

"They're...they're as still as statues," Feledias said.

"Not statues," Matt said quietly. "Puppets."

Cutter frowned back at the feyling, who was studying them with a smile. Puppets, Matt had said, and he didn't think there was any need in asking who their master might be, nor who the master might be of those others who were still exhuming themselves from their icy graves.

"What do you want to do, Bernard?" Feledias asked, his voice sounding strained, afraid.

Cutter glanced at his brother and his son. Both looked frightened—as well they might—worse; though, they looked near panic. And panic, Cutter knew, could get a man killed, could do the job quicker than any blade. "I didn't much care for her song," he told them.

Feledias's darting eyes slowly settled on his, and some small bit of resolve came back into his panicked expression as he took a slow, steadying breath. "Alright, Bernard," he said, swallowing. "Alright. You didn't like the song...let's go tell her."

Cutter turned to regard Matt. His son gave a small, shaky nod. "Alright then," Cutter said. "Stay close. I'll take the front. You handle any that come at us from the sides, but whatever you do, keep moving and do not stop. We won't survive long here, where they can surround us. If we can make it to her, if we can kill the puppet master..."

"Then no one will be controlling the puppets," Matt finished.

"And if she doesn't just stand there and let us kill her?" Feledias asked.

"Then we'll stand a better chance in the pass beyond than here in the open. Now come on."

As Cutter, his brother, and his son started forward at a jog, the feyling began to play. The figures which had emerged from the ice and snow and which, to that point, had stood unmoving, suddenly stirred at the sound of that music. As one, they started toward Cutter and his two companions, the circle that had surrounded them beginning to collapse onto them.

Cutter hefted his axe and continued forward at a jog. The first of the dead to reach him came from the front. It had been some sort of feyling once, he thought, though unlike any he had ever seen before. It had eyes that glowed green in its cadaverous face, and great, curved horns rose above its head. It held no weapon, but didn't seem bothered by that fact as it came at him, did not even seem bothered as his axe cut it down, and its body, now in two halves, fell to the ground.

The next figure had been a man once. He held a weapon, at least of a sort. An old, rusted machete, the blade chipped and dulled from exposure to the elements. He must have died with it in his hand, though it clearly had not served him then.

And it did not serve him now.

The dead man's hand went up, his blade along with it. It flashed down, but even as it did so, too, did Cutter's axe, severing the dead man's hand at the wrist. Then with a quick pivot, Cutter brought the blade back around and his axe struck the dead man in the throat, sending his head sailing out of sight into the growing mass of risen dead.

A wolf came next, not leaping as their kind did but lurching toward him. Cutter swept his axe out, sending it flying and knocking several of the closest dead men and creatures back.

He continued on.

He felt as though he were caught in some nightmare as they fought their way through those silent dead, the only sounds of the battle their own shouts and grunts and exhausted breaths.

More and more came at him, and Cutter cut them down in their turn, the axe flashing this way and that. Yet no matter how many he cut down, there were always more to take their place, and despite his efforts, their forward progress began to slow.

But that was not the worst of it. As they slowed from a jog to a walk and a walk to a halting, forward shuffle, Cutter was able to see those he cut down. And so as he fought more of their number, he saw that even whatever magic the Breaker of Pacts possessed was not enough to overcome the power of the feyling's song, for those he'd cut down slowly began to rise again, unfazed by wounds that would have proven fatal to any living creature.

As the dead came on from all sides, their progress continued to slow until, finally, they were forced to stop altogether. They stood back-to-back as row after endless row of dead came at them, a snare that was slowly tightening no matter how hard they fought.

Cutter was all too aware of what was at stake, and his axe was a blur as it sent one then another of the dead things down to the ground —not that they stayed that way. They did not heal from the wounds he and the others gave them—they simply did not care. Torn and ripped and smashed, they rose. Armless, missing a leg, headless, still they rose, obeying the siren's call of the feyling's lute. And during the time it took them to rise again there were more than enough of their fellows to keep Cutter and his companions busy.

As he fought, he came to the realization of the way the thing would go, the way it *must* go. Retrieving his axe from the head of his latest opponent, Cutter risked a glance ahead and caught a glimpse of the feyling in the distance, still standing where she had. There was an eager smile on the creature's face, for it seemed she knew the truth too— there were simply too many.

For years, nearly his entire life, Cutter's strength had been celebrated. Legends had sprung up about that strength over the years.

Some true, most outright lies. But as he stood with his brother and son fighting a desperate battle, he was confronted with one, undeniable fact.

It was not enough.

No matter how much he tried, how hard he fought, it was not enough to make a dent in the onrushing tide of creatures seeking their death. And if his strength was not good for that, for protecting his son, then what, he despaired, was the point of it at all?

But despair or not, hopeless or not, Cutter did what he had always done. He gripped his axe, set his jaw...

And he fought on.

CHAPTER SEVENTEEN

Maeve was tired.

She felt wrung out, used up. She lay on the cold dungeon floor where she had for the last several hours, searching for sleep and not finding it. Facing imminent torture and death, she'd found, had a way of dampening a person's restfulness.

She'd told herself when she'd lain down that she would rest, would close her eyes and conserve her strength. Now, though, she thought that, if she were being honest with herself, she had little strength left.

They had been in the dungeons for two days—perhaps two and a half. She had discovered that time was funny to a person stuck in a cage. At once, it seemed to mean everything and signify nothing. What *did* mean something, though, was the fact that, until half an hour ago, she and Emille had not been offered food or drink of any kind.

So when the guards had arrived, carrying a tray of moldy bread that Maeve wouldn't have normally thought fit for hogs and water that was, she had strongly suspected at the time—a thought that had been confirmed when she'd tasted it—dirty dishwater, the contents of the tray had looked almost magically tempting to her. Seeming to cast a spell on her. Of course, knowing Bethesa as she thought she did, how cruel the woman could be, how cruel she *enjoyed* being, Maeve had not been particularly surprised by this. Nor had she been all that surprised to find that the two guards who brought the food and drink had been Phillip and Joseph, the two men who had been her bodyguards now her jailers, and no doubt Bethesa got plenty of pleasure from that fact as well.

Phillip had at least had the good grace to look ashamed, but he had not responded to Maeve when she'd ordered, threatened and, now she had to admit, if only to herself, *pleaded* for him to release them. It had been Joseph who had responded instead, tossing the moldy bread on the dirt floor of the cell, the bowl of water as well, spilling nearly all its contents and laughing in surprise and delight like a mean-spirited child as Maeve fell to her hands and knees, lapping at the water like a dog.

Maeve had been ashamed even as she'd done it, but she had not been able to stop. That water, muddy as it was, had seemed to her the way some of those potent herbs to which people became addicted were said to seem to them. She had drunk as much as she could, drunk until her tongue came away with nothing but slightly-damp dirt. She had heard Emille in the cell next to her doing much the same and when Maeve was finished, she had simply lay there to "gather her strength."

That had been a few hours ago now, or so she thought, for while she couldn't be sure, she thought it was around midnight. She had lain there since, covered in her guilt and shame. Following the Skaalden invasion of Daltenia and her homeland, and after that during the Fey War, Maeve had, time and again, been confronted with the truth that what men and women fancied as "civilization" as "progress" was no more than a lie. Or perhaps a game of make believe, a game that might, at any moment, come to an end and reveal one simple truth.

In the end, that civilization, those ideas of proper conduct were simply that—ideas. Ideas that might be cast aside or forgotten easily enough when a man or woman was confronted with the brutality of war, of death. Or, she had come to learn, when they were starving. When their mouths and throat seemed filled with dried ash, and they could think of little else besides what they would do—and a far shorter, ever-changing list of what they *wouldn't* do—for a drink, for something to eat.

Humans, she decided as she lay there covered in dirt and shame, fancied themselves far above the beasts of the world, but the truth was they were not so far at all. Only a few missed meals, a few days without drink separated the two of them from lying on the floor, lapping desperately at the dirt as some crude beast might, as Maeve *had*.

Before Phillip and Joseph had arrived, Maeve and Emille had been trying to figure out some way out of the mess they were in, scheming and plotting. But since the guards had left, they had not talked anymore, Emille, Maeve suspected, feeling much the same shame and embarrassment and despair that she herself felt.

Besides, what was the point? All the talking in the world wouldn't unlock the door to the cell, and the truth was, as weak as she felt, Maeve didn't think it would make any difference even if it had, for she would never be able to make the journey out of the guild before her captors caught her.

Get a hold of yourself, she thought, some distant, increasingly weak part of her mind, her resolve, told her. She made a feeble attempt, thinking about Chall, about Matt and Priest and all the others, but from her spot on the floor of her cell, lying in the darkness, they all seemed very far away, seemed, in truth, to be no more than a dream she'd once had. A pleasant dream...but a dream nevertheless.

Just then, she became aware of a metallic sound, one that she knew well, for she had come to dread it over the last days—it was the sound of the door opening. As the door opened, Maeve forced herself into a seated position, determined not to give them the satisfaction of seeing her despair.

She expected Bethesa or Piralta or, failing that, the torturers they'd heard so much about. But as the figure stepped through the door, she saw that none of those were the case. Instead, it was the doppel, still wearing the skin of the old beggar it had killed. It closed the door behind it, grinning widely. "Ah, hello again," it said. "We were interrupted during our last...conversation. I came back to finish it."

Maeve gritted her teeth, using the wall for support as she leveraged herself to her feet. "Can't say I missed it...all that much," she said.

The old man's mouth split into a wide grin, displaying his few remaining rotten teeth. "Ah, but *I* missed it," the creature said. "I missed it terribly. You see, you said some interesting things before. About King Yeladrian, the heir of Summer. Some things that any right-thinking fey could not abide."

"You came to kill me," Maeve said.

The creature grinned widely. "No, Lady Maeve, Maeve the Marvelous, companion to the Destroyer. I have not come to kill you...that would be too easy, too simple for one such as you, one who would dare mock the heir of Summer. No, Lady Maeve, I have not come to kill you, like some mortal thug in a dark alleyway." The far too-wide grin split the old man's face then like a dagger slit. "I have come to feast on your flesh."

That sent a cold shiver up Maeve's spine. It wasn't just the words—though they were plenty bad enough to make a person lose some sleep; it was the *way* the creature *said* the words. It was the hunger, the eagerness in the feyling's voice that scared her the most.

But she refused to let that fear show. "You might not find me so easy a meal as an old beggar," Maeve said.

"Will I not?" the feyling said as it moved close, taking its time—after all, it wasn't as if Maeve were going anywhere. "Am I to fear you then? You who struggle now to even stand? You have lost weight since you came here, but that is not all you've lost, is it?" The creature moved closer still, cocking its head as it studied her. "You have lost your hope, haven't you? Your despair, your hopelessness, I can smell them."

The feyling paused, breathing deeply, its eyes closed, a twisted pleasure on its face. "I can almost *taste* them. That sweet, slightly sour taste. It is a shame about the weight you've lost, for I would that there were enough of you that I might feast on your flesh for eternity, meatling. For the offenses you have given, I would *rip* and *tear* and *chew* forever onto forever." The bony old man's shoulders went up into a shrug. "A shame, but that is alright. We will take our time, you and I. Not an eternity perhaps, but it will feel like one for you. That is my promise."

"Leave her alone you...monster."

The creature turned to glance at Emille's cell, cocking its head. "Oh, do not worry, fleshling. Your turn will come soon enough."

The feyling moved to Maeve's cell then and any hope she'd entertained that its threats were idle vanished in a moment as it reached into its dirty trouser pocket and retrieved the dungeon key.

"I have looked forward to this moment since last we spoke," the creature said, its voice barely sounding human at all now, coming in a low, throaty, bestial whisper. "I have wondered what you would taste like." The old man's tongue snaked out of the creature's mouth, licking its lips as it fit the key into the lock.

As the door swung open, Maeve tensed, knowing that she had little strength left and that she would have to take the creature out quickly, before her weary body failed her.

The creature took a step toward her, and Maeve braced herself, preparing to launch forward. But before she got a chance, the strangest thing happened.

The creature's smile vanished, as did the rest of its head. Or, at least, it seemed to. In fact, it didn't vanish, only came free of its neck in a spurt of blood, flying into the dungeon wall. As the head and the creature's body crumpled to the ground, they revealed another figure standing behind it.

"Phi...Phillip?" Maeve asked.

The bodyguard stood with his bloody sword held in front of him in a two-handed grip, his eyes slightly too wide around the edges. "Hello, Guildmaster."

And just like that, those two words were enough to tell Maeve that she had judged the bodyguard unfairly. Of course, the doppel that was currently lying dead at her feet instead of chewing on her was also a good sign.

"Can you walk?" Phillip asked.

"I'll do cartwheels if it means getting out of here," Maeve said.

The bodyguard gave a nervous smile then knelt, taking the keys from the dead doppel's hands. He stepped out of Maeve's cell, and she started out after as he unlocked Emille's cell.

"Hello again, Sister Emille," the man said.

"Phillip, wasn't it?" Emille asked.

"Yes, ma'am."

"Phillip, I cannot describe the pleasure it is to see you," she said, then as she staggered out of her cell, she glanced at Maeve, giving a small smile. "Or you, Guildmaster."

Maeve smiled back—she couldn't help it. She knew they were still in terrible danger, and two days spent in the dungeon had taken its toll on both of them, but they were alive, for the moment at least. Alive and free and she found that, considering the alternative, that was more than enough to be getting on with.

"Are you alright, Emille?" A stupid question, probably, for Emille looked exactly how Maeve felt, and Maeve thought she was pretty damned far from alright.

But Emille only gave a weary shrug, glancing down at her dirty, wrinkled clothes, then gave Maeve a small smile. "Oh, I'll live. At least for the moment. Still, I think it best I take a bath before I see my husband. Ned is a kind man—the kindest I've ever met—but he's got a temper, and if he were to see me like this..." She shook her head, trailing off, her eyes getting a distant look as she no doubt thought about her husband, wondered if she *would* see him again. After all, they might have been out of their cells, but they were still trapped in a guild of contract killers.

Maeve found her gaze moving to the dead doppel. They weren't in any danger of getting eaten, at least, but the feyling was far from the only threat facing them. She turned to the bodyguard. "So, Phillip, do you have a plan?"

The man winced. "Forgive me, Guildmaster, but I didn't have a chance. When I realized what that, that *thing* meant to do..."

Maeve nodded. "If either of us owes the other forgiveness, Phillip, then it's the other way around. Anyway, I'm not likely to complain, not considering that I'd be busy being that damned thing's dinner right now if it weren't for you."

"So then," Emille said, glancing at Maeve, "what do we do?"

Maeve considered their options—it didn't take long. Mostly because they didn't have any. "We get moving," Maeve said. "It won't be long before Bethesa comes to gloat or Piralta or someone else happens by. Best we be gone before then."

"Works for me," Emille said. "The hospitality here isn't all it's cracked up to be."

Maeve smiled, turning to Phillip. "Listen, Phillip, thank you, for all that you've done for us. But perhaps it would be better if you made yourself scarce. When that crooked old bitch Bethesa finds out what happened here, she won't be pleased. There might still be a way for you to stay clear of this, but if you're caught trying to help us escape...well. Bethesa doesn't strike me as the forgiving sort."

"Forgive me, Guildmaster," he said, "but I'm your bodyguard—it's my job to keep you safe."

Maeve blinked. Perhaps it was the ordeal she'd gone through or that, moments before, she'd been facing not just imminent death but imminent digestion. Whatever the cause, she felt tears gathering in her eyes at that. "Thank you."

The bodyguard inclined his head, a pleased expression on his face. "Are you ready, Guildmaster?"

Maeve glanced at the cell, at the dead creature lying within it. "Oh, I'd say I've had enough of dungeons to last a lifetime. Lead on."

Phillip moved toward the door, giving Maeve and Emille a backward glance before easing it open and stepping out of the dungeon.

They followed him, Maeve grunting as she nearly tripped on a corpse lying on the ground only a few feet beyond the door. And not just a nameless corpse this but one she recognized as Joseph, the second of the bodyguard pair.

She glanced at Phillip, and the man winced. "He meant to let the creature do...what it planned," the bodyguard explained.

Maeve nodded. "Well, I'll waste no tears over him then." She knelt, retrieving the dead man's sword from the sheath at his waist. She also took his belt knife, glancing at Emille in question as she held the two out. Emille nodded to the knife and so Maeve handed it over, rising with the borrowed sword. She had never been much on that sort of weapon, far preferring her easily-concealed and easily-carried knives, but then there was that old saying, how did it go? Something along the lines of "Guildmasters running for their lives in a guild full of assassins can't afford to be choosy." She glanced back at the bodyguard. "Lead on, Phillip."

"As you say, Guildmaster."

Then they were moving again, Phillip walking at their front, his sword in hand. Maeve and Emille followed, leaning on each other for support. They made their way through the guild corridors, and at each corner they stopped, Phillip checking to make sure it was clear before ushering Emille and Maeve forward. Maeve begrudged each pause, for she wanted nothing more but to get away, to run as fast as her feet would carry her, to get to the castle and lock herself in her room with Chall and leave the world to itself. She was, in short, afraid. Afraid of being discovered, afraid of Bethesa whose evil was beyond even what she had thought.

She had been afraid before, of course, had been in life-or-death situations before, but rarely had she felt so helpless, so much a *victim* as she had while inside the dungeon cell. She had not felt like Maeve the Marvelous. Instead, she had only felt—and felt still—like one of the countless poor souls of the world who could not protect themselves and could only accept whatever grim fate awaited them.

She did not like the feeling.

Emille suddenly staggered where she was leaned against Maeve, nearly causing them both to fall over. Maeve managed to keep her feet and help the woman regain her balance, but only just. She held her free arm wrapped around Emille's shoulder. "Alright?" she asked, looking at the woman.

Emille winced. "Sorry, I'm just...just tired," she said, though the expression on her face showed that she was more than just that. She was afraid, was likely feeling the same sort of feelings of helplessness that Maeve was. It wasn't just that they had been imprisoned, it was that they could *be* imprisoned wrongly and so *easily*. Another reminder that the world was not a safe place at all and that whatever security a woman thought she found was little more than an illusion, one that might collapse around her at any moment.

"Yeah," Maeve said quietly, meeting the woman's gaze. "I'm tired, too."

Emille nodded, giving her a small smile. "I'm ready," she said.

And they were moving again. They reached an intersection, and the bodyguard peered around it, looking both ways before taking the hall on the right. One which, Maeve knew, would take them to the stairs leading out of the bottom floor of the guild and into the Healing Academy above.

They were near the end of the hallway, and Maeve was just beginning to believe they might actually make it out when two guards rounded the corner in front of them, coming up short only a few feet away from the bodyguard.

"What the—" one said, then frowned. "Gods be good, Phillip, you gave me a fright. What are you doin' here anyway? I thought you were s'posed to be in the dungeon watchin' over that old bi—" He cut off then, his eyes going wide as he took in Maeve and Emille standing behind the bodyguard. "Son of a bitch," he hissed. He went for the sword sheathed at his waist but before he could, Phillip lashed out with his own bared blade. The man screamed as the sword cleaved a bloody furrow across his chest, and he staggered before falling to the ground.

Phillip stepped forward and drove his blade into the writhing man's chest. But before the bodyguard could remove the blade the second man was on him, barreling into him with a roar. The bodyguard's sword flew from his hands and he grunted in pain as he was slammed against the wall.

"Traitorous bastard," the guard hissed. He struck the still-dazed Phillip a blow across the face that busted his lip. He drew the knife at his waist and thrust it forward, but Phillip recovered enough of his senses to catch the man's wrist.

The two men struggled then, the guard's attention completely focused on Phillip, which was just as well as Maeve was exhausted from her ordeal and slower than normal as she hurried—or at least *tried* to hurry—forward. The guard had just managed to break free of Phillip's grip and was raising his hand in preparation of another strike when Maeve's borrowed sword cleaved into his back.

She was exhausted and certainly not at her best but then a sharp blade had a way of getting a man's attention whether it was swung by a man of Prince Bernard's strength or a child. And get the guard's attention it did. He screamed in surprise and pain, all thoughts of his struggle with the bodyguard forgotten in the midst of that agony. Phillip, though, did not forget. He wrested the knife out of his distracted attacker's hand and the other man's screams abruptly cut off as the bodyguard sheathed the blade in his heart.

The guard stood, wavering, for a moment before collapsing at their feet.

Phillip looked up from the dead man to Maeve. The bodyguard was panting heavily, blood—his or his attacker's, Maeve didn't know—on his chest and face. "Thank you...Guildmaster."

"Considering that you saved us from the dungeons, risking your life to do it, I'd say it's the least I could do, Phillip," Maeve said.

The bodyguard opened his mouth to answer but before he got a chance there was a scream from the end of the hallway, and they all turned to look. A woman—who might have been a secretary or a personal valet based on her dress—was standing at the far end of the hall, staring at them and, more particularly, the corpse at their feet.

"*Murder!*" the woman screamed. "*Murder!*" Then she was off and running, disappearing down the hallway and screaming all the while.

"Think we could tell her he slipped?" Emille asked.

Maeve glanced at the woman, and Emille winced. "Sorry. That's the sort of thing Ned would say...guess when you're married as long as we've been you start to pick up each other's traits."

"There are worse things," Maeve said. "Anyway, I don't think she'd be in much of a mood to listen just now." She glanced back at Phillip. "Best we get a move on."

"Yes, Guildmaster," the man said.

They hurried forward in an exhausted shuffle which was the best she and Emille could manage, but it wasn't long before Maeve was able to make out the shouts of pursuing guards. Not long after *that,* she was glancing behind them for what must have been the hundredth time when she caught sight of their pursuers, half a dozen guards at least, at the far end of the hallway.

Maeve hissed in frustration. "We can't outrun them," she said. "Not as we are."

"Perhaps we could hide," Emille said.

"Forever?" Maeve asked, glancing at the woman as they continued forward. "I think we both know Bethesa won't stop searching until she finds us."

"What, then?" Emille asked. "If we can't hide and we can't run, what option does that leave us?"

Only one, so far as Maeve could see, and she was just about to say as much when Phillip spoke instead. "Fight," the man said, slowing to a stop and turning to regard the other figures approaching at a jog from the far end of the hall.

Emille gave a weary snort. "Not a great option—I'm more likely to pass out than I am to kill anybody. Still, I don't suppose we're exactly spoiled for choice."

"I didn't mean the two of you," Phillip said. "I meant me."

"What are you talking about?" Maeve asked.

"Go, Guildmaster," the man said. "I will buy you as much time as I can."

Maeve was shaking her head before he'd gotten the words out. "No. No, Phillip, I can't let you do that—it's suicide. I won't allow you to get yourself killed for us."

"I'm not doing it for you, Guildmaster," the man said, meeting her gaze. "Or, at least, not only that. The Known Lands is my home. The people of New Daltenia, the people of the Known Lands are *my* people." Anger flashed in the man's eyes, and he set his jaw. "What Tribu—what Bethesa means to do, it is unacceptable. It's evil. *She's* evil, her and those who support her. And my father, he used to tell me that all evil needs to succeed is for good men—"

"To do nothing," she finished, remembering Priest telling her as much long ago when she'd asked him why he'd left the priesthood to go to war. She shot a quick glance at the approaching guards then looked back to the bodyguard. "Are you sure?"

"I'm sure. Go and save yourselves," he said. "Save our people."

"If I can I will," Maeve promised.

"Maeve—" Emille began.

"Come on, Emille," Maeve said. They started away then, and Maeve glanced back at the man standing there, his sword drawn, facing down the onrushing guards.

"Phillip."

He turned to glance back at her. "Yes, Guildmaster?"

"What a bodyguard you turned out to be," Maeve said quietly.

The man smiled then, she returned it as best as she was able, then he turned away, and she began to run.

They didn't make it far before they began to hear the sounds of fighting from behind them.

"They'll kill him," Emille panted as they hurried forward.

"Then let's make it...mean something," Maeve gasped back. She was exhausted, done-in, her breath coming in ragged gasps, her legs trembling and threatening to give way beneath her with each hurried, staggering step she took, but she forced herself onward.

Soon they reached another intersection. Emille started down the right turn, the one that would lead in short order to the stairs to the Healing Academy. Maeve meant to follow her but found herself hesitating as a thought occurred to her.

Emille turned, looking back at her. "Maeve?" she asked. "Are you alright? It won't take them long to...to get past Phillip."

To kill him. She meant to kill him. She was right, of course. And while Phillip would be killed for freeing them, even his fate was not nearly so bad, she suspected, as that fate waiting on her and Emille should they be captured once more. But even knowing this, she found herself hesitating, her eyes going not to the right hallway but to that on their left, the hall which led to classrooms where assassins were taught their bloody trade and, eventually, to the guildmaster's quarters.

As she stared down the hallway, Maeve found herself thinking not of the guards pursuing them, not even of what Bethesa would do to punish them for trying to escape. Instead, she found herself thinking of her conversation with the Tribune. "She doesn't have it," she said quietly.

"Maeve," Emille said, walking up beside her, "we have to go. There's no time to—"

"She doesn't have it," Maeve said again, turning to regard the woman. "She hasn't found it yet."

"Found what?" Emille asked, shooting a nervous glance behind them. "What are you talking about?"

"The diary," Maeve said. "Agnes's diary. It's still in her quarters."

"So what if it is?" Emille said. "You said yourself you looked through the diary, didn't you? And you didn't find anything. So what difference—"

"Not all of it," Maeve said thoughtfully. "Not even close."

"But what could possibly be in the diary that matters so much?"

"I have no idea," Maeve said, shaking her head. "But it *does* matter. Enough that Agnes's valet tried to kill me over it, if you'll remember. Enough that it was the first thing Bethesa mentioned when she had us imprisoned. Whatever it is, whatever's hidden in the diary, it's vital for Bethesa to achieve her goals."

"And you think that it may help stop her."

"The thought had occurred," Maeve said. "But you go on, Emille—you're right. They'll be on us soon. Best you get out of here while you can. Find your husband. Find Chall and Priest, tell them what's happe—"

"You can tell them yourself," Emille said. "When we get out of here. Together."

Maeve winced. "You should go, Emille. Really. You have already been captured once because of me—I won't let it happen again."

"It's not up to you," Emille said. "You obviously think the diary's important—important enough to risk them finding you. And I agree. If Bethesa wants it so badly then I can only imagine it's in our best interests and the best interests of the Known Lands to keep it from her. Now let's go. Just because I'm going to stay and help you get the diary doesn't mean I want to hang around and see what those bastards chasing us have to say."

Maeve wanted to argue the point further, but the fact was they simply didn't have the time, and it wasn't as if she could have forced the woman to leave. Just then, she doubted she could have forced open a heavy door. "Right. This way."

They walked on. They passed several people on their way to the guildmaster's quarters, servants and clerks, mostly. But while those they passed gave them odd looks—no doubt wondering why they looked like they'd spent the last several days starving in a dungeon somewhere—they did not stop or hinder them. If there was any place in the world where a person learned to mind their own business and keep to themselves, it was certainly in a guild full of men and women who spent their days killing people.

Maeve knew that they ran a risk of word of their passage getting back to Bethesa or Piralta, but it was a risk she decided to take. Mostly because they had no choice. Stealth was out the window now, and so they had to rely on speed. Speed from two people who couldn't have run just then if their lives depended on it. Which, of course, they did.

It took fifteen minutes to reach the guildmaster's quarters. Maeve approached the door, feeling more than a little surprised. She had not expected, in truth, to make it this far, had thought that her and Emille's pursuers would have caught up to them by now. Which only meant that they had thought she and Emille had meant to escape and taken the right turning in the intersection, as she'd hoped they might.

Still, she knew it wouldn't take them long to realize their mistake. She glanced around the hallway then at Emille. The woman nodded, and they moved to the door.

"It could be a trap," Emille said quietly.

"Yes," Maeve agreed. "It could."

"But you're going in anyway," Emille said.

"Yes," Maeve said. "I am."

Emille sighed. "Alright then—let's go get that diary."

Maeve tried the door. It was unlocked, which was just as well as her key had been taken from her along with her weapons and no small part of her dignity when Bethesa and the others had imprisoned her. She pushed it open slowly, tensing in expectation of an attack, but none came. Her quarters, at least so much as she could see of them from her place in the hall, were empty. She glanced at Emille, and the woman shrugged, giving her a small smile.

"Go on then," Emille said. "Guildmasters first."

Maeve stepped through the door, quickly scanning the room but despite her worries no one was there to ambush them. Though it was obvious from a quick glance that someone *had* been there recently. The entire sitting room area had been destroyed in what had obviously been a very thorough search, one that she could only hope had been fruitless.

The table that normally sat between the two divans was turned over on its side, one leg broken off. The divans themselves had been slashed to ribbons, the searchers apparently thinking that she had hidden the diary in one of the cushions. And that was just the beginning of the devastation. Everywhere she looked, things were shattered and broken, drawers left open or pulled off the bureaus altogether, their contents scattered on the floor.

"Well, you were right about one thing," Emille observed quietly. "They really want that diary."

Maeve nodded. "Let's hope they still want it." She moved through the wreckage, stepping around pieces of shattered wood and shattered glass, for even all the dining set which had set on the table had been broken to crystalline pieces. Either the searchers had thought that she had somehow hidden the diary inside transparent containers or, more likely, they had simply destroyed the dining set and the other glasses and carafes of wine in a fit of pique.

But then some spilled wine and ruined furniture were far from the worst of Bethesa's crimes. Maeve reached the other side of the room where the door to the guildmaster's office stood ajar and peered inside. She saw at a glance a devastation to match that of the sitting area, and she felt her heart speed up in her chest. She stepped inside, noting that not so much as a single book remained on the shelves against the wall. They had all been torn through and cast to the ground. Hundreds of crumpled, ripped pieces of pages littered the floor.

The desk at which Maeve had sat poring over the diary, searching for some reason that it had seemed so important, had been turned over as well, all of the drawers ripped out. It seemed impossible, given the thoroughness of the search, to hope that they hadn't found the diary. Her heart hammering in her chest, Maeve moved to the desk. She knelt, pressing against the hidden compartment where she'd secreted the diary, but it remained shut. After a moment, Maeve saw why—when it had been turned over the wood had bent a little, enough to keep it shut. She grunted with the effort of pressing against it and was just about to give up when the secret compartment opened. Her breath in her throat, Maeve leaned forward and was shocked to see the diary sitting there just as she'd left it.

As she stared at it, Maeve realized there'd been a part of her—a very large part—which had been confident she'd find nothing.

"It's there?" Emille asked, her tone making it clear that she was as surprised as Maeve to find it.

"Yes," Maeve said.

"Well, what now?"

"Now we get out of here," Maeve said, snatching up the diary. "Before Bethesa and her cronies show up and take us back to the dungeons. I've had just about enough of their hospitality."

Emille didn't seem prepared to argue with that, so they started toward the door.

Maeve opened it and took a step out into the hall, coming up short before she could take a second. Not that she would have likely been able to anyway, not without running into one of the half a dozen guardsmen on either side of the door, all with swords or crossbows drawn.

And behind the armed men, a small smile on her face, stood Bethesa. "Hello, Maeve," the tribune said. "Fancy meetin' you here."

CHAPTER EIGHTEEN

PRIEST WOKE to the sound of voices. At first, he felt a surge of panic before the thick fog of sleep began to clear from his mind, and he realized that he recognized those voices as belonging to Bert's friends, Eugene and the others, in the next room.

The door was closed, and so he couldn't hear much of what they said, but it was clear from their laughter that they were having a good time. He sat up, wincing in preparation of pain in his side, but was surprised to find that, while it still ached, the crossbow bolt wound did not hurt anywhere near as much as he'd expected.

He grabbed his boots that had been set beside the cot, pulling them on. Then, he took a deep breath and stood, holding onto the wall for support in case he was weaker than he realized. He *did* feel a little weak, a little nauseous but all in all he thought he felt a lot better than a man recently shot with a crossbow ought to feel. There was a full cup of water on the stand beside the cot and he drank it down greedily, unable to remember the last time he'd tasted anything so fine.

He grabbed his shirt from where it lay on the room's only chair, pulling it on before moving to the door. The conversation abruptly cut off as he stepped through, and the four people seated at the table—

cards, money, and ale littering its surface—turned to regard him. "Ah," the old man that Priest knew to be Eugene said. "Decided to grace us with your presence, did you, Your Highness?"

The woman seated at the table rolled her eyes. "Don't mind, Eugene. He's a bit of an asshole, though I'm sure you picked up on that soon as you saw him." She sniffed. "Or smelled him."

The two big men seated at the table—Thunder and Blunder, Priest remembered Bert calling them—guffawed loudly at that.

He might have expected Eugene to be upset at being mocked but instead he grinned as if the woman had just paid him the greatest compliment. "You say the sweetest things, Joan," he said.

The woman rolled her eyes again, but the small smile on her face was enough to show Priest that these four shared the easy camaraderie and familiarity of people who had known each other for a long time. "Forgive me, I did not mean to disturb your game—"

Eugene waved a hand. "Think nothin' of it, lad. Any friend of Neddy's is a friend of our'n, and a fella'd have to be pretty sorry not to lay down a hand of cards for a friend."

"Particularly when said 'fella' is losing," Joan said dryly.

"That ain't got nothin' to do with it," Eugene said. "I was just tryin' to be nice, is all."

Joan snorted, but it was one of the brothers—Thunder or Blunder, Priest wasn't sure which—who spoke. "Nice, is it?" the man said grinning. "Eugene, the last time you did anythin' nice, you still had a full head of hair, and that was only on account of you were tryin' to make time with a pretty little blonde, as I recall."

"One that, as *I* recall," the other brother said, "remembered that she had somewhere else to be."

The two brothers erupted in loud, belly laughs, slapping the tabletop in their mirth and setting the ale glasses on its surface to dancing.

"She had an errand to run is all," Eugene said sourly.

"Sure she did," Joan said, grinning. "Why is it that every woman you speak to always has some place they need to be?"

"Not you," Eugene countered.

Joan winced. "Suppose that don't say nothin' too good about me. Anyway," she went on, turning to Priest, "how are you feelin'?"

"Better," Priest said.

"Aye," Eugene said. "Don't tell him I said so—bastard's head gets any bigger he won't be able to fit through the door—but there's few folks with a knack for puttin' folks back together like Bert."

"Or takin' 'em apart, if he's a mind to," one of the brothers said.

"Anyway," Joan said quickly, shooting a frown at the brother who looked away sheepishly, "I'm guessin' you were lookin' to speak with Neddy?"

"I had thought to," Priest confirmed.

"Yeah, well, he and Bert are catchin' up," Eugene said. "Thick as thieves, those two."

"You'd know, wouldn't you?" Joan said.

Eugene groaned. "By the gods, that was damn near half a century ago now, and I told you I weren't stealin' that horse, just borrowin' it 'til its owner came lookin' for it."

"Which he never did."

"Or she," one of the brothers said. "Never did meet 'em."

That sat the two brothers to laughing again, and Eugene grunted. "Laugh all you want, you bastards," he said. "As I recall, it was my borrowin' of that horse that saved the two of you from walkin' into a bandit ambush. Seems to me some thanks ought to be in order."

"I meant to give you some thanks, Gene," Joan said, "honestly I did, but I'm afraid someone…you know…stole them."

The two brothers busted out laughing again, and Eugene sighed, turning to Priest. "This is what I have to deal with."

"I suppose there are worse things," Priest said, grinning.

"Yeah?" Eugene said. "You let me know when you find 'em. Anyhow, why don't you pull up a chair? I expect they'll be jawin' for a while yet if history's anythin' to go by."

Priest considered that, glancing at the door that led out into the shop proper. He liked the four people seated at the table, had the instant sort of like for them that was rare when meeting someone. They seemed *good*. Good in a simple, uncomplicated sort of way, and the last thing he wanted to do was risk Balderath and the others finding them here.

"If it's your assassins you're worried about, I wouldn't," Eugene said. "You're as safe here as you are anywhere. Leastways, so long as you ain't allergic to fartin'. The brothers there get in their drink, they kick up a mighty dustin'."

Priest laughed at that. He wouldn't have thought that a sentence that began with talk of assassins would end with him laughing, but there it was. "Are you sure?" he asked uncertainly. "I don't want to cause you all any trouble. Perhaps it would be better if Ned and I left. You all seem like nice people and—"

Joan snorted. "Been called a lot of things before. Not sure 'nice' has ever been one of 'em. As for trouble, lad, sometimes at our age, trouble can be good. Distracts us from our bad knees and bad backs."

"Got a wrist that troubles me somethin' fierce,' Thunder, or maybe Blunder, said.

"From his youth," Blunder or maybe Thunder said, then everyone was laughing except the first of the brothers who frowned, or at least tried to before a grin broke through.

"Fella has to keep himself entertained, hasn't he?" he asked.

Joan grunted. "Gods, I sometimes wonder why I spend my days with you twisted bastards. Anyway," she went on, turning back to Priest, "you may as well take a load off. Looks to me like you could use it. Besides, last look I caught at Ned, he didn't appear in danger of runnin' any marathons anytime soon."

Priest hesitated for a moment, then finally nodded. "Just a few minutes," he said. "We really must be going and I don't want to disturb you all."

"Oh, trust me—Priest, isn't it?" one of the brother's said, grinning. "We were disturbed long before you got here."

"Anyway, a few minutes with these bastards'll feel like a lifetime, you mark my words," Eugene said. "Go on and pull up a seat. You want dealt in?"

"No thank you," Priest said, moving toward a chair between Eugene and Joan and sitting down. "I'll just watch, if that's alright."

Eugene shrugged. "It's alright with me. It a religious thing, that it? Playin' cards a sin?"

"When you play them as badly as I do, it probably ought to be," Priest said. "Anyway, I'd hate to get robbed and murdered in the same night."

They all laughed at that, and Eugene clapped him on the shoulder. "You're a lot more fun than the priests I've met."

"Not that he's met many," Joan said as they began to deal out a fresh hand, "avoids them like a child'll avoid baths. Still, he's right, Priest. You are welcome back anytime, alright? Particularly if you don't bring any assassins with you."

"Oh, I don't know," one of the brothers said. "I wouldn't mind a bit of sport. Been a long few years. Nothin' makes a man feel more alive than a good scrap."

"Or more dead if things go sideways," Joan said. "And things just about always go sideways."

The brother grunted. "Yeah. S'pose there is that. Still. Gets borin' sometimes, that's all I mean. Say what you want to of it back then, we weren't never bored."

"You and I remember things differently, Thunder," Joan said. "Anyway, there's worse things than bein' bored. Like bein' dead. The gods know there ain't as many of us seated here as there might have been."

The brother winced at that, remaining silent. Eugene sighed, lifting his glass. "To dead friends and dead enemies," he said.

They all lifted their own glasses and echoed the sentiment before taking a drink.

"So what about it, then?" Eugene asked, glancing at Priest as he set his glass down.

He noted the others turning to regard him as well. "Sorry, what about what?"

"Well, you're a priest, ain't you?" Eugene asked. "Got an inside line to the gods, maybe? So what's the deal with all this dyin' then? What's the point of it?"

Priest saw them all watching him, waiting for what he would say. Finally, he shook his head slowly. "I don't think it's about dying...I think it's about living."

They all sat in silence for a moment then, thinking over his words. Finally, one of the brothers raised his ale mug high. "Shit, I'll drink to that."

"He'll drink to anything," Joan said, giving Priest a wink. "But it was well said." Then she raised her own glass and took a drink.

"So tell me, Priest," Eugene said as he raised his cards, peeking carefully at them, "these assassins, what do they want with you and Neddy?"

"What do assassins usually want, Gene?" one of the brothers asked. "Shit how many of those ales you drink?"

"Not enough to pretty up your ugly mug," Eugene said to which the brother grinned. Eugene, meanwhile, glanced back at Priest.

They were all looking at him then, and Priest shrugged. "To be honest...I'm not sure. I came to Ned's home to speak to him about... about a separate matter, and when I did the assassins were there."

"Damned assassins," one of the brothers—Blunder, Priest thought—said. Then the man winced, glancing at Joan with a guilty look on his face. "Sorry, Joan. I don't mean you."

Priest glanced at her, surprised, and the woman rolled her eyes. "That was a long time ago. Anyway, better an assassin than a bandit," she finished, shooting a meaningful look at Eugene.

Eugene frowned. "Look here, a man's got to eat, hadn't he? Anyway, I ain't proud of it and—"

"*That was a long time ago*," the two brothers said in unison, grinning widely.

"Well, it was, damnit," Eugene said. "I left that life of crime behind me."

"Except when it comes to cheating at cards," Joan said, glancing at Priest.

"Wait, you were a bandit and you were an assassin?" Priest said, surprised by these revelations.

"As Gene said, that was a long time ago," Joan said. "But I wasn't one of these guild-trained professional killers if that's what you mean. Just a lady that had a knack for stickin' people with a blade before they stuck me is all. Anyway, all that was before Bert."

"Aye, before Bert," Eugene said, nodding slowly.

"I...I don't understand," Priest said.

"Go on, Eugene," Joan said. "You tell him. You were the first after all."

Eugene shrugged. "Ain't all that much to tell, really. Just, well, back in Daltenia, I was a bandit, see. Me and some others, we'd find folks on the road, take what they had and send 'em on their way. Anyway, got to the point that the king—that's your Prince Bernard's pa—sent some men after us. Bert was leadin' 'em. Long story short, he tracked us down, tracked *me* down. Had me dead to rights, and instead of killin' me as he might have, he made me an offer, asked if I wanted to do some good to make up for all the bad I done. Asked me to join the army, and I did."

"Easy choice with Bert's blade at your throat," one of the brothers said, grinning.

"Aye, it was," Eugene said, glancing at Joan.

The woman sighed. "I was an assassin, as I said. A fairly good one. At least, there are a few people who might agree with me, if they were able. But of course they're not and that's the whole point. Anyway, as I said, I didn't work for no guild. Was sort of...well, freelance, I s'pose you'd say. Didn't love the work, mind, but I grew up on the street as an orphan, and I loved starvin' a whole lot less. Anyhow, one day, a job came to me, and the target...well, the target was a young prince, one barely in his teens and already celebrated for his strength. I think maybe you know him."

Priest blinked. "You mean...Bernard?"

"That's right," Thunder said, grinning. "Joan here was tasked with slayin' the Crimson Prince himself. The greatest warrior of this age, maybe any age."

Joan winced at that. "Yeah, well, he wasn't the Crimson Prince then. Just a young man—a boy, really."

"And...you took the job?" Priest said.

"Sure I took it," Joan said, not defensively but instead in a weary voice. "I didn't know much about princes then, but I knew something about starving, alright, about what it felt like when the hunger pangs took hold. And livin' on the street, a young woman's got more to worry about than just starvin', I can tell you that. You wouldn't believe what you'd be willin' to risk, willin' to *do* for enough coin to put a locked door between you and the world. Anyway, I took the job and was just set to do it. Made my move while the lad was out one day, him and his retinue of guardsmen and hangers-on, visiting the city. In that press, with everyone pushing forward, tryin' to get a good look at him, well, I figured it wouldn't be all that hard to get close without someone seein'. But Bert just happened to be guardin' the prince that day, and he saw. Even now, I don't know how he done it, how he noticed me in that crowd, but he did. One minute, I was makin' my move toward the young prince ridin' his horse, the next Bert was standin' in front of me. And that one, I can tell you, makes for a damn fine wall when he's a mind to."

"What...what did you do?"

"Well, I went for my blade, of course," she said. "See, I was fast—you had to be, if you wanted to survive on the streets. But Bert, he was faster. I'd barely managed to catch hold of the handle of the knife at my waist when Bert's hand clapped over mine, stopping it." She shook her head, a distant cast to her gaze. "He might have killed me then. Or might have thrown me in the dungeons," she said, frowning at Eugene for some reason.

The man winced. "Damnit, you ever gonna let that go? I mean, you did try to kill a prince, for the gods' sake."

"Anyway," Joan went on, "what Bert did instead was just about the most surprising thing I could have imagined. He offered me a job."

"A job?"

"Sure. As a guard. See, he asked me why I done what I did. I told him, a girl's got to eat. He said that were true. But he said there were ways to make enough coin to live without losin' sleep from nightmares about what I done."

"And you two?" Priest asked, glancing at the brothers.

"Oh, we weren't bandits or assassins, if that's what you're askin'," one of the brothers said.

"Nah, nothin' so serious as that," the other said. "Just a couple of street toughs who spent our time knockin' people around for coin."

"Sort of...fists for hire, you might say," the other clarified.

"Anyway," the other said, frowning at a memory, "when the Skaalden came, we were drunk—"

"Most times we were drunk," the other explained.

"Right, well, we were. Drunk, I mean."

"Meeting Bert changed some of us more than others," Joan said, raising an eyebrow at the ale mugs sitting in front of the brothers.

"Everyone was runnin' around crazy when they come, screamin' and carryin' on. Except us..."

"Too busy being drunk," the other interjected.

"Right, well, except us and Bert. See, while most folks were panicking', shittin' themselves in fear, Bert was roundin' up people and makin' for the docks. We were among those he rounded up. He saved us."

"The drink'll kill you," the other agreed.

"I...I don't understand," Priest said, glancing around at the four of them. "Bert said that you all saved him, back when the Skaalden came."

Joan snorted. "Yeah, well, Bert's a good man. The best, maybe. He's also a damned liar. He show you his hand?"

"That'd be a neat trick," Eugene said.

"I mean," Joan said, frowning, "did he show you where his hand oughtta be?"

"It...came up," Priest said.

"He came for me at my home—this is before we went and found these two drunk fools. Anyway, he might have left, but he didn't. As we were leavin' my little house—not much but mine, bought and paid for with honest coin with not a speck of blood on it—one of those damned frost demons appeared out of the mist. Took a swing at me with this great axe it had and would have cut me in two, I was so terrified at the sight of it. But Bert saved me again, knockin' me out of the way. Managed to get me out of the way in time, but his hand...not so much."

"And so he saved us all," Eugene said. "Got us on the boats and out of Daltenia. Saved a lot of others, too."

"I...I had no idea. He didn't say anything."

"Nor would he," Joan said. "I told you, Bert, he's good at savin' broken things. Good at puttin' back together what's went wrong. But he ain't never much cared to talk about it."

"That's...incredible," Priest said honestly. "I had no idea. But...how does a man like that become a map maker?"

The four shared looks at that, and Eugene shrugged. "Well, now, that was Maddy's idea."

"Maddy?" Priest asked.

"Aye, Madeline," Eugene said quietly. "Bert's wife."

They all nodded slowly, looking far more somber than Priest had yet seen them.

"Fever took her a few years back," Eugene explained. "Bad business. What you got to understand, Priest, Bert and Maddy, well they loved each other more'n any two people I've ever seen. Neddy and that wife of his, Emille, they're the closest. Anyway, when Maddy went...it was hard on Bert. Still is. It's why we stay with him as much as we do. At least one of the reasons."

"He makes some fine ale," one of the brothers joked, but it seemed to be more out of habit than anything, for his expression remained grim when he said it.

"So...he saved you so, in a way, you mean to save him," Priest said.

Eugene shrugged. "Guess I haven't thought of it that way, but sure. We'd save him—if we could. We owe him that much."

"And plenty more besides," Joan agreed.

Priest was just opening his mouth to speak again when suddenly a door opened, and they all turned to see none other than Bert walk inside, followed by Ned. The mapmaker paused, noting the way everyone was looking at him, then frowned. "What's all this then?"

"Oh, nothin' to worry your pretty little head over, Bert," Eugene said, forcing jocularity into his voice. "We just been tellin' some stories is all."

Bert grunted. "Lies, more like."

"That's what I said, ain't it?" Eugene asked, glancing at Joan.

Joan rolled her eyes. "So, how you feelin', Neddy?"

"I'll be alright, Jo," Ned said. "Thanks. Just a little tired. Anyway, I'm not the one that was shot with a crossbow." He turned to regard Priest. "How are you getting on?"

"All patched up," Priest said.

"Good," Ned said, "because we need to get going."

"There ain't no cause to—" Eugene began.

"No need for you to go leavin' so soo—" the brother Priest believed to be Thunder started.

Ned held up a hand. "I appreciate it. And it's good to see y'all. But the longer we stay here, the more danger we put you in."

Eugene snorted. "Danger. We're old, Neddy. You get to our age, gettin' out of bed is dangerous."

"For once, Eugene's right," Bert said. "I stood up the other day—just *stood up*, mind—and my knee was sore for three days. It's tough work, gettin' older."

"So tough there ain't a one that survives it," Joan said.

"Point is," Blunder said, "there ain't nothin' assassins can do to us that time hasn't already or won't soon enough."

"We gotta work on that imagination of yours," Ned said. "Look, I appreciate it, I really do. But we're goin' to get goin' just the same. Those bastards didn't seem the sort to give up the chase on a whim. My guess, they're out there combin' the city for us now, and what with me exhausted and Priest here shot, we weren't exactly all that subtle when we come here, I'm afraid. We need to get gone before they follow us here and—" just then, there was a knock on the door.

Ned glanced at Priest.

"Oh, keep your knickers on," Bert said. "Probably just some drunken bastard mistaken the shop for his home. It's happened before."

"More likely that than someone actually come to buy a map," Eugene said.

The other man scowled at him. "I'll go send him on his way—be right back."

"I'll go with you," Eugene said, rising.

"There really isn't—"

"Oh, come on, Bert," the other man said. "You know that roustin' drunks is one of my favorite things to do."

"So why don't you go roust yourself," Bert grumbled, but he voiced no further complaint as the two turned and headed into the shop.

Priest hoped the men were right and that it was no more than a drunk who had knocked on their door by mistake, but he rose anyway. Death found men sooner or later, no matter their efforts and hopes to the contrary, and when it found him, he'd just as soon it found him standing.

There was another knock, one that seemed to thunder in Priest's ears. If it *was* a drunk as Bert had suggested then the stranger had taken some serious offense at the mapmaker's door, for it sounded as though he were trying to break it down.

"I'm sure it's nothing," Joan said, but Priest didn't miss the way she and the two brothers were staring through the open door, marking Bert and Eugene's progress. The two men were about halfway to the door when a voice called from the other side.

"*Hello!*" the voice called. "*Is anybody home?*"

Priest and Ned shared a look then, the grim expression on the carriage driver's face a match for what Priest was feeling, for it was clear that he, like Priest, recognized the voice. How could it be otherwise? After all, when someone orders a band of assassins to murder a man, he tended to remember what they sounded like.

Bert turned and glanced back at Ned in question, and the carriage driver game a grim nod.

Bert returned the nod, turning back to stare at the shop door. *"We're closed,"* he called back.

"Ah, I see," the voice said from the other side of the door. "Well, my business, it will not take but a moment of your time—it should cause you little enough bother. Unless, of course, you make my business *your* business, say by involving yourself when you need not. In such a case as that, I'm afraid that I and those with me will take considerably more than a moment of your time."

"Fella likes to hear himself talk," Eugene observed.

"Yeah, well, you'd know, wouldn't you?" Bert countered. The other man scowled, but Bert had already turned back to regard the closed door. "What is it you're wantin' then? A map? If so, I reckon I ought to have one to suit your needs."

"I'm afraid it isn't a map I'm looking for," the voice called from the other side of the door, "but a person. Two persons, in fact—"

"They call those 'people,'" Eugene called.

There was a slight pause before the voice spoke on. "Yes, of course, *people*. Two men, to be specific, one a priest the other a carriage driver, though men being complicated, they are both more than just that."

"I don't sell people here," Bert called, "I sell maps. Sounds to me like you got the wrong shop."

"I see," Balderath said from the other side of the door. "And should I insist on checking for myself to make sure that two such men might not have stumbled into your shop?"

"Bert," Ned began, "I'll go out to them, I didn't—"

The other man held up a hand, looking offended that the carriage driver would even suggest such a thing. "That bein' the case," Bert called back to Balderath, "then, fella, I'd say you *really* got the wrong shop. What's between these walls is mine to see to, mine to protect." He paused, glancing at Ned. "And I'll be damned if you or anybody is goin' to come in here and take anythin' under my protection without goin' through me first."

A loud sigh from the other side of the door. "Then through you it will be, mapmaker," Balderath said. "But think it over though, won't you? I will give you ten minutes to do so. After all, I do so abhor violence. At least, that is, violence I do not get paid for. But know that in ten minutes, that door is opening, one way or the other. And either they are coming out, or *we* are coming in. Which transpires, I leave entirely in your care. Your countdown...begins...now."

"Look, Bert," Ned said as the map-maker and Eugene made their way back into the room, "there isn't any call for you to get involved. I'm sorry I brought this to your door—" he paused, glancing at those at the table—"to *all* your door. It ain't Priest they're after either, but me. I'll go out to them and—"

"Damn if you will," Bert said. "Anyway, if you're involved, I'm involved."

"*We're* involved," Joan corrected.

Bert nodded, moving toward the table. "Go on then, Blunder, Thunder. Help me slide this big bitch out of the way, will you?"

"*With pleasure, boss,*" the two men said in unison, and Bert gave them a sharp glance. There was something about the words, about the way they said them, Priest thought, as well as the other man's reaction, that spoke to some familiarity. Words that, he suspected, harkened back to a time long ago, when Bert had not been a mapmaker, and he and the others had not spent their time sitting idly around a card table drinking.

The three men set to sliding the table to the side of the room. Once finished, Bert knelt, grabbing hold of the rug that had been underneath it. As the mapmaker pulled the rug away, Priest was surprised to see that it had concealed a trap door.

He glanced at Ned but by the confused expression on the carriage driver's face, it was clear that he had not been aware of the hidden hatch either.

"Bert, please," Ned said, looking around at everyone in the room. "I don't want you, *any* of you getting involved. This Balderath, I've heard of him. He might not sound like it, but he is, by all accounts, a twisted, psychotic bastard. An assassin, sure, but one that doesn't just do what he does for the money—by all that folks say, he *enjoys* it, enjoys cruelty."

Bert grunted. "Known a few folks like that in my time."

"Had an ex-wife fit the type," Eugene agreed, and despite the fact that assassins were threatening to kill them in less than ten minutes' time, the man sounded relaxed.

"How is Debbie anyway?" Joan said, a small smile on her face.

Eugene frowned. "How in the name of the gods would I know? Still howling at the moon, last I heard."

The two brothers laughed at that. "Like a wolf," one said.

Eugene raised an eyebrow. "That's right. Like a wolf. Or a banshee, maybe."

"Well, now, that's a question," the other brother said. "*Do* banshees howl?"

"Huh," Bert said thoughtfully. "I don't think they howl as such. More of a sort of keenin', ain't it? Like—"

"Damnit, Bert, *listen* to me," Ned said, clearly frustrated. "This isn't a joke! These men out there, they mean business. They will kill all of you, if you don't do what they say. Now, I'm going to go out and—"

"I'd really rather you didn't try to do that, Neddy," Eugene said. "It'd be a damn shame to have to clock you one and tie you up."

"But we would," Joan said.

"I do have the rope," Bert said, and with that he grabbed the handle of the trap door, throwing it open. Dust, disturbed by the movement flitted into the air in a small cloud.

"Gods, this place could use a woman's touch," Joan observed.

"Couldn't we all?" Eugene grumbled.

Priest was barely listening, though, and neither, it seemed was Ned. The carriage driver, like Priest was instead busy staring through the opening at what had been revealed in the hidden cellar. He saw what he thought must have been the rope Bert had mentioned sitting in a bundle in the corner, but as he gazed closer he saw far more than that.

"Gods be good," Ned said, "what is all that?"

"That, dear Neddy," Eugene said, moving to stand beside the man and gaze down into the cellar, taking in the various swords and knives, maces and crossbows, and enough other weapons to outfit a small armory, "is what's left after a life of bad decisions."

"And the scars," Joan said quietly. "Don't forget about those."

"How could we?" Thunder said. "The way Gene bitches about his knee? Anyway, the scars give us somethin' to talk about, don't they?"

"You take a mace to the knee and tell me you don't have thoughts on it," Eugene snapped.

"Enough," Bert said. He spoke quietly, calmly, as he had since Priest had arrived with Ned. But there was something else in his voice too, a sort of quiet, confident authority, one that the others responded to, going silent immediately. Priest glanced over at the mapmaker, his eyes drawn by the sound of the man's voice, only as he turned to regard him, it didn't feel as though he regarded a mapmaker anymore but a warrior and never mind his gray hair.

"You worry over us," Bert said, looking at Ned, "but you needn't. Runnin', fleein', cowerin', that's not the sort of thing we do."

"Not with knees like ours," Eugene agreed.

"Ain't nothin' scarier than gettin' older anyway," one of the brothers said.

"Except your breath, maybe," Joan said.

"Point is," Bert went on, ignoring them, still studying Ned, his gaze moving to Priest as he spoke, "those sorts of things are for younger folks. But even when we were young, we didn't have much interest in it. Never much for runnin' or cowerin'. That's the sort of thing victims'll do. And Neddy," he went on, meeting the man's eyes, "you'll find no victims here." He glanced back at the doorway. "And neither will he."

"Best be gettin' on with it then," Joan said. "He only gave us ten minutes."

"That's alright," Bert said. "We'll only need five."

And with that, he started into the cellar.

CHAPTER NINETEEN

His shoulder ached. His arms burned from lifting the axe and bringing it down again and again. His legs were weary from pivoting this way and that to evade the attacks of the dead, and his chest and back burned from those times when he'd been too slow to manage it and accepted a cut or scratch for his troubles. The dead, while they might have been hard to kill...or rekill, were not so great warriors. Those few who actually held weapons often didn't bother using them, choosing instead to swipe at Cutter and his companions with bony claws. It was only because of this that none of the wounds Cutter had received so far were serious. But while their individual attacks might not have been particularly dangerous, their cumulative effect was beginning to tell.

Cutter was exhausted—he couldn't remember the last time he'd had a full night's sleep, one where he wasn't woken by something or someone trying to kill him.

Worse than his weariness though, was the hopelessness he felt. There were simply too many of them. Hundreds, thousands, pressing in against him and the others, an inexorable wave of dead that they could not help but be swept underneath.

And all the while that they fought, as his brother and his son grunted and growled and hissed in pain from this small scratch or that cut, Cutter could hear the strumming of the feyling's lute as she called on the dead with her song. The melody, in some way that Cutter did not understand, like the strings of a puppet master, pulling the dead up from the ground and tethering them to the feyling's will.

A figure that had once been a man but was now only recognizable as a skeleton reached for Cutter, and he swung the Breaker of Pacts, the blow severing the dead man's arm at the elbow before Cutter's backswing sent the dead man's skeletal head flying free of his shoulders.

No sooner had he done so then two more pushed forward to take the last one's place. Cutter swung his axe at these two, hissing as a clawed hand scratched at his side, managing to make it past his defenses and those of his companions. Another moment and Matt cut the offending hand and its owner down, but it was another pain, another wound to add to the others. Taken by itself, it would have been no big deal, but the problem was that it *wasn't* by itself, and Cutter knew well from years spent in war that such wounds accumulated, robbing a man of his strength and his speed when he needed them most.

"*Father,*" Matt hissed even as he swung his own blade, knocking away a half-rotted wolf. "Look."

Cutter spared a glance and realized at once what his son was talking about. As bad as their situation had been, it had just gotten a whole lot more desperate. Or perhaps *inevitable* was the word. He did not know what errand or imperative had called the Unsated away, but they were back. Back in even greater numbers. He saw in the spaces between swings of his axe that hundreds of them, perhaps as many as a thousand, had gathered around the upper mountain walls surrounding the clearing.

"What's the...point?" Feledias asked, pausing to kick away an attacker. "They can't...kill us...twice."

Cutter'd had the same thought, but both of their questions were answered, at least to a degree, a moment later. A wind seemed to rush across the clearing, filling his nose with the crisp, dried-leaf scent of autumn—an unusual scent in the perpetual winter of the frozen mountains but one that was unmistakable for all that. Then, abruptly, the Unsated surged forward as one, charging down into the milling army of undead.

Cutter watched in confusion as dozens—hundreds—of the dead were torn and ripped and smashed down before they even seemed aware of the Unsated's presence. Not that it mattered much, for even as they were torn and ripped apart, their dead bodies began to rise again, shrugging off the wounds left by the Unsated as easily as they had those left by Cutter and his companions.

But the Unsated continued on, plowing forward. Cutter detected a change in the melody the feyling played, an urgency to it now, and the dead slowly seemed to become aware of the Unsated's presence. As they did, some of the creatures began to fall to their attacks, overcome by the sheer numbers of the dead. Yet those that remained continued to drive toward Cutter and his companions.

As the deads' attention shifted to the onrushing Unsated, Cutter and his companions were allowed a brief moment of respite. He knew he should press the attack, should cut the dead surrounding them down while they were distracted, but Cutter was exhausted and so only stood, as did his brother and son, watching in surprise.

Suddenly, there was a strange feeling in the air, a sort of thickness, a *weight* to it. A weight that seemed to be growing with each moment, pressing against him uncomfortably.

"What...what is it?" Feledias asked, his voice sounding strained as he, too, noted the building pressure. "Some more of that damned feyling's magic?"

"No," Matt said quietly, looking into the air, "not her...it's autumn. Autumn comes."

Cutter frowned, sharing a look with his brother. He turned to ask Matt what he meant but his eye caught on something strange. Leaves. A lot of them. Not so unusual under normal circumstances, but here in the frozen mountains where what scarce vegetation did manage to grow amounted to moss, or thin, pitiful looking bushes no more than a few inches high, it was strange indeed. Stranger still, the leaves rushed down the path he and the others had followed to get here, a great mass of them, leaves of yellow and gold, of orange and red, the colors of autumn, though brighter than any Cutter ever remembered seeing.

Thousands of them all rushing together, carried along in the opposite direction of the cutting wind. The great, swirling mass flew past undead and Unsated alike, aiming unerringly directly at Cutter and his companions. It swept several of the dead nearest them aside with shocking force, scattering them like paper dolls before the leaves began to swirl in a cyclone, and Cutter held up his arm, shielding his eyes from the buffeting wind.

"*What in the name of the gods is that?*" Feledias asked, yelling to be heard over the crackling cyclone.

Cutter opened his mouth to answer but before he could the leaves —which had been swirling more and more rapidly—suddenly burst apart in an explosion of color, of autumn.

Slowly, he lowered his arm, opening his eyes. He wasn't sure what he expected to find—some new threat come to kill him and his brother and son seemed most likely. But when he gazed upon the figure standing before him, ten-feet-tall at least, composed of swirling leaves and bits of bracken and twigs that moved even as it seemed to regard him he realized with a shock that he recognized it.

"It...it's you," he said.

"*It is I, Destroyer,*" the Gray Man said.

Suddenly, the music—which had faltered at the appearance of that great rush of leaves—failed altogether, and the feyling spoke from where she still stood on the other side of the mountain clearing, on the opposite end of an army of the dead.

"The Gray," she said in a voice that was breathy and sounded full of awe. "You have come then, to help me destroy these interlopers? These enemies of our people?"

The shifting mass of leaves slowly turned to regard the feyling. "*No, daughter of twilight, whisper of wind. I have not come to aid you—I have come to stop you.*"

"Stop me?" she asked, recoiling as if he'd struck her. "But...but I do not understand, Elder. The will of the Green is that—"

"*I do not follow the will of the Green, youngling,*" the Gray Man said, and there was something that sounded sad about his voice. "*What once was fine has turned to rot. The roots are poison, and so, too, the fruit. Please, leave this, leave* them. *It is not the way.*"

The feyling's gaze traveled between Cutter and his companions and the Gray Man. "You would...you would that I set them free?" she asked, shocked.

"*It is what must be,*" the Gray Man said. "*Now please, go. Return to the Wood. There you might grow in life and years and perhaps, in time, in understanding.*"

"You want me to let them go," the feyling said again, her voice an angry hiss. "The Destroyer who has taken so much from our people, who killed your own *son*." Slowly, she shook her head. "No. No, I will not. He must die, *they* must die. The Green demands it."

Then she began to play again.

The music seemed far louder than before, shriller and almost painful to Cutter's ears. The dead, who, to that point, had remained unmoving, suddenly roused to life once more. Worse still, Cutter noted that they moved faster now than they had before as they turned to regard Cutter and his companions.

"*You have fought against my people for many years, Destroyer,*" the Gray Man said. "*As have you, Stormborn. Now,*" he went on, turning to regard Cutter, "*will you fight with me?*"

"It would be my honor," Cutter said.

"I'd rather have a drink with you," Feledias said, "but I suppose we're not exactly spoiled for choice."

The great swirling mass of leaves bent as if to incline its head. "*The dead will not stop until the melody comes to an end,*" he told them. "*Go to* the youngling, the daughter of twilight, and do what must be done—I will clear a path."

"You mean to take on all of them alone?" Matt asked incredulous.

"*In this world, youngling,*" the Gray Man said, "*we are never alone.*" The feyling didn't move, or at least not anymore than its swirling leaves already had been, yet something about its regard seemed to grow far stronger as it looked at Matt. "*Even,*" the Gray Man said, "*when it feels like we are. All is connected. Not separate growths with separate roots, but all offshoots of the same great tree. But the time for talk is done. Now we war.*"

And with that, the ten-foot-high figure turned and waded into the dead with long, lumbering strides that were nearly as far apart as Cutter was tall. As he did, he swept out with his great arms, sending dead hurtling through the air with each blow.

Cutter and his companions followed in the massive feyling's wake, cutting down those dead who tried to pour in behind him. They made good progress, for while the dead might not be much bothered by the blow of an axe or sword, they did not so easily recover from being scattered into pieces and launched through the air by one of the powerful blows of the Gray Man's arms.

They had covered nearly half the distance to where the feyling stood on a rock, playing frantically, her hands clawing at the lute strings as she watched them with eyes full of hate and what he thought might have been fear, when Cutter heard a scream.

He cut down the dead thing—unrecognizable due to decay—attacking him and spun to look behind him. At once, his chest tightened, and his breath caught in his throat.

Matt lay on his back. His borrowed machete lay several feet away, apparently knocked from his grip when he fell. But it was not the machete or his son that kept Cutter's attention—instead, it was the figure standing above Matt. The dead thing—which has once been a man—held a sword in its hands and even as Cutter watched, it raised the weapon in preparation of a blow.

Cutter bellowed a roar, charging into the creature in front of him with his shoulder, knocking it away. But no sooner had he done so than others pushed forward, crowding all around him. He struck out with his axe desperately, finding strength buried underneath his exhaustion and weariness that he had not been aware he possessed. Yet as hard as he fought, he knew that it would not, *could not* be enough.

The world seemed to slow to a crawl as he watched the blade of the sword scything down at his son. Matt was reaching for his own blade, but he, like Cutter, would be too slow. Then, suddenly, a figure dove out of the press of dead, one that Cutter recognized in shock as one of the Unsated. The wolf-like beast landed on top of Matt so that the sword strike that had been meant for him struck it instead, and it howled as the blade cleaved into its back, killing it.

The dead man raised his sword, preparing to swing it again—but before he could, two more of the Unsated leapt out of the fray, driving into him. The three struck the ground, and the Unsated began tearing the dead man's limbs off with their razor-sharp teeth and claws.

Cutter backhanded one of the dead in his way, sending its skeletal head hurling from its body into the press, then rushed forward. He grabbed the corpse of the dead Unsated, tossing it off his son to find Matt staring up at him in shock. "It...it protected me," his son said. "But...why?"

"I don't know," Cutter said, "but we've no time to think of it just now. Come on." He offered his son his hand, and he took it.

Cutter pulled him to his feet as Feledias came up to them. His brother bore dozens of scratches and cuts, much like Cutter himself, and he looked like he might collapse from exhaustion at any moment, but he seemed entirely focused on Matt. "Is he okay?" he asked Cutter in a breathless voice.

"I'm...fine, Uncle," Matt said.

Feledias huffed a breath. "Thank the gods. Come on—we don't want to get left behind."

Cutter glanced at the Gray Man and saw that the feyling had hesitated for them. The giant feyling's strikes sent several of the dead sailing through the air with each blow, yet even they were not enough to halt the onrushing horde, and he could see that it wouldn't be long before even the Gray Man was overwhelmed. "Ready?" he said, glancing at Matt.

His son looked pale, no doubt fully aware, as Cutter was, of just how close he'd come to death, but he nodded. "R-ready."

Then they were moving again. Several dead tried to fill the space between them and the Gray Man, but Cutter and the others moved side by side now, cutting them down and soon they were at the Fey elder's back, and they started forward once more.

As they grew nearer to where the feyling woman stood on the rock, the music became increasingly frantic and so, too, did the attacks of the dead. Soon, even with the Gray Man's help, they were forced to a stand still, no more than twenty-five feet away from the feyling woman.

The Gray Man spun, turning to regard Cutter and the others even as his arms swept out again and again. As he did, Cutter saw that while the Fey elder had wrought havoc on the lines of the dead, he had not done so without cost. Large sections of him seemed to be missing. Cutter didn't know how the swirling mass of leaves that comprised him might appear as though it had been torn in places, wounded the way a man might be, but it did.

"*Go, Destroyer. The song must be silenced, the melody quieted, before the restless dead will find their slumber once more. I will hold them off for as long as I can.*"

Feledias snorted. "And how in the name of the gods do you think we'll manage that?" he said, waving a hand at the dozens of dead separating them from the feyling. "Ask them to move?"

"*No, Stormborn,*" the Gray Man said. "*I will ask.*" And with that, the feyling spun and charged forward. As it did, the leaves and forest debris which comprised it *exploded* toward the creatures. A moment later, the Gray Man, at least the form which he had taken, was not there at all. The leaves and debris burst apart and the dozens of undead ahead of them were sent flying, scattered as though some giant had brought its fist down in the middle of them.

"Wh-what happened to him?" Feledias asked. "Is...is he—"

"Worry about that later," Cutter said. "He's bought us a chance—let's not waste it." Even as he and the others started forward into the empty space the devastating attack had left, the dead that had been broken and battered slowly began to rise once more. Cutter's axe swiped out, taking the head off one, smashing into the skull of another and then they were past, nothing between them and the feyling.

"*Curse you, Destroyer,*" she hissed, "*you and yours are a plague upon this land, a disease of rot that festers and ruins all that it touches.*"

"I've been called a lot of things," Feledias said. "Never a disease."

The feyling snarled. "*You think you have won and so mean to gloat. But there is no winning, not here, not in this place. This place belongs to the dead, and you will join them.*"

Cutter didn't see much point in bothering with words. He started forward, only pausing when his son spoke.

"Father..."

He turned and saw immediately what had drawn Matt's attention. The dead were coming. The Gray Man was nowhere in evidence, and while the devastation his final attack had wrought had been incredible, the thing about the dead was that there were always more of them.

"We'll hold them off as long as we can," Feledias said. "Go, Bernard. Finish this."

Cutter glanced at Matt, and his son nodded. "I'll be okay, Father."

"Sure, we will," Feledias agreed. "Just so long as you hurry, huh?"

And with that, they turned and moved to intercept the dead coming toward them.

That left Cutter to turn and face the feyling. Or, more accurately, face her back as she darted down the mountain pass, running even as she played. Cutter growled, searching about him, his gaze sweeping the area. He found a fist-sized stone among the scree and snatched it up, then hurled it with all his might. It struck the feyling in the lower back, and she screamed, her music faltering as she fell to one knee halfway down the mountain pass.

Cutter started forward at a jog but was forced to come up short as two dead leapt toward him. One appeared to be the half-decayed form of a wolf which he swiped away with his axe. Or, at least, tried to. The blade became stuck in the creature's rib bone, and then the second was on him. He was forced to let his axe go and meet this latest attacker with his bare hands. This undead swiped at Cutter with skeletal fingers twisted into claws, and he caught its wrists. Then, aware that every second brought the dead—and *death*—closer and closer to Matt and Feledias, he grabbed the creature by one of its bony legs and with a roar lifted it in the air, bringing it down on his knee, breaking the creature in two halves that fell, shattered, to the ground.

That done, Cutter turned to find that the wolf-like creature lay beside him, the axe still embedded in it as it tried to work its way to its feet. He didn't give it the chance. He brought his booted foot down on its skeletal face, smashing it into bone dust, then grabbed the axe and with a growl ripped it free.

Then he spun to see that the feyling had not been idle. She had used the distraction to gain her feet and was even now barreling down the path which was flanked on either side by the sheer walls of the mountain, nearing its end.

Cutter started forward at a run, his breath rasping in his weary lungs, his body aching from exhaustion and exertion. The feyling fled, but the stone had clearly hurt her, for she favored one leg, limping and leaning against the mountain walls for support as she continued onward.

She disappeared around the corner of the path, and Cutter followed her out at a run, coming to an abrupt halt as he saw that the feyling stood on a ledge, beyond which the world spread out far, far below them.

A path to his left went further up the mountain, toward its peak. The feyling started toward it, but in her haste to flee had ventured too far so that Cutter was able to step forward, interposing himself between her and her only route of escape.

"It's over," he told her.

She sneered, her eyes wide and wild. "*Fool,*" she hissed. "You know nothing. You think that you have won? That you *will* win? You think you have seen even the beginnings of the danger these mountains offer? Death slumbers here, Destroyer. A death beyond your understanding. It has slumbered for many hundreds, thousands of years, but it will slumber no longer." She grinned then, her lips spreading far too wide.

Then she began to play.

A terrible, discordant melody that struck Cutter like a blow. It felt *evil,* that melody, blasphemous somehow.

"*Do not,*" a voice thundered, and Cutter and the feyling spun to see the Gray Man standing in the mouth of the path through the mountain walls. He knew him by his voice, if not by his appearance, for the Gray Man who stood before them was not a giant comprised of leaves and bracken now, but one that looked almost like a man, the way he had when he had visited Cutter and Feledias inside the trunk of the giant tree in which they'd taken refuge what felt like a lifetime ago. "*Do not do this, daughter of twilight,*" the Gray Man said. "*Some of those things which have been forgotten have been forgotten for a reason.*"

"Too late," she hissed. "*You have betrayed your people, Elder, betrayed your son, but I will not. I serve the Fey—I serve the Green!*"

The music grew louder, each note slicing at Cutter like a physical pain.

"*It is forbidden! Stop her, Destroyer!*" the Gray Man yelled. "*Before it is too late!*"

Cutter ran forward, meaning to do just that, and was less than ten feet away from where the feyling stood at the cliff's edge when something began to happen. The ground shook beneath his feet, and he staggered, nearly slipping over the edge of the mountain into a long fall in which he'd have plenty of time to think about the many ways he had failed.

He managed to keep his feet, if only, and was just about to start forward again when a great wave of cold, cold like he had rarely ever felt, swept over him, and mist began to rise from the ground. Mist which, in another moment, coalesced into a figure that was eight feet tall. But it was not the creature's height, not even the mist that coalesced in its hand into what appeared to be an axe forged of ice, that sent a tremble of supernatural fear through Cutter's spine.

It was, instead, that he recognized it, for he had seen its kind before.

"You...you cannot be here," he said.

The Skaalden said nothing, only regarded him silently, either unable or unwilling to speak. Staring at that creature, the creature whose kind had slaughtered so many of his people, including his father, and sent what was left of their kingdom fleeing across the sea only to come to the Known Lands and suffer more at the hands of the Fey, Cutter felt a storm of feelings. Rage, mostly. Rage and fear, and how not? Here, before him, stood the single greatest threat his people had ever faced. An enemy that had, in the space of a day, conquered them, sending the lucky ones of their number fleeing wounded and battered and stricken with grief at their losses onto their ships. Cutter and his people had fled everything, traveled half the world, abandoned their homes and their dead, to escape the creatures...and yet now one stood directly in front of him.

It stared at him with the same blank expression the rest of the dead had, whatever pseudo-life the feyling's music gave it apparently not enough to resurrect any emotion or personality.

He heard Matt shout from behind him, and he turned to look where his son and brother stood holding off the dead. Matt was alright for the moment, but Cutter felt a great sense of urgency rush through him, and he looked back to the creature only to see that it had followed his gaze and was staring at Matt as well. Slowly, its head turned to regard him once more, and Cutter found himself snarling.

"Do not look at him," he said. "Your kind have taken everything from us. You will not take him."

The last time the Skaalden had come, he had fled. They all had. They had fled through the city as their friends, their lives were cut down around them. They had fled onto boats, fled across oceans.

This time, however, he did not flee.

He charged.

He had spent the last hour fighting the dead, so he was accustomed to them moving like puppets or automatons, their movements jerky and graceless. The dead Skaalden moved in the same way, but there were some differences that he recognized in moments.

The first was its strength. Cutter's first strike was aimed for the creature's waist, but the creature knocked the blow away with its axe, nearly knocking Cutter from his feet at the same time.

The second thing he noticed was its speed, for in the brief moment it took him to regain his balance he nearly lost his life. The creature's follow-up attack was instantaneous, its ice-edged axe flashing forward. It was only a life spent fighting and doing little else that saved him. Cutter reacted more by instinct than actual thought, spinning around the strike and narrowly avoiding being cut in two. He swung his own axe again, and again the creature knocked the blow away.

Then they were at it in truth.

The creature of ice fought in a cold, disinterested way, its face expressionless, its arm moving independently of its body. It did none of the foot work, none of the pivoting and positioning that Cutter had learned over years of training and actual fighting, its unnatural speed and strength more than enough to make up for what it lacked in technique.

But if the creature was ice, then Cutter was fire, roaring his anger and hatred, his axe flashing forward again and again as the melody of the lute grew more and more jarring and desperate, as if it were all the feyling could do to hold onto the spell.

The creature suddenly parried with a powerful blow that flung his axe—as well as Cutter himself—backward. Cutter grunted as he hit the ground hard, sliding across the rocks and ice and rolling to one knee, facing the creature. It stood as it had before, seemingly unaffected by their brief, but—for Cutter, at least—brutal struggle. Meanwhile, Cutter's breath rasped in his lungs, and the muscles of his arms and legs felt as if they'd been set on fire.

Laughter drew his attention, and he raised his weary head to look up at the feyling. She still strummed desperately at the strings of the lute, her fingers, Cutter saw, bloody from sawing at it, but she played on anyway, a rictus of concentration and what looked like pain on her sweat-drenched face. "*Do you not see, Destroyer?*" she screeched. "*What is dead cannot die. You have come to your end.*"

Battered and bruised, exhausted as he was, Cutter didn't feel as though he was in much of a place to argue. Certainly, he had little left. His legendary strength was spent, his legendary will faltering. Perhaps it was that he was tired, tired beyond comprehension, a weariness that went far past muscle and sinew but down into his bones, into his soul. Or perhaps it was the appearance of the Skaalden and the realization that despite the many intervening years between now and when they'd first come, despite the many battles he'd fought and foes he'd bested, he was still not enough. He hung his head, sweat dripping from his hair despite the mountain cold. He was tired. He did not think he had ever been so tired.

"*You will die,*" the feyling cooed, her voice strained and ecstatic at once. "*And your brother will die. Your* son *will die.*"

That was enough to make Cutter raise his head once more. As it turned out, he had a little strength, a little will left after all. He stood, retrieving his axe from where it had fallen nearby. "You cannot have them," he told her, told *it*.

The dead Skaalden only stared back at him, its expression as emotionless as it had been. But the feyling laughed. "*Your threats are empty, Destroyer,*" she crooned. "*You have nothing left.*"

"Let's find out."

And with that, he bellowed a roar, charging forward again.

He came on in a flurry of blows, his axe flashing out with every bit of strength and speed he could muster. Driven by his rage and his fear for his son, he fought, in that moment, the best he had ever fought. And in doing so, he managed to land several blows where the axe cleaved through the creature's dead, icy flesh. Not that it mattered. The Skaalden accepted each wounding without a sound of complaint, recovering instantly from blows that would have killed a normal man.

Cutter heard the feyling laughing as she played the lute, no doubt thinking—like Cutter himself—that he could not win. No matter how many times he wounded the creature, it did not seem to care in the slightest, nor did it seem to be growing tired. Meanwhile, he was quickly running out of the little bit of strength he had left.

The creature swung its axe at him again, and Cutter ducked underneath the blow, pivoting, and with a desperate strike brought his own blade into the creature's wrist, severing it and sending it—and the axe it held—flying away.

Whatever satisfaction he felt at this, however, was quickly extinguished, for the desperate maneuver had left him open, off balance. Normally, it wouldn't have mattered, for any living man who had just had its hand chopped off would have been focused on that and that only. The problem, of course, was that his foe was not living, nor was it a man. The Skaalden lashed out with the stump of its wrist, striking Cutter a powerful blow in his shoulder that felt as if he'd been kicked by a horse.

Cutter shouted in pain, knocked backward again where he struck the ground and was sent tumbling by the force of the hit. He rolled over backward twice before he was able to arrest his momentum and find his way to one knee again. Just in time, too, for he was no more than a few feet away from the edge of the cliff and a fall that would end in his death.

His shoulder throbbed, and he knew that if he survived he would have a nasty bruise. He was in so much pain that he felt his stomach heaving with nausea, and it was all he could do to keep from throwing up.

The feyling laughed, and he raised his head to see her—and the Skaalden—moving toward him along the cliff's edge. "*Your end has finally come, Destroyer. So many of my people have sought your life, but you will die at my hands.*"

He found himself thinking of his father. His father, King Dalten, who had died when the Skaalden had come. His father who had told him after one of his duels that it was not the sharpness of a man's blade, in the end, that brought him victory, but the sharpness of his mind.

Cutter had always had far more aptitude for the former than the latter, but another saying he'd learned—this not from his father but from Darius, his master-at-arms—was that when a man's plan failed, he found a different one. And so Cutter watched the Skaalden move closer, watched the feyling approaching behind it, and a plan began to form.

He hung his head, panting, doing his best to look exhausted and used up—it wasn't very hard. As the Skaalden and feyling drew nearer, Cutter's chest heaved with his breaths, and his body slouched in defeat. He gathered what strength he had left, what will he had left, and then, when they were no more than a few feet away, he exploded into action.

He came to his feet in a rush, charging toward the Skaalden. He ducked his head at the last moment so that his shoulder drove deep into the creature. The Skaalden was strong—stronger even than Cutter himself. It accepted blows that would have proved fatal for any living creature with no issue at all, but strong or not, it had not been braced for the blow and so it was driven backward by Cutter's charge.

A charge which he continued, driving the off-balance creature backward and into the feyling who let out a screech a moment before it bowled into her, the lute flying from her hands and finally bringing an end to the infernal music.

But Cutter knew that if he gave the far bigger Skaalden a chance, it would regain its balance and then he, weaponless and exhausted, would not last long against it, so he did not stop. Instead, he continued forward, driving the Skaalden and the feyling toward the edge of the cliff and then, over it.

The feyling let out a scream of terror as the ground disappeared from beneath her feet, and she and the Skaalden plummeted off the side of the cliff into the waiting clouds—and death—below.

Cutter nearly followed them over, one foot actually flying off the edge of the cliff before he was able to spin and, with the other, launch himself desperately away from the empty air. He managed it, if only just, ending with only his chest and arms gripping the mountainside.

Weary and shocked to still be alive, he dragged himself forward and staggered to his feet in time to see the Gray Man, Matt, and Feledias moving toward him from the path opening.

"Father," Matt said, hurrying forward. "Are you okay?"

"Alive," Cutter said, and that was about as much as he could say. "The dead?"

"Dead in truth," Feledias said. He glanced past Cutter at the cliff. "I guess it's hard to cast a spell while you're falling to your death."

"I guess so," Cutter agreed.

"And the other...it looked...was it...?"

"It was a Skaalden," Cutter said, nodding.

"But...how is that possible?" Feledias said. "That it would be here?"

"I don't know," Cutter said. "And I don't care, just so long as its dea—" He cut off then as something wrapped around his ankle with the strength of a vice, his words turning to a shout of pain. He looked down and was shocked to see the Skaalden gripping his ankle, hanging from it along the cliffside.

Cutter stared down at it, was raising his other foot to stomp on its hand or its face—he wasn't all that particular—when the Skaalden did something that sent a shiver of dread through him.

It met his eyes and did what none of the other dead had done before it.

It smiled.

Cutter roared, bringing his foot down, crushing the features of its face, yet even as he did he saw that its smile remained. It remained as he brought his foot down again and again, but when the Skaalden's grip finally came loose from his ankle, it did not fall as it should have. Instead, the figure began to turn into an icy mist, the last to go that crushed and broken smile.

But the mist did not fall away. Instead, it drifted forward, and a great wave of icy shock struck Cutter as the cold mist rushed against him, rushed *into* him. He staggered back, barely aware that he was moving at all. Icy pain greater than anything he had ever felt surged through him, and he collapsed to the ground.

He found himself cast into an icy world of despair and pain, then. Pain, despair like he had never felt before. He stood in a great wilderness of ice and snow, of cold beyond reckoning, one that made the northern Known Lands seem like a tropical paradise by comparison.

He had never experienced such cold in all his life, would not have thought a man *could* experience such cold and still live. There was nothing but the ice and the cold and the pain. And the darkness. That too. Darkness that was drawing into him, carried on the frigid wind that seemed to blow through him.

And past all that pain and ice and cold, he had one thought...

He was dying.

"*Father!*"

The voice sounded as if it came from a mile away, a faint echo carried on the icy wind.

"*What is it, what's happening to him?*" another voice asked. He should have known it, but in that moment he did not, knew nothing but the cold, nothing but the darkness.

"*It is the Winter,*" a voice said. "*It is inside him now.*"

"*B-but please, c-can't you help him?*"

"*Forgive me, but I cannot.*"

"*Of course you can, save him! Save him like you saved me!*"

"*This is different,*" the voice answered. It did not sound urgent, as it might if there was saving to be done. Instead, it sounded sad, the sort of voice a person used when any hope of saving was gone and there was nothing left to do but grieve. "*It is inside him, the Eternal Winter. It has not been conquered nor stayed except by one and one only, and she is beyond our reach.*"

"*So what then?*" Feledias demanded. "*He's just going to die?*"

The other voice, the one that Cutter slowly realized belonged to the Gray Man, didn't answer which, of course, was answer enough.

Cutter felt lost. Lost in the cold, with no hope of shelter or fire. He stood in a great expanse of ice and snow, and he did not need the Gray Man's reaction to know this and know it clearly—he was dying.

"*Please, Father,*" his son said. He was close but, at the same time, was so very far away. "*Please...don't die.*"

I don't want to, he thought, but he could not answer, was past such things as speaking now. Was past moving or trying. Past fighting, even. The fight was done. His fight, at least. There was no more, could *be* no more.

There was only the one thing left to do.

"*Please,*" Matt's voice came. His *son's* voice, and the pain in it made Cutter sorry. It was all he had ever caused his son, he thought. Pain. He had tried to do otherwise but it had made no difference.

"*You cannot die,*" his son said, and a flash of green appeared in that hellish winter's landscape that was Cutter's entire being. Only for a moment, so fast it might not have come at all. Then it was gone. "*I will not let you die,*" his son said.

Only, it did not just sound like his son this time—it sounded like thunder. It sounded like *power*. Not like just a voice at all, or at least, if it were a voice, then it was a voice of strength, not of desperation, but of demand. It was a voice that brought, somehow, warmth to the cold, that chased away the creeping frost that had lined Cutter's heart.

It was the voice, he thought, of summer.

And it brought summer with it.

Suddenly, the cold was torn away, scalded away by a heat that should have burned Cutter along with the rest but did not. He found himself brought back from that gray world of ice and pain, carried back. He found himself opening his eyes. For a moment, it seemed to him that he stared directly at the sun, and he winced at the brightness of it. But slowly, as his vision resolved, it was not the sun at all but Matt.

The young man crouched beside him, and Cutter could feel heat, like that of the sun on his skin, where Matt gripped his shoulders. "Father," his son said, his head bowed. "Please. Please don't leave me."

"I...I won't," Cutter said, his voice a dry crack.

Matt raised his head then, an expression of astonishment on his face, an astonishment that Cutter shared, for his son's eyes were glowing a deep emerald green.

Matt smiled wide then. Cutter had seen a lot in his life, a lot of places, a lot of things, but he had never seen anything as good as that smile.

"Bernard?" a frightened, hopeful voice asked.

Cutter turned his head to see Feledias walking up, the Gray Man beside him. "Fel," he said, smiling wearily.

"Oh, thank the gods, you're alive," his brother said. "I really hated the idea of lugging your big ass all the way down this mountain to find somewhere the ground wasn't too frozen to bury you."

Cutter gave his brother a tired grin. "Love you too, Fel. Now come on—help me to my feet."

Matt took one hand, and Feledias took the other, pulling him up. Feledias clapped a hand on his shoulder, running an arm across a tear that had traced its way down his cheek. "Thought we lost you there for a minute."

"For a minute, so did I," Cutter said.

"What happened, anyway?" Feledias said.

Cutter shook his head. "I'm not sure...it—it was cold. I've never felt a cold like that...didn't know there *was* cold like that." He turned to regard Matt. His son's eyes were normal now. "I thought...I *was* dying, but then...then you were there."

"But...I thought you said he was beyond saving," Feledias said, and they all turned to regard the Gray Man.

The feyling was in his smaller form, one composed of swirling leaves and bracken and shorter than Cutter himself. As the feyling regarded Matt, there was something about the way he moved, his manner, that seemed astonished. But no, Cutter decided as the feyling continued to stare only at Matt, it wasn't just astonishment—the Gray Man seemed awestruck, the way a priest might should the object of his worship suddenly appear before him.

"I will tell you what has happened, Destroyer. Stormborn," the Gray Man said, his eyes never leaving Matt. "Winter came. It has come before to this place, to my people, and many fell to its embrace. It was not defeated, for such a thing cannot be defeated, it is believed. But it was met, and only through the great sacrifice of the Summer Queen was it held at bay. A sacrifice which has kept that winter here, in these mountains, and away from the lands of my people. What the daughter of twilight did...summoning that winter back...it is forbidden. For it is a winter that does not stop or slow, that swept across our lands and threatened to destroy all, *would* have destroyed all, had the Queen of Summer not stood against it, giving her own life to stay its chill."

"The Summer Queen?" Feledias said, glancing at Cutter who gave a shake of his head. "I've never heard of her."

"Perhaps not," the Gray Man said, "but there is not one among my people who does not know her, who does not revere even the sound of her true name. She is the first of the Fey, and hers is the greatest line of my people, one that might be traced back to the beginning. A line that we had believed until this very moment, ended."

Cutter frowned, following the feyling's gaze to Matt. "Wait...what are you saying?"

"I am saying, Destroyer," the Gray Man said, "that your son is more than that. Far, far more. Welcome, last of the ancient line, he who carries the blood of our beginning," he said, turning to Matt and falling to his knees, bowing his head. "Welcome, Lord of Summer."

And now we have come to the end of *A Warrior's Devotion*. I hope you enjoyed journeying with Cutter and his companions once more. The next adventure in Saga of the Known Lands will be coming soon, so keep an eye out!

In the meantime, I have plenty of other reads to keep you busy.

Want another story of an anti-hero in a grimdark setting where a jaded sellsword is forced into a fight he doesn't want between forces he doesn't understand?
Get started on the bestselling seven book series, The Seven Virtues.

Interested in a story where the gods choose their champions in a war with the darkness that will determine the fate of the world itself?
Dive into The Nightfall Wars, a complete six book, epic fantasy series.

Or how about something a little lighter? Do you like laughs with your sword slinging and magical mayhem? All the world's heroes are dead and so it is up to the antiheroes to save the day. An overweight swordsman, a mage who thinks magic is for sissies, an assassin who gets sick at the sight of the blood, and a man who can speak to animals... maybe.
The world needed heroes—it got them instead.
Start your journey with The Antiheroes!

If you enjoyed *A Warrior's Devotion*, I'd really appreciate it if you'd take a moment to leave an honest review. They make a tremendous difference, and I would love to hear from you.

If you want to reach out, you can email me at Jacobpeppersauthor@gmail.com or visit my **website.** You can also give me a shout on **Facebook** or on **Twitter.** I'm looking forward to hearing from you!

***Turn the page for a limited time free offer*!**

Sign up for my new releases mailing list and for a limited time get a FREE copy of *The Silent Blade*, the prequel book to the bestselling epic fantasy series *The Seven Virtues*.

Go to https://www.JacobPeppersAuthor.com to get your free book now!

NOTE FROM THE AUTHOR

And now, dear reader, we have once again come to the end, at least of this story. But then there is always another, isn't there? Another story waiting to be told, waiting for someone to be told *to,* and personally I think there are few things more exciting than that.

Cutter and his brother and son have survived so far, but the danger is only beginning. For to find what the Gray Man has sent them after, they must delve deep into the mountains and discover its secrets. But some secrets are secret for a reason and often barriers—such as the Barrier Mountains—exist for a reason. Not always to keep things out but sometimes...just *sometimes* to keep things *in.*

I hope you enjoyed this latest entry in Saga of the Known Lands and that you have found your time journeying with Cutter and Matt, with Chall and Maeve and Priest and all the rest, time well spent. We have reached the end of this book, and I fear before long the end of the series altogether. But we are not there quite yet—there are still adventures to be had, still stories to be told. Still challenges to be met and overcome... or not. The story is not yet finished, after all, the ending not yet written.

Now, I would like to take a moment to thank all of those who have made this book—and so many of my books—possible.

NOTE FROM THE AUTHOR

My first thanks, as always, I give to my wife. Poor payment for having to deal with me on a daily basis, I expect, but you have them anyway. Andrea, I could not ask for a better partner in this life, a better person with which I might celebrate the good days and face the bad ones, doing whatever is required and doing it together. Plenty of people over the centuries have claimed that they are the luckiest man in the world. The difference between me and them is simply this—I'm right.

Secondly, I want to thank my children, Gabriel, Norah, and Declan. It is the greatest privilege of my life to be your dad, knee kicks and unexpected elbow drops and all. It is a blessing I do not deserve but one that I am forever grateful for. I love you guys.

Next, I want to thank my beta readers and my launch team, the men and women who so kindly dedicate their time and energy—and, I expect, no small bit of their sanity—to helping make my books better. I am very thankful for all that you do, a sentiment any of my readers would share if they were unlucky enough to see my unedited drafts.

Thank you, lastly, to you, dear reader. People often talk about storytellers, about the great bards and playwrights, but they rarely spend enough time, I think, talking about the most important people involved in such pursuits—the listener. Or reader, as it happens. After all, if the bard—even one as humble as I—casts a spell, then it is only by the grace of his listener, his reader that it has any power. So thank you for showing up and making my arm waving and grim intonements more than just the irrational behavior of a madman. Which I still might be—you'd probably have to ask my wife.

Now, if we've both got our breath, then best we stand again and get ready. More adventures are coming, after all...and isn't that exciting?

Happy Reading and until next time,

Jacob Peppers

ABOUT THE AUTHOR

Jacob Peppers lives in Georgia with his wife, and his children, Gabriel, Norah, and Declan, as well as their three dogs. He is an avid reader and writer and when he's not exploring the worlds of others, he's creating his own. His short fiction has been published in various markets, and his short story, "The Lies of Autumn," was a finalist for the 2013 Eric Hoffer Award for Short Prose. He is the author of the bestselling epic fantasy series *The Seven Virtues* and *The Nightfall Wars*.

Printed in Dunstable, United Kingdom